## CRITICAL ACCLAIM FOR PETER MURPHY

'Racy legal thrillers lift the lid on sex and racial prejudice
at the bar' – *Guardian*

'Murphy paints a trenchant picture of establishment cover-up,
and cannily subverts the clichés of the legal genre in his
all-too-topical narrative' – *Financial Times*

'Peter Murphy's novel is an excellent read from start to finish
and highly recommended' – *Historical Novel Review*

'An intelligent amalgam of spy story and legal drama' – *Times*

'A gripping, enjoyable and informative read'
– *Promoting Crime Fiction*

'The ability of an author to create living characters is always
dependent on his knowledge of what they would do and say in
any given circumstances – a talent that Peter Murphy possesses
in abundance' – *Crime Review UK*

'Murphy's clever legal thriller revels in the chicanery of the
English law courts of the period' – *Independent*

'The forensic process is examined in a light touch, good-
humoured style, which will evoke a constant stream of smiles,
and chuckles from nonlawyers and lawyers alike'
– **Lord Judge,** *former Lord Chief Justice of England and Wales*

'A gripping page-turner. A compelling and disturbing tale of
English law courts, lawyers, and their clients, told with the
authenticity that only an insider like Murphy can deliver. The
best read I've come across in a long time' – **David Ambrose**

'If anyo                                                           ok no

# VERBAL

A BEN SCHROEDER NOVEL

## PETER MURPHY

**NO EXIT PRESS**

First published in 2020 by No Exit Press,
an imprint of Oldcastle Books Ltd,
Harpenden, UK
noexit.co.uk
@noexitpress

© Peter Murphy, 2020

ISBN
978-0-85730-424-7 (print)
978-0-85730-425-4 (epub)

2 4 6 8 10 9 7 5 3 1

Typeset in 11pt Minion Pro
by Avocet Typeset, Bideford, Devon, EX39 2BP
Printed in Great Britain by Clays Ltd, Elcograf S.p.A.

For more information about Crime Fiction go to crimetime.co.uk

For my son Christopher, one of the overwhelming majority of British police officers who do, and have historically done, the job as it should be done: with competence, courage, dedication, honesty and integrity.

A good police force is one that catches more crooks than it employs.

– Sir Robert Mark GBE QPM
(Commissioner of Metropolitan Police, 1972-1977)

'A "verbal" is an oral admission made by a defendant when interviewed by the police, which on the advice of his solicitor he later denies.'

– Answer frequently given by Metropolitan Police officers in evidence, in the days before the Police and Criminal Evidence Act 1984, when asked by defence counsel whether they understood the term 'verbal'.

# PART ONE

# 1

*Monday 31 October 1983*

When the phone rang, she was instantly awake and fully alert.

Earlier in her career, as a young solicitor fighting for a place in the dog-eat-dog world of London law firms, Julia Cathermole had made two promises to herself: she would never force her body into the stereotypical female lawyer's black suits and shoes; and she would never keep a phone by her bedside to threaten her few precious hours of sanctuary. These were prices she deemed too high to pay for success. Her resolve had not done her any harm. At the age of fifty-five, the senior partner of Cathermole & Bridger was the moving force of a firm with an enviable client list, on whose behalf its lawyers habitually punched well above their weight. Julia Cathermole had arrived, and she was here to stay. But she was still quite capable of sleeping contentedly through the ringing of the phone in her study, a safe distance away down the hallway from her bedroom.

There was no logical reason why this morning should have been any different. But reflecting on it later, she recalled a sense of foreboding as she had drifted off to sleep, a sense that something nameless was on its way, something that would jolt her prematurely back into the harsh reality of the waking world. Opening her eyes, she glanced at her alarm clock, which told her that it was just after three o'clock. Three o'clock on the morning of 31 October: All Hallows Eve, Samhain Eve, the day when the portals separating the world of the living from the world of the dead stand ajar, enabling the two worlds to collide. Why in God's name had that piece of arcane knowledge drifted into her mind? She got out of bed quietly and threw her heavy dressing gown over her naked body, tying the soft belt firmly around her waist in an effort to keep out the autumnal chill in the air. She glanced back over her shoulder. On the other side of the bed, Imogen was sleeping soundly, breathing softly and rhythmically, her back to Julia. The duvet under which they had slept had shifted towards Julia's side of the bed, leaving her back exposed. Julia gently pulled it back up to cover her, and felt a pleasant sensation of lust run through her body as she remembered their bodies entwined together during the small hours, before they had finally surrendered to sleep, before it fully became Samhain Eve.

Closing the bedroom door behind her, she made her way to the study, switched on her desk lamp, seated herself behind her desk, and gave the phone one last chance to stop ringing, to admit that it was all a mistake. When it failed to oblige, she picked up the receiver.

'Julia Cathermole…'

'This better be important,' she added under her breath.

'Good morning, Julia,' a familiar voice said. 'I'm sorry to wake you up.'

She yawned reflexively, drawing the dressing gown even more tightly around her. She had turned the heating down in the study and it was even chillier than her bedroom.

'Baxter? What are you doing up at this hour? You're supposed to be retired, for God's sake.'

'I'm doing my best,' he replied, 'but they know where I live.'

She laughed sleepily. 'You could always move.'

'Too much trouble; besides, Dianne loves Richmond.'

'How are you both?'

'As well as can be expected in the case of two such aging dinosaurs. She sends her love.'

'And mine to her… So, to what do I owe the pleasure? Falling prey to insomnia in our old age, are we? Craving the comfort of another human voice in the dead of night?'

He laughed. 'Would that be so unreasonable?'

'It's a poor excuse for dragging me out of bed at three in the morning.'

'Insomnia's an occupational hazard in our line of work, Julia, a way of life – you know that – nothing to do with age. And if another human voice was all I needed I'd wake Dianne up – it wouldn't be the first time.' He paused. 'No, it's business, I'm afraid. I need to talk to you; and I'm calling now because I don't have the luxury of waiting until a more civilised hour.'

She nodded to herself. 'I was afraid you'd say that.'

He did not continue immediately.

'Don't tell me: let me guess,' she said. 'I know. Ronald Reagan is about to bomb Russia and start World War Three?'

'Not as far as I know – although if I'm honest about it, I can't say it would surprise me. How's that for a comment on the state of the world? No, slightly closer to home: we're getting worrying signals from our man in Belgrade.'

'Yugoslavia? I thought they were on our side these days.'

'They were moving in our direction while Tito was alive. But since he died – well, let's just say that the direction of travel isn't quite as clear as it used to be. They're wobbling just enough to give the Service a case of the jitters.'

She ran a hand through her hair. 'What's worrying you? Is Moscow throwing its weight around again?'

'No,' he replied, 'and even if they tried, they'd get nowhere. The Yugoslavs are too well armed and too well drilled. The Russians couldn't send the tanks into Belgrade the way they did in Budapest or Prague; they'd be sent packing in short order. No. What's worrying C is that we've had a few doubtful characters crawling out of the woodwork of late. Do you remember all those nationalists Tito put in prison, to shut them up in the great cause of Yugoslav unity?'

'Let me guess: now he's gone, and they're back out on the street?'

'Exactly, and they're finding their voices again: Serbs mainly, but the odd Croat here and there too. They've been on our radar for some time now. Eventually, C felt we had to brief the Minister and – well, you know what happens once you cross that line.'

She smiled. 'The Minister wants C to hold his hand, and C passes the buck to you because you actually know what's going on.'

'Something like that. Well, it's true: the Balkans used to be one of my bailiwicks. So a month or so ago, I get the usual plaintive phone call from one of the minions, don't I? "C sends his very best regards, Baxter, insisted I pass them on personally. He's always thought the world of you, as you know. The thing is, old boy, we've got a bit of a problem – right up your street actually, just the kind of thing you used to deal with back in the good old days. So C was wondering whether you could possibly spare a few days? Shouldn't take too long, and it would really mean a lot, old boy; C would really appreciate it." So here I am, back on the beat for a while. It won't last, obviously. There will be some other hot spot that takes their fancy tomorrow, and I'll be back on the scrap heap. But, for the moment...'

She laughed. 'They'll never let you retire, Baxter, will they? You've been around too long and you know too much, that's your problem. You're too valuable to let go.' She paused. 'But you still haven't explained why you're disrupting my beauty sleep at this hour.'

She heard him exhale heavily.

'No... Julia, you know Imogen Lester, Michael's daughter, don't you?'

Smiling, Julia turned in the direction of the bedroom and the young woman asleep in her bed.

# 2

'Yes, of course. She's been working for my firm since she came down from Cambridge, while she decides what to do with her life. I know Michael and Margaret through my father – well, he was Michael's mentor in the Service when Michael was a young officer. But you know all that...' She stopped abruptly as the sense of foreboding returned to her, her stomach suddenly seeming to tie itself in knots. 'Baxter, what's happened?'

'I don't know the full story yet. We got a message from the embassy in Belgrade an hour or so ago. It seems that Michael had been working on something in Sarajevo. The embassy's not saying exactly what he was doing there, but he had Margaret with him.'

'Diplomatic cover, presumably?'

'Yes: he was officially a cultural attaché or whatever, the usual nonsense. Anyway, it seems that the two of them were set upon by a gang of men armed with blunt objects, in some seedy district away from the city centre, where there was no obvious diplomatic reason for them to be.'

'Set upon...?'

'I'm sorry, Julia. I hate to have to tell you like this, but there's no way to make it any easier. They were both bludgeoned to death. The local police found them at about midnight our time, and their pathologist thinks they'd been dead less than an hour at that point. A witness, who wouldn't give his name and ran off before they could question him properly, told the police there were four men involved, all carrying big sticks of some kind, details unclear, but suggesting that Michael wouldn't have stood much of a chance. This is all second hand from the embassy, you understand, but it's all we have. It's early days.'

Julia put a hand over her mouth. 'Oh, God,' she whispered. She fought desperately against a rising feeling of nausea. Baxter allowed her some time. She took a deep breath and forced herself to think clearly. 'Margaret, too? For God's sake, Baxter…'

'Yes.'

'And we have no idea why…?'

'The police are saying it was a street robbery gone wrong. Complete bollocks, probably, but I'm not sure how we could call them on it without giving the game away – whatever the game is. He would have been carrying diplomatic credentials, of course – they both would – but the police say there's no identification on the bodies or at the scene. His wallet is gone, as is her handbag – and as is his revolver, if he was carrying it. Where they've gone is another matter, but the embassy isn't saying any more.'

'I see.'

'What we got from the embassy is the standard official notification, so it's not going to tell us anything that's not for public consumption. In fact, they're probably sending it to *The Times* for publication as we speak – which is actually the main reason I'm calling you so early.'

She took another deep breath and exhaled slowly. 'You want me to break it to Imogen.'

'I'm really sorry, Julia. But I don't want her reading about it in *The Times*, or even hearing about it from the embassy if I can help it: just out of regard for Michael and Margaret, you understand.'

'Leave it to me,' Julia replied softly.

'Thank you. There's a son too, isn't there?'

'Damian. Yes. I'll find him.'

'I'm really sorry, Julia.'

'So am I.'

She paused. The worst of the nausea was subsiding, but the first pangs of grief and horror were replacing it: these people had been her father's friends, and hers. She fought for control. She knew she had to put her grief aside for now; there were immediate problems to solve; she had to make herself think; she needed her rational solicitor's mind to assert itself.

'The police may just be right,' she suggested tentatively, testing her voice. 'There are probably all kinds of doubtful people in Sarajevo now, with the Winter Olympics coming up in a month or two. And you know Michael. He could be a bit hot headed, and if he refused to give them his wallet, or didn't understand what they wanted, I can see the situation getting out of hand. Are you sure it's related to whatever he was doing?'

'Michael's Serbo-Croat was pretty good,' Baxter replied, 'so I'd take a bit of persuading that it was just a misunderstanding. But what really worries me is what the hell they were doing in Bistrik, south of the river, at that time of night. It's not a tourist haunt. It's not even where you go in Sarajevo for a good night out – no decent restaurants or bars, or anything like that – and it's definitely not on the diplomatic circuit. It's not the safest part of town either, and Michael would have been well aware of that. He had a junior officer working with him, Scottish chap, name of Faraday. He's probably still with the police, but I'll call him later and if he has anything the embassy wouldn't have put in the official communiqué, I'll pass it on to you.'

'Thank you.'

'Please tell Imogen and Damian that everyone in the Service here will be thinking about them. It's as hard as hell when we lose one of our own, as you know. And for them to kill Margaret as well is unspeakable.'

'Yes.'

Julia replaced the receiver and sat in her chair for some minutes. She suddenly realised that she was shaking. She had forgotten about the cold and, remembering it again, felt chilled to the bone. Clutching the collar of her dressing gown, she stood and made her way slowly back to the bedroom. Imogen was still asleep under the duvet. She would let her sleep for another hour, perhaps two. Then, she would have no choice but to wake her.

# 3

When Baxter called again two days later, Julia was wandering randomly around her house, unable to settle in any particular room, reading a book here, looking at some papers there, doing her best to talk herself into going back to the office the following day. She had taken two days off, citing shock and distress following the death of two close friends. Her team had been understanding, but they would expect her to be back in harness soon. There was a lot going on, and in a small firm that meant all hands on deck. She knew she had to pull herself together, but she still felt numb from the sheer unyielding awfulness of the previous two days.

Not long after Baxter's call, before waking Imogen, she had prevailed on the duty sergeant at Hampstead Police Station to send a uniformed officer to the Lester family home near Hampstead Heath, to break the news to Imogen's brother, Damian. She had thought long and hard before calling the police, but in the end she could see no other way. She couldn't bring herself to tell him by phone, and with Imogen to care for she couldn't go herself in time to guarantee that he would not hear about it from a newspaper or the radio. But the visit from the police would be problematic. Damian was not unknown to Hampstead Police Station. At the age of nineteen, five years younger than his sister, only good fortune and one or two timely interventions by his father stood between Damian and a criminal record. In contrast to his sister, who had inherited her parents' drive, had excelled at school and had graduated from Girton College, Cambridge, with a first in classics, Damian had always seemed listless and bored by his teachers' efforts to educate him. He seemed content to drift though life without any obvious goal. When Michael was posted to Belgrade, Damian had resisted his parents' attempts to take him with them to Yugoslavia, promising to pull himself together and get himself a job. But jobs rarely materialised and never lasted long, and when Imogen was away from the house, his life became a never-ending round of sleeping for much of the day, and late nights spent drinking and consuming other substances with his friends.

Julia was keenly aware of this history from Imogen, who in her parents' absence felt responsible for her brother and was racked with guilt that she was powerless to change, or even control, him. It had taken all Julia's diplomatic skills to explain to the duty sergeant that there had been a family tragedy, and that it would mean a lot to the family if the officer could deliver the news without paying too much attention to what he was likely to find when he entered the house. Mercifully, the sergeant was sympathetic. The officer broke the news and offered his help without commenting on the unmistakable aroma of cannabis that greeted him when, after a prolonged assault on the doorbell, a sleepy Damian eventually invited him in.

Julia had woken Imogen at six o'clock. Taking off her dressing gown, she had settled herself next to Imogen in bed, gently drawn her into her arms and, with Imogen's head resting on her breasts, had lovingly stroked her hair while telling her, with a minimum of detail, the embassy's official story of how her parents had met their deaths. Imogen had cried, hardly moving, for more than an hour. When she became quiet and got out of bed they had walked together downstairs to the kitchen on the ground floor, where Julia made coffee. By the early evening, Imogen had recovered sufficiently to be concerned for her brother, and insisted on leaving for Hampstead to see him. Before putting her in a taxi, Julia had made her promise to call regularly. She had so far called three times in two days, and sounded quietly distraught. Damian, she said, was reluctant to talk and had responded to his parents' death with a fresh round of whisky and cannabis. By the time of the third call she was thinking of abandoning ship. But she had not returned.

Baxter's call came as a relief. He was reticent and unwilling to talk over the phone, and instead asked to see her under London Rules, code Echo, at three o'clock that afternoon. As he disconnected abruptly, Julia felt herself smile for the first time since his call two days before. Baxter's caution in such matters was the stuff of legend within the Service, and the explicit reference to the tradecraft he had used with her before came as no surprise. It was, as ever, slightly over the top by more contemporary standards. But Julia found it charming and comforting. Baxter had learned his tradecraft in Vienna from Nigel, his mentor and her father, and he remained loyal to Nigel's classical approach, outmoded as it now seemed to his younger colleagues. A meeting with Baxter under London Rules brought back happy memories of her father. At three o'clock she was waiting for him on Victoria Embankment exactly opposite Temple tube station, as code Echo stipulated, knowing that he would emerge from the station and join her in precisely six minutes, having kept her under observation during that time, just in case she had been followed.

'I've talked to Faraday,' Baxter said, as they began the slow walk towards Charing Cross. 'As I suspected, there's more to it than the embassy's official story. How did the children take the news?'

'Imogen took it hard,' she replied, 'but she's a strong girl; she will be fine. I haven't seen Damian. I asked the police to notify him. I don't know how much Michael told you about him, but he's gone off the rails a bit. He's a young, immature nineteen. He was on a steady diet of booze and drugs before this happened, and obviously, it hasn't helped.'

He nodded. 'We'll have to keep this from Damian then,' he said matter-of-factly, 'but if you think Imogen is trustworthy, I need you to talk to her – and enlist her.'

'Enlist her?'

'Yes. The benefit to her is that, if all goes well, she might just learn the truth about how her parents died: no guarantees, but she might. I appreciate that it may be scant compensation. But the fact is, Julia, I need her help – and yours.'

She stopped and leaned against the Embankment wall, looking out across the river.

'Help with what, exactly?' she asked.

He came to stand beside her.

'You understand...'

'Yes, I understand. Come on, Baxter, I know classified information when I'm about to hear it.'

He nodded. 'Faraday told me that Michael had an agent in Sarajevo, code name Oscar, who has connections to certain criminal elements, specifically, drug dealers plying their trade to facilitate the movement of hard drugs in both directions, East to West and West to East, using the Balkans as their main hub.'

She frowned. 'So? Since when is drug dealing of interest to the Service? Why not pass the intelligence on to Interpol and let them deal with it?'

'The proceeds of the drug trafficking are being used to fund the purchase of arms and ammunition for some fledgling nationalist groups – which is of considerable interest to the Service. The ringleader is a man known as Dragan, real identity unknown, who has the reputation locally of being a bit of a hard man.'

'Hard enough to set four thugs armed with big sticks on someone who might pose a threat to him?' she asked.

'That's Faraday's theory. Unfortunately, Michael didn't tell him exactly why he was making this particular trip to Sarajevo, or why he was taking Margaret with him. He doesn't know of any reason for him to go, other than to see his agent.'

'And there was no diplomatic cover story for the trip?'

'None whatsoever. Also, bear in mind that Michael wouldn't make a trip to Sarajevo unless it was strictly necessary. Yugoslavia may be more relaxed than most places behind the Iron Curtain – especially Sarajevo, since they're trying so hard to establish it as an international destination with the Winter Olympics – but you still wouldn't want to push your luck.'

'Perhaps he thought that the Games would provide some cover?'

'That would be a risky assumption. Yes, they're trying to create the illusion that Sarajevo is some kind of Cold War-free zone, but the reality is that there are just as many watchers as ever, quite possibly even more, with so many foreigners from the West coming to town. All it would take is for Michael's tradecraft to let him down once, and he would be putting Oscar directly in harm's way, as well as himself. And we still have no explanation of why Margaret was with him.'

She turned to look at him directly. 'All right, but where do Imogen and I come into it? If you want to tell Imogen her father was looking into some criminal activity when he died, as opposed to being the victim of a random robbery, I suppose she might take some comfort from that. But…'

'Faraday thinks we need to extract Oscar,' Baxter replied.

She stared at him. 'What? As in, relocate him here?'

'Yes.'

Julia's jaw dropped. 'Well, I repeat my question: Imogen and I fit into this picture how, exactly? Or, let me put it another way: why would you involve two civilians in such a risky procedure behind the Iron Curtain? I thought C was trying to discourage that kind of stuff?'

He smiled. 'Oh, come on, Julia. I'm not suggesting that you would be part of the extraction itself. That's a matter for the Service – assuming we end up agreeing with Faraday that it is, in fact, necessary.'

'Well, what *are* you suggesting, then?'

He exhaled heavily. 'I can't go into detail at this stage, but what it comes to is this: from what Faraday tells me, there are some tricky legal issues involved in relocating Oscar to England.'

As if by an unspoken agreement, they resumed their slow walk.

'Issues with Oscar himself, or issues with the authorities here?' she asked.

'Both: and it would be really useful to have a solicitor at work on both ends. But I need a solicitor I can trust with very sensitive information, Julia, and that's not a large group.'

They walked on for some time in silence.

'Assuming for a moment that I would be willing to do this,' she said, 'there must be no question of exposing Imogen to danger. Unless things have really changed since my father's day, it's not Service policy to put civilians in harm's way in peacetime. And why would she be of interest to you, anyway? She's not a lawyer.'

'Cover,' he replied. 'Imogen wants to find out what really happened to her parents, doesn't she? She's not happy with the embassy's account of it: too many unanswered questions by far. What was going on? What was her mother doing there? So she decides to visit Sarajevo to find out for herself. She asks the embassy to arrange a visit to the local *gendarmes*, so that she can question them in person. The authorities aren't going to stand in the way of that, are they? It's exactly the kind of publicity they want, what with the Games coming up.'

'Is it?'

'Of course. They've had a double murder and the victims were two prominent westerners. If they can't protect visitors like Michael and Margaret, how can they expect anyone to feel safe during the Games? The least they can do is let the world see how seriously they're taking the investigation. Trust me, Julia, they will be falling over themselves trying to help her. And while all eyes are on Imogen, nobody is focusing on you. She's the perfect cover.'

'That's your idea of cover? Really? How does that work? Why am I even there with her?'

'You're her solicitor, Julia. At the end of the day, whatever she finds out, she's going to need legal advice about what she should do, isn't she? Who else would she turn to? Besides, nobody would do this alone, trying to ask questions of police behind the Iron Curtain: it's far too daunting. No. You have every reason to be there with her, and with any luck it should be enough to lull the watchers into a false sense of security – enough for them to let their guard down, even if only for a few hours.'

She nodded. 'During which time…?'

'During which time Faraday quietly takes you to see Oscar, perhaps after a lunch or dinner long enough to allay any suspicion, and you – what is it you solicitors call it? – take instructions, and advise Oscar and ourselves accordingly. Then you come back home and help to facilitate things for Oscar here.' He laughed. 'Besides, you've done this kind of thing before.'

She stopped and turned to face him.

'Excuse me?'

'Don't tell me you've forgotten.'

'You're going to have to remind me,' she said.

'Vienna,' he replied. 'Your father and I extracted an agent called Vladimir Pushkov. Don't tell me you've forgotten that.'

'I was nineteen,' she protested indignantly. 'My mother wasn't feeling well, so I made the coffee and sandwiches at the safe house.'

'Well, there you are,' Baxter replied.

She laughed briefly, and then they were silent for some time.

'We're sleeping together,' she said eventually, 'Imogen and I. If we're going to do this, you need to know.'

Baxter nodded. 'Well, Sarajevo's beautiful in the winter,' he replied, 'very romantic. Bloody cold, of course. You'll have to take some thick sweaters and all the rest of it. But very romantic: just the place for lovers.'

# 4

Julia cursed to herself as yet again the car bounced violently on the uneven tarmac and administered a sudden sharp jolt to her back.

'For Heaven's sake, Faraday,' she complained, 'I feel like every bone in my body is coming loose. Doesn't the embassy have any British cars? I thought we were supposed to be flying the flag, for God's sake, promoting British exports, and all that kind of thing.'

She saw Imogen and Faraday smile at each other in the front seats. Imogen actually giggled. That was good, she thought. Imogen had been uncharacteristically quiet and withdrawn since she learned of her parents' death; but when Julia had put Baxter's proposal to her she had agreed without hesitation, and her energy and determination had returned, increasing noticeably as the date of their departure drew near. Today she seemed calm and composed, and the giggle was a welcome sign that her sense of humour had survived the trauma intact.

'Sorry, Miss Cathermole,' Faraday replied. He was in his early thirties, tall and thin with pale skin, and soft-spoken with no trace of an accent, the only clue to his Scottish antecedents being his addiction to a red and green tartan tie. 'Ambassador's idea. Someone told him it would make us popular if we adopted the local brand instead of endlessly pushing our own. The drive should get smoother once we get out of the airport and on to the main road.'

'I remain to be convinced,' Julia insisted. 'What exactly is this local brand?'

'This is the Zastava Koral, commonly known as the Yugo,' he replied. 'It's not exactly a Rolls Royce, obviously, but they only started production about three years ago, so hopefully it will improve with time.'

'It would improve if they added some suspension,' Julia observed sourly.

'Is it far into town from the airport?' Imogen asked.

'No, not too far, Miss Lester. In normal traffic we would do it in twenty, twenty-five minutes. It might take a bit longer today. They're desperately trying to get all the venues finished for the Winter Olympics and they're a bit behind schedule, so everyone's rushing everywhere and all the roads are clogged up. We'll be going into town with the traffic for the Skenderija Center, which will be the venue for the skating and ice hockey, so it might be a bit slow.'

'That should give this contraption ample time to dislodge my last bone,' Julia said. 'I must remember to thank the Ambassador for sending you to pick us up.'

Imogen laughed. 'Try curling up in the foetal position,' she suggested.

'Point taken, Miss Cathermole,' Faraday said, pulling smoothly out of the airport access area on to the main road, 'but don't be too hard on the Ambassador: remember, you do have him to thank for your room at the New Holiday Inn.'

'I've been reading about this hotel,' Imogen said. 'It's supposed to be quite something, quite a departure for Yugoslavia.'

'It is,' Faraday agreed. 'Well, it's all because of the Games, obviously. We wouldn't have it, otherwise. But people aren't waiting for the Games. Even now, with a couple of months to go, you can't get a room for love nor money.'

'I'm not surprised,' Imogen said. 'I'm sure people are fighting each other to get in. But in that case, how did we end up with a room?'

'The Ambassador pulled some strings.'

'That was nice of him.'

'It wasn't entirely out of the goodness of his heart, I imagine,' Julia said.

'No,' Faraday agreed. 'Actually, it was our idea. The Holiday Inn works on the western model so, unlike other hotels here, it's accessible at all hours of the day and night: much easier for us to keep an eye on you while you're here. Baxter asked someone high up to approach the Ambassador to see what he could do. Apparently, he came up trumps.'

'Good for him,' Julia said.

'I may as well go through all this with you now,' Faraday said, 'while we're still in a secure space. Once we get out of the car at the other end, there are no guarantees. You're used to all this, Miss Cathermole, I know; but, Miss Lester, it may be very new to you. So bear with me while I go through the protocols.'

'I'm all ears,' Imogen said.

'Good. First, although Yugoslavia has a certain reputation for being liberal by Eastern European standards, it is only liberal by those standards. You are behind the Iron Curtain. Surveillance, spying, eavesdropping – call it what you will – is a way of life. They do it to their own people just as much as to us westerners, so don't take it personally. Rule number one is: never talk about anything to do with why you're here unless you're outside walking around. Never talk in the hotel, even in your room – in fact, especially in your room – never in the bar, and never when you're away from the hotel in a restaurant or shop. I don't mean small talk, obviously, but nothing to do with what you're doing here, or about the Service. If you need to have a conversation about anything serious, bundle up and go out into the cold and walk around.'

Imogen turned to Julia. 'Punch me in the arm or something if I start on something I shouldn't.'

'You'll worry and feel self-conscious about it at first,' Faraday replied, 'but you'll get used to it. Rule two: obviously, don't write anything down and leave it lying around.'

'What's the emergency protocol?' Julia asked.

'I'll give you a number you can call any time, day or night. Your code name is Morecambe, and yours is Wise, Miss Lester.'

They both laughed. 'Highly original,' Julia commented.

He smiled. 'We like to give you something you won't forget.' He looked at Julia using his rear view mirror. 'Is it true what they say about your memory, Miss Cathermole?'

'Yes.'

He removed a small slip of paper from the top pocket of his grey jacket and held it out to her, his left hand over his shoulder. She read it quickly and returned it to him.

'Got it?'

'Got it.'

He replaced the paper in his top pocket.

Imogen turned to look at her. 'You memorised the number? Just like that.'

'I was born with a photographic memory,' Julia replied quietly, 'and believe me, it's a curse as much as a blessing.'

'If anything happens in the hotel to make you feel uncomfortable,' Faraday added, 'go down to the bar wearing a white shawl. You'll find one in your room. We'll have someone in the bar around the clock. But don't try to work out who it is. You won't be able to, and it will only make them nervous. Just be aware they're there, but don't use them unless you really have to. It's not easy placing watchers here.'

# 5

They pulled up at a red traffic light. As Faraday had predicted, there was a steady flow of heavy traffic ahead and behind them, most of it apparently destined for the skating and ice hockey venue at the Skenderija Center.

'We have an appointment with Colonel Miroslav Stojanović at Militsija headquarters tomorrow morning at ten,' Faraday said. 'I will pick you up at nine thirty. Stojanović will be anxious to impress on you that they're pulling out all the stops to solve the murders. It's not good for business to have foreigners being attacked on the streets with the Games coming up, so Stojanović is going to bend over backwards to persuade you that everything is under control. But don't forget, his agenda is that this was a random street robbery. It has to be, because that's less of a threat to tourism than organised crime. And you can bet your bottom dinar that the Militsija will round up four of the usual suspects within a few days of your returning home, just to reinforce the illusion.'

'Will he let us see my parents' things?' Imogen asked.

'Yes. The embassy will see to it that they're returned to you once they're no longer needed as evidence. Forgive me, Miss Lester, I don't mean to be crass, but our main interest in them tomorrow is to see what's there and what's not there. The initial report was that all their personal identification items were missing. We need to check that. Hopefully, Stojanović's people will have made a thorough search of the area by now.'

Faraday briefly touched the back of Imogen's hand with his.

'The other thing Stojanović wants to do, Miss Lester, is to take us all to see the crime scene. I think he feels obliged. It's up to you. There's really nothing to see. It's just a back street in a bad area of town. If you don't want to go, I'll tell him to forget about it.'

'No,' Imogen replied softly. 'I've come all this way. I want to see it.'

Julia reached over and touched her shoulder. 'So do I. I want to see what kind of area Michael took himself and Margaret into. Maybe it will give us a clue about what he was doing. I couldn't get much out of Baxter about it.'

'We're speculating,' Faraday admitted. 'I would be very surprised if he hadn't been to see Oscar. But it's all a bit odd. The crime scene is less than a mile from where Oscar lives, but it would be a pretty elaborate piece of tradecraft to end up where they were attacked; so we're not ruling out the possibility that he was meeting, or planning to meet, someone else. I'm hoping Oscar can give us something. If not, I'm not sure where we go. Stojanović's robbery theory may prevail by default.'

'Do you want to tell us about Oscar,' Julia asked, 'given that we have to advise him about the legal issues involved with his extraction – whatever they may be?'

Faraday smiled. 'I'll let Oscar explain the legal issues to you himself. You'll meet him tomorrow evening. All I will say for now is that he's Austrian and his name is Ernst Meier.'

'That doesn't tell us much,' Imogen protested.

'It tells us that his name isn't Ernst Meier,' Julia muttered from the back seat, 'and I'll be very surprised if he's Austrian.'

'Baxter told me you were something of a cynic, Miss Cathermole,' Faraday said, with a grin into his rear view mirror.

'The fruit of long experience,' she replied. 'What's the tradecraft for getting to his place? Given what happened to the Lesters, I assume you have something in mind?'

'After we're finished with the Militsija for the day, you will return to the Holiday Inn, rest for a while, change if you want, and

I will pick you up for dinner at seven. We're going to Star Srbije, Star of Serbia. It's run by a crusty old Serb called Vlado. During the War he ran with Tito's Partisans, fighting with British forces against the Germans and their Croatian fascist allies, the Ustaše. Ever since he's stayed totally loyal to Tito and to us, in that order. Michael put me on to him. He's helped us out in all kinds of ways over the years. One of those ways is tradecraft. The Star Srbije is a natural looking glass.'

'Looking glass?' Imogen asked.

'As in Alice,' Julia smiled. 'If you step through it, it's a portal into another world.'

Faraday nodded. 'The front of the restaurant is on the south bank of the Miljacka, not far from the Princip Bridge, where the First World War started – very respectable looking. But it has a vast cellar, with a back door that dumps you out on to a very unprepossessing side street. You'll be tempted to go straight back inside, but the good news is, you're just a brisk ten-minute stroll from Chez Oscar. Vlado will even lend us replacement coats and hats for the rest of the evening, so we leave wearing something different from what we arrived in – an old Partisan trick for outfoxing watchers. Don't worry – his son Andrej will get yours safely back to the hotel for you, and he will watch our backs as far as he can. Andrej's totally reliable, a chip off the old block. He'll probably take the restaurant over from his father before too long, so it's good to give him a few things to do, just to keep him onside.'

They were drawing up in front of the Holiday Inn.

'My God,' Julia said, surveying the hotel's glaring exterior, 'they went a bit overboard with the yellow and brown, didn't they?'

Faraday laughed. 'It's been a bit controversial,' he replied. 'Not what you'd expect in Yugoslavia – but then, we are in Sarajevo, and Sarajevo does tend to go its own way. To be honest, I rather like it. I won't come in with you, if you don't mind. Did you remember to bring some Deutsche Marks with you?'

'Lots of them,' Julia confirmed.

'Good: they're very popular here. You should buy a few dinars to carry around for small change, for coffee and newspapers and such like, but for anything serious – including paying for things in the hotel – use the D-Marks. The locals are always grateful for hard currency. They're not supposed to have it, but everybody does.'

'I assume you get a better deal with D-Marks?' Julia asked.

'Absolutely. The authorities frown on it officially, but unofficially they turn a blind eye unless someone is dealing in large numbers. That's what happens when you have a currency like the dinar with fifteen to twenty-five per cent annual inflation. As long as you're not flashy about it, no one will bother you.'

He opened the hatchback door, and lifted their suitcases down to the ground as smartly attired hotel employees began to descend on them with offers of help.

'Nine thirty tomorrow, then,' he said. 'Have a good evening. If you don't fancy venturing out on your first night, the restaurant here isn't too bad.'

'High praise indeed,' Julia replied, smiling.

# 6

*Wednesday 30 November 1983*

Lying on her back on the bed, Julia surveyed the room. It was late in the afternoon, but the previous twenty-four hours had been long and draining. Beside her, Imogen was asleep, her breathing calmer and more rhythmic now, suggesting that the emotional toll was beginning, at last, to recede. But Julia was wide awake, her mind racing. What had happened today? Had they learned anything new about the fate of Michael and Margaret Lester? Colonel Stojanović, and the officers who accompanied them to the crime scene, had been models of formal concern and compassion; but they were less than forthcoming about forensic details, and when pressed, their answers were stilted and inconclusive. Imogen had paid a high emotional price for the chance to inspect her parents' last view of this world, but it had brought them no closer to the truth. Whether Faraday had seen anything, she had no way of knowing. Even if he had, in accordance with his own admonitions, he would not reveal it unless and until he was sure that it would be safe. She liked Faraday so far, she reflected. He was competent, thorough and precise, and understated – all qualities her father had taught her to value. And he was right about their room: she was sure of it.

Brought up in the Service residence in Vienna, Julia had learned the mechanics of sweeping rooms for bugs at a young age. As a child, she had innocently followed the Service's technicians around the house as they worked for her father, and they never thought to discourage her, never dreamed how much the child was quietly assimilating as her extraordinary memory instantly recorded their techniques. The sophistication of the devices had evolved dramatically over the years, but the essentials of bugging and sweeping a room remained comfortably familiar. Julia had never formally worked for the Service, and her childhood was now forty years and more distant. But her consciousness of security remained an integral part of her life. As soon as they had arrived in the room the previous evening she had looked slowly around her, carefully taking in the details of the ceiling and walls, the fire alarm, the small black and white television, the telephone, the bedside lamps – looking for any possible hiding place for a camera or a recording device. Now she looked again, just to check her findings. She was sure she was right. She was confident that she could have discovered and removed the bugs, swept the room clean, in a matter of minutes. But she was not about to take such risky liberties on Faraday's patch. With Baxter, perhaps, whom she knew well, but not with Faraday – certainly not yet.

Baxter had been her father's friend and colleague for many years, and because her father had trusted him, so did she. She had been eighteen when they first met in the Vienna residence in 1946. But their paths had crossed again unexpectedly in 1965, in the early days of Cathermole & Bridger, during the notorious case that led to the unmasking of Sir James Digby QC as a Soviet spy. He had been exposed by her American client, Professor Francis Hollander - with significant support from the Service. Since then, and in the aftermath of her father's death, Baxter had been her mentor, friend, and confidante. But Baxter was an officer of the Service, and she was not; and there were two secrets, though only two, that she kept from him. She had never told him the full extent of her knowledge of bugs, and she had never told him of the one room in her house, a comfortable attic sitting room, that she kept regularly swept.

This was partly an old habit dying hard, but she also had a more practical reason for maintaining her sanctuary. She needed a secure place to have certain conversations with clients and sometimes others, conversations that no one else, including Baxter, could be permitted to hear. It was nothing personal. Baxter would never spy on her unless he was convinced that the interests of the Service required it; but she could never exclude the possibility that one day the interests of the Service might, in Baxter's mind, require it. And now she was about to represent a man whose name wasn't Ernst Meier and who probably wasn't Austrian, whose interests were not identical to those of the Service. This man was going to be her client. Sometimes, there had to be secrets.

Imogen awoke abruptly and turned over to face her. Julia bent down and kissed her on the forehead.

'Have I been asleep all this time?'

'Ever since we got back. You lay down and went out like a light.'

She yawned and stretched.

'I don't even remember going to sleep. I must have been ready for a nap.'

'After the day you've had? I would say so.'

She nodded, sitting fully up in bed and stretching again.

'Well, thanks for not waking me. What time is it? Are we late for dinner?'

Julia looked at her watch. 'Six-fifteen. We've got plenty of time. But I'm ready to get out of this room. What do you say we hit the bar and knock back a couple of shots of slivovice before Faraday gets here?'

'I'm up for that,' Imogen replied.

# 7

Advertising was not a big part of Vlado's business plan. Unusually for a man in his profession, it was not his way to draw undue attention to his restaurant. Star Srbije was a pleasant enough establishment, situated on a respectable thoroughfare overlooking the Miljacka River, no great distance from the city centre. But the only indication of its presence was an inconspicuous sign bearing its name, written in the Cyrillic alphabet, and no other information whatsoever. It was the kind of place you probably wouldn't find unless you were looking for it. Vlado's regulars, almost all of Serbian extraction, knew exactly how to find it, and the occasional new customer learned about it by word of mouth from one of the regulars. It was an arrangement with which Vlado was perfectly happy.

The reason for Vlado's modesty was that, in addition to its very acceptable, if plain, cuisine, Star Srbije was also a venue for certain dealings for which publicity was neither necessary nor desirable. Some of those dealings had been instigated by Faraday, and by Michael Lester before him, and had to do with the Anglo-Serbian bond that meant so much to Vlado. It was a timeless bond forged by comradeship during the Partisan struggle against the Ustaše, a bond that would never die while Vlado and his colleagues from those days were around to keep it alive. Other such dealings, however, were in an exclusively Serbian cause. Faraday was careful never to inquire into this cause too closely, and although he did report on it to London from time to time, he did so in very guarded language and took infinite pains not to compromise Vlado in the eyes of the Service.

Vlado welcomed Julia and Imogen as if they were long-lost members of his family, which was how he felt about all the British people he met, but particularly those with ties to the Service. Andrej discreetly disappeared into the cellar with their coats and hats, while Vlado seated them at a table by the wall and close to the door of the cellar, which also offered a good view of the restaurant's main entrance. In the centre of the table, next to a lighted candle in a pewter holder, was a miniature vase that might have held a single bloom but, in fact, held two miniature flags: the Union Flag, and the red, blue and white Tricolour of Serbia. Next to the candle and the vase stood a bottle of slivovice and a jug of ice. He returned a matter of seconds later in the company of a young waiter bearing plates of delicious pastry appetisers filled with meat and vegetables, bottles of water, and two carafes of a vigorous red wine. He poured shots of the slivovice over ice for the table and for himself, and pointed to the flags.

'It is discouraged to do such things,' he said, 'to display Serbian flag. It is discouraged to be Serbian since the War, although we Serbs fought under Marshal Tito against the fascists, with you, our British friends. This is our reward. Even the name of my restaurant, Star Srbije, they would like me to change it to the Star of Yugoslavia. But of course, I will not, and perhaps not in my time, but in Andrej's time, we will once again be allowed to be Serbian. But always we will be your friends. Drink, please. Živeli!'

They raised their glasses in response. 'Živeli!'

Vlado replaced his glass on the table and handed round menus.

'If you need menu, it is here,' he said, 'but menu is only in Serbian language, and so if it would be easier, please allow me to bring you meat and vegetables to your heart's content, and you will tell me when to stop.'

He disappeared in the direction of the kitchen.

Imogen smiled. 'So, the menu is mainly for show?' she asked.

'I'm not sure I've ever looked at it,' Faraday replied, returning the smile. 'If you're wondering what's good here, the answer is: anything that has the word "Serbian" in the title. Personally, I'm going to let him bring me as much meat and veg as he wants.'

Imogen laughed. 'Sounds good to me,' she said.

'That's quite a chip Vlado has on his shoulder about being Serbian,' Julia observed, as they settled down to tackle the excellent grilled beef and pork chops the waiter had brought for them. 'Obviously, he means, as opposed to being Yugoslavian.'

Faraday nodded, refilling their wine glasses. 'In reality, "Yugoslavia" is nothing more than a geographical expression. The Balkan territories have been realigned and redistributed so often, had their borders redrawn so often under some peace treaty or other, that most people don't much care what name the country happens to go by today. That's not where people's loyalties lie. They were loyal to Tito, not "Yugoslavia". You're either a Serb or a Croat, Orthodox or Catholic – or in this neck of the woods, a Bosnian and maybe a Muslim – and now that Tito's gone, there's no one left to hold this country together.'

'So Vlado is the rule, rather than the exception?' Imogen asked.

'Yes,' Faraday replied. 'But there's something you have to understand about Vlado. His loyalties are absolute. That's why he's been so useful to us. But it's also why he remained totally loyal to Tito, even when Tito started locking up Serbs who were too outspoken, in the name of a multi-ethnic Yugoslavia. That must have been a terrible betrayal for him. But Tito had been his commander, his comrade in arms, and for men like Vlado, that's a loyalty you don't question. Also, he understood that Tito was under pressure from Moscow to crack down on nationalism...'

He took a long draught of wine. 'But Tito was a Croat; and for Vlado to see his Serb friends – men who probably sat down to dinner where we're sitting this evening – thrown into prison must have been hard.'

'But won't the Games help with that?' Imogen asked. 'I mean, so much exposure to the outside world can't be bad, can it?'

'I'm afraid that one effect of the Games may be to make our

government, and the West generally, too complacent,' Faraday replied. 'We've underestimated nationalist and religious feelings in this part of the world for centuries.' He paused for some time. 'Your father was pessimistic about it. He gave Yugoslavia twenty-five years at most before the wheels start to fall off. I'm beginning to think he was right.'

It was after ten when their leisurely dinner ended, despite Vlado's best efforts to ply them with further food and drink. They paid the very modest bill using Deutsche Marks and prepared to leave as unobtrusively as possible. The restaurant was quiet now, and Andrej was able to spirit them into the cellar, to begin their journey through the looking glass, without attracting attention. Vlado was keeping a discreet watch inside, and would raise the alarm if any other customers left at the same time. No one did. As Faraday had promised, Andrej had dark coats and hats in the heavy local style ready to replace their own. The cellar door dropped them on the street, and then closed quickly behind them. They stood still and silent for two minutes as Faraday allowed his eyes to adjust to the darkness, before screening the street and finding it apparently deserted.

'Keep close,' he said, as they set off, 'and don't panic if I suddenly turn back or change direction. Andrej will watch our backs for as long as he can. I don't think we have company, but these people are experts, and if there's any real sign of trouble, we're going to abort.'

'I've done this before, with my father,' Julia whispered quietly.

'Not here, you haven't,' Faraday replied.

# 8

It was forty minutes later when Faraday finally stopped outside a detached two-storey house on a narrow side street off Bakarevićeva, a wide, leafy thoroughfare. The house appeared dark, except for a solitary flickering light in one downstairs room. Even in the darkness they could see that the exterior looked dilapidated; the tiny front garden had been abandoned, left to run wild and untended. Julia was aware that they had taken forty minutes to complete a ten-minute walk. She had tried to plot their route in her mind as they went along, but she had soon become disorientated by Faraday's relentlessly fast pace and constant changes in direction. He had led them from Vlado's cellar door by a circuitous route away from the river and deep into Bistrik. Once she had caught a fleeting glimpse of Andrej: that, she was clear about. But then, they had criss-crossed the main road, walked in circles and doubled back on themselves so often and so abruptly that she lost her bearings. She was impressed. Even by Baxter's standards, this was meticulous tradecraft and another reason for warming to Faraday. He had paused in front of the door for a last check and, once satisfied, he knocked on the door three times in quick succession. Beside her, Imogen seemed tense. She had not spoken since they left the cellar.

The door was opened by an elderly man dressed in an open-necked shirt and faded blue jeans. His hair was long and unkempt, he was sporting a long grey beard and moustache, and he wore a silver bracelet on his right arm. At first he opened the door only far enough to allow him to inspect his visitors. Once satisfied, he closed the door and released the chain, after which he opened it fully and stood back to allow them to enter.

'*Willkommen in meinem bescheidenen Zuhause. Bitte, kommen 'rein.*' The man ushered them into what appeared to be the house's living room, and flicked a switch on the wall to allow two large lamps to add to the dim ceiling light they had observed from outside. Surprisingly, the room was clean and tidy. Newspapers and books covered the dining table, but with them was a bottle of slivovice, a carafe of water, and four glasses. 'Oscar' or 'Ernst Meier' had been expecting them. Julia stared at the man intently.

'Ernst, may I introduce Julia Cathermole,' she heard Faraday say, 'the solicitor I told you about; and this is her associate, Imogen Lester.' Imogen shook his hand gingerly.

'Miss Cathermole, this is…'

'This is Sir Conrad Rainer,' Julia said, offering her hand, but still staring. 'Thank you for the warm welcome, Sir Conrad, but there's no need for German, is there? We all understand English perfectly well.'

The man returned Julia's stare for several seconds before bursting out laughing, after which he was overtaken by a fit of coughing that made him bend over, hands on chest, and turned his face a bright shade of red. It took him several seconds of slow deep breathing to recover. He took a drink from a glass of water on a side table. Eventually he took her hand.

'Just plain Mr Rainer these days, I'm afraid,' he said. The accent was standard professional class English. 'The Queen got rather annoyed with me, so I understand, and revoked my K. Can't say I blame her. You are a very perceptive woman, Miss Cathermole. With advancing age and my facial disguise I had hoped I would be somewhat harder to recognise.'

'I have a good memory for faces,' Julia replied.

'What's going on?' Imogen asked.

Julia turned to her. 'Mr Rainer was a High Court judge who suddenly disappeared from London in 1971, just after trying a murder case at the Old Bailey. He left behind him huge gambling debts, and the body of his mistress, a woman called Greta Thiemann, stuffed into a storage area in his flat in the Barbican – allegedly, of course, I should say. There's a warrant out for his arrest. Supposedly, he disappeared without trace, whereabouts unknown, authorities completely baffled, and all the rest of it.'

She turned again and looked pointedly at Faraday.

'But it seems the authorities weren't quite as baffled as they led us to believe. Someone knew exactly where he was, and kindly supplied him with a new identity as Ernst Meier, Austrian. Not the best choice, if you don't mind my saying so. The accent is way off base. I'm surprised he lasted a week.'

'That was nothing to do with us,' Faraday protested. 'He was already Ernst Meier when Michael found him. Conrad told Michael who he was, but his cover had been in place long before we got to him.'

'I didn't have much choice, really,' Rainer said. 'It didn't take him long to see through my Austrian persona. You're quite right, Miss Cathermole: my family German, such as it is, is strictly *Hochdeutsch* – I've never been exposed to *Bairisch* – so I thought I might as well make a clean breast of it. It was better than having him running around asking questions about me. That would have attracted a lot of attention, and God knows what might have happened.'

'What you might call being between a rock and a hard place,' Julia observed wryly.

'Not an ideal situation, certainly.' He paused for another drink of water. 'But I calculated that Michael would think I was more useful to him here, supplying him with information, than I would be rotting in some prison in England. Fortunately, I was right.'

He gestured to the four chairs around the table and lit a cigarette. Immediately, he coughed and almost seemed to choke. He leaned on the table and bent over, trying to regain his breath. Imogen filled his water glass from the carafe and put it in his hand. He drank, nodding his thanks, and allowed some seconds to go by until his breath returned fully.

'If you'd like to have a seat, I'll tell you all about it. Help yourself to a glass of the local firewater, or I can brew some coffee. I have some first rate stuff a friend brings for me from Venice.'

'We've probably had all we need to drink,' Julia said, taking her seat.

'Coffee it is, then,' Rainer replied. He walked unhurriedly, but they heard the coughing welling up from deep in his chest. Moments later, there was the sound of a kettle beginning to boil. He returned and leaned against the door-frame. 'I suppose you want to know everything, from the beginning, Greta and the gambling and all the rest of it?'

Julia shook her head. 'Yes, but not now – not if I'm going to act as your solicitor.'

Rainer smiled. 'Of course. What am I thinking?'

Faraday looked at Julia questioningly. 'I'm not following,' he said. 'How can you advise him unless…?'

'I said, I don't want to hear it *now*,' she replied, 'not that I don't want to hear it at all. As Mr Rainer well knows, with his experience, conversations between solicitor and client are only privileged as long as they don't include third parties. Imogen works for me, so she's covered, but we can't talk about certain things in front of you without losing the privilege, so unless you're ready to leave us to talk alone…'

'I'm afraid not,' Faraday said, 'not at this stage.'

'That's what I assumed,' she said.

'What would you like me to talk about, then?' Rainer asked, after a silence.

'Why don't you start by telling me why you're thinking of going back to England? I take it you do understand what's going to happen the moment you step off the plane?'

He nodded. 'I'm sure you've noticed the cough – you couldn't really miss it, could you? It's been getting worse and worse for a couple of years now. I'd been putting it off, of course, trying to ignore it, as one does; but inevitably, the time came when I couldn't ignore it any longer. So a couple of months ago I finally took myself off to see the quacks at the local hospital for a check-up. I'm sure you can guess the rest. Generally, health pretty good for a man of your age, the quacks reported, but one or two worrying signs we would like to take a closer look at, run a few tests, and so on. Probably nothing to be concerned about, but you might feel better if you cut back on the smoking, maybe even give up altogether – you know the kind of thing. So I go back, they do the tests, and they tell me I have a very nasty type of lung cancer, distinctly antisocial, very aggressive. "Not operable, unfortunately, and actually, to be honest, there's nothing we can do when it's so advanced. If you'd come to see us a year ago, perhaps, but… Sorry to be the bearers of bad news, but you'll be a very lucky man if you're still alive six months from now."' He took a deep drag on his cigarette. 'So, I didn't give up, did I? No bloody point now, is there? But it did get me thinking.'

The kettle whistled loudly, and he returned to the kitchen. Two minutes later he came back, carrying a huge red metallic coffee pot, which he placed on the table. He took four earthenware mugs from the sideboard on the wall alongside the door to the kitchen and placed them close to the coffee pot.

'Let's give that a minute or two to brew.'

'If you did go back to England,' Imogen said, 'at least you could get a second opinion. I don't know what the standard of medicine is here, but…'

'Better than you might think, actually,' Faraday said. 'Health care can be surprisingly good behind the Curtain – if you have access to it, which is another question altogether. The hospital here is as good as anything in Eastern Europe. The doctors are well trained. I doubt they would make a mistake with something like this.'

Rainer nodded. 'You can feel it, anyway, when it gets to this stage. No, they've got it right, I'm as sure of that as I can be. But you see, it means that I have no reason to fear being put on trial. I'm not going to live long enough.'

'They will still put you in prison,' Imogen said, 'won't they Julia?'

'Yes, they will. There must be something more to it than that, Mr Rainer.'

'Conrad, please. No need for undue formality, is there?'

'Conrad. Look, Conrad: you have a choice: you can live out your life here in freedom, or you can go home and die under lock and key. You can breathe the fresh air for as long as you have left, and die at home, or in the hospital here; or you can spend your remaining days in some prison hospital with guards at your bedside day and night. Each to his own, obviously, but I know what I'd choose.'

He nodded. 'I understand. But I want to make amends, to the limited extent open to me.'

'Amends?'

He looked down at the floor and was silent, for some time.

'There are people I need to apologise to. I left my wife, Deborah, behind when I came abroad so abruptly, but I had wronged her in many other ways long before I left. She's divorced me since, I believe.'

'Yes, she has,' Julia said. 'It was in the news: about a year after you disappeared.'

'Yes: well, I don't blame her at all; what else could she do? But if she would agree to see me just once, so that I could apologise, it would mean a great deal to me; my conscience might be clearer when I go. And,' he added, with a grin in Faraday's direction, 'assuming, hypothetically, that I have committed any criminal offence in respect of which I might need Julia to defend me, I might, hypothetically, want to ask forgiveness of any of the victims of such hypothetical conduct – again, so that I can shuffle off this mortal coil somewhat more at peace with myself.'

'I'm still not entirely sure where I fit into this,' Julia said.

'I want you to make a deal for me,' Rainer replied.

# 9

'What kind of deal?' Julia asked.

Rainer thought for some time. 'I would like to live out my days in freedom, if it could be arranged – of course, I would. Most of my remaining time is probably going to be spent in a medical facility of one kind or another, so why keep me in jail when they know I won't last long enough to be tried? I'm not going anywhere.'

'They think you murdered Greta Thiemann,' Julia pointed out. 'You're not being charged with shoplifting, Conrad. You're being charged with murder. You've tried a murder case. You don't need me to tell you how the system works: they will remand you in custody. What makes you think I could make a deal of that kind for you?'

'I have information,' Rainer replied, 'information that could be very useful to them.'

She glanced at Faraday. 'What kind of information? Political or criminal?'

'Both,' Faraday replied. 'Based on what Conrad told Michael, there is a possibility of breaking up a huge drug trafficking enterprise – the proceeds of which are being used to finance the purchase of arms by underground Serb nationalist groups. It's serious stuff, Julia, and it's something that would be of huge value both to the Service and the police. But if he names names, and if those involved work out where the names came from, it wouldn't make Conrad any friends in this part of the world.'

Julia nodded quietly for some time. 'So, it's not just a matter of his conscience: you need to extract him for his own safety?'

'Exactly.'

'I think you'd better tell me the whole story,' Julia said.

Rainer refilled the coffee cups and lit another cigarette, with the inevitable cough as he took his seat.

'When I had reason to leave England in 1971, I did so with the aid of some friends, who will remain nameless. They got me safely across the channel and I found myself in Amsterdam, in what Michael would have called a safe house. I'd had no time to prepare: the chance to leave came and I had to take it. I had nothing, except for five hundred pounds and the clothes I stood up in. But my friends did hand me over to a minder – someone using the name Jan. I didn't know him at all, and I don't know how my friends knew him, but there he was. Jan warned me not to go out under any circumstances. He told me that food would be brought to me, and he gave me some guilders to pay for it. I was to wait in the safe house for someone else to contact me. After the best part of a week, someone came. He called himself Branko. He had a sidekick with him, a fellow by the name of Miodrag. They said they had come to conduct me to my new home.'

He laughed briefly, then coughed again, and took a sip of water.

'They had documents for me – an Austrian passport, birth certificate, driving licence, and some other papers, all in the name of Ernst Meier. They apparently knew that I spoke some German. They insisted that we leave immediately. They took turns driving, and we hardly stopped until we got here. The papers they'd prepared were good quality – well, at least, no one asked us any questions at the borders. We drove for what seemed like a couple of days: I'm not sure. I was out of it. I hadn't slept properly for a week or more, and I had no idea where we were or where we were going. It wasn't until they told me we were in Sarajevo that I had any clue.'

'They brought you straight to this house?' Julia asked.

He nodded. 'Everything was arranged. There was a wardrobe full of clothes upstairs, my size, and I was given enough money to manage for a couple of weeks. They said I would receive further instructions. I've been here ever since.'

'This all sounds remarkably well organised,' Julia observed.

'That's what I thought too,' Rainer replied, 'but I had no idea how well organised it was until they contacted me again. I'd hardly ventured out since I arrived. I went to a couple of shops for supplies, of course, and I walked into town after dark a few times to learn my way around, but other than that I sat here without very much to do.' He smiled. 'But I did find this in a bookshop.' He picked up a book from the table. '*Serbo-Croat for English Speakers*,' he read from the cover. 'It's been a godsend. I had nothing else to do with myself, so I started working my way through it. The more I read, and the more I went out at night and listened to people talking, the more I started to get a feel for it. I even moved on to reading the local newspaper once a week, and now, I'm not exactly what you'd call fluent, but I can hold my own.'

'Which means, he has become a good listener,' Faraday observed.

'I've never given away that I could understand their language,' Rainer added. 'As far as they're concerned I speak English and German and that's it; so they've always chattered away happily in Serbo-Croat, under the impression that I can't understand a word they're saying... But we're getting a bit ahead of ourselves.'

He poured himself a glass of slivovice and added some ice. 'Anyone join me? No?' He took a drink and lit another cigarette. 'Branko and Miodrag came back, closer to three weeks than two, as it turned out, and this time they had a gentleman with them they called Dragan. Dragan was in a different league altogether.'

'Meaning?' Julia asked.

'Well, Branko and Miodrag were pretty scruffy types, if you know what I mean, definitely not officer material. Branko spoke a few words of English – enough to order me around – but Miodrag didn't speak a word. Dragan was very different: immaculately dressed, expensive Italian suit, silk tie, white scarf, patent leather shoes, Balkan Sobranie cigarettes, the whole works. His English is almost perfect – a bit of an accent, but I'd bet my pension, if I had one, that he didn't get it from a book. He's spent time speaking English somewhere.'

'British English or American?' Julia asked.

'British, definitely.' He exhaled slowly and heavily, a rasping noise coming from deep in his throat. 'Dragan was the officer commanding, no doubt about that. He asked me whether I was comfortable, whether the arrangements were to my satisfaction, and so on. I said they were. I tried to find out how he and his people were involved in my escape, what relationship, if any, they had with the people I knew, but he wasn't giving anything away. Then he made his pitch. He made it clear that he knew exactly who I was; that he knew how pleased the authorities back in England would be to know where I was; and that he wouldn't hesitate to convey that information to them if I didn't behave exactly as instructed. If, on the other hand, I agreed to do as instructed, I would be perfectly safe, I would be under his protection, and I would receive a monthly stipend more than sufficient for my needs, in untraceable notes, a mix of dinars and D-Marks.' He took another long drink. 'So, I've been behaving as instructed, and receiving my stipend, ever since.'

'What did the officer commanding instruct you to do?' Julia asked.

'He appointed me one of his innkeepers.'

'What?'

'*Gostioničar* – an innkeeper. From time to time, on average once a week, sometimes twice, I would have guests to stay with me, either overnight or using the house as a rest stop for several hours. These so-called guests are couriers, of course, en route to somewhere else; and they always have large canvas bags with them, containing certain commodities. On other occasions, a courier may drop the commodities off with me for storage for a day or two, for collection by others. There are always two of them, sometimes three, if it's a big shipment.'

'No prizes for guessing what commodities we're talking about,' Julia observed.

'No. But I have the occasional peek inside the bags late at night, after the couriers have passed out from too much firewater, just to make sure. Cocaine and heroin are the staples, but also cannabis resin and other stuff too, sometimes. God only knows what some of it is. But whatever it is, there's a lot of it.'

Julia shook her head. 'It must have occurred to you that you were running a terrible risk, staying put here and helping to traffic hard drugs.'

'What choice did I have?' Rainer asked. 'If I'd tried to run, they would have tracked me down in no time. These are serious people, Julia. You don't have to deal with Dragan for very long to see that. I had nowhere to go – unless I made a dash for the British embassy, and that didn't seem like a very inviting option in the circumstances.'

He drained his glass.

'But about a year and a half ago,' he added, 'the opposite happened. Since I couldn't go the embassy, the embassy came to me.'

# 10

'My father,' Imogen said quietly.

'Yes. Michael was waiting for me in the shadows at the side of the house late one evening, when I returned from my favourite watering hole. I had no guests that night, as I'm sure he knew – evidently, he'd already been watching the place for some weeks by then. He accompanied me into the house without any by-your-leave: all a bit alarming at the time, but within a few minutes we were on our second glass of firewater, and he'd convinced me that he meant me no harm – no physical harm, at any rate. We'd spoken German when he first approached me, but he saw through me straight away, just as you did, so we soon switched to English. As I said before, I told him who I was. I told him the whole story, in fact, rather than wait for him to make inquiries and draw more attention to me; and – not to put too fine a point on it – I offered him all the information I had if he would agree to keep quiet about me.'

'What did he say to that?' Julia asked.

'Not much, at first: he was very non-committal to begin with. We continued imbibing the firewater while he probed me for an hour or so about what I had to offer, during which time I was trying to give him just enough to make him believe me, without reducing myself to having nothing left to bargain with. As good luck would have it, it seems I persuaded him that I did have some worthwhile information, and that I could get even more if he left me alone.'

Imogen stood, walked over to the wall by the front door, and turned back.

'My father promised not to turn you in?' she asked. 'After everything you've done?'

'Allegedly done,' Julia murmured.

'Your father had been on Dragan's trail for some time, Miss Lester,' Rainer replied, 'but Dragan is well guarded and he couldn't get close to him. But then suddenly, here I was – in personal contact with the man and his senior associates. I'm sure Dragan has other innkeepers, but the chances are I'm the only Brit among them, and as far as your father was concerned, I was an asset worth protecting. That's all I was to him – an asset, nothing more – I have no illusions about that. But that was good enough for me, and it was also good for your father, and for his Service. You may not be able to see it from my point of view: I understand that; but please try to see it from his.'

'We're not the police, Miss Lester,' Faraday said quietly. 'We can't always choose who we deal with. We have wider interests to consider.'

Imogen turned her back, shaking her head.

'There's one thing worrying me,' Julia said. 'You'd obviously made good progress with your Serbo-Croat, but to get the level of information Michael would have wanted, that wouldn't be enough, surely. You would have to...' She allowed her voice to trail away as she turned her head to look at Faraday, who had stood, and was leaning on the table. He straightened up. 'Oh, please don't tell me...'

'With Conrad's permission, we've been bugging the house,' he confirmed quietly.

'That's a dangerous game, Faraday,' she replied. 'You could have got him killed, for God's sake. You're playing against professionals here. You don't think Dragan's people know how to sweep a house?'

'We explained the risks to Conrad, Julia. He agreed to work with us.'

'What choice did the man have?'

'That's not our fault,' Faraday replied. 'We play the hand we're dealt. Conrad agreed to work with us. We've kept watch over him as much as we can without giving ourselves away. Periodically, we send people in, dressed as plumbers or delivery boys or whatever, to take the tapes away and make sure the equipment hasn't been tampered with. If there'd been any sign that Dragan's people were on to us, we would have had him out of here before you could say Josip Broz Tito.'

Conrad stood and held out his arms. 'May I suggest that we're all getting a bit carried away? Shall we sit down and focus on the facts as they are?'

Faraday took his seat immediately, followed a second or two later by Julia. Imogen kept her back turned for some time, but eventually followed suit with an obvious show of reluctance.

'Michael did explain the risks to me,' Rainer continued. 'I had no illusions about what I was doing. But Dragan's people haven't rumbled me, and regardless of what Michael may have agreed to in the interests of getting information, I will, in fact, be returning to England very soon to face the music. So why don't you at least let me finish telling you what I found out – including what little I know about what happened to Miss Lester's parents?'

'Go ahead, please,' Julia said.

'All this came out over a lengthy period of time, of course,' Rainer continued, 'but while my friends the couriers thought I couldn't understand them, they were gradually making it clear to me that Dragan is running a major operation on a huge scale, trafficking hard drugs in both directions, buying in the Near East and Eastern Europe and selling it on in the West, and vice versa. Typically, heroin, amphetamines and cannabis resin running east to west, cocaine and some other stuff running west to east. I also found out that the bulk of the proceeds – apart from a healthy chunk devoted to keeping Dragan in the luxurious style he's become accustomed to – is finding its way into the coffers of the Serb nationalist groups. These groups are operating covertly, under the radar, for now; but since Tito's death the pressure on them isn't as intense as it used to be, and they're poking their heads above the parapet from time to time.'

'Which, needless to say, is of considerable concern to us,' Faraday added, 'given its potential to destabilise Yugoslavia in the longer term.'

'Where in the West?' Julia asked.

'All over the place: Hamburg, Frankfurt, Berlin – East and West – Stockholm, Amsterdam, Paris, Brussels, Madrid, and, of course, London.' He hesitated, glancing at Faraday. Faraday nodded. Rainer lit another cigarette. 'One of the advantages of being a judge or lawyer is that one learns how to assemble pieces of evidence into a structure, how to factor in new evidence, how to make the evidence reveal a pattern. Over time, I was able to piece together the likely addresses of some of their safe houses – not always exactly, but close enough to be identified with the aid of a bit of surveillance – and the likely names of some of their contacts in those cities.'

'I can confirm that,' Faraday added. 'I've been passing Conrad's information on to Interpol – without divulging the source, obviously – and they're almost ready to give the green light to police forces in seven or eight countries to act on it. I've asked them to hold off for now, to protect my source, but I can't hold them indefinitely. Conrad's information is crucial. It's the key to clipping Dragan's wings, perhaps even to closing him down altogether.'

Rainer refilled his glass and drank deeply.

'And that brings me to the highlight of tonight's show,' he said, 'the reason why the authorities in England may be tempted to let me die with some degree of comfort, after all.'

'We're all ears,' Julia said.

'I believe I know the identities of several of Dragan's contacts in London,' he replied. 'They are officers serving in the Metropolitan Police. Interesting, don't you think? I'm prepared to name names as soon as we have an acceptable deal.'

Julia nodded quietly.

'So what happened to my parents?' Imogen asked pointedly.

# 11

The question seemed to require another glass of slivovice and another cigarette.

'I don't know the whole story,' Rainer replied. 'But I can tell you one thing: it wasn't a street robbery – or if it was, it was one hell of a coincidence.'

'Why do you say that?' Imogen persisted. 'What *do* you know?'

Rainer exhaled deeply. 'Your father came to see me on the evening he died; eight thirty, nine, that kind of time, out of the blue – I wasn't expecting him. He had your mother with him.'

'Had he ever brought her here before?' Julia asked.

'No, never. I'd never met Margaret before, and I was very surprised to meet her then. I assumed that he had a good reason for having her with him, but he didn't tell me what it was, and I didn't ask. What he did tell me was that they'd been to see someone else, and that since they were in the vicinity, he thought they might call in and partake of a glass or two of vino with me before calling it a night.'

'Meaning that he thought he was being followed and had to get off the street,' Faraday said.

'He didn't say that in so many words, but that was the impression I had. Your father wasn't one to show undue concern, Miss Lester, as you know, I'm sure. He was a cool customer. But the fact that he turned up here unannounced…'

'He must have known he was in trouble,' Julia agreed. 'But

wasn't there some emergency procedure he could have activated?'

Faraday grinned, looking sheepish. 'He had the same number I gave you. But it rings in Belgrade, so it's not exactly like calling 999.'

'Oh, thank you,' Julia replied. 'I feel much safer now.'

'In Belgrade, we would have people on the street within minutes, but we're pretty much on our own here. But Michael knew that. He could have arranged for a couple of big lads to watch his back if he thought he needed them. Vlado has a few such on payroll, and he wouldn't have minded lending them out to Michael for an evening. But you wouldn't want to do that unless you knew you were expecting trouble, and the fact that he had Margaret with him strongly suggests that he wasn't worried at the start of the evening. I would say whatever happened took him by surprise. He didn't see it coming.'

Rainer took a long drink. 'I didn't have any business meetings planned for that night, no guests in residence, so I told Michael that they could stay as long as they wanted. They could have stayed the night as far as I was concerned. I wish to God they had. But he seemed anxious to get back to wherever they were staying, as if there was something urgent he had to do.'

'He was probably worried about you, too,' Faraday suggested. 'The longer he stayed, the more he would be putting you at risk from whoever was following him.'

'What do you know about the place where my parents' bodies were found?' Imogen asked.

'I know it wasn't on any direct route to where they were staying, on the other side of the river. So either they had someone else to see, or...'

'Or,' Faraday added, 'as Colonel Stojanović would have us believe, they were doing a spot of late night sightseeing – which I think we all agree we can rule out – or Michael was doing some serious tradecraft in an effort to lose whoever was after him, but it didn't work.'

They were all silent for some time.

'So we don't really know any more than when we started,' Imogen concluded sadly.

Julia put an arm around her shoulder. 'Yes, we do. We know that this wasn't a random street crime. Your dad was working on something important, and he may have stumbled over some valuable information. Whatever it was, it was enough to make Dragan's people take immediate action. Your mother and father died in the line of duty, Imogen. There's no doubt about that.'

'I will keep my ears open,' Rainer said, 'for as long as I'm here. Dragan's boys get quite talkative after a few glasses of firewater, so I may well pick something up.' He lit another cigarette. 'But on the subject of while I'm still here, have I given you something to work with? It's not that I'm getting nervous, but…'

'Do you have two hundred D-Marks?' Julia asked.

'Yes. Why?'

She held out her hand. Rainer walked to the sideboard, took the notes from a drawer, and handed them to her.

'Thank you,' Julia relied decisively. 'Now that you've paid me my retainer, I'm your solicitor, and I will do my best to work something out for you.' She hesitated. 'But I don't want to hold out any false hope, Conrad. They're not pleased with you back home, and the moment your feet touch British soil the press will be baying for your blood. There will be a lot of pressure on the court and the prosecutors to make sure you stay locked up – even if they know you may not make it to trial.'

He nodded. 'I understand.'

'But I'll do what I can behind the scenes.' She turned to Faraday. 'I assume you don't want to delay his departure any more than he does. It would help if I could cut this trip short and get back to London tomorrow.'

Faraday shook his head. 'Not recommended. It's a matter of your cover. You wouldn't run straight back home after your meeting with the Militsija. You're still a bit shocked, remember, a bit depressed about your lack of progress. You'd be walking around a bit, you'd certainly be visiting the local newspaper office to see if they have anything, and when you finally give the impression of giving up, you'd spend your last day doing some melancholy sightseeing. I can recommend a few melancholy sights. You might want to take a stroll over the Princip Bridge – in daylight. It was where poor old Archduke Ferdinand bought it, after all.'

'At the hands of a Serb nationalist assassin,' Rainer observed quietly.

'Yes. Well, *plus ça change*, as the French say. No, I think a touch of sightseeing would definitely be in order. Just don't venture too far south of the river, that's all.'

'Faraday,' Julia said, 'the kind of meetings I need to arrange take a certain amount of planning. I can't just walk into these people's offices and expect their undivided attention. If I could get to a secure phone I would ask Baxter to make some calls for me. But I'm well aware that I'm in Sarajevo, where such things don't exist.'

'I can pass anything you want on to Baxter for you tomorrow, when I get back to Belgrade.'

'When you get back...? You're abandoning us here with the famous emergency number that rings in Belgrade?' she asked, with more than a little venom.

He laughed. 'You won't be alone at any time, I assure you. All I ask is that you don't stray too far from the hotel after dark, and that you stay north of the river – except to go to Vlado's. Actually, I suggest that you have lunch, or a drink, with him both days. That way, if I need to leave you a message, I'll know you've got it.'

She shook her head. 'All right,' she said. 'I want to see John Caswell. He's the Deputy Director of Public Prosecutions. I also need to book a conference with counsel, Ben Schroeder QC, at Two Wessex Buildings, Middle Temple. That's for starters. I'm not sure where I may have to go after that.'

'Your wish is my command,' Faraday replied.

'You've got that?' she asked.

'You're not the only one with a memory, Julia. It may not be quite as good as yours, but I do have one.'

She conceded a thin smile. 'Once I've seen them, I'll have a better idea of how the land lies. I assume you will have Conrad ready to go?'

'He's on standby as of now, twenty-four hours' notice.'

'Code name?"

'Prodigal.'

'Nice touch'

Rainer nodded. 'I'll be ready,' he said.

Julia glanced around the room. 'Do I take it that everything we've said has been duly recorded?'

'Naturally. But don't worry: we're going to take a few minutes to remove the evidence before we go. Actually, it would save time if you wouldn't mind helping me. Baxter says you're quite good at this kind of thing.'

'Baxter talks out of school too much,' she replied. But then she laughed. 'Oh, why not? No harm in keeping one's hand in, is there? By the way,' she added, as they started work, 'you do realise, don't you, that Conrad won't be the only one with the press on his trail once he's back home? They're going to be asking why it took you so long to bring him back. Do you really think you can keep the lid on this?'

'Why not? He's got a decent cover story. Ever since his chums smuggled him out of England in 1971 he's been hiding out in Sarajevo, posing as Ernst Meier. But his luck ran out when the local police stumbled across him while investigating a murder committed close to his house. The police alerted the embassy and we did the rest: and now he's facing a murder charge of his own. Simple enough story: what's not to believe?'

He put down the screwdriver he was using and walked over to her.

'The press are welcome to run that story as much as they like. In fact, we'll probably encourage it. But his work for us, the information he's supplying us, can't go anywhere near the public domain, Julia. You know that. I'm sure Conrad understands, too, but we will be making it clear to him before he leaves, just to make sure.'

'I have to deal with people on his behalf.'

'And we will expect you to impress upon them how important this is.'

'But if there's a trial…'

'There won't be,' Faraday replied definitively.

# 12

It was almost nine o'clock in the evening when Imogen finally arrived back in Hampstead. She gratefully paid the driver, and climbed out of the taxi as he deposited her suitcase on the pavement in front of the large nineteenth-century terraced house in Willow Road, the house that had been her family home. After the stifling warmth of the cab's heater, the freezing air came as a shock. Wearily, she hauled the suitcase along the icy stone path that led from the street to the front door. On her left, the path ran alongside the privet hedge that separated the small front garden from the neighbouring property; while on the right, a metal railing, painted a smart glossy black, protected visitors against a sudden precipitous drop down to the level of the basement. Reaching the end of the path, she hauled the case up the four stone steps, also icy, that led up to the front door. Having rummaged impatiently through her handbag for some time before finding her keys, she unlocked the door, pushed it open and, with one last effort, dragged the suitcase over the threshold.

With a sigh of relief she closed and locked the door. She closed her eyes and allowed her body to lean against the door for some moments, until her breath returned. It wasn't simply her modest exertion with the suitcase. She felt exhausted, physically and emotionally. She had not slept well since seeing that god-forsaken street, little better than an alleyway, where her parents had died; since seeing their personal effects, defaced by grey identifying tags, impersonally displayed on a trestle table under the clinical fluorescent lights of the Militsija's evidence storage room. And today, their flight had been delayed, a particular annoyance when both she and Julia were already frustrated at being forced to spend the two previous days in Sarajevo. As Faraday had asked, they had paid pro forma visits to the local newspaper office, dutifully admired every tourist attraction they could find, and reported to Vlado in case he had some message for them, which he had not. It struck her as a lot of trouble to go to, just to maintain what she had always thought of as an improbable cover story – a story they nonetheless had to repeat in detail on arrival at Heathrow to an inquisitive customs officer, who showed great interest in the fact that they had ventured behind the Iron Curtain, and questioned them at length about their movements. Their luggage was then mysteriously delayed, and surfaced only after all the other bags from their flight had long since been reclaimed. Finally, when they had escaped the airport, came the long trek into town.

The house was in darkness, as far as she could see. She switched on the light in the hall. The air seemed stale and musty, but she also detected the unmistakable, familiar aroma of cannabis.

'Damian?' she called out. 'Dame, are you here?'

There was no reply. She lifted the suitcase past the coat stand and parked it against the wall. She took off her scarf and gloves, crammed them into the pockets of her coat, hung the coat up and walked to the end of the hall, where the house's massive dark wooden staircases led up to the two upper floors, and down to the basement. She pressed two other switches, which shed light on the passage leading to the living room, dining room and kitchen.

'Dame, where are you?' She raised her voice now. 'I know you're here. Where are you?'

'Kitchen,' a voice replied, without enthusiasm, several seconds later.

The kitchen was also in darkness. She switched on the lights, causing him to wince and cover his eyes with his hands. He was seated at the table, wearing an old brown sweater over a green shirt, and casual khaki trousers. He was surrounded by a half-empty bottle of whisky, a number of glasses, a plastic bag containing herbal cannabis, a packet of cigarette papers, a lighter, and a large glass ashtray filled with roll-up cigarette ends and the remains of several joints. In and around the sink were a number of unwashed plates, cups, knives and forks. The cupboard under the sink was open, revealing a bin overflowing with tins and food packages; some had spilled out on to the floor.

'So, the traveller returns. How was Commie-land? Full of pictures of Comrade Stalin, and workers queuing up for food, was it? Did you bring me a stick of Sarajevo rock?'

She shook her head. 'It wasn't like that at all, actually. Is this what you've been doing all the time I've been away?'

'"This?"'

'Yes: "this". Sitting around in the kitchen in the dark, drinking and getting stoned?'

He pretended outrage. 'Certainly not: I'm offended by the suggestion. One has been taking one's morning constitutional on the Heath, playing one's regular eighteen holes each afternoon, dining at one's club with one's chums, all the usual stuff.' He glanced up at the functional, black and white electric clock on the wall above the sink. 'I say: is that the time? Almost time for me to change into my DJ and make my way into town for the evening's entertainment.'

She made her way to the sink, turned on the tap, and allowed hot water to splash liberally over the items piled on top of each other there, before adding a generous dose of washing up liquid. As it percolated, she seized a rubbish bag from under the sink and emptied the overflowing debris from the bin into it, adding a tin and three packages from the floor, before stowing it away next to the bin.

'You are such a child, Dame,' she said quietly. 'When are you ever going to grow up? If Mum and Dad dying hasn't done it, what is it going to take? No one's going to look after you all your life, you know. You're going to have to take some responsibility for yourself at some point.'

She heard him pour himself another drink.

'Oh, for God's sake, stop lecturing me, Girton. I'm grieving, OK? This is how I grieve.'

She snorted and began washing the dishes, getting angry now, banging them down into the rack and leaving them to drain. He watched her for some time.

'So, how is your employer-lover, lover-employer, or whatever you call her? I'm surprised the two of you didn't get arrested over there. I don't think the Commies are very keen on that kind of thing, are they?'

She took a deep breath. 'Julia is fine,' she replied, 'thank you. But it was a long few days, I'm very tired, and I could do without your juvenile attempts at humour.'

'Well, we don't all have your gift of timeless wit and repartee, do we, Girton?' His tone suddenly changed to sullen. 'And anyway, what do you expect when you bugger off with your lover-employer, employer-lover, and leave me here on my own with only the pigeons for company? You're not the only one with feelings, you know. I loved them too.'

She paused, dish in hand, for a moment, then looked back at him.

'I know you did, Dame.'

They were silent. She finished the task she had set herself, dropping the last dish into the rack to drain. She dried her hands on the none-too-clean towel hanging from the hook beneath the draining board, and sat down opposite him at the table. He held up the bottle of whisky questioningly. She looked at him for some time before nodding. He poured into a clean glass.

'So, what's it really like over there?' His voice was calmer now, more reasonable. 'Did you have to eat boiled cabbage three times a day?'

She smiled. 'No. Actually, I was surprised – the food there is pretty good, and I didn't see anyone queuing up to buy it. The city is really beautiful – well, the centre anyway, the parts they let the tourists see. There are some lovely old buildings, churches, mosques; it's surrounded by mountains; and the air is incredibly fresh compared to London.' She paused. 'I wish I could have seen it under different circumstances, you know... But...'

He nodded. 'You were there on a mission. How did it go? Did you find out what happened to them?'

She took a good swig of the whisky, and was grateful for the rejuvenating effect as its warmth produced a sudden surge of energy. Her body relaxed for a moment, but the relief was short-lived. Almost at once she started to feel tense again. There was no mystery about that. In addition to the frustrations of the past days, she had been carrying the burden of her guilt about what she was about to do. Her brother was grieving: for all his immature reaction to her she did not doubt that, and she desperately wanted to offer him some consolation. But, having no consolation herself, she had none to offer. Not only that, but she was about to lie to him, and she had no way of avoiding it. Both Julia and Faraday had made it very clear to her that at least one life depended on her doing exactly that, not to mention the breaking up of an international drug ring and nameless political repercussions. Perhaps one day she would be able to tell him the whole story, but not today.

She shook her head. 'Not really. The police were very nice, and they did their best to be helpful. They took us to see the place where it happened. But there was nothing to see, Dame. It was just a street, like all the others. They said south of the river in Sarajevo isn't the safest of places. Street robberies aren't uncommon there, and Mum and Dad were probably just in the wrong place at the wrong time.'

'They were supposed to be in Belgrade. That's where Dad worked. Why were they even in Sarajevo?'

'The embassy said he had something work-related to do there. Obviously, he had to travel from time to time for work. They haven't said exactly what he was doing. But they wouldn't, would they? You know what it's like. They can't talk about everything people like Dad do.'

He seemed unconvinced. 'There's got to be more to it than that. Are the police still investigating?'

'Yes, of course. They said they would let us know as soon as they make an arrest. They're up to their necks in work, what with the Olympic Games coming up and everything, but they are taking it seriously. They did have a witness come forward, who said there were four men who attacked them. They have a couple of potential suspects in mind, and they're hopeful that may lead somewhere. If they arrest one, they think he may give the others up in return for some sort of deal. They even let us see the evidence, you know, Mum and Dad's things. They're going to return them once they don't need them as evidence any more... But... well, that's about it, for now, at least.'

He was silent for some time.

'So, it was all a bit of a waste of time, was it?'

'No, I wouldn't say that,' she replied. 'I think the fact that we went all that way showed them how concerned we are, and how much we want the case solved. Also... well, you know, at the moment they're keen on having good relations with the West, and they're worried about visitors not feeling safe during the Games, so they do have some incentive to solve it.'

'Nothing to do but wait, then?' he said.

She smiled. 'Well, there are things one can do. One can still take one's usual constitutional, play one's eighteen holes, dine with one's chums at one's club. No need to just sit around in one's dark kitchen brooding over it.'

For the first time, they laughed together, and the tension subsided. He pushed the plastic bag and the cigarette papers across the table in her direction.

'You could do with unwinding a bit,' he observed. 'You were wound tight as a drum when you came in.'

'If you'd had the kind of day I've had,' she replied, 'you'd be wound pretty tight yourself.'

'I'd be in a far worse state,' he admitted. 'I don't have your capacity to duck and weave and let the bullshit go by you. So I have more bad days than you do. But suffering so much, as I do, I also happen to have a decent remedy for it.' He nodded in the direction of the bag. 'Roll yourself one. Let yourself go for once, Girton. Prove to me that I have a sister with normal human urges, not some desperate bluestocking whose idea of a good night out is a seminar on the siege of Troy.'

'I don't have to do drugs to unwind,' she replied primly.

'Really? So how do you unwind? In all the years I've known you, in other words, all my life, I've never been able to figure that out about you.'

'I don't do it with drugs,' she insisted.

He laughed and leaned across the table. 'Right. Now, look me in the eye and tell me that never once, in your three years away from home at Cambridge, surrounded by hedonistic undergraduates, never once during that whole time did you take a drag from a joint.'

She grinned, but did not reply.

'As I suspected,' he said. 'So, please, loosen up, Girton. Just for tonight, OK? Just for me. Tomorrow, I promise, I will start cleaning the place up and getting my act together.'

She scoffed. 'That, I would like to see.'

'I swear. Look, Mum and Dad may be disapproving, looking down on us, or up at us, from wherever they are, but there's nothing they can do to us now, is there? We both need to take the edge off tonight. The only difference is, I know that, and you don't. Except, you do now, because I've just told you.'

She did not reply.

'You don't need their approval anymore, Girton. Cut yourself some slack. Come to that, cut both of us some slack.'

She took a deep breath and exhaled heavily as the lies she had told him played and replayed in her head without pausing, as if on some perpetually repeating tape.

'If I do, will you stop calling me "Girton", and will you shut up about Julia, and promise that you will not call her my employer-lover, or lover-employer, or… will you just shut up about her?'

He bowed his head to her. 'You have my word, my Lady.'

She seized the packet and pulled out a cigarette paper.

# 13

*Sunday 4 December 1983*

Her first thought or, more accurately, her first instinct – in those first moments thought was still elusive – was that there must have been an explosion, a bomb must have gone off. What else could make a noise like that, and follow it with such an incomprehensible silence? The noise had assaulted her physically: it was a stomach-churning, bone-rattling act of brute force. It had jolted her out of a profound, dreamless sleep; turned her stomach inside out; and made her bones shake inside her like twigs in a gale. In response, her body had shot up into a seated position without any conscious act of will on her part. She was sitting bolt upright in her bed, shaken to the core, shivering, shocked and confused, conscious but unable to get her bearings. She was staring blankly straight ahead, trying to salvage the most basic information: where she was, and even who she was. Then suddenly, as that information began to return to her, she found herself running as fast as her legs would carry her out of her bedroom and along the landing, her eyes beginning to pick out patches of light here and there in the darkness, her ears picking up formless sounds in the silence.

It was cold, colder than it should have been, on the landing. The cold penetrated her easily, without resistance, through her thin pyjamas and the soles of her bare feet. But the shock of the cold began to force her mind into gear. The information was coming back fast now. She was Imogen Lester; she had a brother, Damian; they lived here. She was at home, on the landing, staring down at the hallway below her, but something was wrong with the picture. As she pondered what it was that was wrong, the formless noises began to take on a form; there were noises of men shouting, running through the house, cursing as they knocked over chairs and small tables in their hasty progress through the darkness, eventually locating light switches, but still shouting. As they began to climb the stairs towards her, she saw what was wrong with the picture. She was looking at the privet hedge, except, of course, that she couldn't be seeing the privet hedge because the privet hedge was outside, and the front door was closed and locked, shielding the outside from her view. But it wasn't: and shifting her gaze slightly, she caught a brief glimpse of what remained of the front door, fractured, splintered, lurching drunkenly down towards the floor, a half-dislodged hinge its only remaining contact with the doorframe, its absence exposing the privet hedge to anyone who cared to look. She took in all these details just before they reached her.

There were two of them, or perhaps three, and they were shouting something about being police officers, ordering her to give it up, ordering her not to do anything stupid, ordering her to get down on the floor. She was given no choice about that. They had hold of her and they were leaning on her. Her knees buckled under their weight. She crumpled and went down like a sack of bricks. One of them twisted her right arm behind her back. She screamed in pain. That brought an order to shut the fuck up, and a knee in the back, on the left kidney, which emptied the air out of her lungs. She fell flat on her face, gasping for breath. Her other arm was wrenched behind her back. Her wrists were forced together into handcuffs that were too tight. One of them pulled her to her feet by her hair. She was dragged downstairs bodily and dumped on the floor, near where her front door had once prevented her from seeing the privet hedge. She could see it again now. She was fully awake now, and she saw that there were lights on throughout the house. There were two men standing by her now, both in suits and ties, one a fair bit older than the other. Looking towards the staircase, she saw several uniformed officers walking briskly, some upstairs, others downstairs. One, who had a sergeant's stripes on his sleeves, called over towards the men with her.

'We're ready for you down in the basement, sir, whenever you are.'

'Right you are,' the older of the two men replied. 'Where's Jack the Lad?'

'He's down there, sir.'

'What about the rest of the house?'

'Just getting started now, sir. They've found some stuff in the kitchen – personal use, by the look of it. No word on anything else as yet.'

The older officer nodded. 'Right, carry on, then.' He looked down at her. 'Would you like to confirm your name for us?'

'Imogen Lester,' she replied, automatically.

'Right, Imogen Lester, on your feet. Let's show you what my lads have found downstairs.'

'Can I get something to put on?' she asked quietly. It was the only thing that came to mind. 'I'm freezing.'

'Where's Roberts?' the older officer asked.

'She's downstairs, I think, sir.'

'Right, there will be a female officer down in the basement. She'll fetch you something if you tell her where to look for it.'

# 14

The officers marched Imogen downstairs towards the basement. As they arrived at the door leading into the dark, low-ceilinged room, the comforting touch of the smooth wood of the stairs under her feet gave way to the shock of the rough, cold stone of the cellar floor. There was a strong smell of cannabis in the damp air. The room was lit by a single naked bulb hanging from the ceiling, and one or two officers were using torches to aid their inspection of some objects on the floor. Allowing her eyes to follow their light, she saw that the objects were seven large black canvas bags lying together at the far end of the room under the basement's only window. Next to the canvas bags she saw Damian, sitting on the floor and holding a handkerchief to what looked like a swollen left cheekbone; there was a cut and the first signs of bruising were emerging.

'Dame? What have you done to him?' she demanded angrily.

'Nothing,' one of the officers replied. 'Walked into the door when we were bringing him in, didn't he? He'll be all right. He's your brother is he, Jack the Lad?'

'Yes, he is: and his name is Damian.'

'Damian. Damian and Imogen. Very nice. Very Hampstead.'

'We've brought you down here,' the older officer added, 'so that you can see for yourself what we've discovered already. If you've got any more stashed away, you can rest assured we're going to find it. So why don't you tell us now, so we don't have to tear the whole house apart looking for it? Young Damian here doesn't seem inclined to assist us, so we're hoping you're the one in the family with a bit of common sense.'

'I know nothing about this,' she replied, 'whatever it is.'

The older officer shrugged. 'Suit yourself. But it's a shame. You've got a nice house, and my lads are going to make a right mess of it, believe you me.' He paused. 'No? Right. Well, they should have cleaned up the kitchen after your party last night by now, so why don't we go back up there so that we can ask you a few questions?'

'Where are you taking Damian?'

'Straight down the nick, I should think. He's confessed already, so there's no point in him hanging about, is there?'

'What? Damian…?'

Damian turned his head away.

'Oh, God,' she said. 'Dame…?'

'PC Roberts, please escort Miss Lester back upstairs to the kitchen.'

'Yes, sir.' PC Roberts turned Imogen around and led her from the cellar.

'Would you like me to bring you some warmer clothes?' she offered in a whisper as they reached the landing.

'Thank you. It's the middle bedroom on the first floor.'

PC Roberts sat her down in a chair at the kitchen table. Looking around, Imogen saw that the kitchen had indeed been cleaned. All trace of the whisky and cannabis of the previous evening had been removed. Someone had washed the kitchen table down with water and detergent – no doubt after taking possession of the evidence of what they had been doing. The two officers who had overpowered her had entered the room. The younger officer approached her and deftly removed her handcuffs. She clenched and released her fists several times in quick succession, and rubbed her wrists reflexively. He seated himself opposite her and took a notebook and pen from his jacket pocket. The older officer took the chair next to him. PC Roberts quietly left the room.

'Now then, Miss Lester, I am Detective Chief Superintendent Mellor,' the older officer began, 'and this is Detective Inspector

Beech. I'm sure it won't come as any surprise to you when I tell you we're attached to the Drug Squad, and we would like to ask you a few questions about what we've just seen in the basement.' He looked around him. 'We won't know the full extent of the haul until the experts have had a look, but clearly we're looking at a valuable consignment of class A controlled drugs. We'd like to know how they come to be in your house.'

Imogen felt completely disorientated.

'Excuse me… I'm sorry… could you tell me what time it is?'

'What time it is?' He looked at his watch. 'Nearly five, ten to five.'

'In the morning?'

The officers exchanged glances. 'Yes, in the morning. Bloody hell. How much did you smoke last night?'

Her mind seemed to have stopped in its tracks, and she was feeling faint.

'It's not that… it's just that I…'

She had no sense of how long had passed before PC Roberts returned with a blouse, a cardigan and a pair of slippers.

'Are these all right?' she asked.

Imogen nodded. 'Yes. Thank you.'

For some moments no one moved. Imogen looked inquiringly at Roberts. She nodded. 'Would you like to give her a moment, sir?'

'What?'

'A moment, sir, so she can get dressed.'

Still, there was no sign of movement.

'Sir?' Roberts insisted; she sounded authoritative, this time, even harsh.

'Oh, right,' Mellor replied.

The two male officers stood slowly, Beech with the suggestion of a grin on his face, and moved towards the door.

'Don't talk to her while we're outside,' Mellor ordered.

'Are you all right?' Roberts asked quietly, once the door was closed.

'No. I'm not feeling well,' Imogen replied. 'I feel faint. I don't seem to know where I am, although I'm obviously at home... but... it just doesn't feel right.'

'I'll tell them,' Roberts said.

The familiar clothes made her feel better and warmer. For the first time she felt her body relax slightly.

'Have you had anything to drink, anything to eat?' Roberts asked.

Imogen shook her head.

'All right. I'll put the kettle on. Where's the coffee?'

She had to think about it. 'Cupboard on the left, top shelf.'

Mellor and Beech came back in without knocking as Roberts was making her way to the sink with the kettle.

'What do you think you're doing?' Mellor inquired brusquely.

'Making her some coffee, sir. She hasn't had anything and she's feeling faint.'

'Not without my say so, you don't. She's in custody.'

'She's not feeling well, sir.'

'Don't you worry your pretty head about that, Constable Roberts. We're not likely to be long with her. I'm sure she'll want to give it up and cooperate with us, just like Jack the Lad, and once she's done that and we've got her down the nick, she can have a nice warm cell and drink as much coffee as she wants.'

'Sir...'

'That's enough, constable. I'm not running a canteen here. I'm interviewing a suspect. Go on. Hop it.'

Imogen looked up.

'I'd feel safer if this officer could stay with me. I'm not feeling well. And I would like a glass of water.'

'You'll be perfectly safe with us,' Mellor replied. 'Constable Roberts is required elsewhere, I'm sure.'

'Actually, sir...'

'Get her a cup of water on your way out,' he added, resuming his seat, 'and as soon as you've done that, make yourself scarce.'

# 15

'Now then,' Mellor began, once PC Roberts had departed with an obvious show of reluctance, 'let me put this to you again. We've just found a large haul of illegal, mostly class A drugs stashed away in your basement. You're saying that's all there is. My lads are making a search of the house as we speak, so we shall see. But even assuming there's no more, we've already got you bang to rights for conspiracy to supply drugs, and permitting your premises to be used for the supply of drugs. That means you and Jack the Lad are already going down for a good stretch. If there's anything you'd like to say to us that might enable us to help you, you'd better say it now. Once we take you down the nick and charge you, it may be too late.'

She looked at them in turn. She was recovering slowly, but the feeling that she might faint had not subsided completely. She was finding it difficult to focus her mind. 'What do you mean, help us? I don't understand.'

'Well, if you cooperate, we could put in a good word with the judge, couldn't we? All judges are impressed by defendants who cooperate with the police, supply them with useful information, and such like. A judge might knock quite a bit off the sentence in a case like this, wouldn't you think, Tom?'

'Very likely, sir, yes.'

She stared at them again. 'What is it you think I can tell you?'

'Well, you might start by telling us who supplied the drugs you've got stashed away downstairs, and who was due to collect them. If you can give us some people higher up in the chain, that's always good.'

She looked down, shaking her head. 'I'm not in any chain. I've already told you, I know nothing about this.'

'For example, Jack the Lad has already given us…'

She exploded. 'For God's sake, stop calling him that. My brother's name is Damian.'

'All right, then, Damian. Damian has already told us about someone called Sean. What can you tell us about Sean?'

'I don't know anyone called Sean.'

'Really? Because Damian says that Sean delivered the drugs to these premises, and that he was paying rent for them.'

'Rent?'

'Rent, storage fee, whatever you want to call it. You were taking money for looking after these drugs until someone collected them to move them on. You do live at this address, I take it?'

'Yes.'

'Right. So, in law, you're the occupier and if drug transactions take place on your premises, you're committing a serious offence.'

She was silent for some time. 'You think I'm an innkeeper?' she asked.

Mellor and Beech exchanged looks. There was silence for some time. Beech took advantage of the lull to put down his pen and massage his writing hand.

'What did you just say?' Mellor asked.

'What?'

'Did I hear you use the word "innkeeper"?'

'Yes,' she replied. 'Innkeeper, *gostioničar*. Is that what you're suggesting?'

There was a long silence.

'*Gostioničar*?' Mellor asked. 'That's a foreign word, isn't it, Tommy? Doesn't that sound like a foreign word to you?'

'It's Serbo-Croat, I believe, sir,' Beech replied. 'I believe it may be the Serbo-Croat word for "innkeeper."'

'Is it really?' Mellor said. 'Well I never. How do you come to know how to say "innkeeper" in Serbo-Croat, Miss Lester?'

She froze, and then, for the first time, her mind belatedly started to focus. As it did, she began to realise with horror what she had said. Suddenly it all came back to her: the information she had, the information Faraday and Julia had warned her to keep secret at all costs, the information she had kept from Damian, the information that might hold the key to the murder of her parents. With her guard down she had spoken without calculation, without thought, and she had betrayed herself and others. She also sensed that she had played into the hands of her interrogators.

'I know nothing about any of this. The first time I knew anything was when you took me down to the basement this morning. This has nothing to do with me.'

'That's not what I asked you, Miss Lester,' Mellor persisted. 'I asked you how you come to know the Serbo-Croat word for "innkeeper?"'

'I've just got back from Yugoslavia,' she protested. 'Sarajevo. I got back last night. You can check my passport. It's upstairs in my bedroom.'

'What were you doing in Yugoslavia?' Mellor asked.

'Perhaps she was doing a spot of skiing, sir,' Beech suggested. 'Sarajevo's in a skiing area, isn't it, from what I hear? Isn't that where they're having the, what d'you call them, the Winter Olympics?'

'I believe so,' Mellor replied. 'Is that what you were doing, Miss Lester? Bit of a winter holiday, was it? Behind the Iron Curtain?'

'My parents were murdered in Sarajevo recently,' Imogen replied quietly. 'My father was a diplomat, at our embassy in Belgrade. The local police haven't been able to find out who did it yet. I went because I wanted to know what they were doing to investigate.'

'I see,' Mellor replied. 'Well, I'm very sorry to hear about your parents, Miss Lester. But surely, the embassy would have made some inquiries for you, wouldn't they, especially as it was one of their own who was murdered?'

'I felt I had to see for myself.'

'Did you? In that case, why did you go on your own? Why didn't you take your brother with you, for example?'

'I went with Julia Cathermole. She's the solicitor I work for.'

'But why not take your brother? Wasn't he interested in finding out what happened to your parents?'

'Perhaps she needed Damian to take over as innkeeper in her absence, sir,' Beech suggested.

'Perhaps she did. Is that what happened, Miss Lester? Damian stayed here to take in the drugs – and the money – while you were away in Yugoslavia?'

'I don't know what Damian did in my absence.'

'You still haven't explained how you come to be able to say "innkeeper" in Serbo-Croat,' Mellor pointed out. 'It's not a word you use every day, innkeeper, is it? What have innkeepers got to do with the investigation into your parents' deaths?'

She shifted uncomfortably. 'Nothing. We stayed at the Holiday Inn, that's all. It was probably a word I picked up there.'

'I see,' Mellor said, after a pause. 'Well, that's all very interesting, Miss Lester. I don't suppose you happened to run into a gentleman by the name of Dragan during your stay in Sarajevo, by any chance, did you?'

She froze again. 'Dragan? No. I don't know anyone of that name.'

'You see, the reason I ask is that, according to police intelligence, a man called Dragan is a major supplier of illegal drugs throughout Europe. He has a vast operation, so we're told, and sometimes, some of his merchandise even ends up here in Britain. And according to police informants, "innkeeper" or "gostioničar" is a term Dragan uses for people he pays to make their premises available to him for drug transactions. So it's quite a coincidence that you go to Sarajevo and pick up the word "gostioničar" in the Holiday Inn just as a shipment of illegal drugs is making its way to your basement, don't you think? Any comment on that at all?'

She took a deep breath.

'Do I have to answer your questions? Can I speak to a solicitor?'

The officers exchanged smiles.

'Didn't I explain that when we started?' Mellor said. 'Remiss of me; I do apologise, Miss Lester. You are not obliged to say anything unless you wish to do so, but anything you do say may be put into writing and used in evidence. I'm not sure about a solicitor at this precise moment. I'll have to think about that.'

'But…'

'I'm not sure I can allow it at the moment. There may be accomplices still at large – such as Sean – who a solicitor could tip off about you and your brother getting nicked, and who might in turn destroy or conceal evidence. Once I'm convinced there's no further danger of that, I will allow you to see a solicitor. Obviously, if you were to supply us with some helpful information that would enable us to make further inquiries, I might be able to eliminate those possibilities sooner rather than later. But as I said, you're not obliged to answer any questions.'

'I can't tell you anymore. I just don't know.'

Mellor glanced at Beech, who nodded. 'All right, Miss Lester. I'm now arresting you on suspicion of conspiring to supply controlled drugs and permitting your premises to be used for the supply of controlled drugs. Again, you are not obliged to say anything unless you wish to do so, but anything you do say may be put into writing and used in evidence. Stand up, please.'

As she stood, Beech re-applied the handcuffs and led her from the room, closely followed by Mellor. PC Roberts was waiting nearby.

'Go back to her bedroom and see if you can find her passport,' Mellor said to Roberts. 'You'd better bring her a change of clothes too.'

'Yes, sir.'

'Oh, and while you're at it, have a look around for Jack the Lad's passport; and see if you can find any papers anywhere in the house suggesting foreign travel – especially travel to Yugoslavia.'

'Right you are, sir… Sir…?'

'What?'

'She needs something to eat and drink when you get her down the nick.'

'I'll see to it personally, Constable Roberts,' Mellor replied.

'Thank you, sir.'

# 16

Imogen had been alone in the cell for more than eight hours. She knew that because PC Roberts had smuggled her watch into the police station with her change of clothes, and she had been able to keep it out of sight. Another female officer had brought her breakfast. Although she was still feeling weak and tired, she surprised herself by also feeling ravenously hungry and clearing her plate quickly. The same officer took her to the toilet whenever she asked. She tried to get information about Damian, and quizzed the officer about whether he had been given medical treatment for the injury to his face. The officer said that she had no information about Damian, but would take it up with the custody sergeant. If she did, it was apparently not a matter anyone felt it necessary to report back on to Imogen.

Mellor and Beech came to her cell just after three in the afternoon.

'Are you all right?' Mellor asked perfunctorily. 'Have they given you something to eat and drink?'

'Yes. Thank you.'

'Good. Well, Constable Roberts will be glad to hear that, I'm sure.'

'I appreciate PC Roberts's kindness and consideration,' Imogen replied. She felt herself gaining in confidence for the first time. 'And I would be grateful if that could be recorded and reported to a senior officer.'

'You heard the lady,' Mellor said to Beech.

'Duly noted, sir.'

'Right. Now, the reason we've come to see you is this. This morning I told you that your brother Damian had admitted his role in the supply of the drugs we found in your basement.'

'Was that before or after someone punched him in the face?' she asked.

'Don't get clever with me, young lady...'

'Has he received medical treatment?'

'If your brother requires medical treatment, it is the duty of the custody sergeant to make sure he gets it, and I assure you, that will have been done. So far, as the investigating officer, I have not heard anything to that effect.'

'So when people walk into doors, they don't automatically qualify for medical assistance in this police station?'

'Inspector Beech will make inquiries about it once we have finished this interview and we will make sure you are informed of any developments,' Mellor replied. 'Will that be satisfactory?'

'Thank you,' she said.

'Now, as I was saying, your brother admitted his role this morning. This afternoon, we spoke to him again with a view to clarifying what he had said, and at that time he asked to make a written statement under caution. I would like to show you his statement and invite you to comment on it. Obviously I can only do that if you agree. Would you like to read it?'

'Yes, I would,' she replied.

Beech handed her a copy. She took it and sat down in the one chair in the room. The officers leaned against the wall.

'Take your time,' Mellor said.

HAMPSTEAD POLICE STATION
4 December 1983
2.00 p.m.
Statement of: Damian Lester
Address: 102 Willow Road, London NW3
Age: 19
Occupation: Unemployed

I, Damian Lester, wish to make a statement. I want someone to write down what I say. I have been told that I need not say anything unless I wish to do so, and that whatever I say may be given in evidence.

Signed: Damian Lester
Witnessed: Alfred Mellor, Det. Chief Supt.

My name is Damian Lester. I am 19 years of age and I live with my sister Imogen at 102 Willow Road, NW3, in Hampstead. This is my family home, in which Imogen and I grew up with our parents, Michael and Margaret Lester. Our parents were killed recently in Sarajevo, Yugoslavia, as a result of an assault on them, which remains an unsolved crime. Imogen and I continue to live at the same address.

Imogen works for Julia Cathermole, a solicitor, so she is at work in the West End during the day. She also often works late, and then stays overnight with Miss Cathermole. So I spend a lot of time on my own at home during the day. I am unemployed. I have tried to get a job, and I have worked for short spells, but I'm not sure what I want to do and I can't seem to keep a job for very long. Unfortunately, I have had some experience with illegal drugs. Some friends I met at our local pub introduced me to cannabis, and I have tried heroin once or twice, though I didn't like it. I also drink more than I should. Being unemployed, this means that I am often short of money, and I have had to borrow from my friends or ask to buy cannabis on credit. I estimate that, at present, I owe various people a total in excess of £400. I have no way to repay all this money.

Several months ago, a man known to me only as Sean, who I met in the pub, offered to wipe out £50 of my debt if I would let him bring some cannabis over to the house during the day and store it in the basement, until another man came to collect it the following day. I agreed to do this. It seemed like easy money. At that time I did not believe that Imogen would ever know about it, because she is out at work all day and rarely goes down to the basement. Also, she knows that I smoke, so any smell from the cannabis would not make her suspicious. After this, there were two other occasions when Sean again asked me to store drugs in the basement. On these other occasions, he gave me other drugs, which he said were heroin and amphetamines, as well as cannabis. Also, while the quantity on the first occasion was quite small, just one holdall, on the two later occasions there were two or three large canvas bags, which obviously contained much larger amounts. I told him I was worried and didn't want to do it, but he said he would pay me more money, so I agreed. He paid me £100.

The last occasion was this weekend, including this morning when we were arrested. Last Thursday I was in the pub, and Sean asked me to take a consignment, which would be picked up on Saturday morning, yesterday. I didn't really want to do it, because I didn't know exactly when Imogen was getting home. I think she told me, but I may have been stoned at the time, and couldn't really remember. Also Sean told me that the consignment would be at least as big as the last time. I told him I didn't want to do it, but he, sort of, insisted, if you know what I mean, saying he knew a lot about me, which I took to be a threat. Also, this time he agreed to pay me £200 and said there could be more where that came from.

Imogen was away. She'd gone with Miss Cathermole to Sarajevo. Imogen said it was to try to find out more about how our parents died. In the end, they were away for four or five days. Imogen didn't get back until yesterday evening, the night before we were arrested, so there shouldn't have been any problem. But the man who was supposed to pick up the drugs didn't turn up on Saturday morning, and I couldn't reach Sean, so the drugs were still in the basement when Imogen got home.

[Clarifying question by Det. Chief Supt. Mellor: Just before you go on, Damian, you mentioned Sean to us this morning, and we asked other officers to make inquiries about him via sources in your area, but we're not coming up with anything. Can you tell us any more about him?]

Like what?

[Det. Chief Supt. Mellor: Well, could you describe him?]

Quite tall, about five foot ten, maybe six feet, well built, black hair, a few spots on his face, like he has, what do you call it?

[Det. Chief Supt. Mellor: Acne?]

Acne, yeah.

[Det. Chief Supt. Mellor: Does he have an accent at all?']

Not really – just a basic London accent, I would say.

[Det. Chief Supt. Mellor: And there's nothing else you can tell us about him? Where he might live, any associates he might have?]

No. He keeps himself to himself. But there was one thing he said that was strange.

[Det. Chief Supt. Mellor: What was that?]

Well, it was this last time, on Thursday night, when we were in the pub. I'd agreed to look after the stuff, and we were having a drink, and he said: 'You're a real something – I didn't get the word he used – now, aren't you?' I asked him what the word was that he'd said, because I didn't understand it. He repeated it several times. It sounded like 'Gost-something', or 'Gostion-something'. I still wasn't getting it, so he scribbled it down on the back of a beer mat.

[Det. Chief Supt. Mellor: Do you have the beer mat?]

No. But I'm pretty sure it was 'Gostionicar'. Let me write it down.

[Det. Chief Supt. Mellor: OK, you've written it down for me. And you think it's as you wrote it, 'Gostionicar'?]

Yes. Except that there was a squiggle over the letter C, like an accent of some kind. Sean told me it meant 'innkeeper' in Yugoslavian. So I was an innkeeper. Well, I suppose that's one way of putting it. But it seemed like quite a coincidence.

[Det. Chief Supt. Mellor: You mean, with your sister and the solicitor she works for being in Yugoslavia at the time?]

Yes.

[Det. Chief Supt. Mellor: Did you know of any reason why he would be using a word in Yugo... actually, I believe it's called Serbo-Croat, to give it its proper name?]

No.

[Det. Chief Supt. Mellor: Well, here's another coincidence for you,

Damian. When we interviewed your sister Imogen this morning, she used exactly the same Serbo-Croat word for innkeeper.]

What, Imogen? I don't believe you.

[Det. Chief. Supt. Mellor: Straight up, I promise you. She came right out with it. So, how would she know about that, do you think?]

I have no idea.

[Det. Chief. Supt. Mellor: Did it occur to you that your sister might have some connection with Sean, a connection you didn't know about, perhaps?]

[Laughs.] What, Imogen? Imogen, deal in drugs? God, no. No way. My sister is pathetically, depressingly law abiding. She picks up litter on the street; she stops her bike at red lights. She went to Cambridge, for God's sake. All right, she did smoke a joint with me last night when she got home, which I must admit, rather blew me away. But she was in a real state. The trip had obviously upset her, which I understand completely. If it had been me, I'd have been mainlining something a lot harder than weed when I got home. But knowing someone like Sean, getting involved in dealing drugs? No way. It did strike me as strange that he used a Yugoslavian word, but it must be a coincidence. I think that's it, really. I don't know any more.

[Clarifying question from Det. Chief Supt. Mellor: Just one more thing, Damian. Were there any other drugs at the house, other than what we seized in the basement, and what you and your sister had for your own use in the kitchen? My officers didn't find anything, but I thought I'd ask, just in case there's anything else you want to tell us.]

No.

[Det. Chief Supt. Mellor: And you do understand, we haven't got the full analysis back yet, but you do understand that we've recovered a substantial commercial quantity of heroin and amphetamines, in addition to some cannabis resin. Do you understand that?]

Yes.

[Det. Chief Supt. Mellor: All right, Damian, if there's nothing else, read your statement through for me. You can correct, alter or add anything you wish. Take your time, and when you're ready, I will ask you to sign it.

That's fine.

Signed: Damian Lester

Witnessed: Alfred Mellor, Det. Chief Supt.

I have read the above statement. I have been told that I can correct, alter or add anything I wish. This statement is true. I have made it of my own free will.

Signed: Damian Lester

Witnessed: Alfred Mellor, Det. Chief Supt.

Statement taken by me, Det. Chief Supt. Alfred Mellor, between 2.00 and 3.00 p.m. No breaks for refreshments.

Signed: Alfred Mellor, Det. Chief Supt.

'Now,' Mellor said, pushing himself off the wall, 'once again, Miss Lester, you are not obliged to say anything unless you wish to do so. But do you wish to comment on this statement?'

Imogen handed the document back to him. She was shocked, and she was sure that her shock must be obvious to the officers.

'For example, this morning I asked you whether you knew anyone called Sean, and you told me you didn't. Having read what your brother has said, do you wish to change that answer?'

She shook her head firmly. 'No. I don't know anyone called Sean.'

'So, yet again, we have this coincidence that your brother knows this man Sean – who, like yourself, knows how to say "innkeeper" in Serbo-Croat – and Sean has been using your brother to keep drugs in your house, which is exactly what an innkeeper does. I must tell you, Miss Lester, that I don't believe that any of this is coincidental. I believe you've been working with agents acting for Dragan to supply controlled drugs.'

She stared at him, open-mouthed. 'Can I speak to Damian?'

'Not at the moment.'

She was silent for some time. 'I don't know what to say. I can't believe Damian has been doing something so stupid. All right, he's immature, and he's made some bad choices in his life, and I know he's been using drugs himself. But this...? I just can't believe it.'

'You know exactly what he's been up to, Miss Lester, because you are involved yourself, along with your brother.'

'No. I've never been involved with drugs.'

'Well, that's not entirely true, is it?' Beech asked. 'You were smoking cannabis with your brother in your house last night, weren't you? Celebration, was it? Celebrating the money you made from Sean for acting as his innkeeper?'

She exhaled heavily. 'All right. Yes. I smoked a joint last night. I also drank some whisky. But it wasn't a celebration, for God's sake. I was hoping to get away from the pain for a while. I'd been in Yugoslavia for five days. I'd been taken to see the place where my parents were murdered. I'd seen their effects laid out in the police station, with the blood still on them. Do you have any idea what that's like ...? So yes, I was upset, and I smoked a joint. But I have never in my life been involved with supplying drugs. I would never do that. Read Damian's statement, for God's sake. He told you I wouldn't be involved with drugs.'

'He did indeed,' Mellor replied. 'Unfortunately, I don't believe him – or you. You will be charged later this afternoon and kept in custody to appear before Hampstead magistrates tomorrow morning. You will have access to a solicitor at court, who will explain to you where we go from here, and who can make a bail application for you – although I must be honest with you: I shall be opposing bail for both you and your brother, on the ground that you're flight risks, and would be likely to commit further offences while on bail. I'm sure PC Roberts will make sure you get something to eat for supper in a little while.'

They opened the door of the cell, and made as if to leave. But abruptly they turned back and closed the door again.

'Of course, there is another possibility,' Mellor said.

'What do you mean?'

'You're an intelligent woman, Miss Lester. You graduated from Cambridge, so I'm told.'

'So what?'

'So, you should be clever enough to see which side your bread is buttered on. You're in a very privileged position.'

She looked up. 'Really? What position would that be?'

He smiled. 'Let's not play games, Imogen. Come on. It's not every day we come into contact with one of Dragan's innkeepers. From what we hear, Dragan doesn't pick just anyone to do what you do for him. You're a rare breed, a special breed.'

She stared at him and decided to say nothing.

'It's not hard to work out how much money you're pulling down in a year, working for Dragan. If you were to give us a good drink – let's say ten per cent – and perhaps throw us the odd bone like Sean now and then to keep our superiors happy, we might see our way to turning a blind eye when Dragan needs to offload some merchandise on our patch. If you know any other innkeepers in London, you could tell them that the same applies to them.'

She still said nothing.

'Think about it,' he added. 'You could walk out of here tonight. It could turn out to be all Sean's fault. You and your brother had nothing to do with it, after all. We could even supply you ourselves from our evidence room if you ever need some merchandise to pass on in future. Obviously, we'd need a drink for that, but it could be arranged.'

'I have nothing to say to you,' she replied eventually.

He shrugged. 'If you change your mind before tomorrow, let someone know you need to see me. Otherwise, I'll see you in court, as they say.'

# 17

Ben Schroeder QC had been standing for some time, looking silently down over the serene garden of the Middle Temple outside the window of his room in chambers at Two Wessex Buildings, a majestic edifice at the foot of Middle Temple Lane. His two visitors had not interrupted his reverie. They were conscious of having put him in the unusual position of conducting a conference and offering advice without being allowed to make any written note of what was said. Ben was a senior member of chambers now, having completed twenty years of practice, and having recently taken Silk. The lean figure that had characterised him in his younger days had filled out, but he still gave the impression of carrying not an ounce of extra weight, and the eyes that had intimidated a generation of witnesses, not to mention the occasional judge, had lost nothing of their power. At length he turned back to face them.

'As I understand it, then,' he said, 'the plan is to bring Rainer back as quietly as possible, perhaps as soon as the end of next week?'

'We will do our best not to draw attention to him,' Baxter replied. 'But there's only so much we can do. Eventually the press are bound to catch on to him.'

'Well, as soon as he's been charged with the murder of Greta Thiemann, he will have to appear in front of the magistrates. The press will know all about it by then, at the latest.'

'We're going to try to keep it quiet until then,' Baxter said, 'but it's not a hundred per cent guaranteed. We'll need a bit of luck. All it takes is one person outside the Service recognising him, and the balloon goes up.'

'He should be arrested the moment his feet touch British soil,' Julia confirmed. 'We can't stop that. But, if he consents, Baxter will arrange for him to be stashed away in a safe house to be interviewed, so that we have a shot at keeping him out of the court system for some time.'

'During which time, he will be interviewed by who, exactly: Special Branch?'

'What I'm going to propose to John Caswell at the Director's Office,' Julia replied, 'is that we ask the two officers who originally investigated Rainer's disappearance and the murder of Greta Thiemann to do it. That way, we don't have to reinvent the wheel: they will have access to the files they developed themselves, and they can go from there.'

'Are they both still available? Rainer disappeared twelve years ago.'

'I made discreet inquiries,' Baxter replied. 'Webb retired in 1980 with the rank of Detective Chief Inspector. But he's still living in London, he's fit and well, and I hear he's bored out of his mind and thinks this retirement lark is strictly for the birds. So I don't think we'll encounter any resistance there. Raymond is still in the job. He's now also a Detective Chief Inspector. They're both well thought of, reliable, safe pairs of hands, and so on; and neither has ever had any involvement with the Met's specialist squads, which may be important, depending on what Rainer has to tell us.'

Ben nodded. 'They were the officers in the murder case I was doing at the Bailey in front of Rainer just before he disappeared. They seemed capable enough – except for letting Rainer escape the net and make his dash for freedom, obviously.'

Baxter grinned. 'That should make them even more anxious to help,' he observed. 'They can clear up some unfinished business.'

'So,' Ben said, 'there are three areas you would want Webb and Raymond to ask him about: firstly, the murder of Greta Thiemann...'

'They've got to start with that,' Julia pointed out. 'It's an open murder case, and there's a warrant out for his arrest.'

'Right. Then, secondly, how he was able to vanish into thin air from his flat in the Barbican and end up in Sarajevo, without anyone noticing.'

'And who was helping him,' Julia added. 'He didn't do that all on his own.'

Ben walked over to his desk and resumed his seat.

'You know, of course,' he said after some time, 'that that's a slightly delicate subject in these chambers.'

'Oh?' Baxter asked.

'My head of chambers, Aubrey Smith-Gurney, was a close friend of Rainer's and spent a lot of time talking to him about his gambling habit, and God only knows what else, in the weeks leading up to his departure. I can't believe that Aubrey would have stepped over the line, certainly not to the extent of helping to spirit Rainer out of the country. But he was interviewed by Webb and Raymond at the time, and I daresay they would want to come back for a second look.'

'Does that cause you any difficulties in representing Rainer, Ben?' Julia asked. 'I didn't think of that.'

'No. Obviously, I couldn't play any part in representing Aubrey – if it were to come to that – but that's not a problem. I'm sure Harriet Fisk would do it. She was Aubrey's pupil.'

He was silent for some time.

'Then, thirdly, they would want to ask him what he knows about this man Dragan and his drug trafficking operation – including anything he may know about villainy in the Metropolitan Police.'

'That's our best hope of making a deal,' Julia said. 'That information could blow the lid off whatever corruption is going on in the Met these days.'

'Well, he's picked a good time,' Ben commented. 'Operation Countryman, the corruption in the Flying Squad, is recent history. The Met is still sensitive about it, as is the Home Secretary. So if Rainer really does have some worthwhile information about corruption, that might just get the Director's attention. After all, we're not asking them to let him off, are we? It's just a matter of where he spends what little time he has left. The Director might agree to a condition of residence in whatever care home or hospital he may need.'

'That's as much as we can hope for,' Julia agreed. 'Conrad knows that. He's under no illusions.'

'Then finally,' Baxter said, 'Rainer may well have some information about political developments in Yugoslavia. That's not a police matter. The Service will deal with that aspect of it, and I won't be able to share Rainer's product in that area with you.'

'We wouldn't expect you to,' Julia replied.

'But if he can give us what he's promised, we can make it clear to whoever needs to know that he's provided us with some extremely valuable intelligence, and hopefully that will count for something.'

'It would be a good idea for me to talk to him about the murder case as soon as he's been charged,' Ben said. 'Even if he's never going to trial, I need to understand what he says about it before we ask Carswell for a deal.'

'I assume you won't mind if Ben and I come to the safe house to see him?' Julia asked Baxter.

'Not at all, as long as we have the usual ground rules in place: we give you a lift to the house, you wear blindfolds en route, and you don't talk to anyone about it. Subject to that, you can make yourselves at home and talk to him to your hearts' content.'

'And you would respect our legal professional privilege?'

'You mean, will we be bugging the conference room?'

'You know that's what I mean.'

'Only if it's necessary in the national interest.'

They laughed together. There was a knock on the door, and Ben's clerk, Alan, poked his head inside the room.

'Sorry to disturb, Mr Schroeder. Miss Cathermole, there's a call for you from your office. They say it's urgent. Would you like to take it here, or in the clerk's room?'

'You can put it through in here,' she replied. She smiled as Alan left the room. 'I still keep waiting for Merlin to appear. How is he enjoying retirement?'

'I gather he and Sylvia are enjoying it enormously,' Ben replied. 'They spend almost all their time in their house on Guernsey. He pays us a visit once in a while, just to check on us, but I don't think he's missing being senior clerk at all. Fortunately, he's taught Alan well.'

'He has,' Julia agreed.

The phone rang. Julia walked over to Ben's desk to answer it. Ben watched her face turn from its usual robust colour to an ashen white in just a few seconds. For some moments she seemed to be unsteady on her feet, and leaned against the desk. Ben stood. She listened for some time and eventually whispered, 'I understand,' very quietly, before shakily replacing the receiver. Ben walked around his desk and, with Baxter taking one arm, helped her back into her seat.

'Julia,' Ben said, 'you look like you've seen a ghost. What on earth is the matter?'

She looked up at him. 'Imogen's been arrested,' she replied. 'I need to go to her.'

# 18

'Arrested? What for? When?'

'Yesterday, apparently. The Drug Squad raided the family home in Hampstead and found something. I don't know what, or how much, but they're saying it's commercial. She appeared before the magistrates this morning, and they've remanded her in custody. It's that bloody brother of hers,' she added savagely. 'Damian. They've arrested him too, the worthless, stupid little git.'

She raised herself out of the chair.

'I need to go and see her. She had some idiot local solicitor who obviously didn't make a proper bail application. I need to take over and see if I can get it back before the bench this afternoon. You'll represent her, Ben, won't you?'

Ben took both her hands in his.

'Julia, calm down for a moment. Yes, of course, I'll represent her. But you can't. You can go to see her, but you can't represent her.'

'But…'

'She's a friend, and she works for you, Julia. Not a good idea.'

She allowed her body to sink back into the chair, and held her head in her hands.

'The Drug Squad's got its claws into her, Ben. What am I going to do?'

'Let me see if I can reach Barratt Davis,' Ben suggested. 'You know Barratt. I'm sure he'll be very glad to help.'

She nodded. Ben returned to his desk and called through to the clerk's room.

'Alan, would you do something for me? I want you to call Barratt Davis's office and ask how soon he can come to chambers. Tell him it's about a new client, and it's urgent.'

'You're in luck, as it happens, Mr Schroeder,' Alan replied cheerfully. 'Mr Davis is in conference with Mr Overton as we speak, about that robbery they've got coming on next week. They've been going for almost an hour, so I would expect it to end in the next ten to fifteen minutes or so. I'll put my head round the door and ask Mr Davis to come to see you as soon as he's finished with Mr Overton.'

'Thanks, Alan. And would you bring a very strong cup of coffee for Miss Cathermole, please?'

'I will, sir. Be right with you.'

Baxter stood and put an arm around her. 'I'm really sorry about this, Julia, but you're in good hands and there's nothing useful I can do here. I'll go back home and see if anything's showing up on the bush telegraph.'

'Call Faraday,' Julia suggested. 'Please. See if he knows anything.'

'I will.'

He kissed her briefly on the forehead and shook hands with Ben, who walked him to the door.

'Keep me informed,' he said quietly, as he left the room. 'I'm not sure I like the sound of this.'

Alan brought coffee, and showed in Barratt Davis less than five minutes later.

'Good timing, Ben. Clive and I were just finishing up.'

'I'm very glad you're here, Barratt. You know Julia, of course.'

'Of course,' Barratt said, shaking hands. 'Ever since the case of our mutual friend Sir James Digby. What seems to be the problem?' He took a seat at the side of Ben's desk and produced a notepad from his briefcase.

'Julia's…'

'Lover,' Julia said.

'What? … really?' Ben asked. Neither could resist a smile at the look of surprise that had crossed Ben's face.

'Julia's… lover, Imogen Lester, was arrested yesterday during a raid by the Drug Squad on her house in Hampstead.'

Barratt looked up. 'What did they find? Type, quantity?'

'Unknown.'

'But it's her house?'

'She and her brother Damian live there. It was the family home, but their parents died recently in tragic circumstances, so it's theirs now. Damian was arrested too, and we think he's probably to blame for whatever's happened.'

'There's no "probably" about it,' Julia interrupted. The coffee seemed to be reviving her. 'He has a history with drugs. He's a horrible little bastard, complete waste of space.'

Barratt made a note. 'So, they're probably going for permitting premises to be used. Where are we with it? Has she appeared before the magistrates?'

'This morning apparently, at Hampstead. We think some local solicitor may have made a bail application, but it wasn't successful.'

Barratt snorted. 'No surprise there. They don't approve of bail in Hampstead – it's against their religion – so don't be too hard on whoever it was. That's a job for counsel, getting bail in Hampstead.'

'I want you and Ben to represent her, Barratt,' Julia said. 'I have to do something. She'll go crazy in jail. I have to get her out on bail. I'll stand surety for her myself. I can get them a decent amount if they want recognisances.'

'I understand. Previous good character, I assume?'

'Previous *exemplary* character. She works for me in our office.'

He finished his note. 'Good.' He looked at his watch. 'Almost three o'clock, so it's too late to do anything about bail today. But if I leave now, I can get to court before they close, and I'll see if they'll give me another hearing tomorrow. If not, I'll get it listed as soon as possible. I'll find out who the arresting officer is, see if he's willing to talk to me, and I'll get as much information as I can about the case. And while I'm at it, I can make a legal aid application.'

Julia shook her head. 'This isn't going to be a legal aid case,

Barratt. I'm instructing you privately on this. I want you to retain Ben as counsel.'

Barratt looked at her and at Ben in turn. 'I'm happy to do it that way, Julia, of course, if that's what you want,' he replied slowly. 'But… I have to be frank with you: it's going to be expensive. Ben isn't as cheap as he once was. Now he's in silk, he has to have a junior to hold his hand.'

'Yes. I know that, Barratt. I'm in the business too. That's what I want.'

'All right. If I may make a suggestion, I would fancy Clive Overton as junior in this kind of case. He's a wizard on bail – magistrates seem to love him.'

Ben smiled. 'I agree.'

'That will be fine,' Julia replied..

Barratt nodded. 'I'll sort it out with Alan on my way out, then. Presumably, the brother will apply for legal aid?'

'I neither know nor care,' Julia replied.

'We don't have to care,' Barratt said, 'but we do need to know. We will need to talk to them and find out what they have to say for themselves at some point, whether he's going to plead or fight it, and so on. I'll see what I can find out.' He stood and replaced the notepad in his briefcase. 'Look, we'll get Clive up there as soon as we can to charm the pants off the good ladies and gentlemen of the Hampstead bench. But until I get the lie of the land, I can't tell you how long it will take. By all means, go and see her at Holloway this evening, but you know the drill…'

'There's no privilege,' Julia replied with a thin smile. 'So no talking about the case. I know the drill.'

'I'm sorry. I know I'm teaching my grandmother to suck eggs,' he said. 'But I have to…'

'Yes. I know you do,' Julia replied. 'I understand. Thank you, Barratt, and I promise – we'll behave ourselves.'

# 19

With a glass of champagne in each hand and the cold bottle tucked under her arm, Julia was seriously hampered, and was eventually reduced to kicking the bathroom door open, overcoming the weak resistance of the old, pliant latch. 'Your Bollinger, madam,' she proclaimed. She walked over to the huge tub, set the bottle and the glasses down on the elegant white marble ledge behind the tub, slipped out of her dressing gown, and climbed carefully into the hot, rose-scented water. Once settled, she handed one of the glasses to Imogen and raised the other in the air.

'Here's to bail,' she said. 'I'm sorry it took so long. Barratt had a devil of a time getting the magistrates to agree to another hearing so soon. But he's a persuasive fellow.'

Imogen raised her glass in turn, and they clinked glasses. They drank deeply and Julia immediately refilled the glasses.

'God, I'm so glad to be out of there,' Imogen said. 'Thank you for standing surety for me, Julia. I know you're taking a huge risk for me, but it made all the difference with the magistrates – even I could see that.'

'You're not such a big risk, really,' Julia replied with a grin. 'I only lose the money if you don't show up for your trial; and since the police have your passport, so you can't get very far – unless you have friends who can help you do a Conrad Rainer.'

Imogen laughed. 'I'm not going anywhere, Julia. It's just that…

oh, never mind.' She raised her glass again. 'Here's to Clive Overton. He's really good, isn't he?'

'He is,' Julia agreed. 'But if you think *he's* good, wait till you see Ben Schroeder in action. You're in good hands, Imogen.'

She nodded. 'I hope so. I can't go back to prison, Julia.'

'You won't need to,' Julia replied, with more confidence than she felt. 'This is going to turn out well. We know Damian is going to plead guilty and take full responsibility, which takes at least some of the pressure off you. The prosecution have to prove that you knew what was going on. They can't get a conviction for permitting the use of premises unless they prove that you knew. And now they've looked at your passport, they know you were with me in Sarajevo when the drugs were delivered to the house. You'll be fine.'

Imogen did not reply immediately.

'The thing is, Julia... I made things worse for myself... I...'

Julia put her glass down on the ledge. Reaching under the water she lifted Imogen's legs and rested her feet against her breasts. She started to massage them gently with her thumbs.

'I was so disorientated,' Imogen continued quietly. 'I was so tired after our journey. They broke the door down at about four o'clock in the morning, when I was dead to the world. After the joint and the whisky, I passed out the moment my head touched the pillow. You know what it's like when you wake up suddenly, after you've been out like that. When they came in it sounded like the whole house must be falling down around me, like someone had set a bomb off. I was terrified, Julia. I didn't know where I was, or what day it was. They had me in handcuffs before I even knew what was going on.'

Julia interrupted the massage for a moment. 'Did you say anything that they could have taken as an admission?'

'No. I told them the truth – that I knew nothing about it.'

She resumed the massage. 'Well, in that case...'

'Julia, they were accusing me of agreeing to keep the drugs at the house for someone to collect. I told them that must mean they were accusing me of being an innkeeper. Of course, then, they wanted to know why I'd used the term "innkeeper".

'Imogen...'

'It just came out. I thought it must be a term everyone uses in the drug trade. But apparently not: they told me it was a term Dragan's people use, and then they said they suspected that the drugs must have come from Dragan. I'm sorry, Julia, I wasn't thinking straight. But I didn't tell them anything else about what had happened in Sarajevo, I swear.'

'Did they ask you about our trip?'

'They asked me what I'd been doing in Yugoslavia. They said I must have been in Sarajevo for a meeting with Dragan or his people, leaving Damian to handle the delivery at home. I explained to them I was only there to find out how far the police had got with solving the murder of my parents. I didn't tell them what else I'd been doing, obviously.'

Julia nodded. 'But if...'

Imogen closed her eyes. 'That's not all, Julia. I... also used the Serbo-Croat word – *gostioničar*, you remember?'

'What? Why would you...?'

'I don't know,' Imogen replied simply. 'I don't know, Julia. Please don't be angry with me. I was tired. It just came out. But later, when I was at the police station, they showed me Damian's statement under caution. Damian told them that the drugs came from a man called Sean – and Sean had also used the words "innkeeper" and "*gostioničar*".'

Julia stared at her. 'Sean used the word "*gostioničar*"?'

'That's what Damian told the police. He said that Sean had written it down for him on a beer mat while they were in the pub. He didn't keep the beer mat, but he remembered how to spell it. Damian knew how to spell "*gostioničar*", Julia.'

Julia thought for some time.

'Do you believe that – that Damian knew that word?'

'I don't know what to believe. But it was there in his statement. He'd signed the statement, and he'd answered Mellor's questions about it.'

'Did you have any chance to talk to Damian before they took him away to the police station?'

'No. They told me he'd already confessed when they first took me down to the basement. They couldn't have been in the house more than ten, fifteen minutes at the most. At the time, I didn't know what to think about that, but now...'

'What I'm thinking,' Julia said, 'is that it must have been one of the quickest confessions on record. All right, he'd been caught red-handed with the drugs, but still...'

'And they'd hit him, Julia.'

'What? Are you sure?'

'He had a cut, and some bruising was just starting to show on his cheek – his left cheek – and he was obviously very, very frightened. He was almost curled up on the floor.' She hesitated. 'Julia, have I screwed up my case?'

Julia gently raised a foot from her chest and kissed it.

'No. But I think you need a consultation with Ben and Clive as soon as we can arrange it,' she said. 'I'll call Barratt on Monday. You need to tell them everything you've told me – in fact, you need to tell them everything that happened during the raid and at the police station.'

Imogen smiled. 'Thank you, Julia, but I'll call Barratt myself. I'm his client. You can't represent me, remember?'

Julia returned the smile. 'I remember. But make sure you do it. Oh, and when you see them, I want you to warn them that both you and Damian may have been "verballed". Do you know that word, "verballed?"'

'Can you translate it into Serbo-Croat for me?'

Julia playfully splashed some water up into her face. 'Smart Alec. No, Imogen, listen, I'm serious. Bring up the subject of "verbal". Don't forget.'

Imogen sat up, leaned forward and kissed her. 'I won't forget.' She reached over Julia and grabbed the bottle. 'Let's have another glass of this. And then, could we please not talk about the case anymore tonight? I really want to get back to normal things in the normal world. I want to forget about drugs and innkeepers and Sarajevo and verbal for the weekend. Is that all right?'

Julia kissed her in return. 'Of course. As a matter of fact, I've already taken the first steps towards returning you to normality. Jean-Claude and his band of helpers will be here bearing delicious morsels for our dinner – in less than an hour. So let's drink up, and we can look forward to dining – informally, no need to dress up for dinner tonight, I think.'

They kissed again, 'Sounds wonderful,' Imogen replied.

# 20

'If we're all agreed, then,' John Caswell said, 'I'll ask Webb and Raymond to join us.'

They were gathered in the conference room of the Office of the Director of Public Prosecutions in Queen Anne's Gate, an elegant, if ageing building, a stone's throw from Green Park and a short walk to Buckingham Palace or Parliament Square.

'Yes, I think we're ready,' Julia replied.

Ben and Baxter nodded.

Caswell left his place at the head of the huge conference table, and put his head outside the door.

'Jenny, ask the officers to come in, please.'

'Right you are, Mr Caswell,' a female voice replied.

Moments later, Jenny ushered in Detective Chief Inspector Phil Raymond of E Division, and Detective Chief Inspector Johnny Webb, retired. Both were dressed in their best suits and ties, and both seemed apprehensive. Neither had been given any inkling of why they had been summoned so urgently to the Director's office, and in Webb's case, the summons had been particularly unexpected, given that he had retired from the force almost four years before. They looked around them, anxiously. Three of the four people present in the room were strangers to them, but the fourth provoked a flash of recognition, and both offered a slightly forced smile.

'Mr Schroeder,' Webb said, extending his hand, 'it's been a long time: the trial of Henry Lang, Old Bailey, 1971, if I'm not mistaken. You're looking well, sir.'

'So are you, Chief Inspector,' Ben replied, taking his hand. 'Chief Inspector Raymond.'

'Mr Schroeder.'

'Perhaps I should do the honours,' Ben said. 'This is Mr John Caswell, Deputy Director of Public Prosecutions, who asked you to come today; Miss Julia Cathermole, my instructing solicitor; and…'

'Baxter. I'm with the security services.'

When the handshakes had been completed, Caswell waved the officers into their seats at the table. Baxter's reference to the security services had dampened down the smiles, and the anxiety was starting to bubble up to the surface again. But there was no time to ask questions. Caswell pushed a form and an office biro across the table for each of them.

'Mr Baxter has asked that we all sign the Official Secrets Act form,' he explained, matter-of-factly. 'Mr Schroeder, Miss Cathermole and I have signed already, and I would be grateful if you would do the same. I don't know whether you've ever encountered these forms before, but if not, by all means take a moment to read through them.'

After exchanging glances, both officers signed with little hesitation.

Caswell smiled. 'Thank you: and now that you've signed, I'm authorised to give you some good news. We're here to offer you the chance to clear up an old case – one, I imagine, that must have caused you a certain amount of frustration over the years.'

'Sir…?' Webb asked.

'We've found Sir Conrad Rainer,' Caswell said. He sat back, unable to resist a smile at the shocked looks on the faces of both officers. As they both appeared speechless, he continued. 'I suppose I should call him Mr Conrad Rainer, strictly speaking, since the Queen revoked his knighthood after he went off-radar so abruptly, but as you knew him as Sir Conrad, I thought I'd use his former title just the once.'

'Do you mean he's... back in England, sir?' Raymond asked tentatively.

'He's...'

'He's abroad,' Baxter interrupted quickly.

'Yes, quite,' Caswell agreed. 'He's abroad, but his whereabouts are known and it is possible that we may be able to bring him back to this country. In that eventuality...'

'In that eventuality, sir,' Webb interrupted in his turn, recovering rapidly now from his initial shock, 'Mr Rainer will be arrested and charged with the murder of Greta Thiemann, among other things. I believe the correct procedure is for arrangements to be made with the government of the country he's hiding in for the arresting officers to attend with a warrant and detain him, with the assistance of the local police.'

Caswell glanced at Baxter. 'It's not quite that simple in this case, Chief Inspector.'

'Mr Rainer is not known to the authorities in the country in which he's been hiding,' Baxter said. 'They're unaware of him – at least as far as we know. He's been living there using a false identity since he departed our shores in 1971. But he became known to my Service some time ago, as a result of a coincidental contact with one of my colleagues who is – was – attached to our embassy there. He has recently expressed an interest in returning to this country.'

Raymond looked up. 'He wants to come back? I beg your pardon, sir, but I must say, I find that hard to believe. Why on earth would he want to come back now?'

'For several reasons,' Baxter replied, 'the most compelling of which is that he is terminally ill. He is aware that he will be arrested and charged as soon as he arrives. But as he won't live long enough to be tried, that's not the main factor. Connected to that is a wish to apologise to his wife and certain other people he deceived and stole from, so as to clear his conscience.' He paused. 'And finally – and this is why I've asked you to sign the Official Secrets Act form – since my colleague made contact with him, he has been providing my Service with information, much of it extremely useful, about political developments in the country concerned, and about serious criminal activity that has an impact here at home. But we've now reached the point where he's at risk; it's becoming too dangerous for him to remain where he is.'

Webb sat up in his chair. 'Excuse me, sir: but are you telling us that your Service has known where Sir... Mr Rainer has been hiding, but hasn't taken any steps to have him arrested?'

'I would prefer to say that we have chosen to leave him in place subject to certain conditions.'

'Sir, with all due respect...'

'You believe that people should be prosecuted for criminal offences they may have committed,' Baxter continued, 'especially when the offence is murder. So do I. But the information Rainer has been supplying has been directly relevant to our national security, and to efforts to break up a powerful organised crime operation.' He smiled. 'Don't look so unhappy about it, Chief Inspector. We're bringing him back now, aren't we? So he will be charged with murder.'

'But he won't be brought to trial,' Webb commented, 'will he?'

'I'm sorry about that. But my colleagues and I had to balance different interests – all of them important – and in this case the balance came down firmly in favour of keeping him in place. If it's any consolation, he may not have been in prison where he belongs, but he hasn't exactly been living *la dolce vita*. In fact, I would say, his existence has been pretty miserable on the whole – and now it's coming to an end. There's nothing about his present life to envy, I assure you.'

'He's been shielded from justice for as long as it suited you,' Raymond observed quietly. 'You would have turned him in if the information had dried up, wouldn't you? With all due respect, sir, I have no sympathy for Rainer, but isn't that a form of blackmail?'

Baxter smiled. 'Blackmail isn't a word we use in the Service. We would prefer to say that favourable circumstances presented themselves, and we took advantage of them in the national interest. Rainer has always known that, if he had nothing to offer us, we would have no choice but to repatriate him. It made sense for him to cooperate with us, and it made sense for us to leave him alone for as long as he cooperated. Now, those circumstances have changed.'

'It's been my experience, sir,' Raymond said, 'that information delivered under duress isn't always very reliable.'

'We don't just take his word for it, Chief Inspector,' Baxter replied. 'We do have protocols for evaluating intelligence.'

'Well, in any case,' Webb said, after a silence, 'it's water under the bridge, isn't it? For whatever reason, he's coming back. But you don't want us to go out there – wherever it is – and get him?'

'No. We can't have the local authorities finding out what we've been up to for the past few years. We don't want to make our Ambassador's life any more complicated than it already is. So we can't bring him out through any of the normal legal or diplomatic channels. We'll have to be creative about how we get him back, and I'm not going to elaborate on that – suffice it to say that it's a matter for my Service, not the police.'

'Then, with all due respect, sir, why are we here?'

'Because once he arrives back in this country, it does become a police matter,' John Caswell said. 'As police officers you are then duty-bound to execute the arrest warrant, interview him, charge him with the murder of Greta Thiemann, and prepare the case against him until it becomes clear that he will not be well enough to stand trial.' He paused. 'In addition, I expect you might want to ask him a few questions about his sudden departure from this country – how it was done, who helped him, and so on, and make recommendations about whether proceedings should be brought against anyone else.'

Webb was nodding. 'Yes, sir.'

'And finally,' Caswell added, 'Rainer has indicated that he has further information about a very significant organised crime venture which has its hooks into us here, in England. He's offered to name names.'

'Including some in your own profession,' Baxter added.

'Police officers?' Webb asked.

'Yes. Mr Schroeder and Miss Cathermole will be representing Rainer on the murder charge. They have asked me to agree that, if he does supply the information he's promised us, he should not have to spend the little time he has left in prison.'

'You're joking, sir,' Raymond said, glancing up at Julia and Ben in turn. 'In a murder case, after having fled the country and been on the run for twelve years? You want a court to give him bail?'

'No,' Caswell replied. 'Obviously, there's no chance of any court granting him bail, so there would have to be some kind of arrangement independent of the court. As you rightly point out, Chief Inspector, Rainer's record is not sympathetic. But on the other hand, the information he has may be of the highest importance.' He looked around the room. 'So we've arrived at a... well, a compromise. We've agreed that Rainer will not be placed on remand in prison. Instead, he will nominally be remanded to police custody.'

'"Nominally,"' Baxter added, 'meaning that he will, in fact, reside in one of my Service's safe houses, where he can be questioned without anyone noticing, and where we can ensure that he receives the medical care he needs. The information he's going to give us is highly sensitive, and it would be too much of a risk – for him and for us – to keep him anywhere not under our direct control.'

'He's not going anywhere, Chief Inspector,' Julia said. 'He's going to need the equivalent of nursing home or hospital care for almost all the time left to him, whoever he's with. All it really comes to is that if he's not in prison he will have a nicer view from his window while he's dying.'

'I see,' Webb said.

'We've asked you here today,' Caswell said, 'because we felt that, with your knowledge of the case, you would be the obvious choices to deal with the murder of Miss Thiemann and with Rainer's sudden disappearance. We also felt that you might derive a certain satisfaction from, shall we say, tying up the loose ends – after all, let's be honest, gentlemen: Rainer's disappearance wasn't the most glorious chapter of your careers, was it? But, of course, if you prefer not to be involved, I'm sure we can find other officers to step in.'

There was silence for some time.

'There is one point everybody seems to be overlooking,' Webb said. 'I'm no longer a police officer. I'm retired.'

'A technical matter,' Caswell replied with a smile. 'We can sort that out this afternoon.'

He waited for some seconds, observing the looks that passed between the two officers, before taking two file folders that had been lying at his left hand under a copy of *The Times*, and placing them directly in front of him.

'These files contain the reports of your earlier investigation, and current information about Rainer, including his present whereabouts and a summary of the information he is expected to provide. If you want to work with us, you can have them now. If not, then as far as you are concerned this meeting never took place. I hope that's clear.'

Both officers slowly extended an arm along the table. Caswell pushed the files towards them.

'His code name is "Prodigal,"' Baxter said. 'To be used at all times.'

# 21

The officers were waiting for him in a miserable unfurnished hut, with glazed windows and fluorescent lighting, about a hundred yards from the runway of the RAF base in East Anglia where the anonymous transport plane had just landed. The aircraft's arrival did not correspond with any flight plan notified to the tower, but air traffic control had nonetheless guided it down on to the runway discreetly, with no fanfare. Conrad Rainer looked tired and old, but on seeing them, he volunteered a thin smile.

'Mr Webb, Mr Raymond: how nice of you to come and meet me. You've aged rather better than I have, I must say.'

'Welcome back to England, Mr Rainer,' Webb said, 'and to celebrate your return I am now arresting you on suspicion of the murder of Greta Thiemann. You do not...'

'I do not have to say anything unless I wish to do so, but anything I do say may be put into writing and given in evidence. Yes. I know. I haven't forgotten.'

'I couldn't have put it better myself, sir,' Webb said. 'Come with us, please.'

'Any problems *en route*?' Baxter asked as Rainer was led away.

'Nothing serious,' Faraday replied.

'Meaning?'

Faraday hesitated. 'Somebody took a pot shot at us as we were leaving his place in Bistrik. Don't know who, but fortunately he wasn't a very good shot.'

'What?'

'Apparently we got Prodigal out just in time. I had a couple of Vlado's lads with me, so it didn't get out of hand, but someone had obviously been watching the place. If we'd left it much longer it might have been a bit dodgy.'

'Anything the Ambassador needs to know about?'

'I don't think so. The lads don't think they hit anyone, and there were no incidents getting to the plane. What about this end?'

'A couple of grumblings about the absence of a flight plan – the only important one being Yugoslavia. After you left Yugoslav airspace you were among friends, and we'd warned them to expect you. They're not bothered as long as we're not landing on their territory, and they know we'd do the same for them.'

'Can we deal with Yugoslavia?'

'The Ambassador's been briefed. God only knows what legend C has given him, but I'm sure it will pass muster. All the same, just in case, I don't think you should go back straight away. Take a couple of weeks off here, and let's see how the land lies.'

'I can manage that,' Faraday said, with a contented smile.

'How's Prodigal doing?'

'Not good. He hardly stopped coughing the whole bloody flight. If you ask me, he doesn't have much time left.'

'He'd better bloody-well have long enough left to talk to us,' Baxter replied, 'after all the trouble we've gone to, to bring him home.'

# 22

'Mr Rainer,' Webb began, 'on the morning of Saturday 9 October 1971, DCI Raymond and I – we were DI Webb and DS Raymond at the time, based at Holborn Police Station – had occasion to visit your flat in the Barbican. We had some questions for you about a complaint made to us by three barristers who were members of your former chambers. You were not at home. We became concerned and asked the building manager, a Mr Ensley, to let us in. On entering the flat, we noticed a strong smell coming from a storage area behind a door to our left; and on examining this area we found the body of a woman, later identified as Greta Thiemann. The pathologist estimated that she had been dead for two or three days. The cause of her death was a blunt force trauma to the right side of the head causing a fracture of the skull, and administered using...'

'Administered using a cast iron bust of Wolfgang Amadeus Mozart,' Rainer replied. 'Deborah and I bought it in some antique shop in Vienna years ago. Quite a nice little piece, actually.'

He was sitting at the table in khaki trousers and a borrowed blue police sweater, a large jug of water and an array of pills in their foil wrappings in front of him, a grey inhaler within easy reach.

'I'm sure it is. We took possession of this nice little piece, and asked our forensic colleagues to examine it. They reported that Mozart had your fingerprints and traces of blood on him. They also found traces of blood on the floor, on a rug, on a chair and on a coffee table, despite apparent efforts made by someone to clean the room. The blood was later tested and found to be that of Greta Thiemann. It appears that, by the time we arrived at your flat, you had already left, or were in the course of leaving, the country, apparently to avoid being questioned about the circumstances of Miss Thiemann's death. We have reason to believe that you then remained absent from this country, living under a false name in Sarajevo, Yugoslavia, until you returned voluntarily two days ago, on Monday 19 December 1983.

'It is now eleven o'clock on the morning of Wednesday 21 December 1983. We are in premises whose whereabouts are an official secret. We wish to question you about the matters I have just mentioned. Before we do so, I must caution you that you are not obliged to say anything unless you wish to do so, but anything you do say may be put in writing and given in evidence. Do you understand the caution?'

'Yes, I do.'

'I also wish to ask whether you have any concerns about being questioned now, in the light of your medical condition?'

'No. Thank you. The quacks examined me yesterday and said I could stagger on for a short while yet. I've got my inhaler and some medication. I'm sure I'll be fine.'

'Very well, Mr Rainer. I understand that everything we say is being recorded electronically. Is that also your understanding?'

'So I've been told.'

Webb nodded. 'Well, let me ask you, then: did you kill Greta Thiemann?'

'Yes, I did.'

'By striking her on the head with the bust of Mozart?'

'I struck her once with Wolfgang Amadeus Mozart, yes.'

'What was your intention when you struck her with the bust of Mozart?'

Rainer thought for some time. 'That's a rather complicated question, Chief Inspector,' he replied. 'I'm really not sure how to answer it. It's a bit of a long story.'

'Take all the time you need,' Webb said.

Rainer nodded and took a long drink of water. 'I met Greta Thiemann the year before – April, May, that kind of time.'

'That would be 1970, then?'

'Yes. I met her at the Clermont Cub – you know, John Aspinall's place in Berkeley Square. She was with some very boring fellow, whose name escapes me. Doesn't matter. Anyway, we hit it off, and we agreed to meet at Annabel's a couple of nights later. You know Annabel's, the nightclub in the basement of the Clermont?'

'The Clermont Club is a gaming establishment, is that right?'

'Yes: very exclusive, high stakes. John handpicked the members personally – all very well-heeled, needless to say: Jimmy Goldsmith, Kerry Packer, Lucky Lucan, people like that.'

Webb smiled. 'Speaking of Lord Lucan, you started something of a trend, didn't you? I don't suppose you know where we might find him, do you? He hasn't been hiding out in Sarajevo with you, by any chance, has he?'

Rainer laughed out loud, but quickly doubled up in his chair, coughing and gasping for breath. He seized the inhaler, rammed it into his mouth, and inhaled several times. He took another long drink of water. Even then, he continued to cough for some time.

'Sorry,' he said eventually. 'Bloody nuisance, not being able to breathe. Lucan? No. I have no idea where he is, I'm afraid. I only found out that he'd scarpered through reading my weekly Serbo-Croat newspaper, which wasn't really a great source of British gossip. No. You'd need to ask around at the Clermont – some of the members who were there at the time. If anybody knows, they do.'

'Our colleagues tried that,' Raymond observed. 'I don't think they got very far.'

Rainer shrugged. 'Sorry. Anyway, I started seeing Greta. I was looking for a bit of excitement, you see. Deborah's a wonderful woman in her own way, but she was always far more interested in her church than she was in me.'

'Why did you marry her, then?' Raymond asked. 'Just out of interest.'

'I forget,' Rainer replied. 'Probably because she had money – a lot of money, actually, family trust fund.'

'You had a house down in Surrey, in Guildford, I believe?' Webb asked.

'Yes: and I was bored out of my mind with it all. Deborah's idea of sex was once a week in the missionary position. I couldn't even have a decent drink – she wouldn't have it in the house. Jesus wouldn't approve, apparently. So after I took silk I got my flat in the Barbican, and made up excuses for staying up in town as much as I could. And it was then I joined the Clermont and finally started living life the way I wanted to instead of the way she wanted me to.'

'I appreciate that you were a successful QC,' Webb commented, 'but I wouldn't have thought that put you in the same league as the likes of Lord Lucan and Sir James Goldsmith. Where did you get the money to play at the same table as people like that?'

Rainer smiled, coughed again. More water. 'Believe it or not, I won a lot of money when I first started. Beginner's luck, I suppose. We played *chemin de fer*. I don't know whether you've ever…?'

'No.'

'Well, it doesn't matter. Suffice it to say that money can change hands very quickly. You can win a lot and lose a lot in a night playing chemmy. And for the best part of a year, I did well – very well. I didn't always win, obviously, but in any given month I was at least breaking even, and there were times when I was a long way ahead.' He paused. 'It was almost as if I could see the energy of the cards, as if I knew where the energy was, and which way it was going; as if I could control it, and guide it in my direction. It was easy…' His voice trailed away.

'And then…?' Webb asked.

'Something changed,' Rainer replied. He hesitated. 'Almost overnight. It was as if I'd suddenly lost the ability to read the game. I was worrying too much about winning and losing instead of playing the table. And that's when it all started to unravel. This was March, April 1971, around the time they told me they wanted me to become a judge – and that was even more pressure, you know: you can't afford any scandal as a judge, and they make that pretty clear to you when you take the job.'

'How much did you lose?'

'Between March or April and August, September, I probably lost in the region of £30,000, £40,000.'

Raymond whistled softly. 'What did you do? Why didn't you just quit?'

Rainer laughed again, and coughed for some time.

'Ah, well, that's the question, isn't it? That's where Greta comes into the picture.'

# 23

'What did Greta Thiemann have to do with you losing money at the Clermont Club?' Webb asked.

'That was how she got her kicks, I believe the phrase is,' Rainer replied.

'You're going to have to explain that to us.'

'Greta Thiemann liked to watch, Chief Inspector. She liked to watch men risking large sums of money. If you won, that was great: you'd go out and drink the best champagne your winnings could buy. If you lost, then you had to go and find more money to play with so that her entertainment wasn't interrupted. And if you were cautious – which to Greta was anything short of downright reckless – you got punished.'

'Punished, how?'

'You'd be taken home, stripped, and thrashed with a ping pong bat until she decided you'd learned your lesson.'

'You're joking,' Raymond said, barely suppressing a laugh.

'I'm perfectly serious, I assure you. And before you ask: yes, you could walk away – in theory. But you wouldn't want to walk away. Greta was a very alluring woman, and after she stopped thrashing you she would give you the best sex you ever had in your life. Call it weakness, call it whatever you like, but she was an addiction – rather like gambling in many ways.'

'Well,' Webb said, 'whether or not she gave you the best sex ever, that didn't solve your immediate problem, did it? You were down £30,000 or £40,000, and you couldn't keep Greta entertained without money. What did you do about that?'

Rainer nodded. 'Ah. Well, Chief Inspector, I'm afraid the answer to that question doesn't reflect much credit on me.'

'Tell me anyway,' Webb replied.

'Well first, I raided Deborah's trust fund, to the tune of about £20,000. I worked out that I needed that kind of float to keep me at the table long enough to allow my luck to change. You can't win all the time, you see. It ebbs and flows. You've got to have enough funds to see you through the losses until you can turn it around.'

'When you say you "raided" her trust fund, what you mean is that you stole from it?'

'Forged her signature, yes. I honestly didn't think it would do any harm. I fully expected to be in a position to repay it before anyone noticed.'

'But that wasn't the way it turned out?'

'No. So I took out a mortgage on our house in Guildford, for another £10,000.'

'The house being in joint names, which means that...'

'I forged her signature again, yes. I got rather good at it, actually. And then the next step was to steal cheques from my former friends in chambers, which, of course, is the complaint you were investigating when you came to my flat.'

'To the tune of about £16,000?'

'That's what they said, isn't it? I honestly didn't think it was that much, but there's no point in arguing about it, is there? I'm sure you've got all the paperwork.'

'You forged their signatures too, just like you forged Deborah's?'

'Yes, and deposited the cheques into an account in my name. Bloody silly thing to do, obviously – I could have been caught straight away. But you don't see that when you're addicted to the cards, Chief Inspector. You always think your luck is about to change, so why would you need to worry about it?'

'Let's focus on Greta again, shall we?'

'Yes. Well, after I'd lost most of the proceeds of my forgeries, Greta offered to introduce me to a man who could lend me money, but who obviously wasn't a banker or trust fund manager.'

'A loan shark?'

'Quite so.'

'Daniel Cleary, also known as "Danny Ice?"'

'The very same. And you know the rest of the story. I've been appointed a judge. I'm trying my first murder case at the Old Bailey, the case of Henry Lang. And lo and behold, up pops Danny Ice as a character in the case I'm trying as a judge. Complete bloody nightmare. He'd been up to his tricks in the Henry Lang case, too. Lang's counsel, Ben Schroeder, produced evidence that Cleary had threatened the defendant with violence unless he gave up custody of his children – which was the alleged motive for his murdering his wife. As my luck would have it, Danny Ice and the deceased Mrs Lang were good mates. What were the odds on that? But that's the way it goes when you're on a losing streak.'

'So you saw it all unravelling? The Lang trial could have brought everything out into the open?'

'Yes. And when I confronted Greta, she pretty much admitted to me that she had set me up. Not in so many words, of course, but it was obvious enough.'

'What do you mean, set you up?'

'Cleary was keeping Greta supplied with cocaine. She never told me about that, of course, and she never took it while she was with me; but it turns out that she was using and he was her dealer. She had the same problem as me – she was living beyond her means. So when she'd run out of money and exceeded her credit limit, Danny gave her a choice: either have her face carved up, or send some of the gamblers she knew his way when they ran out of money from more conventional sources, such as raiding their wives' trust funds. That's all I was to her – another fool who didn't know when to stop: another fool to keep her supply of cocaine coming.'

He seized the inhaler and used it several times.

'And that's when it happened – two or three days before you came. I'd had a terrible night at the Clermont. I'd nearly won enough – can you believe it? It was almost like the old days, when

I first started. I was up the best part of £20,000. If I'd quit then, while I was ahead, I could have paid Danny off, and… But I didn't quit, because Greta kept egging me on – win more, risk more – which, of course, like the fool I was, I did. We ended up at my place, and I was beside myself – out of my mind, literally. I called her out about setting me up. She told me I was a fool; that I should grow up and take responsibility for myself. It was all my fault, she kept saying. This from a woman I thought cared about me. It was just too much. My life was falling apart…'

'And there was Mozart…?'

'There was Mozart. You began by asking me what I intended when I hit her, Chief Inspector, but you see, I'm really not sure. Intention requires thought, doesn't it? But I wasn't thinking. The mist descended, and when the mist descends you don't think. Thought is suspended and you just act. I hit her. I can't say I intended to kill her, because I don't know what I intended, if I intended anything at all. I lashed out, and I had Mozart in my hand. That's all I can tell you. I think I did exactly the same as Henry Lang. He stabbed his wife when she told him that his children might not be his, didn't he? I doubt that he had any real intention. There are times when intention isn't the issue. You act because you have to. You can't stop yourself. You are compelled.'

Webb nodded. 'Is there anything you would like to add, Mr Rainer?'

'No. I don't think so.'

'All right. You're looking rather tired to me. We don't have to go any further today if you'd prefer to stop now.'

'Yes. I think that might be best.'

'In that case we will see you tomorrow. I have a few other things to ask you. After that, you will be charged with the murder of Greta Thiemann, and if there is anything else you would like to add, you will be given the opportunity to do so then. I'm not sure whether we will charge you with anything else. I'll have to get the Director's advice on that. There doesn't seem much point, as far as I can see. But it's not up to me.'

'As a matter of interest,' Rainer asked, 'what happened to Danny Ice?'

'He got sent down for seven years for blackmail and assault,' Webb replied, 'didn't he, Phil? About two months after you left the country. Nothing to do with either you or Henry Lang, as it happens. Different case altogether.'

Rainer nodded. 'Good,' he replied, before the coughing overcame him again.

# 24

*Thursday 22 December 1983*

'How are you feeling today, Mr Rainer?' Webb asked.

'Well enough,' Rainer replied. 'But I haven't heard anything from Baxter. I asked him to get in touch with Deborah and find out whether she's willing to come to see me. Has he said anything to you?'

'Not to me,' Webb said. 'Phil?'

'No. But I'll remind him once we've finished here.'

'Thank you, Chief Inspector.'

'Now today, Mr Rainer,' Webb began, 'I want to ask you about what happened after you'd killed Greta Thiemann. Once again, I must caution you that you are not obliged to say anything unless you wish to do so, but anything you do say may be put into writing and given in evidence. Do you understand the caution?'

'Yes. I do.'

'When did you actually set out to leave the country?'

'Immediately after the Lang trial ended.'

'What, on the Friday night? If you recall, it finished very late. The jury didn't return their verdict until after eleven.'

'Yes, well it would have been early Saturday morning. After I'd sentenced Lang I went straight back to the Barbican. I knew I couldn't risk any delay. I knew you would have received the complaint from my old chambers by then, and you would want to talk to me about it. I had to assume that you had a search warrant.'

'You assumed correctly,' Webb confirmed.

'I had no way of getting rid of Greta's body; and I had Daniel Cleary on my tail. I'd missed a payment to him and Greta had told me he was after me. So I had no choice – I just had to make a run for it. I got changed, grabbed my passport and some money, and got out. It must have been between two and three o'clock, I suppose. What time did you get there?'

'About eight o'clock,' Webb replied. 'Look: quite obviously, you didn't just walk out of the Barbican on a whim and take the first available ferry to the Continent. This was a carefully planned escape. Why don't you tell us how you did it?'

Rainer sat back in his chair and drank some water. He gazed at the wall for some time.

'Is this really necessary, Chief Inspector? You've got me for killing Greta. I've told you all about that. Why does it matter how I got to Sarajevo?'

'Because I have reason to believe that criminal offences may have been committed by whoever arranged your journey, and whoever actually took you out of the country,' Webb replied. 'I need to know.'

'That would mean giving up my friends,' Rainer replied quietly, 'men who have been very loyal to me.'

Webb put his file down on the table and leaned forward. 'Let me make something very clear to you, Mr Rainer. Your disappearance was a source of considerable embarrassment to DCI Raymond and myself...'

'That wasn't my intention...'

'I don't give a damn what your intentions were. Our superiors thought we should have barged into your flat in the early hours instead of buggering about waiting until the next morning, and they were right, weren't they? But I said, "No, leave it, he's probably exhausted, we can't interview him in that state". I thought I was being fair to you, but as it turned out I was just being bloody stupid, wasn't I? And I've been hearing about it ever since, from the press as well as my superiors. I've never been able to live it down, and neither has Phil. So I don't give a damn about your intentions or your ideas of loyalty. You made an agreement to supply us with information and, so help me, if you don't live up to that agreement, I'll have you remanded back to Wandsworth so fast your feet won't touch the ground. Try seeing Deborah then.'

Rainer had turned white. Raymond put a hand on Webb's forearm.

'Take it easy, Johnny,' he said quietly. 'Look, Mr Rainer, after you'd gone, obviously we carried out an investigation into how you were able to disappear so easily. We came up with the names of two of your friends, Gerry Pole and Aubrey Smith-Gurney. Neither of them was willing to admit to having helped you, and they both said they had no idea where you were. So we were stuck. But we had a pretty shrewd idea of what had happened, what with Mr Pole rather conveniently having a house and a boat on the Isle of Wight; and now we know where you ended up, it won't take Interpol long to supply the missing pieces of the puzzle. So we're going to get there eventually.' He paused. 'In any case, I don't know whether you know this or not but Gerry Pole died last year – heart attack, apparently.'

Rainer held his head in his hands, and suddenly seized the inhaler.

'No. I didn't know,' he replied, after some time.

'I think we'd have had Gerry bang to rights,' Raymond continued, 'but it's too late for that now – which leaves us with Aubrey Smith-Gurney.'

'Aubrey wasn't involved,' Rainer said immediately.

'All right. Tell us what happened, then.'

'Aubrey was trying to help me in other ways.'

'What do you mean, other ways?'

'I'd confided in him about my gambling, including the money I'd stolen from chambers, and he volunteered to try to sort it out.'

'Sort it out?'

'He went to see the three barristers concerned and told them I would repay them as soon as I'd repaid Daniel Cleary. He asked them to wait until I'd got Cleary off my back, for obvious reasons. But it didn't work: they went to the police.'

'So you told Aubrey about Daniel Cleary?' Webb asked. He seemed to have regained his composure.

'He already knew about Cleary, before I told him.'

'Really? How did that come about?'

'Aubrey and Ben Schroeder are in the same chambers. I don't know how much you remember about the Lang trial, but there was a legal question about some evidence involving Cleary, and they'd consulted Aubrey about it.'

'Did Aubrey know about Greta?'

'He knew everything.'

'Including the fact that you'd killed her?'

'No,' Rainer replied vehemently, almost shouting. He thumped the table, and immediately collapsed back into his chair, coughing violently. Raymond poured him a glass of water and put it in his hand. He drank it quickly, which produced another bout of coughing.

'Let's take a break,' Raymond said.

# 25

'No one knew I'd killed Greta,' Rainer said when they resumed, some ten minutes later, 'except for Gerry. I had to tell him because of what I was asking him to do. He wouldn't have taken a risk like that just for a few gambling debts. But killing her… well, that was a different matter, obviously. I didn't tell Aubrey. I didn't tell anyone else. There was no need. Aubrey knew what I'd done to fund my gambling habit, but I wasn't completely honest with him even about that.'

'In what way?'

'He made me promise that I would stop going to the Clermont Club, stop gambling, and stop seeing Greta.'

'But you kept on despite his advice?'

'I didn't know what else to do. I needed to win some money back, to pay my debts. Obviously, I wasn't thinking clearly. You don't, in that situation. But I knew that if Aubrey found out what I was doing that would be the end – he wouldn't help me anymore. He told me as much.'

'So, what happened then?' Webb asked.

'Aubrey called Gerry and they had a meeting. Gerry then called me, and I asked him whether I could hide out at his house on the Island if it came to it, and whether he could take me over to Le Havre, or wherever, if I needed it. He said he would help me.'

Webb shook his head. 'Sorry, Mr Rainer, I'm not buying it. What would be the point of landing in Le Havre? Where were you going to go from there? By that time, we would have alerted Interpol and every police officer in Europe would have been looking for you. It was a very high-profile case. You wouldn't have lasted a week. How did you end up in Sarajevo?'

Rainer nodded. 'Gerry obviously knew some people. By the time I actually got to his house, there was a plan.'

'What plan?'

He hesitated. 'All I can tell you is that when I got to Gerry's house, he told me that he would drop me off at the harbour in Amsterdam, where I would be met by a man called Jan. I have no idea who this man was, Chief Inspector. That's the truth. We didn't go straight away. I lay low for three days, just to let things cool off a bit. I didn't shave for a couple of days, I dressed up in some old clothes, and I threw my passport over the side once we were underway. I had some money, not much but some, and that was it.'

'What did this man, Jan, do?'

'He took me to a safe house, where I spent about a week, at which point two other gentlemen, Branko and Miodrag, came to give me my new identity as Ernst Meier and take me to my new home in Sarajevo, courtesy, as it turned out, of Dragan. Look, you know all this from Faraday and Julia...'

Webb nodded. 'We will ask you about Dragan tomorrow. But all this planning must have been in place already by the time you arrived on the Isle of Wight?'

'So it would seem. I knew nothing about it before it happened, and that's the truth.'

'These documents you were given in the name of Ernst Meier,' Raymond said, 'included photographs, didn't they?'

'Yes.'

'How did they get photographs of you?'

'Gerry took some pictures before we left, passport size. I didn't question him about it at the time; I assumed he had a reason for needing them. As I say, my documents arrived almost a week after I'd arrived in Amsterdam.'

'So what you're saying,' Raymond commented, 'is that Gerry Pole had contacts who had access to a safe house in Amsterdam, and who could rustle up good-quality false identity papers within a week?'

'It goes further than that, Phil, doesn't it?' Webb added. 'These people could also arrange accommodation for Mr Rainer in Sarajevo, behind the Iron Curtain, and recruit him to participate in the trafficking of controlled drugs.'

'Very true,' Raymond agreed.

'In other words,' Webb said, 'your friend Gerry Pole of blessed memory, to whom you are so loyal, was working with Europe's biggest drug kingpin: working quite closely with Dragan. But you didn't know any of that, Mr Rainer, did you?'

'I did not.'

'How much did you pay Gerry Pole for services rendered in organising your escape?'

'Nothing. Our relationship wasn't like that. Gerry and I had known each other all our lives – since primary school. You don't ask for money for doing a favour for a friend. That's not how it works.'

The officers exchanged glances. 'How does it work, then, Mr Rainer?' Webb asked. 'It's the old boy network, is it? If someone's in trouble, you do what you have to, no questions asked, and you don't give a tinker's cuss about the law?'

Rainer did not reply.

'When we interviewed him just after you disappeared,' Raymond said, 'Aubrey Smith-Gurney told us that he was a member of your little club too. The "Gang of Three": is that right?'

Rainer laughed. 'That's what we called ourselves at school. We grew out of it. But the three of us were always very close. Aubrey and I read law at Cambridge together and went to the Bar together. He did his best to help me out of the mess I'd got myself in, but it was too late.'

'And it was Aubrey who first contacted Gerry for you?'

'I didn't know he was going to do that. He only told me after he'd done it.'

'But you did go to meet Gerry?'

'Yes.'

'Did Aubrey know about Gerry's house and his boat on the Isle of Wight?'

'Yes, of course.'

'So Aubrey knew perfectly well that you were going to do a runner, didn't he?'

'I'm sure he suspected it. I don't know how much Gerry told him. I didn't ask. Aubrey told me that as a QC there were certain lines he couldn't cross, certain things he couldn't know. I respected that.'

'And that's all he said to you about it, was it, after he'd contacted Gerry on your behalf: that there were certain things he couldn't know?'

'He told me that if I was going to do anything, I should do it immediately,' Rainer added.

'Did he indeed?' Webb asked. 'When did he say that?'

'It was on the Thursday, the day before the Lang trial ended. He said that I shouldn't even stay to finish the Lang trial – if I was going to do anything, I should do it there and then. I told him I couldn't, I had to finish the trial.'

Webb smiled. 'Yes. You had to tell the jury to return a verdict of manslaughter by reason of provocation, didn't you?'

Rainer bristled. 'Judges don't tell juries what verdict to return, Chief Inspector. They explain to the jury what the law says, and what their options are. The jury did what they thought was right. As it happens I agreed with them, but it was their decision.'

'But you learned a lot about provocation in that case, didn't you? Was that useful when you were concocting your explanation of why you killed Greta Thiemann?'

'I have no idea what you mean,' Rainer replied.

'Of course, you don't.' Webb stood up. 'That will do for today.'

Rainer stood also. 'And you'll ask Baxter if he's heard from Deborah?'

'Mr Baxter will be with us when we speak tomorrow,' Webb replied, 'after you return from court. You'll be able to ask him yourself. Just make sure you don't hold anything back, that's all. I don't think Mr Baxter would like that any more than we do.'

'I suppose the press will be all over us when we go to court, won't they? Can't blame them, I suppose. It's a good story.'

'I'm not aware of any mention of you yet,' Raymond replied. 'Baxter seems to have kept it quiet so far. But the court list for tomorrow will be out this afternoon, and there are always reporters covering Bow Street, so brace yourself – you're probably going to get some coverage tomorrow. We'll get you in and out of the building safely – we're used to doing that kind of thing – but when they call your case on, it will probably be standing room only.'

Rainer smiled. 'Well, I suppose it was always just a matter of time,' he said.

# 26

'May it please you, sir,' John Caswell began, once the hubbub produced by the appearance in the dock of Britain's most notorious fugitive had died down, 'I appear to prosecute in this case. My learned friends Mr Schroeder QC and Mr Overton represent the defendant, Conrad Rainer.'

'Yes, Mr Caswell.' Oliver Holden, the old-school metropolitan stipendiary magistrate presiding in court one at Bow Street Magistrates' Court, gave Conrad Rainer a disapproving stare over the rim of his horn-rimmed spectacles.

'The charge in this case is one of murder, sir. The case will in due course be committed to the Central Criminal Court for trial. But the prosecution is not in a position to proceed today. Mr Rainer was only charged yesterday after being interviewed by the police, and the prosecution still has to prepare the evidence. My learned friend Mr Schroeder has been good enough to tell me that he will not be opposing committal for trial, and will reserve his defence at this stage. But Christmas is almost upon us. It is not possible to prepare the case before the break. I would invite the court to adjourn this matter to Wednesday 11 January for committal proceedings, by which time the prosecution hopes to be ready.'

Holden nodded, conscious of the eyes of the numerous journalists representing the world's press, and those of some curious spectators, fixed on him.

'What's the position on bail?' he inquired innocently. 'I must say, Mr Rainer seems to be rather late getting to court.'

He paused to allow the chuckle in the public gallery to die away. Holden had worked hard at building a reputation for himself as a minor public wit, and even at Bow Street, with its steady diet of notorious cases, it wasn't every day that a chance like this came along to add to his reputation, with a full house hanging on his every word.

'About twelve years late, isn't he, Mr Caswell, if my calculations are correct? Extended holiday of some kind, was it?'

Another chuckle rippled around the courtroom. Caswell, with Baxter sitting unobtrusively behind him, was in no mood to waste time propping up Holden's image of himself as a master of repartee. His goal was to get the hearing over with as quickly as he could, and ignoring the magistrate's attempts at humour seemed the most promising way forward.

'My learned friend and I agree that there is no question of any application for bail in this case, sir. In fact, we have agreed that Mr Rainer should be remanded in police custody pending further proceedings.'

'In police custody? But he's already been charged. It seems most irregular to remand him in police custody once he's been charged. Why shouldn't I simply remand him in custody in the usual way?'

Holden scanned his audience again. He was on technical ground now, nothing very much to amuse them.

'Because, sir, there are other matters to be considered – matters that form no part of the case before you today, and to which I will not refer in open court. As I've already indicated, my learned friend and I have agreed that this is the most satisfactory course to allow us to deal with those matters.'

Holden appeared to be gearing up for another public protest, searching for another witty riposte to keep him in the eye of the world's press for a few seconds longer. Caswell felt Baxter getting nervous behind him and decided to pre-empt him.

'And if I may respectfully remind you, sir – I *am* speaking as the Deputy Director of Public Prosecutions.'

The implication was that there were higher powers to whom Caswell could, and would, appeal if Holden insisted on throwing his weight around – as indeed, there were. Caswell had not come to court without a back-up plan, one in which Baxter's Minister would play a vital role. He hoped it would not come to that – they were going to get quite enough publicity as it was, and they didn't need to give the press even more fodder with irregular goings on behind the scenes. But one way or the other, Conrad Rainer was not going to be remanded to prison. Fortunately, it seemed that Holden had drawn a blank and had nothing else suitably amusing to say about bail.

'Do you want to say anything about this, Mr Schroeder?' he asked.

'No, thank you, sir. I agree with the course Mr Caswell has proposed.'

'Very well,' Holden conceded, shaking his head in an obvious public show of reluctance. 'Stand up, then, Mr Rainer. Irregular as it may be, I shall do as I have been invited to do by the Deputy Director of Public Prosecutions. You will be remanded to police custody until 11 January, on which date the court will deal with the committal proceedings. Take him down. Next case, please.'

After Rainer had been taken back down to the cells and they had left court, Ben approached John Caswell, who was talking discreetly to Baxter.

'Well done, John. Not the easiest of tribunals, Holden, is he?'

'He's a pompous old windbag,' Caswell replied. He smiled. 'That's my personal view, obviously, Ben, not the Director's official line.'

Ben laughed. 'Don't worry – no one's going to hear it from me. He's insufferable, always has been – and he's been doing it for donkey's years, long before I came to the Bar.'

'Isn't he ever going to retire? Someone must be planting the idea in his mind, surely?'

'Let's hope so… Look, Mr Baxter, I don't want to hold you up, but we'd like a few minutes with him in the cells before you take him back to wherever you've got him. I'm not sure when we will be able to see him again, and…'

'Not a problem,' Baxter agreed. 'Take your time. I have no plans for him today, except to let him rest. Webb and Raymond said their interviews seemed to wear him out, and now he's had court to deal with, and I didn't think he was looking too bright by the time we finished. We'll give him a few days off, let him enjoy Christmas as best he can, and see how he's feeling then.'

'Are you worried about him?' Ben asked.

'I wouldn't say "worried" exactly, but he's obviously not a hundred per cent. The doctors say his condition is stable, but he does seem to tire easily. We're not unduly concerned at this stage, but we're keeping a close eye on him. But by all means go and see him. We're not in a hurry. Take as long as you like … Oh, there is one other thing…'

'Go on.'

'He's been asking me to contact his ex-wife, Deborah. He wants to see her, says he wants to apologise to her. It seems to be quite important to him.'

Ben nodded. 'It is. Julia got the impression that it was his main reason for coming back.'

'It could well be. He asks me about it twice or three times a day. Anyway…the thing is, I've spoken to Deborah, and between us, she doesn't want to know. I've done my best to persuade her – I've appealed to the national interest, I've appealed to her Baptist sense of charity, I've appealed to everything I can think of, but she's not having it. I don't really want to tell him that yet, so if he asks you, would you mind trying to change the subject? I think it would be in everybody's interests just now.'

# 27

'It sounds a bit soon, to be having the committal on 11 January,' Rainer complained.

'That's just a date Caswell came up with to keep the court happy,' Ben replied. 'He had to give the magistrate a date, but I don't think they'll be anywhere close to ready for committal so soon after Christmas.'

'Very little chance,' Clive Overton added.

'But what if they are? What's the wait for a trial at the Bailey?'

'In a case like this?' Ben replied. 'It wouldn't come on before early summer, at the earliest.'

They were in a dark, cramped cell in the bowels of Bow Street Magistrates' Court and Ben had noticed, as Baxter had suggested, that the short proceedings had been enough to drain Rainer's energy.

'I'll try my best to be gone by then,' Rainer said, with a thin smile. 'But assuming that I have the misfortune not to die before the early summer, how does it look? Does my defence of provocation have a chance?'

'Probably not, in all honesty,' Ben replied at once.

'In Henry Lang's case...'

'Henry Lang killed his wife when she suggested that someone else might have fathered the two children he loved above all else in life,' Ben pointed out. 'Greta Thiemann told you some home truths about a situation you'd created for yourself. We can give it a run, but your average London jury isn't going to buy that a High Court judge totally loses control just because he gets into an argument of that kind with his mistress. I'm sorry, Conrad, I've got to be honest with you. In the end, it's a question of what the jury think is reasonable.'

'A jury may think you were just taking your frustration about Daniel Cleary out on Greta,' Clive added.

Rainer was silent for some time.

'Actually, I have to agree.' He smiled again. 'I must admit, if I were trying the case, I'd probably have some difficulty summing the defence up with a straight face.' He paused. 'Has Baxter said anything to you about Deborah?'

Ben and Julia exchanged glances.

'He has no definite news yet,' Ben replied.

'I don't suppose she'll come,' Rainer said, almost to himself. 'Can't blame her, really.'

He sat down.

'Are you all right, Conrad?' Julia asked. 'You look a bit peaky.'

He nodded. 'I'm fine... Julia, I take it you're representing Imogen Lester on this trumped up drugs charge?'

'I'm not her solicitor because she's a... personal friend,' Julia replied, 'but Ben and Clive will be defending her. I didn't know you'd heard about all that.'

'Faraday told me while we were flying back. Look, my money's on Dragan for this. Michael obviously had him rattled and he lashed out in all directions. Imogen's just collateral damage.'

'It seems a bit over the top,' Julia replied. 'He'd already had her parents murdered in Sarajevo. Why would he try to fit Imogen up with drugs offences in London? What good does that do him?'

'Dragan doesn't think like that, Julia. He strikes me as a very thorough man. He doesn't like loose ends, and he wants the word to get around about what he does to anyone who poses a threat to him.'

'It's a lot of trouble to go to just to send a message.'

'On the other hand,' Ben said, 'the mention of innkeepers is quite a coincidence.'

'Who was talking about innkeepers?' Rainer asked.

'There's a character called Sean,' Ben replied, 'who, the prosecution say, delivered the drugs to the house. He used the expression to Imogen's brother – said he was a real innkeeper now, a *gostioničar*.'

'He actually used that term, in Serbo-Croat?'

'So the brother says.'

Rainer thought for some time. 'Sean, you said?'

'Yes.'

'It's not a coincidence – can't be.'

'What's not a coincidence?' Julia asked.

He paused. 'I was going to save this for when I talk to Baxter again, to give him the information I promised him about Dragan and his organisation. But I don't know when that will be, probably not until after the New Year at this rate; and in any case, I'm not a hundred per cent sure I trust Baxter to pass this on to you, and I can't let Imogen suffer because of that...'

'Go on,' Julia said encouragingly.

He took a deep breath, coughed, then took another breath.

'As I told you in Sarajevo, I was an innkeeper for Dragan for years. I heard a lot of things late at night when my guests had had a drop too much to drink. From time to time they would talk about their contacts in whatever city they were shipping drugs to or from. One of the things I heard several times was that Dragan had people in the police in London.'

'People?' Ben asked.

'Agents – people capable of facilitating his business dealings in various ways. Obviously, police officers could be very useful in making sure that deliveries were not obstructed, throwing colleagues off the scent – or even fitting people up if Dragan thought it necessary. They were pretty proud of having people in high places in cities like London, I can tell you that. One of the names I heard in connection with London was Sean. There were two others – Wally and Franco. I heard three names, and Sean was one of them.'

'Code names, presumably?' Julia observed.

'Yes, of course. But I heard about these men several times, and in context I had the impression that they were probably police officers, and senior officers, at that..'

'What do you mean, "in context?"' Julia asked.

'My guests would talk about how one or other of these men would direct them to a safe house, or even sometimes meet them with a car and escort them to wherever they were going. They would have a good laugh about it; they would call it "being given the keys to the city". There was talk about how much Sean and the others charged for their services, which apparently was above average – hence my conclusion that they were senior in rank, able to pull some strings.'

'That would explain a lot of what we know about Sean,' Ben said. 'The problem is: who is Sean, and how do we find him?'

'I can't help you there, I'm afraid,' Rainer said. 'But if I were you, I suspect I might start with officers who have been involved in recent large-scale drug investigations. That might narrow the field down a bit.'

Ben glanced at Clive.

'I'll get started on that with Barratt after Christmas,' he said.

'It still seems over the top to me,' Julia insisted, 'to go after Imogen like that.'

'It may have been a back-up plan,' Ben suggested. 'Perhaps they weren't sure they could get close enough to Michael to kill him. Perhaps arresting Imogen was designed to get Michael's attention if they still had to deal with him.'

'Perhaps.'

'Besides,' he added, 'Conrad is right. It can't be a coincidence that Sean turns up in Hampstead talking about innkeepers, can it?'

Conrad nodded. 'I think I would like to go back to where I'm staying now,' he said. 'It has taken it out of me – the crowds, the noise, and appearing in front of that bloody windbag, Holden. I feel myself starting to sink.'

'Of course,' Julia said. 'We don't need to keep you. How are they looking after you, wherever you are?'

'Can't complain. My room is comfortable enough; the quacks check up on me regularly; the food isn't bad; and they allow me a tipple in the evenings. They tell me there are medical facilities I can go to when the time comes. So, all in all, I would say they're treating me well so far. Probably best not to try to gaze into the future too much. We shall see.'

They wished each other a good Christmas.

# PART TWO

PART TWO

# 28

'All rise!'

The hubbub died away quickly. Everyone present in court two at the Central Criminal Court rose from their seats in unison in response to Mary's command. Tall and imposing, a retired officer of the City of London Police, Mary wore her long black usher's gown over a pristine white shirt bearing an image of the City's coat of arms, the cross of St George with a raised red sword in the top left white quadrant. Mary had never experienced any difficulty in dealing with jurors, police officers, witnesses, lawyers, or even judges who were not as familiar as she was with what was necessary to keep the court she was assigned to running smoothly; and today was going to be no exception.

Judge Andrew Pilkington walked briskly to his seat on the bench. Seeing Ben Schroeder sitting in counsel's row he flashed him a brief, but warm, smile, which Ben returned. Before his appointment as a judge at the Central Criminal Court three years earlier, Andrew Pilkington had been one of the Old Bailey's small cadre of prosecutors, known as Treasury Counsel. He had been the prosecutor in Ben's first case at the court, and they had subsequently crossed swords many times in the courtroom; and because of, rather than despite, that history they had become friends, trusting each other and sometimes working together behind the scenes on sensitive matters, including the infamous conspiracy to cover up widespread child sexual abuse in private schools facilitated by Father Desmond Gerrard.

After the judge had taken his seat, Anthony Norris, a member of Ben's chambers, remained standing. Norris was regarded as a competent lawyer and advocate, but he also had a well-earned reputation for being capable of treating anyone in his sights – including witnesses, opposing counsel and even judges – with a barely concealed contempt, although it was sometimes difficult to say whether he was speaking seriously or out of a warped sense of humour. Ben had defended cases prosecuted by Anthony Norris before, but it was a prospect he never relished. Some of that was personal. Norris was senior to Ben in chambers, and when Ben had applied to join chambers, some twenty years before, had objected to him for no reason other than that he was Jewish. Although chambers had deplored Norris's attitude and had welcomed Ben as a member, and although Ben was now well established in his profession, it was a history that would always come between them. Norris had subsequently apologised, apparently sincerely, but there had never been any prospect of closeness between them.

'May it please your Lordship,' Norris began, 'I appear to prosecute in this case. My learned friends Mr Schroeder QC and Mr Overton appear for the defendant, Imogen Lester.'

'Yes, Mr Norris.'

'My Lord, we are ready for trial, and I would invite your Lordship to have a jury panel brought down to court.'

The judge nodded to Mary, who bowed towards the bench and silently left court.

'There are one or two matters I should mention to your Lordship before we begin,' Norris continued. 'Firstly, we were unable to sit this morning because your Lordship was occupied with another case. If your Lordship agrees, my learned friend and I suggest that we should swear a jury and that I should make my opening speech this afternoon, but we should then adjourn for the day and start on the evidence tomorrow.'

'Yes, that makes sense,' the judge agreed.

'As your Lordship knows, the defendant is charged in the sole count of this indictment with knowingly permitting premises at 102 Willow Road in Hampstead, the defendant's home address, to be used for the purposes of supplying controlled drugs. The charge arises from a raid on those premises made by the Drug Squad, pursuant to a search warrant, in the early hours of Sunday 4 December last year. During the search, officers led by Detective Chief Superintendent Mellor and Detective Inspector Beech found significant commercial quantities of controlled drugs, including quantities of heroin, cocaine, cannabis resin, and one or two other items, with a total street value in excess of £20,000. The owners and occupiers of those premises were this defendant, Imogen Lester, and her brother Damian. Damian Lester was jointly charged with this defendant. He has already pleaded guilty to the charge , and he will be brought up for sentence at the end of this trial.'

'Yes, very well, Mr Norris,' Andrew Pilkington replied. 'Mr Schroeder, do you want to add anything?'

'Two things, my Lord,' Ben replied. 'The first is that Damian Lester made a written statement under caution. As your Lordship knows, that statement would be evidence against Damian as the maker of the statement, but it is not evidence against his sister Imogen. As Damian is not before the jury, ordinarily the jury would not see it. But I anticipate that the jury will also hear that, in the course of interviewing Miss Lester, Chief Superintendent Mellor and DI Beech confronted her with Damian's statement and invited her to comment on it. I can't really deal with that without the jury seeing the statement, so in the circumstances of this case I've told my learned friend that he is free to refer to it, and indeed to give the jury copies of it.'

'That is correct, my Lord,' Norris acknowledged immediately. 'I'm grateful to my learned friend for that. Juries always find it difficult to understand why they can't see statements made by other defendants, and it makes life easier in those cases where they can.'

'The second matter, my Lord,' Ben continued, 'is bail. Miss Lester has been on bail since shortly after her arrest. She has attended court, and there have been no problems while she has been on bail. I would ask that bail be continued throughout the trial on the same terms as imposed by the magistrates. Miss Lester is a woman of previous good character, a Cambridge graduate working for Cathermole & Bridger, a highly reputable and respected firm of solicitors.'

Andrew Pilkington nodded. 'I assume there's no difficulty about that, is there, Mr Norris?'

Norris stood. 'My Lord, I'm afraid there is a serious objection to bail. The prosecution objected when Miss Lester was first arrested, and the magistrates at first agreed, although they were subsequently persuaded to change their minds by my learned friend Mr Overton.'

'What is the objection?' the judge inquired.

'My Lord, the allegation in this case is that the drugs seized by the police can be traced to a shadowy figure based in Sarajevo, Yugoslavia, known to the police only as "Dragan". The evidence will be that the man "Sean", who, the prosecution say, brought the drugs to the house, was responsible for recruiting both Damian and Imogen Lester to assist Dragan in this country by acting as what Dragan terms "innkeepers"; that is to say, persons who make their premises available for storage and safe-keeping of drugs pending onward transmission to customers.

'One of the crucial pieces of evidence against this defendant is that when interviewed by the police, she herself, without any prompting from the officers, volunteered the term "innkeeper" and even used the Serbo-Croat word for innkeeper, *gostioničar*. Not only that: but for several days immediately before the drugs were delivered to 102 Willow Road, Miss Lester was in Sarajevo, in company with the solicitor for whom she works, Julia Cathermole. The Crown say that Miss Lester was there to meet one or more persons in Dragan's chain of command. We say it is no coincidence that she was in Sarajevo just as a delivery from Dragan was taking place at her home, overseen by her brother.

'My Lord, if she is granted bail, she is likely to abscond – she has the money and the means – and she may well commit further offences while on bail.'

Ben rose to his feet immediately.

'My Lord, that's absurd. Where would she go? As my learned friend knows, but omitted to mention to your Lordship, the police have Miss Lester's passport – it's evidence in the case.'

'That's no problem in the world of commercial drug dealing,' Norris interrupted, 'as I'm sure your Lordship knows all too well. Drug dealers have the means to produce false documents, and do so regularly.'

'She's had since before Christmas to disappear if she was going to disappear,' Ben retorted, 'but she has appeared today and answered to her bail. And may I remind your Lordship that Julia Cathermole, one of the most distinguished solicitors in London, has stood surety for Miss Lester, who is currently residing with her and whom she continues to employ in her practice. Miss Cathermole is in court if your Lordship wishes to hear from her.'

Norris was pushing himself up to reply, but the judge cut him off.

'I'm satisfied with the terms of bail,' he said, 'and I will continue bail during the trial.'

Mary returned within a few minutes with the jury panel, eleven men and five women. Ben challenged two members of the panel – older, conservatively-dressed men who seemed to him to have a military bearing – but otherwise did not intervene as the jury was sworn. The jury of twelve, nine men and three women, was selected within a few minutes and the jurors took their seats in the jury box. The judge gave them a few preliminary instructions, warning them not to discuss the case with anyone outside their own number, and invited the prosecution to make its opening speech.

'May it please your Lordship, members of the jury, my name is Anthony Norris, and I appear to prosecute in this case. My learned friends Mr Ben Schroeder QC and Mr Clive Overton appear for the defendant, Imogen Lester, the lady in the dock.

'Members of the jury, the Crown say that this is a straightforward case of drug trafficking. We say that Imogen Lester and her brother Damian found a way to make what they thought was some easy money. They agreed to open their home, a large house in a nice residential area in Hampstead – the kind of place unlikely to attract suspicion – to an international ring of drug dealers, to use for the storage of drugs pending onward transmission to customers. I won't take up too much of your time, but let me outline briefly what they did, as well as how the police discovered what they were doing, and were able to put a stop to it, and arrest them. Briefly, this is the evidence you will hear...'

# 29

It was after eight when Baxter called. Imogen had been exhausted by the sheer stress of the first day of her trial at the Old Bailey. Julia had fed her spaghetti bolognese, accompanied by a couple of glasses of wine, and packed her off to bed. She was reading downstairs at her kitchen table when Baxter called and said they needed to meet urgently, London rules, code Delta. Code Delta was the Caxton Bar at St Ermin's Hotel, a stone's throw from Westminster and a veritable cliché, given the Service's long association with the hotel, which had started during the War. Julia had been there many times over the years, at first with her father and, since his death, with Baxter, and had always assumed that those present probably included at least one foreign agent of some kind. But she also assumed that the Service had a way of keeping the place relatively safe, at least for meetings such as this. She left Imogen a note saying that she had popped out and would be back soon, and made her way to Caxton Street.

The Caxton Bar is on the first floor of the hotel, at the top of a dizzying set of steep, winding stairs. As she ended her climb, slightly out of breath, she saw that Baxter had arrived first and had commandeered a corner table in a private spot towards the back of the bar, which allowed him a view of the hotel's main entrance on the ground floor below. He had a bottle of champagne on ice waiting on the table. She took her seat opposite him.

'Are we celebrating something?' she asked. 'That would be nice to hear after the day I've had.'

'I wish,' he replied. 'It's not good news, I'm afraid, Julia. I thought a glass of something decent might at least soften the blow a bit.'

'Oh, God,' she muttered, as he poured two glasses. 'I knew it was too good to be true.'

He handed her a glass. They raised glasses and drank.

'Conrad Rainer is dead,' he said.

Her glass stopped in mid-air in its arc back down towards the table. She set it down slowly and deliberately.

'When?' she asked.

He leaned forward in his seat.

'What John Caswell will tell Bow Street Magistrates' Court on Friday, at the adjourned committal hearing, is that Conrad died this evening of a previously-diagnosed terminal cancer. He will have a death certificate and medical report with him to support that statement, if anyone should wish to see them.'

She stared at him.

'Whereas, in fact...?'

'Whereas, in fact, he hanged himself in his room on New Year's Eve. His supposed minder has been left in no doubt of the scale of his negligence, as I'm sure you can imagine.'

She reacted immediately.

'New Year's Eve?' she said, far too loudly. He placed a finger across his lips. She lowered her voice. 'New Year's Eve was 31 December, Baxter. Today is 14 February. Clive Overton was due to duck out of the Old Bailey for the afternoon tomorrow to see Conrad and get him ready for the committal.'

'Which is why you and I are having this meeting now,' he replied. 'Faraday and I agreed that natural causes would be our best bet. The case is going to get enough publicity as it is. The last thing we need is yet another Conrad Rainer scandal, and you know what the press are like. You tell them it's a suicide, and an hour later they're speculating about whether he might have been done to death in nefarious circumstances.'

'Was he?' she asked. 'I'm sorry,' she added a second or two later. 'I didn't mean that.'

'He hanged himself because his former wife wouldn't come to see him to allow him to purge his conscience. He left a note, saying so quite explicitly.'

They drank in silence for some time.

'You'll never get away with it,' she said quietly. 'Deborah might not have wanted to see him while he was alive, but she might be curious about how he died. What if she wants to see the body?'

'I doubt she will. But even if she does, I'm afraid it won't be possible. It seems that he was cremated once our friendly coroner had provided the death certificate. A bit premature, obviously: administrative error, which the Minister regrets and for which those responsible have been appropriately disciplined.'

'You won't get away with it,' she repeated. 'There's too much public interest in Conrad. It's not just Deborah.'

'We can't have certain elements in Yugoslavia thinking that his death might have something to do with them, or information he might have given us,' Baxter said. 'Suicide would be bound to fuel such ideas. It's a critical moment in some ways. We'll have to take our chances with the press, but as you know, we've cleared that hurdle often enough before.'

He refilled their glasses.

'I take it, then,' she asked, 'that he didn't give you all the information you'd hoped to get from him?'

'Sadly not. I'm fairly sure he was holding back because he thought we weren't putting enough pressure on Deborah to visit him. Actually, we were doing all we could, but she just wouldn't have it. Conrad didn't want to accept that.'

'Was what he gave you useful?'

'Time will tell. There's a question mark over it, at least as far as I'm concerned. Faraday thinks he walked on water, of course, but that was because Rainer was his agent – when an agent's giving you something that glitters like gold, you always want to believe it's the real thing. It's only natural – I was the same way in my day. But in my old age I'm sceptical of any intelligence until we've confirmed it with a second source. Some of it will be useful, I'm sure.' He paused. 'I don't suppose he...?'

'The only thing he told us,' she replied, 'was that Dragan had three agents working inside the Met. They were believed to be senior officers, and they had the code names Sean, Wally and Franco. That was it. It was of some interest to us, because the prosecution in Imogen's case say that Sean was the name of the man who talked her brother into becoming an innkeeper, and Sean also supposedly knew the Serbo-Croat word for innkeeper. But other than that, it wasn't very enlightening.'

Baxter reached down to his side and extracted a file from his briefcase.

'I felt I owed you something, your client having died while supposedly in our safe custody,' he said. He handed her the file.

'What's this?'

'Conrad told me about Sean and company too.'

'Did he give you any more details about them?'

'No. But it got me thinking: if Sean, Wally and Franco were going to be of any real use to Dragan, there's one obvious possibility, isn't there?'

'The Drug Squad.'

'Exactly. These are photographs of all officers currently serving, or who have served in the Squad over the past five years. There's also some biographical information about them – commendations, complaints, dates of promotion and so on – which may help you to rule certain officers out, or in. If you run into a brick wall making your own inquiries, let me know. If it's something I can help with, I will. We still have something of a common cause over Conrad.'

'It's Imogen I'm worried about now,' Julia replied. 'She's my only concern.'

'Of course,' Baxter said. 'But if you could link one or two Drug Squad officers to Dragan, I would imagine that might help her case along a bit.'

She nodded. 'Yes. It just might.'

'There is one other piece of news that might help too.'

'Oh?'

'Faraday says that Colonel Stojanović and his Militsija colleagues have arrested someone in connection with the attack on Michael and Margaret, a man calling himself Miloje. Apparently they're expecting him to confess to being officer in command of the attack, acting on instructions from Dragan or someone close to Dragan. Faraday is asking Stojanović to find out what Miloje knows about corruption over here, and specifically within the Met, linked to Dragan, and he will send us anything of interest. I'm not holding my breath, but you never know.'

'I wouldn't expect anyone close to Dragan to give out that kind of information,' Julia observed. 'If he does, he'll have to start worrying about his own life expectancy, won't he?'

'True,' Baxter replied. He smiled. 'But there again, I don't think the Judges' Rules apply in Yugoslavia, so you never know – he may feel his choices are limited.'

'Thank you,' she said.

'You're welcome. By the way, I've been meaning to ask you: what do you think of Faraday?'

'He's a good man,' she replied immediately.

He nodded. 'I agree. I think we'll have to pull him out of Yugoslavia, though.'

'Oh?'

'It's not his fault, but he's probably become slightly too conspicuous. He's due a move anyway. We don't leave people in place as long as we used to – certainly not as long as your father was in Vienna – not nowadays. We'll find him somewhere he can make himself useful.'

'He reminds me of you – and my father,' she said. 'You don't find officers of that quality every day. You should look after him.'

'We will,' Baxter replied.

# 30

Julia sat down at her kitchen table, poured herself a glass of red wine, and started to thumb through the file of photographs Baxter had given her. None of the faces rang any bells with her, though Baxter had provided more than she had expected in the biographical information, which in some cases was detailed enough to suggest that one of his subordinates had been assigned some challenging and time-consuming homework.

After half an hour or so a sleepy Imogen appeared, barefoot, her hair hanging loosely down her back, in one of the long thin T-shirts she habitually slept in. She came to stand behind Julia, put her arms around her neck, yawned, and leaned forward to kiss her on the cheek.

'Did you get some sleep?' Julia asked.

'Yes, for a while. But then I missed you and came to find you.' She looked at Julia's note, which she had left out on the table. 'You've been out? Where did you go?'

'Baxter called and wanted to see me,' she replied. 'Conrad Rainer died.'

Imogen walked around the table and sat down opposite Julia.

'What? Do they know...?'

'The cancer got him,' Julia replied, 'earlier than expected.'

'Oh? When was this?'

'Earlier this evening, apparently. He didn't give Baxter any more information about Dragan and his cohorts than he gave us. But Baxter did tell me that he'd had a call from Faraday. The police in Sarajevo have arrested a man in connection with the murder of your parents.'

She nodded. 'Good. Has he confessed? What's his name?'

'Miloje, so Baxter said – that's his first name, presumably; he didn't give me a surname. Whoever he is, he's apparently confessed to being involved in the attack, and he's confirmed that Dragan was behind it. Baxter didn't seem to know any more than that, but he will tell us if he hears from Faraday again.'

'This is really good news,' Imogen said.

'Baxter also gave me this,' Julia said, pushing the file of photographs across the table to her. 'These are photographs of Drug Squad officers. Why don't you look through them and tell me if there's anyone you recognise – apart from Mellor and Beech? I'll get you a glass of wine.'

'Does Baxter think some of them may be working for Dragan?'

'It's possible. If Conrad was right about Met officers working for Dragan, the Drug Squad is the obvious place to start.'

Julia set the glass of wine down on the table next to Imogen and silently resumed her seat, watching her go through the file slowly and methodically, page by page. Eventually, she raised her eyes.

'I recognise these two, of course, Mellor and Beech. I'll never forget them.'

Julia walked around the table to stand behind her. 'Yes. Anyone else?'

She turned back a few pages. 'This one looks familiar too. But I can't be sure.'

'DC Wild? Yes: he was one of the officers at the house during the raid. I think he may have been one of the officers who arrested Damian. Anyone else?'

'No,' Imogen replied, flicking through the pages again. 'I don't think so. But everything happened so quickly, and I was out of it for most of the time. You know what, you should ask Damian. He was down in the basement while they were all there, and he had far more chance to see them all than I did.'

'That's a good idea,' Julia said. 'Perhaps I'll take myself off to

Wandsworth tomorrow, assuming he will agree to see me.'

She walked to the phone.

'Tell him, if he doesn't, I'll send someone to break his legs,' Imogen said. 'Who are you calling?'

'His solicitor, Fahmida Patel... Hello, Fahmida? It's Julia Cathermole.'

'Julia? How are you?'

'Fine, thanks, how are you? '

'Good. Actually, I'm glad you called. It's nice to talk to an adult again after having dinner with my beloved children. What can I do for you?'

Julia laughed. 'It's a pleasure I've never had, but I can imagine. Look, Fahmida, I'm really sorry to disturb you so late. But something's come up in Imogen's trial, and I really need to ask Damian to look at some photographs for me – photographs of some police officers, including the officers on the raid, but some others as well. I can't barge into Wandsworth on my own – I'm not even Imogen's solicitor, as you know. They're not going to let me in unless I have his solicitor with me. Is there any chance you could spare a few minutes?'

There was a short silence.

'When would this be, Julia?' Fahmida asked. 'I'm asking because I have a busy week, you know, and...'

'I know. I hate to be a nuisance, but I have a feeling it could be important. The trial is going to move pretty quickly once the evidence gets underway.' She paused. 'Is there any chance at all you could do it tomorrow?'

She turned to Imogen and made an embarrassed face. Another short silence.

'Tomorrow? Oh, dear... well... I can't do it myself, Julia. But... I tell you what, I have a new clerk called Penny. I can pull her off whatever she's doing and tell her to meet you at Wandsworth. Come to think of it, it will be a new experience for her, going to see a client in prison, and there's no harm in that. Would that be all right?'

'You are an angel, Fahmida.'

'What kind of time?'

'Could we say ten? That way I'll be back at the Bailey by lunchtime.'

'Julia, there's nothing in any of this that could harm Damian, is there?'

'Nothing at all. There's an outside chance it could help him – though I can't make any promises about that. But nothing to hurt him.'

'All right. I'll call Penny now. Just one thing, Julia: Penny is what you might call young and impressionable, so...'

'I will be on my best behaviour,' Julia replied, and they both laughed. 'You are wonderful, Fahmida. Thank you.'

'Any time,' Fahmida said.

# 31

Wednesday 15 February 1984

A burly officer, carrying just a little too much weight around the midriff, stepped into the witness box and took the New Testament from Mary. He was dressed in a dark grey suit, with a blue and black striped tie over a slightly wrinkled cream shirt.

'I swear by Almighty God that the evidence I shall give shall be the truth, the whole truth, and nothing but the truth.' He returned the book to Mary and turned towards the judge. 'Alfred Mellor, my Lord, Detective Chief Superintendent, attached to the Drug Squad.'

Andrew Pilkington nodded to him.

'Yes, Mr Norris.'

'Much obliged, my Lord. Detective Chief Superintendent, did you make notes in relation to the evidence you are about to give to his Lordship and the jury?'

Mellor reached into the left inside pocket of his jacket and took out a bulging blue police notebook, which he placed in front of him on the edge of the witness box.

'I did, sir.'

'When did you make those notes in relation to the events you are going to deal with?'

'We made our notes between two and four o'clock on the afternoon of Monday 5 December, after we returned from the magistrates' court.'

'When you say "we"...?'

'I was with DI Beech, sir. We were in charge of the operation, and we had worked together throughout. We had arrested Miss Lester and her brother and had interviewed them the previous day, and we accompanied them to court on the Monday morning. We made our notes of the events together at Hampstead Police Station after returning from court.'

'The raid on the house took place at about four o'clock in the morning of Sunday 4 December: is that right?'

'Yes, sir.'

'Can you explain to his Lordship why you waited so long before making your notes?'

'That was the first real chance we had to do it… if I might just explain what we did over those two days?'

'Yes.'

'As I say, I was with DI Beech, and we were essentially in charge of the operation. Acting on information received, we had obtained a search warrant in respect of premises at 102 Willow Road NW3, where we had reason to believe we would find a large consignment of controlled drugs awaiting collection by a purchaser. With other officers, we raided the premises at about four o'clock on the morning of 4 December.

'We searched the premises and found a large quantity of controlled drugs contained in seven heavy canvas bags in the basement. We arrested Damian Lester, who was present in the premises, and who immediately admitted his role in the offences. Other officers then conveyed Mr Lester to Hampstead Police Station, leaving the house at about five thirty. Other officers completed the search of the rest of the house. Meanwhile, DI Beech and I remained at the house with PC Roberts, a female uniformed officer, and we questioned Imogen Lester regarding her involvement. We arrested Miss Lester at six thirty that morning, and conveyed her to Hampstead Police Station, arriving at six fifty-five. We ensured that the custody sergeant booked in both persons we had arrested,

'We then had to book the evidence in, and ensure that it was identified and catalogued, and delivered to the evidence room for storage, pending being sent for analysis. All of that took some time, and we were anxious to interview Miss Lester and her brother as soon as possible. But due to the early hour they hadn't had anything to eat or drink – and neither had we, come to that – so we were all provided with breakfast, or lunch or whatever it was, before we began the interviews. If I may, sir…?'

He picked up the notebook and flicked quickly through several pages.

'We gave both persons arrested time to rest after their meal. We interviewed Damian Lester between twelve and two o'clock, at which point he told us that he wished to make a written statement under caution, and that was done. I believe…'

'Yes, we've got that statement,' Norris said. 'Members of the jury, you haven't seen this yet, though you may well see it at a later stage of the trial, if it becomes evidence for any reason.'

'Yes, sir. We then interviewed Miss Lester between three twenty-five and four thirty that afternoon. During that interview we confronted her with her brother's written statement and offered her the opportunity to comment on it. Miss Lester did not wish to make a written statement herself, but she did make a full admission of her involvement in the offences.'

'And what happened between the conclusion of Miss Lester's interview and the time when you made your notes?'

'DI Beech and I arranged for both defendants to be charged, sir, and for them to appear in front of the magistrates the following morning, Monday 5 December, at ten o'clock. By then, DI Beech and I had been up since one o'clock that morning so, to be perfectly honest sir, we went home for a meal and a few hours' kip at that point. Damian and Imogen Lester were detained overnight at the police station, pending their appearance before the magistrates the following morning. After their appearance, they were remanded in custody by the magistrates, and we had some paperwork to do in connection with that. Once all that was done, and we'd had lunch, we made our notes.'

'I see. And you've already explained that you and DI Beech made your notes together.'

'Yes, sir. That is the usual police practice, since we had worked together throughout, and this enabled us to pool our recollections and produce the most accurate notes possible.'

'All right, Superintendent, let me turn to the raid itself. You've told my Lord and the jury that it began at about four o'clock on the Sunday morning, 4 December: is that right?'

'Yes, sir.'

'How many officers took part in the raid?'

'Apart from myself and DI Beech, sir, there were four other plain clothes officers from the Drug Squad, DS Martin, DC Wild, DC Fisher and DC Crane. There were six uniformed officers from Hampstead Police Station led by Sergeant Walker, and they included a female officer, PC Roberts, as I mentioned earlier.'

Norris paused. 'You had a search warrant. But how did you gain access to the house?'

'We approached the house and knocked on the door. There was no reply, at which point Sergeant Walker and his uniformed officers broke the door down using a very heavy battering ram.'

Norris nodded. 'You're bound to be asked about this, Superintendent,' he continued, 'so let me ask you now. How long elapsed between your knocking at the door and Sergeant Walker's officers breaking it down?'

'Following standard procedure in drugs cases, sir, we entered immediately after knocking.'

'So, being frank about it, you didn't give anyone inside the house time to answer the door, did you?'

'No, sir.'

'But you say that this is standard police procedure?'

'I said it was standard police procedure in drugs cases, sir. If I may explain...?'

'Yes, please.'

'In cases involving illegal drugs, sir, it has been our experience that as soon as the dealers realise that the police are at the door, they will immediately attempt to destroy or conceal any drugs on the premises. Depending on the quantity and type of drugs, it may take very little time for them to accomplish this, and so we have to enter the premises without delay to prevent that from happening. In appropriate circumstances – if a mistake has been made for example – the Metropolitan Police will reimburse the householder for any damage caused to the door.'

'All the same, Superintendent,' Norris continued, 'the jury may think that it must be a very startling experience for anyone inside the house, having the door forced open in that way in the early hours of the morning.'

'It is, sir. That is regrettable, of course, and we do our best to calm things down once we are inside. But it is important to preserve the evidence.'

'Yes, thank you, Superintendent,' Norris said. 'Well, let's turn to what happened once you were inside the house, shall we?'

# 32

'We entered the house as soon as the front door had been disabled, sir. All of us were shouting, "Police! We have a search warrant! Show yourselves!" and the like, to identify who might be present and where they were. It was obviously a big house, and we were concerned that we didn't know who might be in the house and where they might be. Also, of course, it was dark. We had flashlights, but we needed to locate the house lights. We were able to locate a light switch by the front door. As we progressed into the house we found other switches. But our main concern was to locate the occupants of the house as soon as possible.'

'Did the officers disperse to search different parts of the house?'

'That was the intention, sir. But I observed that DS Martin and DC Wild had progressed to a staircase at the far end of the entrance hall, which seemed to lead both up and down. DS Martin and DC Wild made their way downstairs to the basement, and after a short time, I heard DC Wild shout, very loudly, "Down here, sir, we've got it!" On hearing this, the other officers proceeded quickly to the basement.'

'Did you and DI Beech go with them?'

'Not at that time, sir. We were about to do so, but at that moment our attention was drawn to the staircase leading down from the upper floors. We saw a female, who I now know to be Imogen Lester, the defendant.' Mellor turned towards the dock and nodded towards her. 'Miss Lester is in court today; she's the lady in the dock.'

'What, if anything, did you observe about Miss Lester?' Norris asked.

'I observed that she seemed to have just got out of bed,' Mellor replied. 'She was wearing pyjamas, and no shoes.'

'What else did you observe?'

'She was running downstairs, sir. She was angry and aggressive. I learned later that she had consumed cannabis and alcohol on the previous evening, and...'

Ben was on his feet. 'My Lord, I'm going to ask my learned friend and the Superintendent to take care how the evidence is presented...'

'I wasn't aware that there was any dispute about it,' Norris replied.

'I don't object to the Superintendent giving evidence about what he says he saw,' Ben said, 'but I do object to his speculating about what may have caused it – unless, of course, he's being offered as an expert witness...?'

'Mr Norris?' the judge asked.

Norris seemed vexed, but said, 'Superintendent, please just answer the questions I put to you.'

'Of course, sir.'

'What leads you to tell the jury that Miss Lester was angry and aggressive?'

'Well, as I said, sir, she was running downstairs quickly towards us.' He turned over a page in his notebook. 'And I heard her shout in a loud voice, "Who the fuck are you? What are you, the Old Bill? Where's your warrant? You'd better bloody have one, mate, or I'll have your badge. What have you done to my fucking door? I'll have you for that!"'

In the dock, Imogen involuntarily broke into laughter, then quickly stifled the outburst and put both hands over her face, where they failed to conceal the incredulous smile she was unable to suppress. Every eye in court turned to the dock and two or three members of the jury smiled in response.

'That will do, Miss Lester,' Andrew Pilkington said, though not unkindly.

'If I may continue…" Mellor said. When no one replied, he went on. 'Being concerned for our safety, and that of the other officers, DI Beech and I decided that we should restrain Miss Lester. We ran part-way upstairs to meet her, and with some difficulty we were able to restrain her and handcuff her.'

'When you say, "with some difficulty", Superintendent,' Norris asked, 'are you suggesting that she resisted attempts to restrain her?'

'Yes, sir, she resisted arrest and assaulted both DI Beech and myself in the execution of our duty.'

'What did you do once Miss Lester had been safely restrained?'

'We escorted her the rest of the way downstairs, sir, feeling that it was safer to have her on the ground floor. By that stage she had calmed down somewhat, and asked if she could have some clothes to change into. I advised her that PC Roberts, the female officer, would assist her with that.

'However, I determined that it was necessary for me to see what had been found in the basement. A uniformed officer advised me that it was safe to proceed downstairs, and that they had detained Miss Lester's brother, Damian Lester, in the basement. DI Beech and I made our way down to the basement and saw Mr Lester sitting on the floor near to seven heavy canvas bags, which were later examined and found to contain commercial quantities of various controlled drugs.'

'Yes, let's not bother with that now. I will call other evidence of what exactly was in the bags, Superintendent.'

'Yes, sir.'

'What was Miss Lester's reaction to what you found in the basement?'

'Her first reaction, sir, was to her brother; and I must say, in fairness to Miss Lester, that Damian had been slightly injured, purely by accident, while officers were attempting to restrain him. I'm not able to speak to that, as I didn't witness it, but I believe that DS Martin and DC Wild are prepared to give evidence about that, if required.'

'Yes. What was Miss Lester's reaction?'

'She saw that Damian was bleeding from what appeared to me to be a small cut on his cheek, sir. She started to become agitated again, and accused us of having assaulted him. However, when I pointed out to Miss Lester what I believed was in the canvas bags, she looked at her brother and said, "You fucking moron. I don't know why I bother." At this point, I decided to take Miss Lester back upstairs and interview her away from her brother. I instructed DS Martin and DC Wild to convey Damian Lester to Hampstead Police Station, and to ensure that he received medical attention in respect of his injury. I also requested PC Roberts to escort Miss Lester back upstairs to the kitchen, and to ascertain where she could find some clothing for Miss Lester to put on, and to make that available to her. DI Beech and I then briefly looked around the basement, and gave instructions to the remaining officers to continue the search of the house.'

'Were you concerned that there might be further drugs on the premises?'

'We were, sir, yes. I was aware that a uniformed officer had found evidence of personal consumption of cannabis in the kitchen, and a number of items had been seized there. But also, typically, in a drug house you can find other items that might be of interest as evidence.'

'What kind of items?'

'It could be unexplained large amounts of money, sir, foreign money, travel documents, or items of practical use to drug dealers such as sets of scales, cutting boards, plastic storage bags. It all depends on what use has been made of the premises.'

'Did the officers find any other items of evidential interest, apart from the evidence of personal use of cannabis in the kitchen?'

'Officers took possession of two British passports, in the names of Imogen and Damian Lester, which were seized as evidence, sir. But other than the passports, no, we did not find any other items of interest.'

'All right. Let's move on to the kitchen, shall we?'

# 33

'When we arrived in the kitchen, sir, I noticed that the evidence of personal consumption I referred to earlier had been removed and the kitchen had been cleaned. However, there was still a noticeable smell of cannabis – as there had been in the basement, due to the presence of a substantial quantity of cannabis resin there.'

'Do I take it, Superintendent, that the smell of cannabis is something you are familiar with because of your training and experience?'

'It is, sir, yes.'

'Thank you. Please continue.'

'I asked Miss Lester to sit down at the table, which she did. Once she was seated, DI Beech removed Miss Lester's handcuffs, as she appeared to be much calmer at this stage and there was no continuing need to restrain her. DI Beech and I sat down at the table with Miss Lester. At that point PC Roberts was with us. I asked Miss Lester whether she would like PC Roberts to make some tea or coffee. She declined, but PC Roberts brought her a glass of water on her own initiative. I then instructed PC Roberts to join the other officers who were still engaged in searching the house, and she left the kitchen. I introduced DI Beech and myself to Miss Lester as officers of the Drug Squad, and informed her that I wished to question her about what we had found in the basement, and cautioned her.'

'Yes, Superintendent. Please tell the jury the words of the caution.'

'The words of the caution, sir, are: "You are not obliged to say anything unless you wish to do so, but anything you say may be put into writing and given in evidence."'

'Did Miss Lester reply to the caution?'

'Yes, sir. She said, "What do you want to know?" I then said: "Well, we've just found a large haul of illegal drugs stashed away in your basement. My lads are making a search of the house as we speak, so we shall see. But even assuming there's no more, the evidence points to you being involved in a conspiracy to supply drugs, and permitting your premises to be used for the supply of drugs. That is a serious matter. If there's anything you'd like to say to us that might enable us to help you, you'd better say it now."'

'How did Miss Lester respond to that?'

'She said, "I don't know where to start." I said: "Well, you might start by telling us who supplied the drugs you've got stashed away downstairs, and who was due to collect them. If you can give us some people higher up in the chain, that's always good. For example, your brother has already given us the name of someone called Sean. What can you tell us about Sean?" She replied, "I don't know anyone called Sean." I said, "Really? Because Damian says that Sean delivered the drugs to these premises, and that he was paying rent for them."'

'Yes.' Norris interrupted. 'Superintendent, based on your long professional experience of drugs cases, what is meant by the term "rent" in this context?'

'"Rent" refers to a payment made to the occupier of premises in return for the occupier allowing a dealer to store drugs on the premises for some time.'

'Did Miss Lester appear to understand the meaning of the term?'

'She did, sir. I said, "You were taking money for looking after these drugs until someone collected them to move them on. You do live at this address, I take it?" She replied, "Yes." I said, "Right. So, in law, you're the occupier, and if drug transactions take place on your premises, you're committing a serious offence."'

Mellor paused for effect. 'Miss Lester then said, sir – and I made a careful note of her exact words: "You're saying I'm an innkeeper?"'

'Yes,' Norris intervened. 'Before you go any further, Superintendent, I want to make this clear. Who was the first person to use the word "innkeeper" during the interview you're describing?'

'Miss Lester, sir.'

'Did you or DI Beech suggest that word to her, or prompt her to use it in any way?'

'No, sir, we did not. Miss Lester came up with the word on her own.'

'Tell my Lord and the jury, please, Superintendent, what, if any, significance that word has for you in the context of drugs cases.'

'My Lord, "innkeeper" is a term used by certain individuals who are part of organised crime organisations based in Eastern Europe, particularly in Yugoslavia, involved in the trafficking of illegal drugs on a large scale, including importing such drugs into this country. It refers to persons who are prepared to make their premises available for this purpose in return for the payment of rent.'

'How did you respond to what Miss Lester had said?'

'At first, sir, both DI Beech and I were extremely surprised and it probably took us a few moments to say anything. Eventually, I believe I asked Miss Lester to repeat what she had just said.'

'Did she do so?'

'She did, sir. She replied: "Innkeeper, *gostioničar*."'

'I'm sorry, Superintendent, I didn't catch what you said at the end of your answer. Would you mind…'

'I used a Serbo-Croat word, sir: *gostioničar*. It is the word for "innkeeper" in Serbo-Croat. I can write it down if you like…?'

'Even better,' Norris said, reaching back to the desk behind him, 'My Lord, we have a Serbo-Croat to English dictionary, and we have inserted a bookmark at the relevant page. If my learned friend has no objection…'

'No objection,' Ben confirmed.

'Then may that please become Exhibit one, and if the usher would be so kind, your Lordship and the jury can see the word in print with its English translation.' Norris waited until Mary had made the rounds with the dictionary. 'And I'm sure everyone knows this, but just for the sake of completeness, is Serbo-Croat the language spoken in Yugoslavia?'

'That is correct, sir.'

'Thank you. Before we go on,' Norris said, 'you mentioned a moment or two ago that there were certain individuals involved in organised crime, drug dealers based in Yugoslavia, who have come to your attention. Is there anyone of particular interest to the Drug Squad?'

'Yes, sir. We have reason to believe that one such individual, who goes by the name of Dragan – we don't know his full name, or even whether Dragan is his real name – but we have reason to believe that he is a major figure in the trafficking of illegal drugs, including importing such drugs into this country.'

'As a result of that, were officers of the Drug Squad already familiar with the Serbo-Croat word for "Innkeeper?"'

'I can't speak for the Squad as a whole, sir, but DI Beech and I were familiar with it as a result of certain other investigations in which we had been involved.'

'Thank you, Superintendent. Then, returning to the interview, what happened next?'

'Again, sir, it's fair to say that DI Beech and I were taken aback that she knew the Serbo-Croat word. I think I said something like, "That's a foreign word, isn't it, Tommy?" I was referring to DI Beech, sir. "Doesn't that sound like a foreign word to you?" DI Beech replied: "I believe it's Serbo-Croat, sir. I believe it may be the Serbo-Croat word for "innkeeper." I said, "Is it really? Well I never." I was speaking in an ironic vein at that point, sir.'

'I think you mean a sarcastic vein, Superintendent,' Norris said, with a grin towards Ben, 'rather than ironic. But thank you for pointing that out.' Andrew Pilkington and a few members of the jury chuckled.

'I wouldn't know, sir,' Mellor replied. He paused for a few seconds. 'I then said to Miss Lester, "How do you come to know how to say 'innkeeper' in Serbo-Croat?" She replied, "I've just got back from Yugoslavia, Sarajevo. I got back last night. You can check my passport. It's upstairs in my bedroom."'

Norris reached behind him again and produced Imogen's passport.

'Yes, and, in fact, if you would look at this please, Superintendent...'

'No objection, my Lord,' Ben said.

'I'm obliged. Then, if this may become Exhibit two? Superintendent, looking at the stamps in Miss Lester's passport, do they confirm that she did, in fact, visit Yugoslavia between 29 November and 3 December last year, 1983, which would mean that she arrived back in London the evening before you carried out the raid?'

'That is correct, sir.'

'Thank you. Continue with your account of the interview, please.'

'I said to Miss Lester: "What were you doing in Yugoslavia?" She replied: "My parents were murdered in Sarajevo recently. My father was a diplomat, at our embassy in Belgrade. The local police haven't been able to find out who did it yet. I went because I wanted to know what they were doing to investigate."'

'And pausing there, Superintendent, were you at that point aware of what had happened to Miss Lester's parents?'

'No, sir. But I subsequently made inquiries with the police in Sarajevo, who confirmed that Miss Lester's parents had indeed, sadly, been murdered; and that Miss Lester had had a meeting with the police and had been taken to the crime scene during her visit to the city. But as I was unaware of that at the time, I said to her, "Well, I'm very sorry to hear about your parents, Miss Lester. But surely the embassy would have made some inquiries for you, wouldn't they, especially as it was one of their own who was murdered?" She replied, "I felt I had to see for myself." I said,

"Did you? In that case, why did you go on your own? Why didn't you take your brother with you?" She replied, "I went with Julia Cathermole. She's the solicitor I work for."'

'And did the police, in fact, later confirm that Miss Cathermole had travelled to Sarajevo and had attended the meeting with Miss Lester?'

'They did, sir. However, at that time, given Miss Lester's familiarity with the Serbo-Croat for "innkeeper", I was suspicious of the reasons for her visit to Yugoslavia at the very time when controlled drugs were being stored in her basement. I suggested to Miss Lester that her brother Damian was taking charge of stashing the drugs in the basement while she was in Sarajevo.'

'How did she respond to that suggestion?'

'She replied, "I don't know what Damian did in my absence". Finally, I pointed out to Miss Lester that she had still not explained how she knew the word for "innkeeper" in Serbo-Croat. I said, "It's not a word you use every day, 'innkeeper', is it? What have innkeepers got to do with the investigation into your parents' deaths?"'

'Did she answer that question?'

'Yes, sir. She replied: "Nothing. We stayed at the Holiday Inn, that's all. It was probably a word I picked up there."'

'What happened then?'

'I said to Miss Lester: "Well, that's all very interesting, Miss Lester. I don't suppose you happened to run into a gentleman by the name of Dragan during your stay in Sarajevo, by any chance, did you?" She replied, "Dragan? No. I don't know anyone by that name."'

Mellor turned over another page of his notebook.

'I said: "You see, the reason I ask is that, according to police intelligence, a man called Dragan is a major supplier of illegal drugs throughout Europe. He has a vast operation, so we're told, and sometimes, some of his merchandise even ends up here in Britain. And according to police informants, 'innkeeper' or '*gostioničar*' is a term Dragan uses for people he pays to make their premises available to him for drug trafficking purposes. So it's quite a coincidence that you go to Sarajevo and pick up the word 'gostioničar' in the Holiday Inn just as a shipment of illegal drugs is making its way to your basement: don't you think? Any comment on that at all?"'

'How did she respond?'

'She asked if she could speak to a solicitor, sir. I told her that she could do so in due course at the police station, but that I was arresting her on suspicion of conspiring to supply controlled drugs and permitting her premises to be used for the supply of controlled drugs. I cautioned her again, in the same terms as before: "You are not obliged to say anything unless you wish to do so, but anything you say may be put into writing and given in evidence."' She made no reply to the caution, sir, and DI Beech and I then conveyed her to Hampstead Police Station.'

Norris looked up at the judge. 'My Lord, we are now moving on to events later in the day. I'm sure the jury would welcome a short break, as would Superintendent Mellor...'

'Yes, very well, Mr Norris. Twenty minutes, members of the jury.'

# 34

Julia suppressed a smile as a startled Penny, already nervous about her first experience of the confines of a prison, gasped and turned around to look as the prison officer slammed the door shut with a well-rehearsed reverberating clang. He turned the key in the lock, leaving them alone inside the small cell with Damian Lester. Julia gestured to Penny to take one of the two chairs at the small table, where she recovered stoically, took a notepad and pen from her briefcase and sat poised, ready for action.

'Thank you for seeing me, Damian,' Julia said. 'I'm not your solicitor, and I hope it was explained to you that I'm not even Imogen's solicitor, so you certainly weren't under any obligation to talk to me.'

They shook hands.

'Fahmida said you had something to tell me, or ask me, that might help Imogen,' he replied. 'It's my fault that she's in this mess in the first place, so it's the least I can do. Did Fahmida tell you I will give evidence for her if they want me to?'

'Yes, she did. Thank you. That will be up to her solicitor, Barratt Davis, and her barristers.'

'Why did you come then, rather than her solicitor?'

'Barratt's got his hands full at the Old Bailey now that the trial's started, and actually it was Imogen's idea that I should see you and ask you something.' She smiled. 'After all, I am her lover-employer, or employer-lover, or whatever it was you called me, aren't I?'

Glancing down at the table, she saw Penny's eyes open wide. He returned the smile sheepishly.

'Yes, well, sorry about that. I was just giving her a hard time. I call her "Girton" too, sometimes. It's just to wind her up… anyway, sorry. What should I call you?'

'How about Julia?'

He nodded. 'All right.'

'So, let's get on with it, shall we? Why don't you sit down?'

She placed the file on the table in front of him.

'This file contains photographs of current and past members of the Met Drug Squad. I want you to look through it and tell me if you recognise anyone. Take your time.'

Damian began to work his way methodically through the photographs. He stopped a few pages before the end, and turned back two pages.

'Well, these two were the ones who arrested me,' he said, looking up and pointing to two pictures in turn.

'DS Martin and DC Wild?'

'Yes. Martin was the one who punched me in the face, the bastard.' He glanced across the table at Penny. 'Sorry. Pardon my French.' He turned over to the next page. 'And these two questioned me at the police station when I made my written statement.'

'Chief Superintendent Mellor and DI Beech?'

'Yes.'

'Did they hit you?'

'No. They didn't need to. I was intimidated enough by then.'

'Yes, I get that. You told Fahmida about being hit, I hope?'

'Yes. She took pictures while we were at the magistrates' court.'

'Good. All right: just on the off chance, why don't you look through the rest of them? The witness statements don't mention any other members of the Drug Squad being involved with you during the raid, but we might as well make sure.'

He turned forward several pages. 'This one, possibly. He seems familiar, but I'm not sure.'

'DC Fisher?'

'Yes.' Damian turned forward several pages again, to the end of the file. Suddenly, he sat bolt upright in his chair, rescuing the file just before it fell through his fingers. He had turned pale.

Julia touched him on the shoulder. 'Damian, what's the matter? Are you all right?'

He did not reply immediately, but placed a finger on a photograph and looked up.

'This one? DS Doug Isherwood?' she asked.

He nodded silently.

'I don't recall that name. Was he there during the raid?'

He shook his head.

'That's Sean,' he replied eventually.

# 35

Julia pushed herself up from the table and walked slowly around the cell before stopping to lean against the wall behind Penny's chair. There was silence for a full minute.

'The same Sean who paid you money to stash drugs in the basement of your house without Imogen's knowledge?' she asked. 'That Sean?'

'Yes.'

'The Sean you met in the pub on several occasions?'

'Yes.'

'The Sean who told you that you were an innkeeper, and who wrote the word *gostioničar* down on a beer mat for you? That Sean?'

'Yes.'

'Are you taking notes?' she asked Penny.

'Yes, Miss Cathermole.'

'Good. Write down the word "entrapment" in big capital letters, and make sure you show it to Fahmida as soon as you get back to the office. Understood?'

'Yes, Miss Cathermole.'

'How sure are you about this?' Julia asked.

'I'm sure.'

Julia walked back to the table and placed both hands firmly on the surface, bending down until she was inches away from his face.

'Listen very carefully, Damian, because I don't want to hear on some future occasion that you're not sure about your identification of Sean, because you were pissed or stoned when you saw him, or because you just weren't paying attention, or because the lighting in the pub wasn't good enough. I can't tell you how upset I'm going to be if I hear any shit like that. I can't even begin to tell you what a disaster that would be – for Imogen and for you. I have very limited sympathy for you. If you fuck up your own case I'm not going to lose too much sleep over it. On the other hand, I care a great deal for Imogen, and if you fuck her case up, so help me, I will destroy you, if it takes me the rest of my life. Now: do you understand what I've just said?'

He nodded.

'I didn't hear you.'

'Yes. I understand what you said.'

'Do you believe that I am capable of doing what I say I'm going to do?'

'Yes.'

'Good. Now, listen very carefully. On a scale of one to ten – one being not sure, ten being completely sure – how sure are you that DS Doug Isherwood is Sean?'

'Ten,' he replied defiantly, without hesitation.

She stared at him for some time. She turned to Penny and snatched her notebook from the table, indicating with her fingers that Penny should also give her the pen. Penny complied instantly. With a wave of her hand she ordered Penny to stand and move away, and again she complied immediately. Julia sat down in her place.

'I'm now going to write down something we call a declaration,' she said. 'This declaration is going to say that you have read the statement you're about to make; that the statement is true to the best of your knowledge and belief; and that you make it knowing that you will be liable to prosecution if you wilfully state anything you know to be false or do not believe to be true. When I've finished writing the declaration, you're going to write a statement, in which you're going to say that you are sure, ten out of ten, that

DS Doug Isherwood and Sean are one and the same person. You're then going to describe each occasion when you met Sean, and all the agreements you made together, and how they were carried out. When you've done that, you're going to sign the statement, and I'm going to witness your signature. Is that a problem for you?'

'No.'

'Let me explain one thing to you, Damian. Bad as your situation is now, if you make a false statement about this, it's going to get far, far worse – you have my word on that. Now, let me ask you again: is it a problem for you to make that statement?'

'No.'

She nodded and wrote furiously for several seconds. She stopped and suddenly smiled brightly.

'Good. Off you go, then. Start just under the declaration. Take your time.'

'Imogen was right,' he said, almost forty minutes later, handing her the pen after signing as she directed.

'About what?' she asked, signing quickly as his witness.

'She said she'd never met anyone who could put the fear of God into someone like you do. She certainly got that right.'

Julia smiled sweetly. 'Thank you,' she said. 'How kind of you to say so.'

Half an hour later, Julia and Penny left Wandsworth Prison together.

'How are you finding your first experience of working for a solicitor, Penny?' Julia asked. 'Do you think it's the kind of work you're going to enjoy?'

Penny hesitated. 'I'm not sure, Miss Cathermole,' she replied. 'I did think of doing teacher training.'

'Well, it's never a bad idea to have more than one plan,' Julia said breezily. 'You never know what suits you until you've tried it, do you? Tell Fahmida I'll call her later.'

They shook hands briefly.

'Oh, and Penny...'

'Yes, Miss Cathermole?'

'Not a word to anyone else about this: understood?'

'Yes, Miss Cathermole.'

'Good girl.'

Julia went straight to her office and called in a message for Baxter, requesting a meeting, London rules, code Echo.

# 36

'Now, Superintendent,' Norris began, once court had reassembled after the break, 'I want to move on. You've told us already that, when you returned to Hampstead Police Station, everyone had what I'm sure was a welcome rest and some refreshments, after which you and DI Beech interviewed Damian Lester: is that right?'

'Yes, sir.'

'And at the conclusion of that interview, did Damian make a written statement under caution?'

'He did, sir.'

'Look at this, please, Superintendent.' Norris reached behind him to the young man from the prosecuting solicitor's office, who handed him a document with a number of copies. 'May this be Exhibit three, my Lord? I understand there's no objection…'

'No objection,' Ben confirmed.

'Yes, very well,' Andrew Pilkington said.

'I'm obliged. There are copies for your Lordship and the jury.'

Norris waited for Mary to distribute them.

'Superintendent, I'm not going to read it out now. The jury will have the chance to read it themselves at their leisure. In essence, did he say that he had met a man who called himself Sean at his local pub?'

'Yes, sir.'

'That he had run up some debts because of his personal drug use?'

'Yes, sir.'

'And that Sean offered to pay him to store drugs at the Lester family home in Willow Road, including the consignment you found in the basement, for which he was paid £200?'

'That's correct, sir.'

'And did he also tell you that Sean had introduced him to the word "innkeeper" to describe what he was doing, and had written the Serbo-Croat word for innkeeper, "*gostioničar*", down for him on a beer mat?'

'He did say that, sir, yes.'

'Pausing there, Superintendent, I see that you asked Damian a number of questions about this man, Sean, and that Damian gave you a description of him.'

'Yes, sir. Obviously, if this man Sean existed and was a link in the chain of supply of these drugs, we were anxious to identify and question him.'

'Were you able to find him?'

'No, sir. We made extensive inquiries in the area, but we had no luck at all. Unfortunately, we have no idea who he is, or where he might be.'

'Thank you. Now, returning to the statement: in fairness to Imogen Lester, did Damian tell you in the clearest terms that his sister was not involved with the supply of drugs in any way, and knew nothing about the arrangements he had made with Sean?'

'He did, sir. He was very emphatic on that point.'

'Not only that: did he tell you that she was a young woman of excellent character? And, in fact, did he say this: "What, Imogen? Imogen, deal in drugs? God, no. No way. My sister is pathetically, depressingly law abiding. She picks up litter on the street; she stops her bike at red lights. She went to Cambridge, for God's sake." Is that what Damian said about her?'

'Yes, sir. That's correct.'

'Thank you. Now, the statement indicates that it was completed at three o'clock that afternoon: is that right?'

'Yes, sir.'

'What did you do then?'

'I told Damian Lester that he would be charged with knowingly permitting premises to be used for the supply of drugs, and cautioned him. He made no reply to the caution.'

'Was Damian Lester later charged with that offence, and did he plead guilty to the sole count of this indictment at a hearing at this court some time later?'

'He did, sir, yes.'

'Thank you, Superintendent. Now, moving on to later events on the afternoon of 4 December, what did you do next?'

'Having concluded our interview of Damian, DI Beech and I then interviewed Imogen Lester. We showed her Damian's statement and invited her to comment on it, if she wished.'

'Tell my Lord and the jury what was said.'

Mellor turned over several pages of notes. 'If you would give me just a moment, sir… Yes: when we showed her the statement, Miss Lester read through it, and asked if she could speak to Damian. I said, "Not at the moment". I told her that I did not believe that both she and Sean knowing the Serbo-Croat for "innkeeper" was a coincidence, and that I believed that she was involved, with her brother, in storing drugs for Dragan and his associates. I reminded her of the caution again, in the same terms as before.'

'How did Miss Lester respond?'

'She said: "No. I've never been involved with drugs." DI Beech then pointed out that Miss Lester had, in fact, smoked a joint with her brother the previous evening.'

'Yes: but in fairness, did she explain that by reminding you that she had been upset by her trip to Sarajevo in connection with the murder of her parents?'

'She did, sir, yes.'

'What did she say with respect to the supply of drugs?'

'She said, "I have never in my life been involved with supplying drugs. I would never do that. Read Damian's statement, for God's sake. He told you I wouldn't be involved with drugs".'

'What did you say?'

'I told Miss Lester that I didn't believe her, or Damian, and that

I proposed to charge her with the same offence as her brother. I explained that she would be detained at the police station overnight and taken to the magistrates' court the following morning, and that she would be entitled to be represented by a solicitor.'

'Did she say anything in response to that?'

'Not at first, sir. But just as DI Beech and I were leaving her cell she called us back, and said: "Look, all right, you've got me bang to rights. It's obvious what's been going on. Will you take a good drink to make this go away?"'

For the second time in the trial, Imogen responded with a burst of laughter in the dock. Norris seemed irritated, and looked at the judge questioningly, but Andrew Pilkington showed no inclination at all to intervene. Two or three jurors were smiling.

'I'm sure the jury know this already,' Norris said, as ingratiatingly as he could, 'but just in case, would you explain to us what "bang to rights" means?'

'It's an expression frequently used by suspects, sir, to acknowledge that they've been caught fair and square for the offence.'

'And if someone uses the phrase "a good drink", what would you understand by that?'

'A "drink" refers to a sum of money offered to a police officer as a bribe, sir. A "good drink" means a substantial bribe, perhaps running into hundreds of pounds.'

'What, if anything, did you say to that?'

'I said that DI Beech and I were not interested in being bribed, sir, but that on this occasion I would not charge Miss Lester additionally with an attempt to bribe us. This was taking into account the stress Miss Lester had suffered by reason of the deaths of her parents and her trip to Sarajevo. I thought it right to make an allowance for that.'

'What happened next?'

'Later in the day, Miss Lester was charged with knowingly permitting premises to be used for the supply of drugs, and further cautioned. She made no reply to the caution. She was detained overnight at the police station, and appeared before Hampstead magistrates the following morning.'

Norris looked up at the judge.

'My Lord, I believe I'm right in saying that I'm prosecuting in an application in another case before your Lordship this afternoon, which may take some time. I've spoken to my learned friend Mr Schroeder, and rather than keep the jury waiting until late in the afternoon, we would both be content if your Lordship were to release them for the day and allow my learned friend to cross-examine tomorrow morning.'

Pilkington nodded. 'Yes, very well. Members of the jury, as Mr Norris has told you, I have to deal with another matter this afternoon, so I will release you now until ten o'clock tomorrow morning. Remember, don't discuss the case with anyone outside your number.'

# 37

They gathered in the magnificent foyer outside court two, huddled together in a corner. Imogen was clearly upset and sounded subdued.

'I can't believe it. How could Superintendent Mellor tell so many lies about me, about what I said? I never said that I'd been involved with Sean or Dragan. And I certainly didn't offer to bribe him. It was Mellor who came up with the idea of a "good drink", or whatever you call it.. I'm sorry for laughing out loud in court, but for God's sake… and that language: that's not anything like me. That's not how I speak. Is this what police officers do, make up things people never said, just to incriminate them?'

'It's called a "verbal,"' Ben replied. 'Police officers "verbal" people to make life easier for themselves. It always helps with a jury if they can produce a confession, especially when they don't have much else in the way of evidence. Parliament is going to change the law eventually, so that all police interviews have to be recorded, and that may help – but we're not there yet.'

'I take it you will be looking at Mellor's notebook?' Julia asked.

'Oh, yes. Andrew Pilkington will give us as much time as we need tomorrow morning before we cross-examine. We're going to be especially thorough since it took him, and Beech, so long after the event to write up their notes. Clive and I will go through it line by line and look for tell-tale signs.'

'Such as…?' Imogen asked.

'Alterations, crossings-out, long passages of questions and

answers, supposedly verbatim, going on for page after page, written down hours after the statements were supposedly made. All of those things are suspicious when you don't have a contemporaneous note. We've got a few questions he won't find it easy to answer.'

'I hope so, Ben,' Barratt commented. 'I've heard a few verbals in my time, as have you. But they really went overboard with this.'

Ben smiled. 'Yes. But that's not necessarily all bad, Barratt. It can be one of the things that gives them away. That's up to us to point out to the jury. Now, Imogen, this is probably going to sound strange, but tomorrow I want you to bring a book to court with you.'

'A book? What book?'

'It doesn't really matter: something you like and you're familiar with. What kind of thing do you like?'

'You have Dickens at home, don't you, Julia? What about *A Tale of Two Cities*?'

'Perfect.'

'But why…?'

He smiled. 'You'll see. Get some sleep tonight, and we will see you tomorrow morning. Clive, Barratt, come on, let's get a cup of coffee and go through our notes.'

Julia allowed them enough time to turn the corner before taking Imogen's hand. They sat down on a bench.

'I saw Damian this morning,' she said.

'How is he?'

'He seems well. He's in good spirits. I showed him the photographs, as you suggested, and he came up with something. I'm not going to tell you now.'

'Julia…'

'It's better this way. All I'm going to say is that I'm going to meet Baxter in a couple of hours and, depending on how that goes, you and I may both have a meeting to go to tomorrow after court.'

'But who with…? Why…?'

'I understand you want to know more, Imogen, but I'm asking

you to trust me. I don't want anyone knowing about this just yet.'

'Not even Ben and Clive?'

'Especially Ben and Clive.'

Imogen looked at her searchingly. 'But they're my barristers...'

'Exactly. Barristers can't be involved in investigations. It risks making them into witnesses, in which case they can't act as barristers any more. That doesn't apply to solicitors.'

'What investigations? And you're not even my solicitor: Barratt is.'

'Yes, well... that is a slight technical irregularity,' Julia admitted, 'but necessary in the circumstances.'

'But...'

'Make your way home, and I will see you as soon as I've finished with Baxter. Do you want me to pick up some Chinese?'

Imogen shrugged. 'Sure. Why not?'

'Good,' Julia said with a smile, climbing to her feet. 'See you later. Put some Chablis in the fridge.'

'Will you tell me then?'

'No.'

# 38

By the time Ben arrived back in chambers it was almost six thirty. He was tired and hungry, but his session with Clive and Barratt had been worthwhile: it had given him a basic outline for his cross-examination of Chief Superintendent Mellor. He decided to make the more detailed notes he would need later in the evening, once he was home and had eaten. He put his head around the door of the clerk's room, where Alan was sifting through some briefs newly arrived in chambers from solicitors' offices.

'Part heard, sir?' Alan asked mechanically, looking up.

'Part heard. We've got at least another three days. Any messages?'

Alan glanced at his small pink message pad. 'Miss Farrar called, sir. This would be...' he glanced at this watch, 'about half an hour ago. She said to tell you her case went well, she was still in chambers, but she was about to pick up your son from his friend's house and head home. She will see you there.'

'All right, Alan, thanks.'

Backing out of the clerk's room, Ben found himself bumping into someone trying to make his way in. He apologised automatically and turned to face the man. When he saw who it was he was momentarily speechless.

'Good evening, Mr Schroeder,' DCI Webb said cheerfully. 'Don't be alarmed, sir. Nothing for you to be concerned about. Phil and I just need a quick word with one of your colleagues.'

Ben nodded. 'Mr Webb, Mr Raymond.'

'Mr Schroeder.' They shook hands.

Before Ben could inquire further, Alan walked briskly out of the clerk's room and ushered the two officers along the corridor.

'Come this way gentlemen, please. He's ready for you.'

From the other end of the corridor Ben heard a knock on a door, and a muffled invitation to enter given by a familiar voice. He waited for Alan to return.

'What's that all about?'

Alan took just a little too long to put on his neutral, unconcerned clerk's face.

'They didn't say, sir. They called on Friday and asked if they could see Mr Smith-Gurney after he finished in court this afternoon. He got back from the High Court just before five, but he asked me to put them off for a while. He's had Miss Fisk in there with him.' He paused, as he saw Ben staring at him. 'I don't like to say anything, but I assume it has to do with… you know…'

Ben nodded. 'Yes. I'm sure you're right. Does anyone else know?'

'No, I don't think so. Most people have gone home. I think one or two of the pupils are still in chambers, but they're over the other side of the staircase and I doubt they would know anything about the history anyway. Let's hope it's nothing to worry about. Are you going straight home, sir?'

'I was,' Ben replied, 'but I've got some work to do for tomorrow. I think I might stay in my room and work there for a while.'

'All right, sir.'

Ben entered the room in chambers he shared with Harriet Fisk – an arrangement they both enjoyed and which had started when they were first taken on as members of chambers, some twenty years earlier. Both had encountered resistance in that vital first step in their professional lives, she for being a woman, he for being Jewish. They had fought back together, and had been close ever since. Both were now highly successful QCs, though Harriet preferred the relative calm of the civil and commercial courts, and had never competed with Ben for criminal cases. She had been Aubrey Smith-Gurney's pupil, and the fact that he had turned to her when a visit from two senior police officers was imminent seemed to confirm Ben's worst fear – that something serious was rearing its ugly head again after twelve years.

He sat down at his desk and called home. His son Joshua answered.

'Hi, Dad.'

'Hi, Josh. What are you up to?'

'Homework,' Josh replied miserably. 'Maths. It's making my head hurt.'

Ben laughed. 'You take after me in that department, I'm afraid,' he replied. 'I was never much good at maths. That's why I decided on law. Is your mum there?'

'Yes. Hang on… Mum? It's Dad.' He heard the sound of the receiver being laid down on the small table by the door, and his son's footsteps as he went upstairs to renew his struggle with maths.

'Hi, darling,' Jess said. 'Are you coming home?'

'In a while,' Ben replied. 'There's something going on in chambers. Two police officers are here to see Aubrey. Harriet's with them, but I have a feeling I should stay, just in case I'm needed. I just wanted to hear your voice. Alan said your case went well.'

'Very well. We got full custody of the children and she gets to keep the house, so she's pretty happy. Have you eaten anything? You must be starving.'

'I'll grab something when I get home.'

'I'm making Josh a quick beef stew from that recipe I found the other day. I'll make enough for you and put it in the fridge.'

'Sounds great. I'll look forward to it.'

'I'm sure Aubrey hoped that had all gone away,' she said, after a pause. 'But I suppose, once Rainer decided to come back…'

'The writing was on the wall,' Ben replied. 'I knew the moment Julia told me they'd found him.'

# 39

Aubrey Smith-Gurney stood to shake hands with his two visitors. He introduced Harriet Fisk QC as his colleague in chambers. They took their seats: Aubrey behind his desk, Harriet to his right, the two officers in front of the desk. The officers took out notebooks and pens.

'When we were last here all those years ago, sir,' Webb began, 'you had another gentlemen with you, a Mr Morgan-Davies, I see from my notes.'

'Sir Gareth Morgan-Davies is no longer a member of chambers,' Harriet replied. 'He's a Lord Justice of Appeal. So you've got me instead.'

'It's your turn to see fair play then, is it?' Raymond asked with a grin.

'I'm quite sure that won't be necessary,' Harriet replied. 'I'm just here to keep an eye on things and I'm not going to interrupt unnecessarily.'

Webb nodded and flicked through several pages of his notebook.

'You know, of course, that sadly, Mr Rainer passed away last week as a result of an advanced, very aggressive cancer.'

'Yes.'

'I know you were close friends, Mr Smith-Gurney, and I'm sorry about that.'

'And Mr Gerry Pole died last year too, sir, didn't he?' Raymond added. 'So regrettably, two members of the "Gang of Three" are no longer with us.'

Aubrey remained silent.

'We'll come back to that, sir,' Webb said. 'When we interviewed you in this very room back in 1971, Sir Conrad Rainer – as he then was – had just left England for foreign parts unknown, leaving the body of his mistress, Greta Thiemann, in his flat in the Barbican. Sadly, we missed him by four or five hours, as it now turns out. If we'd gone in earlier, we could have saved everyone a good deal of trouble. But that's all water under the bridge, as they say.'

He appeared to study his notes again.

'You told us on the last occasion that Mr Rainer had confided in you about his gambling problem, and that he'd asked you for help in trying to resolve certain matters relating to the amount of money he had lost at the Clermont Club. Do you remember that?'

'Yes. That was in early October, not long before he disappeared.'

'What did he tell you, exactly?'

'He said he had lost a large sum of money – from memory, somewhere in the region of £30,000 to £40,000. He'd compromised himself by taking money from his wife's trust fund and putting a mortgage on their house – without telling her. He'd also stolen money from three members of his former chambers.'

'Yes,' Webb said. 'And you knew that those barristers were going to make a formal complaint to us, because they told you that was what they were going to do, and you passed that information on to Mr Rainer.'

'Quite correct.'

'And when we interviewed you, you told us that Greta had introduced him to a man called Daniel Cleary, otherwise known as "Danny Ice", a man with ties to organised crime, and that Mr Rainer had also borrowed money from this man.'

'He borrowed £20,000, if I remember correctly, at an exorbitant rate of interest. It was a stupid thing to do, but he was feeling desperate about having defrauded his wife and his colleagues.'

Webb nodded. 'Now, to bring things up to date, we were able to question Mr Rainer to a limited extent before his death, and one of the matters we raised with him was the question of how he had managed to escape, as we now know, to Sarajevo, Yugoslavia.' He paused for several seconds. 'And at this point, Mr Smith-Gurney, it is my duty to caution you that you are not obliged to say anything unless you wish to do so, but anything you do say may be put into writing and given in evidence. Do you understand the caution?'

Aubrey sighed deeply. 'Yes.'

'And the reason I've cautioned you is that I have reason to believe that you may have committed a serious criminal offence in aiding Mr Rainer's escape. Mr Rainer told us that you had contacted Gerry Pole and told him of the problems he was having. Is that correct?'

'Yes.'

'When was that, do you remember?'

'I don't remember exactly, but again, just a matter of days before he disappeared.'

'And Mr Pole had a house and an ocean-going yacht on the Isle of Wight, is that right? Were you aware of that?'

'Yes, of course. We were close personal friends. I'd stayed there with my wife.'

'What was your purpose in speaking to Mr Pole about Mr Rainer's problems?'

Aubrey shifted uncomfortably in his seat. 'Conrad was worried about everything that was going on in his life at that time, but his main worry was Daniel Cleary. I'm sure you know that, Chief Inspector, because Cleary was also involved in the case you were working on, which Conrad was trying at the Old Bailey.'

'The Lang case.'

'Yes. Not only did he have to worry about Cleary coming after him for his money, he also had to worry about all that becoming public – in addition to everything else he had done.' He paused. 'I thought he might be a bit safer on the Isle of Wight until we could sort something out to make Cleary go away.'

'Sort something out?' Raymond asked.

'Conrad wasn't entirely without resources, Chief Inspector, even then. He could have gone to his wife and made a clean breast of the situation. There was still enough money in the trust fund to bail him out. All right, it would probably have cost him his marriage and it would have been hugely embarrassing, but if he could have paid Cleary off and repaid his chambers, there was a way to deal with it. I'd suggested that, but he wouldn't do it. I thought that if he had to make a run for it to the Island, it might focus his mind and get him to face up to reality.'

'So all you wanted was for Gerry Pole to hide him away from Cleary for a while?' Raymond asked.

'Yes.'

'Did Gerry Pole understand that that was what you wanted?' Webb asked.

'I think so, yes.'

Webb paused for some time. 'The problem with that, Mr Smith-Gurney, is that Mr Rainer told us a rather different story. Would you like to hear what Mr Rainer told us?'

'I have a feeling you're going to tell me whether I want to hear it or not,' Aubrey replied.

# 40

'Mr Rainer told us,' Webb said, 'that he didn't hide away on the Isle of Wight. He told us that, within two or three days of arriving at Mr Pole's house, Mr Pole spirited him away in his yacht to Amsterdam, where he was met by a gentleman calling himself Jan. Jan took him to a "safe house" – Mr Rainer's words, not mine; and shortly after that, two other gentlemen called Branko and Miodrag brought him some spanking new identity documents – passport, driving licence, and so on, in the name of Ernst Meier, Austrian. Branko and Miodrag then drove him to Sarajevo, using these false documents, and set him up in a flat there.'

Aubrey sat back in his chair, and the colour drained away from his face.

'I know nothing about any of that.'

'Gerry Pole took the photographs for the false documents himself before they left. All this, Mr Smith-Gurney, suggests that Gerry Pole not only provided Mr Rainer's transport to the Continent, but also had access to people who could produce very professional identity documents in a matter of a couple of days.'

'Not only that,' Raymond added, 'but when they set Mr Rainer up in his flat in Sarajevo, they paid him to store drugs there on behalf of a man known as Dragan, who just happens to be one of the most prolific drug traffickers in Europe: the inference being, obviously, that Gerry Pole also had close links to Dragan.'

'Needless to say,' Webb went on, 'if Mr Pole were still with us, we would be asking him about all this. But since he's not, we're asking you instead.'

He waited for a reply. Aubrey suddenly seemed unsure of himself, and turned to Harriet.

'Perhaps Mr Smith-Gurney should consult a solicitor?' she suggested.

'I thought that's why you were here, Miss,' Webb said. 'But he's free to consult whoever he wants, as far as we're concerned. Is that what you want to do, Mr Smith-Gurney?'

Aubrey made a massive effort to recover.

'I know nothing about any of this,' he insisted. 'It was nothing to do with me. You asked me last time whether I knew where Conrad was. I told you I had no idea, and that was the truth. I just wanted Gerry to give him a bolthole where Cleary wouldn't find him for a few days, while we worked out what to do.'

'Well, the problem with that, sir,' Webb said, 'is that Mr Rainer also told us that you had advised him to make a run for it immediately – by which I mean, even before the Lang case was over. He wanted to stay and finish the case, but you said it was too urgent for that, and he should leave there and then.'

Aubrey ventured a smile. 'So, Conrad verballed me, did he, Chief Inspector?' He actually chuckled. 'Cheeky old bugger.'

'It's interesting that you use that expression, Mr Smith-Gurney,' Webb replied, '"verballed". Are you implying that Mr Rainer was lying to us about a fellow member of the Gang of Three? That's a bit disappointing, isn't it, given the strong bond of loyalty you're supposed to have had?'

'I think you gave him good advice, sir,' Raymond said. 'You were exactly right. You realised the game was up, because you knew that we were about to question Mr Rainer about the theft from the three barristers. He would have been arrested, and we would have searched his flat, at which point we would have found what was left of Greta Thiemann. You were right: he couldn't afford to delay; he had to make a run for it straight away. But he didn't.'

'And if I hadn't been so nice to him,' Webb added, 'we would have collared him the night the trial finished, and he would never have got anywhere near Sarajevo.'

'I never knew he'd killed Greta Thiemann,' Aubrey insisted.

'I'm having a problem with that too,' Webb replied. 'You see, if it was just a matter of the theft of – what, £16,000 or thereabouts? – well, I can see Gerry Pole hiding him away for a few days on the Island, to buy him some time. But he's not going to lay on a full-scale disappearing act, complete with professionally-produced identity documents, bringing in Jan and Branko and Miodrag, is he? Not for the sake of £16,000. But if he's killed Greta Thiemann, and he's looking at a murder charge – well, suddenly it all starts to make sense, doesn't it? It's definitely worth it then, isn't it?'

Aubrey stood. 'I'm not going to answer any further questions now,' he said, after some time.

Webb nodded. 'Fair enough. I did caution you that you're not obliged to say anything, so you're fully entitled not to answer. Obviously, we're not finished yet, but you certainly don't have to say any more today. Perhaps you'd like to think it over, talk over your options with Miss Fisk, or your solicitor, and then get back to us?'

Harriet took a deep breath. 'If you were thinking of arresting Mr Smith-Gurney, Chief Inspector, we would ask you to consider giving him the option of surrendering voluntarily. This is obviously a highly sensitive case, one that's bound to continue attracting press attention. It's going to be hugely embarrassing, not only for Mr Smith-Gurney but also for this entire set of chambers.'

'I can't give you any guarantees about that, Miss,' Webb replied, with a glance towards Raymond. 'But I can tell you this much: we haven't made any decisions about an arrest as yet. We will have to evaluate what Mr Smith-Gurney's told us today, anything he may say on a future occasion, and report back to the Deputy Director of Public Prosecutions. He's aware that it's a sensitive case and he's decided to handle it personally. So nothing's going to happen immediately. But we will pass on what you've said.'

The officers quickly stood and packed away their notebooks.

'But please don't get any ideas about foreign travel, sir, will you?' Webb added as they left.

Ben looked up as soon as Harriet came into their room.

'How bad is it?' he asked.

'Very bad,' she replied, collapsing into a chair. 'Very bad indeed.'

# 41

'My Lord,' Ben began, 'before I cross-examine Chief Superintendent Mellor, I'm going to ask your Lordship's indulgence to do something rather unusual. It won't take long. Miss Lester has brought to court a copy of *A Tale of Two Cities* by Charles Dickens, and I'm going to ask her to read aloud the first few words of that novel, so that everyone in court can hear her.'

Anthony Norris was on his feet at once.

'My Lord, I fail to see how the question of whether it was the best of times or the worst of times can possibly help the jury in deciding this case,' he observed. Both Ben and the judge smiled. 'It seems to me that my learned friend is simply indulging his taste for theatre.'

'Is that what you're doing, Mr Schroeder?' Andrew Pilkington asked.

'No, my Lord. I simply want the Chief Superintendent and the jury to hear Miss Lester's speaking voice and her accent. Mr Mellor has given evidence about statements said to have been made by Miss Lester during the raid and while being interviewed. We say – I will tell your Lordship and the jury quite candidly – that much of that evidence has been fabricated. In common parlance, we say that Miss Lester has been verballed. The jury will recall that more than once, Miss Lester was reduced to laughter in the dock on hearing some of the language attributed to her. I would like the jury to hear why.'

'Whether or not Miss Lester chooses to laugh while she's on trial is completely irrelevant,' Norris insisted. 'It's not right that my learned friend should be allowed to play games like this with the jury.'

'It's not a game, my Lord,' Ben retorted immediately.

Andrew Pilkington held up a hand. 'It's an unusual request,' he said, 'but I will allow it, as long as it is confined to a fairly short passage. As we all know, Dickens was given to being rather prolix and I'm sure the jury doesn't need to hear an entire chapter about the French Revolution.'

The jury chuckled.

'It will be very short, my Lord,' Ben promised.

He turned around to the dock and nodded. Imogen stood, book in hand. She felt desperately nervous. Ben had given her simple instructions. He wanted nothing but her own voice, her own accent, to the extent that she had one. 'Read slowly and deliberately,' he had told her, 'but be yourself: no acting required.' Even so, in this large courtroom with its high ceilings, stage fright was gnawing away at her just as fiercely as if she were about to take the stage at the Old Vic to play Madame Defarge. She had marked the page with a bookmark. She opened to it, and began to read. Her voice sounded clear and strong – at least to her. Ben had promised that he would signal to her if she wasn't clear or strong enough for him, but to her relief, he gave no such sign and turned back towards the front of the court to listen.

'"It was the best of times, it was the worst of times, it was the age of wisdom, it was the age of foolishness, it was the epoch of belief, it was the epoch of incredulity, it was the season of Light, it was the season of Darkness, it was the spring of hope, it was the winter of despair, we had everything before us, we had nothing before us, we were all going direct to Heaven, we were all going direct the other way...."'

She glanced at Ben, who smiled and gave her a surreptitious thumbs up. She closed the book and sat down.

'Thank you, Miss Lester,' Ben said. 'Now, Superintendent, you heard that, didn't you?'

'I did, sir.'

'Can we agree that Miss Lester has a nice, clear reading voice?'

'We can, sir.'

'And she has what we might call a standard English voice, doesn't she? In other words, she doesn't have any particular accent, would you agree?'

'Well…'

'She doesn't have a London accent, does she, Superintendent? She's certainly not a Cockney, is she?'

'No, sir.'

'And you know that because you have a Cockney accent yourself, don't you?'

'I do, sir, and I'm very proud of it.'

'Quite rightly so, Superintendent. Is Miss Lester a woman of previous good character?'

'Yes, sir, she is.'

'In other words, she has no previous convictions, and she's never been in any trouble with the police, has she?'

'That's correct, sir.'

'Tragically, she lost both her parents recently, didn't she? They were both murdered in Yugoslavia?'

'Sadly, sir, they were, yes, in Sarajevo.'

'Before his death, her father was a senior diplomat attached to our embassy in Belgrade, was he not?'

'Yes, sir.'

'Is it your understanding that Miss Lester was privately educated, and that she graduated from Girton College, Cambridge, with a first class degree in classics?'

'I believe so, yes.'

'And that she works for Cathermole & Bridger, a well-known firm of solicitors in London, a firm that does civil and commercial work?'

'Yes, sir.'

'Thank you, Superintendent. Now, you learned from what Miss Lester told you, and from looking at the stamps in her passport, that she had been in Sarajevo for several days and only returned home to London the evening before the raid: is that right?'

'Yes, sir.'

'She'd had meetings with police officers in Sarajevo, officers who were investigating the murder of her parents, which you verified by contacting the police there?'

'Yes, sir.'

'The raid began at about four o'clock on the morning of the day after her return?'

'Yes.'

'You found out that she and her brother had stayed up late, talking about her trip and about their parents, and indeed drinking some whisky and smoking some cannabis: yes?'

'Yes, sir.'

'Oh, and by the way: what they were smoking was herbal cannabis, wasn't it? It wasn't cannabis resin, which is what you found in the basement.'

'That's quite correct, sir. It didn't come from the stash in the basement.'

'Thank you. If I were to suggest to you that Miss Lester went to bed late, that she was very tired, and was still in some distress; and that she was woken up abruptly at four in the morning when Sergeant Walker and his officers used a battering ram to break down her front door, you wouldn't dispute that, would you?'

'No, sir.'

'And yet, when you first saw her, you told the jury that she was running downstairs towards you and DI Beech, and that she was "angry and aggressive": is that right?'

'It is, sir.'

'So much so that you had difficulty in restraining her? You had to handcuff her?'

'Correct.'

'She resisted arrest, and assaulted both you and DI Beech?'

'Yes.'

'Is DI Beech about the same size as you, Superintendent?'

'He's about the same height, I suppose, but, of course, I've put on a bit of weight over the years. He's younger, and probably a bit fitter.'

Several members of the jury grinned.

'You saw Miss Lester when she stood up to read just now, didn't you?'

'I did, sir.'

'This rather slight young woman assaulted both you and DI Beech, did she?'

'She did, sir.'

'And let me see if I've got this right, Superintendent: she said – or shouted, you said, in a loud voice – "Who the fuck are you?" Is that right?'

Ben glanced in the direction of the jury, and was pleased to see several jurors smiling.

'Yes, sir.'

'"What are you, the Old Bill?" Yes?'

'That's correct.'

'"Where's your warrant? You'd better bloody have one, mate, or I'll have your badge." Is that what she said, Superintendent?'

'That is what she said, sir.'

'"What have you done to my fucking door? I'll have you for that!"'

'Yes, sir.'

'So, what the jury have to picture is this, is it? This young woman of previous good character running downstairs, taking on two burly police officers single-handed, and shouting, "Who the fuck are you? What are you, the Old Bill? Where's your warrant? You'd better bloody have one, mate, or I'll have your badge. What have you done to my fucking door? I'll have you for that!" – shouting all that in the voice the jury has just heard reading from *A Tale of Two Cities*. That's what you're telling the jury, is it?'

'That is what she said, sir, yes.'

'And, so that the jury will be aware, Mr Overton and I had the chance to inspect your notebook before court sat this morning, didn't we?'

'Yes, sir.'

'Your note of all this is written clearly and without any crossings out, isn't it?'

'Yes, sir.'

'Even though you made your notes some thirty-six hours after you first encountered Miss Lester?'

'Both DI Beech and I remembered what had been said, and we compared notes about it before writing it down.'

Ben nodded. 'I'm not going to beat about the bush, Chief Superintendent. Are you familiar with the term, to "verbal" someone?'

'Yes, sir, I am.'

'Would you please explain to the jury what you understand by that expression?'

'I would be very pleased to explain it, sir. A "verbal" is an oral admission made by a defendant when interviewed by the police, which on the advice of her solicitor she later denies.'

A number of jurors sniggered.

'Is that a prepared answer, Superintendent?'

'I don't know what you mean, sir.'

'I'm suggesting that the answer you've just given to the jury is a standard answer given by police officers whenever they are accused of fabricating evidence of alleged admissions.'

'I can't speak for other officers, sir.'

'Well, speak for yourself, then. Is it an answer you've given before?'

He hesitated. 'I'm sure I have, sir.'

Ben paused to look at his notes. 'She said, "What are you, the Old Bill?" did she?'

'Yes, sir.'

'Is "the Old Bill" a term commonly used in London to refer to the police?'

'It is, sir, yes.'

'Is it a term often used by people who've been involved with the police?'

'Well, not exclusively sir, but yes, you do come across it quite a bit in my line of work.'

'Is it a Cockney phrase?'

'Again, not exclusively, but certainly it's Cockney – and also south London.'

'So when you hear the expression "the Old Bill" you get used to hearing it from people with east or south London accents, don't you?'

'Yes, obviously.'

'Can we agree that you would expect to hear it less often from women living in Hampstead who have standard English voices?'

Norris stood. 'Is my learned friend inviting the Superintendent to speculate?'

'I'll move on,' Ben replied. 'Miss Lester didn't say a word of that, did she?'

'She most certainly did, sir.'

'You didn't give her the chance to say anything, did you? You ran halfway up the stairs to meet her, threw her to the ground, and handcuffed her before she had any chance to speak?'

'No, sir.'

'And far from being angry or aggressive, I suggest that she was barely awake, desperately tired, and utterly bewildered by what was going on?'

'No, sir.'

'All right,' Ben said. 'Let's turn to the basement.'

# 42

'It was a cold morning, wasn't it, Superintendent?'

'It was very cold, sir.'

'Imogen Lester was wearing pyjamas, and she was barefoot, wasn't she?'

'When I first saw her, yes.'

'Well, it wasn't just a question of when you first saw her, Superintendent, was it? You took her down to the basement dressed – or undressed – in that way, didn't you?'

'I did that only because I knew that the female officer, PC Roberts, was in the basement, and I intended to ask PC Roberts to find out where Miss Lester's clothes were and fetch her something to wear.'

'She had asked to be allowed to get dressed before you took her down to the basement, hadn't she?'

'Yes, and I was arranging that as quickly as I could within the demands of the investigation.'

'In what way would it have prejudiced the investigation to let her get dressed before taking her to the basement?'

There was no reply.

'Well, let me ask you this, then: was it significantly colder in the basement, with its stone floor and no heating, compared with other parts of the house?'

'I daresay it was, sir, yes.'

'The officers working down there were wearing their coats and scarves, weren't they?'

'I'm sure they were, sir, as were DI Beech and myself.'

'But Imogen was barefoot, in her pyjamas. Was that intended to soften her up a bit before you interviewed her?'

For the first time, Mellor showed signs of agitation, shifting his weight from foot to foot, his face reddening.

'That is an outrageous suggestion, Mr Schroeder. I am offended by the idea that I, or any officer under my command, would behave in such a way.'

'I'll take that as a "no" then, shall I?' Ben asked. There was no reply. 'I'll move on. Miss Lester's brother Damian was in the basement when you arrived there, wasn't he?'

'Yes, he was.'

'He was sitting on the floor and he had an injury to his face, didn't he?'

'He appeared to have a slight cut on his face, as I said before, caused accidentally when officers were restraining him.'

'And Miss Lester saw the cut?'

'Yes. She accused us of assaulting him.'

'Was she concerned for him then, would you say?'

'I presume she would have been. He is her brother.'

'Well, yes. But in answer to my learned friend, you told the jury that she looked at Damian and said, "You fucking moron. I don't know why I bother."'

'She did say that, sir, yes.'

'This young woman of good character from Hampstead said that to her brother, did she, "You fucking moron. I don't know why I bother?"'

'Yes.'

'She doesn't sound too concerned about her brother then, does she?'

Norris stood. 'Is that a question, my Lord, or a comment?'

'I'll move on,' Ben replied. 'She said no such thing, did she?'

'Yes, she did, sir.'

# 43

'You assigned PC Roberts to escort Miss Lester up to the kitchen from the basement, didn't you, Superintendent?'

'I did, sir, yes.'

'And PC Roberts fetched some clothes and slippers for Miss Lester to wear when you interviewed her in the kitchen: is that right?'

'Yes, she did.'

'So PC Roberts would have had every opportunity to observe Miss Lester's condition during that time, wouldn't she?'

'Yes, I'm sure she did.'

'How would you describe Miss Lester's condition when you interviewed her in the kitchen?'

'Her condition? Well, it depends what you mean when you say "her condition". I'm not sure I understand the question.'

'If I asked you whether or not she was in a fit state to be interviewed, would you understand that question?'

'Well, yes. She wasn't under the influence of drink or drugs by that stage. So, yes, she was in a fit condition to be interviewed.'

'Was she still angry and aggressive?'

'No. She had calmed down by then. In fact, we didn't feel like we needed the cuffs any more, and we took them off once we were all sitting down in the kitchen.'

'Did she complain of feeling faint, feeling unwell?'

Mellor seemed to hesitate. 'Feeling unwell? No... I don't think so; not that I remember, no.'

'Really? You don't remember PC Roberts telling you that Miss Lester was complaining to her of not feeling well?'

'No, sir.'

'PC Roberts was alone with Miss Lester while she put on her clothes. You and DI Beech had left the room while she changed, hadn't you?'

'Yes, that's correct, sir.'

'And while you were out of the room, didn't PC Roberts start to make Miss Lester some coffee?'

'I was the one who offered Miss Lester coffee. She declined it.'

'I suggest, Superintendent, that it was PC Roberts who tried to make coffee, and that you ordered her to stop, telling her that you weren't running a canteen. Do you remember saying that?'

Mellor hesitated again. 'If I did say anything like that, sir, I'm sure it was just by way of a bit of levity. If Miss Lester had wanted coffee, she could have had some. I daresay DI Beech and I could have done with a cup of coffee ourselves, come to that. But Miss Lester didn't offer us any.'

'Miss Lester didn't offer you coffee? Is that a serious answer, Superintendent?'

'All my answers are serious, sir.'

'I suggest to you that Miss Lester was obviously extremely tired, and was feeling unwell and disorientated?'

'Disorientated?'

'Didn't she ask you at one point what time it was?'

'I believe she did, sir, yes.'

'And when you told her it was five o'clock, she asked whether you meant five o'clock in the morning? And you made a joke of it, didn't you? You asked her how much she'd had to smoke the previous evening.'

'I don't remember that, sir.'

'Was PC Roberts so concerned about Miss Lester's condition that she asked to stay with her during the interview?'

'She offered to stay, yes. That wouldn't be unusual in the case of a female suspect being interviewed by male officers. Female officers are often asked to be present. But I didn't see any need for it in the circumstances, and I needed PC Roberts to assist the other officers with the continuing search of the house.'

'She even told you to make sure Miss Lester got something to eat and drink as soon as she arrived at the police station, didn't she?'

'I believe she did say that, sir, yes; and, of course, that was done, as it would be in the case of any person who's been arrested.'

'In fact, later, when Miss Lester was at the police station, she told you how much she appreciated PC Roberts' kindness and concern, and asked you to pass her appreciation on to PC Roberts' superiors, didn't she?'

'Yes, sir, which DI Beech and I noted, and we did as she asked. PC Roberts is an excellent officer.'

'Miss Lester made no admission of being involved with drugs during the interview in the kitchen, did she?'

'She told us she knew about innkeepers, and...'

'Yes, Superintendent, she did use that word, and she knew the Serbo-Croat word for "innkeeper". I don't dispute that. But I'd like an answer to my question. She denied all knowledge of the drugs, didn't she?'

'She did, sir.'

'She denied knowing anything about Dragan?'

'Yes.'

'Even though it slipped your mind to caution her until the very end of the interview, when she asked to see a solicitor?'

'That's not correct...'

'And even though you offered to put in a good word for her with the judge, offered to see if you could get her a lenient sentence, if she cooperated with you in naming people involved in the trafficking of drugs: isn't that right?'

'Certainly not.'

'But you did ask her for names, didn't you? You told the jury yourself, Superintendent, in answer to my learned friend. I made a note of your evidence at the time. Correct me if I'm mistaken. You told the jury that Miss Lester said she didn't know where to start, and you said, "Well, you might start by telling us who supplied the drugs you've got stashed away downstairs, and who was due to collect them. If you can give us some people higher up in the chain, that's always good." Wasn't that your evidence?'

'I didn't offer to put in a good word with anybody.'

'Did you not? What did you mean by, "If you can give us some people higher up in the chain, that's always good." What did you mean by "that's always good?"'

There was no reply.

'Both of those things – failing to caution her, and promising to put in a good word for her with the judge – would be serious breaches of the Judges' Rules, wouldn't they?' Ben asked.

'They would, sir.'

'The Rules are there to be obeyed, aren't they? Where there has been a breach of the Judges' Rules, that's something the courts, and judges such as His Lordship, take very seriously, isn't it?'

'Yes, sir.'

'It can have serious consequences for the officers concerned, can't it?'

'It can, sir, and both I and the officers under my command are very much aware of that.'

'Well, aware of it as you may have been, you and DI Beech committed those two breaches of the Rules, didn't you?'

'No, sir, certainly not.'

'Would it also be a breach of the Judges' Rules to deny refreshments to a suspect who is not feeling well, and needs them?'

'Miss Lester was given water, sir. That's all she wanted.'

# 44

'At the conclusion of the interview in the kitchen, you arrested Miss Lester, and she was taken to Hampstead Police Station: is that right?'

'That's correct, sir.'

'And later that afternoon, after Damian had made his written statement under caution – the jury have copies of that statement – you saw Miss Lester in her cell and invited her to read the statement and comment on it, didn't you?'

'Indeed we did, sir.'

'And she did read it, didn't she?'

'Yes, she did.'

'I suggest to you that she was visibly shocked by what she read.'

'I'm sure she was shocked that Damian had told us all about it, yes.'

'Well, you say "all about it". But, in fact, Superintendent, what Damian had said was that he was the one who had agreed to store the drugs because he needed the money. He specifically said that his sister had no knowledge of it, and that she was not the kind of person who would be involved with trafficking drugs. He said that in so many words, didn't he? The jury have it in front of them, Superintendent.'

'I'm not denying that, sir. That's what Damian said, yes.'

'You told her that you didn't accept what Damian said about her?'

'Yes, I did.'

'But she continued to deny being involved, didn't she?'

'Yes, she did.'

'So the interview ended, you told her that she would be charged and brought before the magistrates, and so on. And you told us that as you and DI Beech were leaving her cell she called you back.'

'Yes.'

'And she said to you, "Look, all right, you've got me bang to rights. It's obvious what's been going on. Will you take a good drink to make this go away?" Is that right?'

'Yes, sir.'

'And in answer to my learned friend, you kindly explained that having someone "bang to rights" means that they have been caught fair and square for an offence.'

'Yes, sir.'

'And that a "drink" is a term used in the London underworld to mean a bribe offered to a police officer, and a "good drink" means a substantial bribe. Yes?'

'Yes.'

'Well, Superintendent, this young Cambridge classics graduate of previous good character has quite a command of London underworld lingo, doesn't she? In addition to "the Old Bill" she is also fluent enough to talk about having somebody "bang to rights" and offering somebody "a good drink". It took me a couple of years of practice in the criminal courts to achieve that level of fluency…'

There was an outburst of laughter in the jury box, which Ben acknowledged with a brief smile.

Seeing Norris rising to his feet, Andrew Pilkington raised a hand. 'Mr Schroeder…'

'Sorry, my Lord. She said nothing of the kind, did she, Superintendent?'

'She did, sir.'

'Let me suggest what really happened, Superintendent. You were the one who raised the question of a drink, weren't you?'

'Certainly not. That is…'

'You said there was "another possibility" and when she asked you what you meant by that, you replied by saying that she was an intelligent woman, a Cambridge graduate…'

'No …'

'You told her that she should be clever enough to see which side her bread was buttered on, and that she was in a very privileged position.'

Mellor threw his hands up. 'Why would I say something like that?'

'That's what she asked you, isn't it? And this is what you told her, isn't it? It may not be word for word, but this is Miss Lester's recollection, and I suggest that it's substantially correct. "Let's not play games, Imogen. Come on. It's not every day we come into contact with one of Dragan's innkeepers. Dragan doesn't pick just anyone to do what you do for him. You're a rare breed, a special breed."'

'That is outrageous. Absolutely not.'

'You then went on, "It's not hard to work out how much money you're pulling down in a year, working for Dragan. If you were to give us a good drink – let's say ten per cent – and perhaps throw us the odd bone like Sean now and then to keep our superiors happy, we might see our way to turning a blind eye when Dragan needs to offload some merchandise on our patch."'

'Absolutely not.'

'Would ten per cent amount to a good drink?'

'What?'

'Or would it be more like fifteen? What's enough to count as a good drink these days?'

He hesitated slightly. 'I'm sure I couldn't say.'

'You went on, "Think about it. You could walk out of here tonight. It could turn out to be all Sean's fault. You and your brother had nothing to do with it, after all."'

'Absolutely not.'

'And to cap it all off, you offered to provide her with drugs seized in other cases if she needed any to supply her own business – in return for a further drink, of course.'

Mellor threw his notebook down from the witness box on to the floor below. His face had turned purple and he was shouting.

'I've had enough of this. You've accused me of verballing her, intimidating her...'

'Superintendent...' Norris and the judge tried to intervene almost in unison.

'No, I've bloody had it with you lot. You defence lawyers are all the same, and I've had enough of it. You've accused me of all that, and now you're accusing me of corruption...?'

'Yes,' Ben replied quietly, 'that's exactly what I'm doing. I'm sorry if I've touched a nerve.'

He resumed his seat. No one spoke for some time.

'Any re-examination, Mr Norris?' Andrew Pilkington asked.

Norris pushed himself slowly to his feet.

'Superintendent, I imagine that, on reflection, you would probably wish to apologise to his Lordship and the jury for your outburst, wouldn't you?'

Mellor was outwardly quiet now, but still seething inwardly.

'Yes, sir,' he almost spat through his teeth. 'I apologise.'

'I'm sure that's not the way you usually act in court.'

'No, it's not, sir. I got carried away. I'm very sorry, my Lord.'

'Superintendent, how long have you been a police officer?'

'For more than thirty years, sir.'

'If you had offered to accept money in return for making a case go away, that would be a very serious thing for a police officer to do, wouldn't it? A corrupt thing?'

'It would, sir.'

'If such a thing were to come to light, and if it were to be proved against you, what would happen to you?'

'I would be dismissed from the force immediately with loss of pension, and in addition to that, I would be prosecuted, I'm sure.'

'Yes, quite. Are you a family man?'

'Yes, sir. I have a wife and three children – one of whom is a police officer in Norfolk – and two grandchildren.'

'Would you ever act in the way my learned friend Mr Schroeder has suggested?'

'No, sir, I would not.'

'You presently hold the rank of Detective Chief Superintendent, obviously a very senior rank. That means, I take it, that you have risen through the ranks over the years, starting out as a police constable, then being promoted to sergeant, inspector and so on: yes?'

'Yes, sir.'

'And what has been involved in the promotions you have achieved?'

'Well, sometimes there are exams. But it's also about the work you've done, your reputation within the force, the opinion of more senior officers, and so on.'

'If an officer were to be suspected of corruption, or even for bending the rules, would that officer be likely to rise anything like as high in the force as you have?'

'No, sir. No chance.'

'For how long have you worked with DI Beech?'

'For the best part of seven years, sir.'

'From your knowledge of DI Beech, would he be likely to act in that way?'

'No, sir, he would not.'

Norris looked up to the bench. 'Unless your Lordship has any questions…?'

'No, thank you, Mr Norris,' Andrew Pilkington replied at once. 'You may stand down, Chief Superintendent.'

After court had risen for the day, they gathered outside.

'My God,' Imogen said, 'are trials always like this? I'm a basket case. What's going to happen tomorrow?'

'Tomorrow,' Ben replied with a grim smile, 'we do it all again with DI Beech.'

# 45

*Friday 17 February 1984*

'My Lord,' Anthony Norris said, as DI Beech left the courtroom, 'my learned friend Mr Schroeder has asked me to call PC Roberts, and it may be convenient if I do that now. I don't propose to examine her myself. I will simply tender her for cross-examination.'

'Yes. Thank you, Mr Norris,' the judge replied.

PC Roberts, a slight, slim figure of a woman, looked barely substantial enough to fill the regulation police uniform she wore. But an unmistakable air of competence and composure went before her. With her dark brown hair neatly tied up in a bun, she entered the witness box briskly and took the oath in a matter-of-fact but unhurried tone.

'Officer,' Norris said, 'I have no questions for you. Please answer any questions my learned friend may have.'

'Yes, sir.'

Ben stood. 'I'm obliged. Officer, if you have notes about the events of Sunday 4 December of last year, please feel free to use them to refresh your memory.'

'Thank you, sir.'

PC Roberts took her notebook from her jacket pocket and placed it on the ledge of the witness box in front of her.

'Officer, on that day, together with other officers based at Hampstead Police Station, did you take part in a raid in support of the Drug Squad at residential premises, number 102 Willow Road, NW3?'

'Yes, I did, sir. I was part of the uniformed support led by PS Walker.'

'Was the object of the raid to search those premises for controlled drugs, to seize any drugs found, and to arrest anyone suspected of committing an offence in connection with those drugs?'

'Yes, that's correct. The Drug Squad had intelligence that there might be a female suspect on the premises, so they wanted to have at least one female uniformed officer available.'

'Thank you. Officer, I don't need to take you through all the details of the raid. The jury has already heard about it at some length from two other officers. But did there come a time when Detective Chief Superintendent Mellor instructed you to join other officers in searching the basement of the house?'

'Yes, sir. That's correct.'

'And the basement is accessed by means of a staircase leading down from the ground floor of the house, where the kitchen, dining room and living room are located: is that right?'

'Yes, sir.'

'Describe for the jury, please, what you saw when you first went down to the basement.'

'I saw other officers examining a number of what looked like large canvas bags. There was a very strong smell of cannabis, and it was clear from an examination of the bags that they contained substantial quantities of controlled drugs.'

'Yes.'

'I also saw a young man I now know to be Damian Lester. Mr Lester was sitting, or crouching, on the floor quite close to the bags, and I noticed that he was bleeding from a cut on his cheek'

'Did you see how his cheek came to be cut?'

'No, sir. I only know what I was told.'

'Which, I take it, was that he had accidentally collided with a door while being escorted down to the basement by other officers: is that right?'

'That is what I was told: yes.'

'Did there come a time when Superintendent Mellor and DI Beech came down to the basement?'

'Yes. That was just a few minutes after I'd arrived there.'

'Did they have anyone with them?'

'Yes, sir. I had been alerted that Superintendent Mellor had detained a female suspect who might need help with finding some clothes to put on. So I was aware that I might be asked to deal with her.'

'Yes. And was that woman Imogen Lester, the defendant in this case, the lady in the dock?'

PC Roberts glanced over to the dock with a suggestion of a smile.

'Yes, sir.'

'What, if anything, did you notice about Miss Lester when she came down to the basement?'

'The first thing I noticed was her dress – or lack of it. She was in pyjamas and in her bare feet, and it was freezing down in the basement. I'd been told that at some stage I should ask her where I could find some clothes for her to put on, which I did while I was escorting her back upstairs to the kitchen.'

'Yes: we'll come to that in just a moment. But what did Miss Lester do or say while she was in the basement?'

PC Roberts picked up her notebook and scanned it briefly.

'Miss Lester saw that her brother had been injured and asked what had happened to him. It was then that DI Beech told her that Damian had "walked into a door" while they were bringing him in, and assured Miss Lester that he wasn't seriously hurt.'

'Did DI Beech say anything else about Damian?'

PC Roberts exhaled slowly, and replied with some reluctance. 'Yes, sir. He asked Miss Lester whether Damian was her brother.'

'But he didn't refer to him as Damian, did he?'

'No. He called him "Jack the Lad". That was a nickname some officers present had apparently given him.'

'How did Miss Lester respond to that?'

'She confirmed that he was her brother and added that his name was Damian. DI Beech then said, "Damian. Damian and Imogen. Very nice. Very Hampstead."'

'Is that the kind of comment…?'

'It wasn't something I would have said,' she added. 'It wasn't necessary.'

'Thank you, officer. Was anything else said?'

'She was asked about the drugs and she said she had no knowledge of them.'

'Thank you. Anything else?'

'Miss Lester asked Superintendent Mellor what was going to happen to her brother, and the Superintendent told her that he had admitted his part in the offences, and that he was going to be taken to the police station. She appeared to be distressed by that, and Superintendent Mellor then asked me to take her upstairs to the kitchen.'

'Officer, you say that she was distressed. At any time while she was in the basement, would you describe Miss Lester as angry and aggressive?'

'Angry and aggressive? No. Not at all. She was obviously concerned for her brother, but no, nothing like that.'

'Did you ever hear her say to her brother anything like this: "You fucking moron. I don't know why I bother?"'

'No, I did not.'

'If anything like that had been said, were you in a position to hear it?'

'Yes, I was.'

'And did you then take Miss Lester back upstairs?'

'Yes, I did.'

# 46

'While you were en route upstairs, did you speak to Miss Lester?'

'Yes. I asked her where I could find some clothes for her to put on. She directed me to one of the bedrooms on the floor above, and I promised her I would go in search of clothes as soon as there was another officer with her in the kitchen.'

'Was Miss Lester at all angry and aggressive with you?'

'No, she was not.'

'How would you describe her when you arrived at the kitchen?'

PC Roberts had been holding her notebook. She now put it down and looked directly at Ben.

'Actually, I was quite worried about her.'

'For what reason?'

She thought for some time. 'The best way I can put it is that she seemed disorientated, almost as though she wasn't focusing on where she was and what was happening.'

'Did anything in particular happen to give you that impression?'

'Yes. Superintendent Mellor and DI Beech entered the kitchen not long after Miss Lester and I got there. I then left the room to find Miss Lester some clothes and shoes, which I did. By the time I came back, they'd taken her handcuffs off and sat her down at the kitchen table. But she was looking very pale and she was looking around her, almost as if she didn't quite know where she was. I was left alone with her while she got dressed.'

She picked her notebook up again and turned over a page. 'I asked her whether she was all right, and she replied: "No. I'm not feeling very well. I feel faint. I don't seem to know where I am, although I'm obviously at home ... but ... it just doesn't feel right."'

'How did you respond to that?'

'I said I would let Superintendent Mellor and DI Beech know that she wasn't feeling well. I asked her if she'd had anything to drink, and she said she hadn't. I offered to make some coffee, and she agreed. But when I asked her where the coffee was it took her some time to answer, as if she was trying to remember where she kept it.'

'In the event, did you make coffee?'

The reluctance returned. 'Unfortunately, no, I did not.'

'Why was that?'

'Superintendent Mellor instructed me not to do so.'

'What exactly did Mr Mellor say to you, officer?'

She bit her lip. 'He said, "What do you think you're doing?" I said, "Making her some coffee, sir. She hasn't had anything and she's feeling faint." Superintendent Mellor then said, "Not without my say so, you don't. She's in custody."'

'How did you respond to that?'

'I said, "She's not feeling well, sir." But Superintendent Mellor told me there was no need to make coffee.'

'Again, officer,' Ben persisted, 'if you remember, please tell us exactly what was said.'

She hesitated for just a moment. 'Superintendent Mellor said, "Don't you worry your pretty head about that, Constable Roberts. We're not likely to be long with her. I'm sure she'll want to give it up and cooperate with us, just like Jack the Lad, and once she's done that and we've got her down the nick, she can have a nice warm cell and drink as much coffee as she wants."'

Ben heard some sharp intakes of breath in the jury box.

'What did you do or say?'

'I began to protest, but Superintendent Mellor cut me off. He said, "That's enough, constable. I'm not running a canteen here. I'm interviewing a suspect. Go on. Hop it." Miss Lester said, "I'd feel safer if this officer could stay with me. I'm not feeling well. And I would like a glass of water". Superintendent Mellor then said, "You'll be perfectly safe with us. Constable Roberts is required elsewhere, I'm sure." I began to say that there was nowhere I had to be, that other officers were already searching the house; and I was trying to remind Superintendent Mellor, sir, that it was supposed to be my role to be with a female suspect.'

'Yes, quite. How did the Superintendent react to being reminded of that?'

'He said: "Get her a cup of water on your way out, and as soon as you've done that, make yourself scarce."'

'And is that what you did?'

'That's exactly what I did, sir: yes.'

Ben paused. 'Officer, have you yourself received any training in the interviewing of suspects?'

'Yes, sir, some basic training – not to the same extent as they do with the detectives, of course, but some.'

'Have you been taught that there are circumstances in which a suspect may be unfit to be interviewed, and that in such a case the interview should be postponed until the suspect is in a fit condition for it?'

'Yes, sir. Typically, this occurs when the suspect is under the influence of drink or drugs.'

'Was that the case with Miss Lester?'

'No. But for whatever reason, she was clearly in a fragile condition, she was complaining of feeling faint and she was disorientated.'

'If you'd had to decide how to deal with Miss Lester, would you have interviewed her at that time, while she was in that condition?'

'No. I would not. I would have taken her to the police station and called the police doctor to examine her. I wouldn't have interviewed her until the doctor gave me the all clear.'

'Did you see Miss Lester after that?'

'Yes, I saw her later when she was in custody at the police station. I had brought her a change of clothes from the house, and the custody sergeant said I could take them into her cell for her. This would be around lunchtime, or just after.'

'And how did Miss Lester seem then?'

'Much better. She'd had something to eat and drink. She still looked tired and she was obviously anxious, but she was fully aware of her surroundings and she wasn't complaining of feeling faint. She didn't ask me to stay with her again.'

'Thank you very much, Police Constable Roberts,' Ben said.

As the officer left the witness box, he turned around to Clive and Barratt, seated behind him.

'Brave woman,' Barratt whispered. 'I hope they don't take it out on her too badly.'

'Well, I'm not sure I'd fancy her chances of promotion after today,' Clive observed. 'It's a bloody shame, isn't it? The Met could do with more officers like her, preferably at the top.'

'All it takes is one senior officer to stand up for her,' Ben replied. 'I just hope they don't make her life so miserable that she packs it in before she gets the chance.'

'If she does leave, I might offer her a job myself,' Barratt said. He sounded serious.

# 47

The driver executed a quick right turn from Old Bailey on to Ludgate Hill, and deftly made use of the black cab's tight turning circle to manoeuvre it into position for his left turn, down towards the Embankment, once the lights turned green. Julia relaxed slightly. It had taken some time, after court had adjourned for the day, to separate herself and Imogen from Ben and Barratt without any show of undue haste, to deflect questions about their plans for the evening without arousing suspicion. There had been a lot to talk about, reliving the day's evidence and anticipating the evidence they expected to be called the following day, and she was all too aware of her own tendency to a touch of paranoia when she saw herself as operating under the radar. There was no reason at all to suppose that Ben knew anything about the meeting, and Imogen knew very little more. But she had been feeling anxious nonetheless. Now, as the cab completed its left turn and began to fight its way through the early evening traffic, the anxiety began to subside.

She put an arm around Imogen's shoulder. 'Another long day,' she commented. 'How are you doing?'

Imogen lowered her head on to the arm. 'I'm all right. But I keep thinking that these days will never end. Today seemed to drag on and on – though Beech wasn't as bad as I expected. Ben didn't take as long with him as he did with Mellor, did he?'

'No. He'd covered the ground with Mellor, and the jury have got the message – or so we have to assume. No point in going back over everything and sending them to sleep. I thought he did it very well. And Roberts was great for us.'

'She was wonderful. But then we had to listen to that expert for God knows how long – it felt like hours on end – telling the jury all about the drugs they found: what type of drugs they were; what everything weighed; what they sell for on the street; what effects they have on people who take them; and God only knows what. And producing all of those bags – actually bringing them all into the courtroom – and showing the jury what was in them. You could see from the look on their faces that they were totally shocked. They kept looking over at me, as if... It seemed to go on forever and it's so unfair, Julia – it's got nothing to do with me. I feel the same way about that kind of thing as the jury. It's just so frustrating.'

'I know,' Julia replied, kissing her on the cheek. 'But you'll have your chance to tell them that when you give evidence. It's always hard to sit through the other side's case, but you will have your turn very soon now.'

'It can't come soon enough,' Imogen said. 'This is a nightmare, Julia.'

'I know.' She squeezed the shoulder and brought her arm back down so that they could hold hands.

Imogen gripped her hand briefly, then reached into her handbag for a tissue and wiped her nose. With a huge effort she forced her mind to leave the courtroom and focus on what was happening now.

'So, where are we going? Surely there can't be any harm in telling me now that we're actually on our way?'

'We're going to the DPP's office in St Anne's Gate for a meeting with John Caswell, the Deputy Director,' Julia replied. 'I'm expecting Baxter to be there too, and with any luck we will have the detectives involved in the Rainer case. It's been short notice, but John said he would do his best to get everyone together.'

'What are we going to talk about? My case? Surely, we can't...'

'No, not about your case – well, at least not directly. But if I'm right about what's going on, it could be good for both you and Damian, not to mention causing some people in high places to lose a lot of sleep – as they bloody well should.'

Imogen turned towards her. 'My God, Julia, you are so opaque sometimes. Why can't you just tell me?'

'Because if you think about where you are for a moment,' she replied very quietly, 'you will notice we're not in a secure place. I know I can be over-cautious about certain things, but if I'm right about this, there's dark work afoot in the woods, and the trees have ears.'

Imogen shook her head. 'I give up,' she said, allowing her body to slide down in her seat.

# 48

John Caswell made the introductions, and arranged his visitors around his conference table. Coffee and water were available on a large table pushed against the wall. Julia and Imogen helped themselves gratefully.

'Now, Julia,' he said, once they were all settled, 'you said you have something urgent for us. We've all dropped whatever we were doing, and here we are. We're waiting with bated breath. The floor is yours.'

Julia opened the large briefcase she had brought with her, and removed several folders. She asked Imogen to distribute them while she donned her reading glasses and opened her own file.

'What you have in these files,' she began, 'are photographs provided to me by Mr Baxter, photographs of all police officers currently or recently assigned to the Met Drug Squad, with a certain amount of detail about the officers' careers.'

'To be regarded as confidential,' Baxter interposed.

'To be regarded as confidential. My interest in this material is that Imogen is presently on trial at the Old Bailey for having – allegedly – allowed her house in Hampstead to be used in connection with drug trafficking. The charge arose from a raid on her house by the Drug Squad early in December.'

'An offence to which her brother Damian has pleaded guilty,' John observed.

'Correct. Damian made a written statement, also in your files, in which he said he had been recruited in his local pub by a man calling himself Sean. Damian says he agreed to store drugs at the house for Sean because he needed the money. Be that as it may, he didn't take Imogen into his confidence about it.'

'Well, that's what the jury has to decide, isn't it?' John commented. Imogen shot him a sour look.

'Yes, it is,' Julia agreed quickly. 'But what's interesting, for the purposes of both Imogen's case and Damian's, is that whoever Sean is, he was using the word "innkeeper" and its equivalent in Serbo-Croat.' She paused to look around the table. 'I'm sure I don't have to elaborate on that. You're all aware of the connection to Dragan; you're all aware of what Conrad Rainer told Imogen and myself when we were in Sarajevo, and what he told Mr Webb and Mr Raymond after he returned to England.'

Webb nodded. 'Phil and I are also aware of what happened to Miss Lester's parents, and the connection between that sad event and Dragan. We're really sorry about your loss, Miss Lester. It was a terrible thing.'

Raymond nodded. 'It was.'

'Thank you,' Imogen said quietly.

'Yesterday morning,' Julia continued, 'I went to see Damian at Wandsworth, where he's on remand awaiting sentence – with the consent of his solicitor, Fahmida Patel, obviously. I gave Damian the photographs and asked him to point out to me anyone he recognised. He pointed to the officers who had arrested him and the two senior officers in command of the raid – which is what you'd expect. But – if you will please turn to page ten – he also picked out DS Doug Isherwood, who wasn't involved with the raid and, as far as we knew, had nothing to do with his case.'

John Caswell shrugged. 'Perhaps he knew him from some prior matter?'

Julia shook her head. 'Damian Lester is a man of previous good character – somewhat fortuitously, I grant you, but, in fact, he is.' She paused deliberately for effect. 'No, gentlemen, Damian identified DS Isherwood as the man he knew as Sean, the man who recruited him in the pub. I thought you should know this before Damian gives evidence about it at the Old Bailey in a couple of days' time.'

There was a long silence.

'And you're saying we should believe him, are you, Julia?' Phil Raymond asked. 'I mean, let's be honest: Damian wouldn't be the first defendant to lash out at the police after he's got himself nicked and finds himself looking at a fair stretch inside.'

'When he saw Isherwood's photograph he looked as though he'd seen a ghost,' Julia replied. 'He looked frightened, Phil, very frightened. He also made a formal witness statement at my request. There's a copy in your files.'

She allowed them time to find and read the statement.

'Damian made this statement after he and I had had a very frank discussion about the legal consequences of his lying, or even of being mistaken. So yes, actually I do believe him, and I think the jury will believe him. But this goes a long way beyond one particular case. If Damian is right about this, the Drug Squad has a problem that could make the Flying Squad brouhaha of recent memory look like a storm in a teacup.'

'Well, we can't ignore it,' John Caswell admitted. 'There's no doubt about that. This file has to go somewhere. The question is, where? I'd have to ask the Director to consult with the Attorney General. My guess is that the Attorney would want to tell the Commissioner of Metropolitan Police and ask him to set up an investigation without delay.'

'There are problems with that,' Baxter intervened. 'All right, I'm not on the criminal law side of things, but as Julia said, this may have far-reaching implications, and I think those implications may go beyond the Met. I take it Sean was the only one of Conrad Rainer's names Damian knew? I'm sure you'd have told us if he'd recognised Wally or Franco?'

'No. It was only Sean.'

'So Wally and Franco are still out there,' Baxter observed, 'and the moment word gets out that Sean's cover has been blown, panic sets in among Dragan's crew and the whole operation disappears underground, taking with it years of work by Interpol – and by my Service: we have a stake in this too.'

'How so?' John asked.

'Within these four walls, Dragan has close connections with various nationalist groups in Yugoslavia we're trying to keep a watchful eye on. These groups depend on Dragan for a big slice of their funding. If Dragan goes underground, the chances are so do they, and then the door closes on an important source of our intelligence in the region. We had hoped to get a lot more information about how these connections work from Rainer – but obviously, it's too late for that now.'

'We could pick Isherwood up ourselves without going to the Commissioner,' Webb suggested, 'see what we can get out of him.'

John shook his head. 'Isherwood isn't going to give up Wally and Franco, is he – even assuming he knows who they are – not without a very good reason? We'd have to offer him something or threaten him with something. What have we got?'

'Nothing,' Raymond replied. 'All he has to say is that he recruited Damian while he was doing some undercover work in the Hampstead area, during which time he happened to be using the name Sean. We don't have any proof that he's Dragan's Sean, or that he had any connection at all with Dragan.'

'He knew about innkeepers,' Julia pointed out.

'As, presumably, do most members of the Drug Squad,' Raymond replied. 'It's the kind of jargon any specialist officer becomes familiar with. It's not enough.'

'I'll get him to talk if you give me the chance,' Imogen said quietly.

# 49

There was a ripple of polite laughter around the conference room. Involuntarily, Julia put an arm around Imogen and kissed her on the forehead.

'Really?' Webb asked, with obvious scepticism. 'And how exactly are you going to do that, Miss Lester?'

She sat up in her chair defiantly. 'I speak the language, don't I, Mr Webb? I know all about being bang to rights and offering the Old Bill a good drink.'

Webb and Raymond laughed. 'That's very good, Miss Lester, but...'

'No. Wait a minute,' Julia intervened. She had been looking closely at Imogen. 'Let her finish. Let's hear what she has to say.'

Imogen took a deep breath.

'When I was interviewed by Superintendent Mellor and DI Beech at Hampstead Police Station, they said they could make my case – and Damian's – go away if I would give them a good drink. I know that's not the story they're telling in court. Now, they're saying I suggested giving them a drink to make the case go away. But that's not what happened. I think Mellor and Beech really believe I'm connected to Dragan. It's not such a stretch, is it? I'd just been to Yugoslavia, and I knew how to say "innkeeper" in Serbo-Croat. I think they actually believe that I was, as they put it, "pulling down" a lot of money, and they wanted in on the action. They were ready to deal. Not only that, they offered to make drugs from other cases available to me for future transactions.'

'It's not impossible that Mellor and Beech are Wally and Franco, is it?' Julia suggested. 'Conrad Rainer thought they had to be high-ranking officers of the Drug Squad, and I don't remember any of us dismissing that possibility.'

'Or they just wanted to get in on some of Dragan's action,' Raymond added, 'as Miss Lester concluded.'

John Caswell seemed exasperated. 'Assuming all that to be true,' he said, 'how does it translate into Miss Lester getting Isherwood to talk?'

'Simple,' Imogen replied. 'I arrange a meeting with him. I explain that I tried to do business with Mellor and Beech, but they didn't want to know. I imply that they're too small time. I tell him I've been to Yugoslavia and that I know that he's Sean. I tell him I'm already working for Dragan – I know where the consignment found in my house came from, just as much as he does. I'm one of Dragan's innkeepers. Damian? You must be joking. Damian is just my runner, nothing more – I mean, come on, who would trust Damian with anything important, for God's sake? He's a user who works to feed his habit. No, I'm the one Sean's been dealing with. We're colleagues now, partners, and I'm prepared to offer him a good drink if he can help me with my case and work with me on future consignments.'

She looked brightly around the room.

'What is it the Old Bill say: he'll sing like a canary?'

Webb and Raymond burst out laughing, and gave her a round of applause. She simply stared back at them.

'My God: you're serious, aren't you?' Webb asked, quietly now.

'These people killed my parents, Mr Webb, and they're trying to ruin my life, and Damian's,' she replied, 'and it's still possible they're going to succeed. But I'm not going down without a fight. I'll get Isherwood to say enough to incriminate himself ten times over, and if he doesn't give me Wally and Franco, he'll give them up to you.' She paused. 'And maybe – just maybe – it will help me prove my innocence.'

John Caswell was shaking his head. 'Out of the question,' he said.

'It might just work, John,' Baxter said.

'Whether or not it might work is neither here nor there,' Caswell insisted. He sounded exasperated. 'With all due respect, Miss Lester is on trial for drugs offences, and this officer, Isherwood, is a potential witness in her case.'

'Not as a prosecution witness,' Julia replied. 'According to Mellor and Beech, they have no idea who "Sean" is, or where they might find him. They made inquiries, they told the court, but they couldn't get any information about him. The defence might call him, but I don't think the prosecution will, do you?'

'Be that as it may,' John persisted, 'it can't be right – not while she's on trial for offences Sean was involved with.'

'Not even if it would help her defence?'

'Miss Lester has a solicitor, Julia. Why isn't he here? If anyone should be involved in investigating the case and interviewing DS Isherwood, it's Barratt Davis.'

'He won't give it up to Barratt Davis,' Julia insisted. 'Barratt doesn't have any leverage. That's the whole point: Imogen might.'

John shook his head. 'Not with my blessing.'

'Well, you have mine,' Baxter said, 'and – no disrespect to anyone present – but if this does go ahead, my people should be the ones to set it up. We have experience of this kind of thing: we know what we're doing. And if we do it, we will do it discreetly. That's essential from everybody's point of view, particularly Imogen's.'

'You know I'm with you on that,' Julia said. 'But it has to be tightly controlled, Baxter. I don't want Imogen being put in danger.'

'It has to be a public place,' Baxter said, 'and there has to be a ground rule that she doesn't leave that place with Isherwood under any circumstances. Just to be sure, we pack the place, and we have a lot of backup. We wire her up, and as soon as the listeners judge that Sean has said enough, Miss Lester excuses herself to go and powder her nose, and we pounce. As Imogen says, hopefully he will be very anxious to cooperate by then. If it doesn't work, we give her a clean bill of health so she's protected if Isherwood tries to turn her in. I don't see any reason not to do it.'

'I'm sorry, Mr Baxter,' Webb said, 'I have to agree with Mr Caswell. Quite apart from the risk to Miss Lester, I don't see how the police can be involved in an undercover operation using someone who's on trial herself – while the trial is still going on. It would raise all kinds of questions.'

'Fine,' Baxter said with a shrug. 'I'd like to have police officers there, but if you're squeamish about it, I'll ask Special Branch. That way, you're not compromised if it all goes south. Besides, DS Isherwood might not be quite so confident about holding out once he realises that this is about national security, not just police corruption. We can be quite persuasive in security cases if we need to.'

He looked at Imogen for some time.

'The only thing is, Imogen: I know from long experience that any operation can go wrong, even with the most careful planning. There's no such thing as risk-free. When you corner people like Isherwood, there's no way to tell how he – or his associates – might react. And I'm not sure what effect any of this will have on your case – Julia would be the one to ask about that. We would dearly love to get inside Dragan's operation in London, and I won't pretend otherwise. It might be the break we've been waiting for. But I'm not going to do this unless I'm satisfied that you know what the risks are.'

'I understand the risks, Mr Baxter,' she replied, 'and I'm ready.'

# 50

'I thought this should be just between the silks in chambers,' Harriet Fisk began, 'at least for now, until we see what develops.'

They had waited until after seven, by which time it was a fair assumption that they would have chambers to themselves for the evening. Harriet had put the 'conference' sign in place on the door, to discourage any over-conscientious pupils still roaming the corridors in search of legal tomes or a helpful word of advice from barging in unannounced.

'You don't think Anthony Norris ought to be here, Harriet?' Kenneth Gaskell asked. 'He may not be in silk, but he's senior in chambers to everyone except Aubrey.'

'No.' she replied. 'At this point this is a conversation for those of us in silk. We'll include Anthony later, of course – and eventually we'll have to call a full chambers meeting. But let's keep it to ourselves for now.' She smiled. 'In any case, we all know how excitable Anthony can be when it comes to chambers politics, and what we need this evening is a gathering of cool heads.'

'I agree,' Sir Gareth Morgan-Davies said, 'but I'm only here as a guest, so you must tell me if I'm speaking out of turn.'

'You never speak out of turn, Gareth,' Harriet said, 'not in these chambers.' She turned to the others present. 'Aubrey and I invited Gareth to join us this evening, not only because – as you all know – he was Aubrey's predecessor as head of chambers, but also because – as you may or may not recall – Gareth sat in with Aubrey the first time the police came to see him in 1971, as I did this time.'

'And because I never come empty-handed,' Gareth replied with a smile, indicating the two bottles of white burgundy those assembled were sampling.

'I think the wine's got even better since you went up to the Court of Appeal, Gareth,' Ben said.

'Well, I'm glad I still have my uses, Ben.'

They laughed, though the laughter was subdued.

'The floor is yours, Aubrey,' Harriet said.

He nodded and took a long drink of wine.

'As you all know, Conrad Rainer and I were friends for almost all our lives. We read law together and we started at the Bar together. There was another friend too, Gerry Pole, who did very well for himself in the City and, among other things, had a very nice place – and a large ocean-going yacht – on the Isle of Wight. Dead now, both of them – Gerry last year and Conrad this year. I'm the last remaining member of the "Gang of Three" as we called ourselves during our misspent youth – not that it was particularly misspent, really, but still…

'Not long before he disappeared, Conrad asked me to meet him and told me that he'd become addicted to gambling – high stakes stuff, *Chemin de Fer* at the Clermont Club, with Goldsmith and Lucan and that crowd. He had a mistress, a woman by the name of Greta Thiemann, who was egging him on – not that he needed much egging on – and by the time he confided in me, he'd lost at least £30,000, probably more like £40,000, possibly even more. Conrad had done pretty well in silk, and he had his judicial salary, so he wasn't short of a few bob. But he didn't have the money to keep pace with those people at the Clermont Club. His wife, Deborah, had some family money in a trust fund. Conrad had already raided that fund, taken out a mortgage on the house, and stolen money from members of his former chambers. He had also borrowed £20,000 from a loan shark called Daniel Cleary. By the time he came to me he was desperate. He asked me to help him find a way out. I said I would do what I could – but looking back now, I can see that it was already too late by then.

'I tried to negotiate with his chambers, but they wouldn't budge. They were all set to call in the police. At that time Conrad was trying a murder at the Bailey. Ben was defending, and it turned out that Daniel Cleary had a starring role in the trial. So a day or two before Conrad disappeared, it was just a matter of who would get to him first – the police or Daniel Cleary. There was nothing more I could do. I spoke to Gerry about it…'

'If I may, Aubrey,' Gareth said, 'obviously this is the crucial part of the story, and I just want to make sure you realise that this is not – can't be – a privileged conversation.'

'We've talked that through,' Harriet replied.

'It doesn't matter now,' Aubrey said. 'Nothing's changed since 1971. I didn't know he had killed Greta. I thought his main problem was Daniel Cleary. I thought Gerry would keep him hidden on the Isle of Wight for a few days until we came up with the next move, which was probably to confess all to Deborah and ask her to bail him out – which she could have done if she'd chosen to. Obviously, the chances were that his career was over, come what may, but at the time, Cleary seemed a more immediate problem.

'I swear to you, I had no idea that he was going to disappear, or that Gerry was going to help him do it. And I certainly had no idea that he was going to end up in Sarajevo, or involved in trafficking drugs. There are some things the mind simply does not allow you to imagine. When the police first interviewed me…'

'They weren't even focusing on you, Aubrey, at that point,' Gareth said, 'were they? They were trying to find Conrad, they were trying to work out who had killed Greta Thiemann, and they had the eyes of the world's press on them. You were the least of their worries. All they could come up with was accessory after the fact to theft – which was never going to fly, and was a complete waste of their time. When they left, I didn't think there was any real chance of them going after you.'

'But now,' Harriet said, 'the game has changed. They spoke to Conrad Rainer. They know exactly where he disappeared to, and they know exactly how it was done. They know about his connection with Dragan, and since they know it was Aubrey who contacted Gerry Pole for help, they think they see a link between Aubrey and Dragan too.'

'Conrad also told them,' Aubrey added, 'that I had advised him to leave immediately – that it wasn't even safe for him to wait another day to finish the trial. Conrad didn't listen, and he only got away because the police didn't charge in and get him straight away.'

'Did you tell him that?' Ben asked.

Aubrey hesitated, taking a deep breath.

'Yes, I probably did. I'm not sure I was that specific about it – maybe I was. But I swear, it was only because of the threat from Daniel Cleary.'

'Not because you knew he'd killed Greta Thiemann?' Gareth asked.

'No. I swear.'

'And not because his former head of chambers was about to call in the police?' Ben asked.

He hesitated. 'I don't know. Perhaps. It's difficult to keep all these things separate when you're under that kind of pressure. You tend to cater for the most immediate threat and leave the rest until later…'

There was a long silence.

'My feeling,' Harriet said, 'is that the police now think they have a solid case against Aubrey for helping Conrad to disappear – not to mention that they're carrying a thinly-veiled grudge because Conrad made them look like fools, and they need someone to blame for that.'

'I'm seeing the net suspended above my head,' Aubrey said.

# 51

'It may all come to nothing,' Harriet continued. 'If Conrad and Gerry were still alive to give evidence – if even one of them were alive to give evidence – they might have a more compelling case. But as things are, they can't prove any direct connection between Aubrey and how Conrad got to Sarajevo.' She paused. 'All the same…'

'It's different this time,' Gareth agreed.

'There's no getting away from it,' Aubrey said. 'There's a real risk that they will try to prosecute me, and even if they don't, there may well be a terrible scandal – which will affect everyone in chambers, not just me. So with Harriet's help, I've come to a very difficult and painful decision. I can't carry on as head of chambers. I must stand down. I'm not even sure I should continue to practise as a member of chambers – at least until this has been resolved one way or the other. But it's certainly too risky with me as head of chambers.'

'Sadly,' Kenneth Gaskell said, after a long silence, 'I think you are probably right. When would you step down?'

'Immediately,' Aubrey replied.

'I agree,' Harriet said.

'The new head of chambers should take over on Monday morning,' Gareth added.

'We can't get it done that quickly, Gareth,' Kenneth said. 'We have to talk to Anthony and we have to call a chambers meeting.'

'Anointing the next head of chambers has never been an exercise in democracy, Kenneth,' Harriet pointed out. 'It's always gone to the next silk in order of seniority. I'm not suggesting an election: I'm suggesting that we make a decision and present it to chambers as a *fait accompli*. We can let them know over the weekend and hold a chambers meeting on Monday.'

'The only real question is, who should succeed me,' Aubrey said, 'which brings us back to where we started. Anthony is the most senior in chambers, but he's not in silk.' He hesitated. 'And as I'm the person standing down, I suppose it falls to me to say what we all know, but would prefer not to have to say: Anthony is not the kind of man we want as head of these chambers, silk or not. He's arrogant; he offends everyone he comes into contact with – which is the main reason why he hasn't got silk, in my opinion; he's disruptive in chambers; and he will alienate solicitors. Not to mention that the clerks might actually walk out in protest.'

'I'm not hearing any dissent,' Gareth observed quietly after some time.

'Which brings us to you, Kenneth,' Harriet said. 'You're the next senior silk. How would you feel about it?'

Kenneth closed his eyes and shook his head. 'I've been back at work for almost six months now, as you all know. My doctors signed me off to return to practice, but only on condition that I don't expose myself to any unnecessary stress. Being head of chambers is a huge responsibility. Anne and Simon would probably lock me up under house arrest just for thinking about it – let alone my doctors.' He paused. 'I can't say I blame them – after all, I am lucky to be alive. I'm not saying I wouldn't take it on if there's no alternative, but I really don't want to be in that position if there's any other way.'

'I'm sure everyone in chambers understands that, of course, Kenneth,' Harriet said, 'and that's why I asked. No one wants to put your health at risk. So…moving on… Until two years ago the line of succession would have continued with Peter Elliott and Roger Horan. Peter got silk while he was still with us, but left for pastures new to set up his own set; while Roger took the Queen's shilling and went off to be a resident magistrate in some far-flung corner of the Empire…'

'Bermuda,' Ben said.

'Bermuda. Then we lost Donald Weston to the county court bench. Which brings us to…'

'Which brings us to you and Ben,' Aubrey said. 'You joined chambers at exactly the same time and you're both in silk. It doesn't have to be a man – unlike the old days.'

'Quite right,' Gareth agreed. 'There are a number of sets of chambers with a woman in command now, and there's no reason why these chambers shouldn't be one of them.'

'So what do we do?' Aubrey asked, with a smile. 'Show of hands, secret ballot, cut the pack, toss a coin for it?'

They laughed. Ben was about to speak but Harriet touched him lightly on the arm.

'I would love to do it,' she said, 'and neither Ben nor I think my being a woman would be an issue – it's something we've talked about often over the years.' Ben nodded. 'But this isn't the right time for me. As you know, I spend as much time in Cambridge as I do in London these days. I have a busy practice. Monty is going to be senior tutor at the College next year. Jenny and Harry have so many activities at school now that we can hardly keep up with them; and my parents are both rather fragile – they're both much slower than they once were.' She paused. 'So much as I would love to throw my hat into the ring, it's not practical for me at the moment.'

No one spoke for some time. Ben felt himself go hot and cold in turn.

'If I'm not mistaken, Ben,' Gareth said with a smile, 'you've just been anointed as the next head of chambers. Speaking as your former pupil-master, may I be the first to congratulate you? I feel very proud.'

After they had drunk a toast and discussed arrangements for notifying Anthony Norris and the fifteen more junior members of chambers, Gareth made his excuses – he was already late for dinner with his wife. Ben stopped him just outside the door.

'Gareth, tell me honestly: do you think I'm ready for this?'

'Of course, you are.'

'I don't feel ready.'

Gareth laughed. 'You didn't feel ready for your first trial in the magistrates' court, your first trial at the Bailey, your first outing in the Court of Appeal, your first case as a silk… I could go on. I know this because I was the one you always came to when you needed to talk about it.'

'And you always reassured me.'

'Of course, I did, and I was right. And I do so again now. Ben, listen to me. You will be a brilliant head of chambers, if for no other reason than that you understand how hard it is for young barristers and pupils. God only knows, you fought your way through enough horrors just to be allowed to join chambers and start your practice – as did Harriet: you both came up through the school of hard knocks. I would have been happy for either of you to take over as head of chambers – either of you would do a great job – but obviously, for personal reasons, I'm quite looking forward to telling people that I am a former member of Ben Schroeder's chambers.'

They shared a smile. Ben shook his head. Gareth turned to leave, then turned back.

'Ben, when I took over as head of chambers from Bernard Wesley, he called me in for a drink – a real drink, his best twenty-year-old single malt, not the industrial amontillado he usually dished out – and he said to me: "Gareth, you will do very well if you remember two things. The first is: when you have a hard decision to make, don't be afraid to ask for advice, but always remember, it's your decision and yours alone. And the second is: whenever you deal with the younger members of chambers, or the pupils, never forget that you once stood where they are standing now. If you remember those two things, you won't go far wrong." And he was absolutely right,' Gareth added, as he made his way out.

# 52

As Baxter had predicted, on a Sunday evening the Lamb was relatively quiet. The venerable pub in Lamb's Conduit Street in Bloomsbury was one he had used many times over the years for rendezvous of different kinds. It was small enough to allow him to check the whole place in a matter of a few seconds, and the two narrow front doors at either end of the bar were easy to keep under constant surveillance. During the week the Lamb could be busy and crowded, an advantage for certain encounters and a disadvantage for others. Tonight it was perfect; he simply needed to keep observation from a distance and be prepared to intervene if anything went wrong. One thing that wasn't going to happen at the Lamb was DS Doug Isherwood, otherwise known as Sean, taking Imogen Lester anywhere else. To do that he would have to walk straight past the two well-built minders Baxter had brought with him. Baxter felt relaxed about that.

Imogen saw Baxter as she entered the Lamb, a good twenty minutes before the time of the appointment a female colleague of Baxter's had made for her the day before. As instructed, she did not react or acknowledge him. Instead she bought herself a tonic water and made her way to a table with seating for two on a plush booth-style padded sofa, which two Special Branch officers had been holding for her and vacated as she approached. She had worried about being too conscious of the minute recording device Baxter's people had installed inside the locket they had given her to wear around her neck. 'Try not to fiddle with it,' they had told her, 'and don't worry about distance or background noise. This thing will pick up every sound there is to pick up, and we can filter out what we don't need later. Just focus on what you're doing and let the device do its work.'

DS Doug Isherwood arrived exactly on time and bought himself a pint of beer, looking carefully around the bar area. When he was satisfied, he approached her.

'May I join you?' he asked.

'Please do,' she replied.

He examined her. She was simply dressed in a navy sweater and jeans, under a short grey coat and a red scarf. She looked somehow innocent: which couldn't be the whole story about her, given what he had been told before he agreed, with some reservations, to the meeting.

'So, you're Imogen?'

'You can call me Maggie,' she replied.

'I thought your name was Imogen,' he said uncertainly.

'I thought your name was Doug,' she countered.

'It is. Damian told me your name was Imogen.'

'You're not dealing with Damian now: you're dealing with me.'

'So I see. But he told me your name was Imogen.'

'He told me your name was Sean.'

He smiled. 'That's just a name I use sometimes when I'm working undercover.'

She took a drink of her tonic. 'That's what you call it when you recruit innkeepers, is it then, Sean, "working undercover?"'

He paused, glass in hand, taken aback by her directness. He experienced a momentary anxiety, an urge to call it off, to get up and leave there and then with no damage done. A meeting he hadn't initiated, with a woman on trial for drugs offences, carried obvious risks and offered no immediately obvious benefit. On the other hand, it seemed that Imogen Lester was connected, and he was intrigued. He wasn't sure of what he was getting himself into, but the intrigue refused to go away. Surely it couldn't do any harm to hear what she had to say for herself? He could always find a way to leave later.

'With all due respect to Damian, Maggie, he's not the most reliable source about what names I use and what I do.'

She smiled. 'Oh, I agree completely. I wouldn't believe Damian if he told me his own name, never mind somebody else's. But someone in Sarajevo, who I would believe, also told me that your name was Sean.'

'Oh, yes? And who might that be?'

'The same person who told me what you do for Dragan – you recruit the odd innkeeper, the odd *gostioničar*, for him and you handle the safe passage of merchandise.'

He took a long drink of his beer, sat back in his seat, and stared at her.

'I don't think I know anyone by the name of Dragan.'

'Really? It's funny you're so well known in Sarajevo then, Sean: don't you think?'

He started to speak, but then checked himself. 'What do you want, Maggie, or Imogen, or whoever you are?'

'What do I want? You conned my idiot brother into looking after merchandise for you in my house – *my* house, Sean – as a result of which I got nicked by your mates in the Drug Squad. I'm on trial at the Old Bailey. What do you think I want?'

'I'm a police officer. It's my job to get people nicked when they commit offences.'

'That's not the way they see it in Sarajevo.'

He laughed. 'You keep going on about Sarajevo. What do I care about what people think in Sarajevo? Where is Sarajevo?'

She nodded. 'Apparently, I'm not explaining myself very well, so let me spell it out for you. Your orders to fit me up using Damian were countermanded long before the Squad hit us. It was always a backup plan, in case Dragan couldn't get close enough to my father to kill him. The point was to send a message to my father to back off, to show him what Dragan was capable of. Once my father was dead, the plan wasn't needed. It wasn't supposed to happen.'

He was silent for some time. She didn't seem inclined to rush him. He drank his pint, evaluating.

'So,' he said cautiously, 'assuming that I understand what you're talking about, what do you expect me to do about it?'

'I want you to get real and see how much trouble you're in.'

'I'm listening.'

'Ordering my father's assassination was the biggest mistake of Dragan's life. Dragan can make the Yugoslav police go away, we all know that – a dinar here, a Deutsche Mark there, you know how it goes, does the trick every time. But not the people my father worked for. Dragan can't them buy off with a few dinars, and now he suddenly has to start worrying about his future.'

'So?'

'So, anyone working for Dragan – let's say a police officer he might have recruited over here, for example – should be feeling just as insecure as Dragan, because now they're on the radar of the security services and the security services are royally pissed off. Of course, if you don't work for Dragan, you don't have anything to worry about, do you?'

'It wasn't my fault,' he said after some time.

She looked at him closely. 'What wasn't your fault?'

'You getting nicked. I don't know what happened. Obviously, I didn't get the message. Wires got crossed, that's all.'

Her heart missed a beat, and at a table close to the door at the other end of the bar, Baxter permitted himself a small smile.

'Wires got crossed?'

'Obviously. Look, I do what I'm told to do within the Squad. If they'd told me to back off you, I would have backed off. It wasn't up to me to call it off. I don't operate on that level. I have no idea where my orders come from.'

'Who was it up to, then? Wally? Franco?'

'No,' he replied impatiently, 'Look, I don't even know who those people are, OK? I just do what I'm told. I'm not saying any more unless you tell me what I'm doing here. What do you want from me?'

She took a deep breath.

'I want to make you a proposition,' she replied.

# 53

'What kind of proposition?'

'A business proposition,' she replied at once. 'What did you think I meant?'

She actually gave him the ghost of a smile, which he returned in kind.

'I went to Sarajevo,' she said, 'to find out why my parents had died. The police didn't know very much – or if they did, they weren't about to tell me – so I had to make my own inquiries.'

'How did you do that?'

'That doesn't matter. What matters is what I found out. I found out that my father was close to bringing Dragan down. So Dragan had him – and my mother – killed, and now I'd shown up on his doorstep: which left Dragan with two choices. He could either take me out too, which would have been easy enough for him, but would have pissed off the security services even more than they were already; or he could make a deal with me, by way of saying, "Sorry, Imogen, it was just business, nothing personal, you understand." Sensibly, he decided to make a deal.'

'What deal?'

'Well, the first and most obvious thing, Sean, was to call off your plan to fit me up with the drugs your Squad found in my house.'

He shook his head. 'Wires must have got crossed.'

'So you said, but I wouldn't like to have to explain that to Dragan: would you?'

She waited for a reply, without result.

'So from now on, I'm under Dragan's protection. If I want to act as a *gostioničar* for a suitable reward, he will make sure that the merchandise is channelled through me, and Wally and Franco will be instructed to cooperate with me. I have a house – well, I had a house, until the wires got crossed, so I assume I'll have to acquire other premises for future consignments. But I will need someone to work with me. That's where you come in. In addition to a good drink, you will also be under my protection – which means Dragan's protection. If I say I'm not holding a grudge for being fitted up, nothing will happen to you.'

'And they gave you the name Maggie, did they?' he asked.

'They said I should use a name. I picked Maggie because it was my mother's name. Her name was Margaret, but my father always called her Maggie... Anyway...'

He was silent for a long time. She sipped her tonic water and studied his face.

'Who else knows about this?' he asked.

'No one,' she replied. 'I tried to proposition Mellor and Beech while I was at Hampstead nick, but they weren't having it. They wanted to cut their own deal with me – a good drink of ten per cent, plus occasional supplies from the evidence storage room, but with them in charge. We never got as far as talking about Dragan, but I thought they might be Wally and Franco.'

He snorted. 'Mellor, maybe. Beech couldn't organise the proverbial piss up in a brewery. Beech's idea of the big time is for some south London low life to slip him a drink of fifty quid. To be honest, I don't think either of them has the imagination for anything on the scale you're talking about. – but definitely not Beech.'

'But Mellor, possibly? We have to know who we're dealing with, Sean.'

'I told you: I don't know. I'm not on Dragan's Christmas card list. Why didn't he tell you, if you and he are such good mates these days?'

She shook her head. 'They said they would tell me when I needed to know.'

They drank silently for some time.

'How are you going to do any business if you get convicted at the Bailey and get sent down?' he asked.

'I'm not going to get convicted,' she replied, 'and even if I did, I'm not going to get a long stretch, am I? I'm what they call a person of previous exemplary character. I graduated from the same university as the judge, I work for a highly respectable solicitor, and I only got involved because my druggie idiot brother dragged me into it, didn't I? Don't worry about me, Sean. I'll be open for business.' She braced herself. 'What I need to know is: are you in or out?'

'I'm interested,' he replied. 'But there are some things we need to talk about – some assurances I would need.'

'That's fine,' she said. 'Look, I need the loo. Get me a Jameson straight up, a double. And whatever you want. On me.'

She stood up as casually as she could and made her way to the ladies.

As she did, Baxter approached the table with his two minders. Sean started to get to his feet to buy the drinks, but one of the minders gently lowered him back down.

'Evening, Sean,' Baxter said.

'Who the hell are you?' Sean asked.

'My name's Baxter, Sean. I'm with the security services, as are my two colleagues here. We have two officers from Special Branch waiting for us by the door, and you're going to accompany us outside without making a fuss about it.'

Sean banged his pint glass on the table, hard. 'That fucking bitch. I'll...'

'Language, Sean, language,' Baxter said reprovingly. 'Remember where you are. You're not down the nick now, you know. This is a nice place. Shall we go?'

Julia had been waiting anxiously in the Italian restaurant next door, drinking endless cups of coffee. When she saw the unmarked car pull away from the kerb she threw some money down on her table and rushed out of the restaurant and into the Lamb. She found Imogen at the bar with Baxter. She pulled her into her arms.

'Are you all right? How did it go?'

'I'm fine,' Imogen replied with a smile.

'She was magnificent,' Baxter said. He seemed in an exceptionally good mood. 'I was about to ask: you must have done some acting somewhere in your past, Maggie, haven't you?'

She nodded, smiling. 'I did several shows with ADC when I was up at Cambridge.'

'Well, you were amazing,' Baxter said. 'Look, obviously, you're not planning to work for Julia for the rest of your life. If you'd like to talk about working with us, I'd be happy to...'

Julia took Imogen's arm and led her to the door.

'I think Imogen's had enough of the cloak and dagger stuff for one night, Baxter,' she said.

'I was just saying...'

'And I'm sure Imogen will let you know if she's interested,' she replied. 'But not until she and I have had a good talk first.'

# 54

Monday 20 February 1984

Baxter led DCI Webb and DCI Raymond into the interview room, closely followed by a minder, who stood just inside the door, leaning against the wall, his arms crossed in front of him. The room had no windows; the lighting was fluorescent and tubular. The air was warm and stale. Sean looked tired and dishevelled. He leapt to his feet and thrust both hands into his pockets.

'Where am I?' he demanded loudly.

'I do hope they've been looking after you, Sergeant,' Baxter said, 'given you some breakfast, that kind of thing, have they?'

Sean waved a fist in Baxter's direction. 'What am I doing here?'

'Do sit down, Sergeant Isherwood,' Baxter replied quietly.

'Not until you tell me where I am and what I'm doing here.'

'These gentlemen are DCI Webb and DCI Raymond. We thought you'd feel more at home with a couple of fellow police officers.'

'I want to know what's going on.'

'All will become clear in due course. Please have a seat.'

The minder pushed himself ever so slightly off the wall on which he had been leaning. Sean sat down with a gesture of defiance.

'Am I under arrest?'

'Not yet,' Webb replied.

'So I'm free to go?'

'Free as a bird as far as we're concerned,' Baxter replied. 'But I'm not sure Mr Webb takes the same view.'

'Technically, at this precise moment, you're free to leave,' Webb replied. 'But if you try, I will arrest you before you can get through that door.'

Sean banged a fist on the table. 'Don't give me that crap. I'm a police officer, just like you. I know my rights. You can't treat me like this. You either have to take me before the magistrates' court or take me to a police station, and I'm entitled to a brief...'

'Don't get stroppy with us, son,' Webb replied. 'It's not a good idea to shout the odds when you're not holding the hand to back it up. You've nicked enough villains over the years to know that.'

'I'm telling you...'

'And I'm telling you,' Webb said, more firmly this time, 'you'd be well advised to shut up and listen, instead of shooting your mouth off.'

'What exactly would you arrest me for?' Sean asked, doing his best to look outraged.

Webb shrugged. 'Well, for starters we've got you bang to rights for conspiracy to pervert the course of justice, haven't we? I could nick you for that right now and get you remanded in custody, and you would stay banged up while we build a case for conspiracy to import and supply controlled drugs, perhaps even for conspiracy to commit murder.'

The outrage suddenly turned to shock. 'Murder? What the hell are you talking about? What murder?'

'The murders of Michael and Margaret Lester,' Webb replied.

Sean's jaw dropped. 'That happened in Yugoslavia,' he protested. 'I've never even been to bloody Yugoslavia.'

'But you know what I'm talking about, don't you?'

'Yeah, I know what you're talking about, but that was nothing to do with me.'

'Perhaps he was only involved with fitting up the daughter, Johnny,' Raymond suggested.

'Perhaps he was, Phil. But it's still perverting the course of justice, isn't it? And they must all have been in on it, mustn't they

– what were their names, again, Sean, Wally and Franco? They're all Dragan's lads, aren't they?'

'You people are out of your minds,' Sean exploded again. 'I didn't fit anyone up. I got them nicked for being involved in supplying, which they were – and that's all there is to it.'

'That's not what you told Maggie last night, is it,' Webb said, 'when you were talking about the two of you working for Dragan? You admitted that Dragan asked you to fit her up if he couldn't get rid of her father, and because wires got crossed you went ahead even though Dragan had called it off. The law calls that perverting the course of justice. The tape came out a treat, by the way. You can hear every word, clear as a bell.'

'That was illegal,' Sean shouted, banging his fist on the table again. 'You set me up. You entrapped me. You can't go near a court with that. It's not admissible. You can't tape record people without their permission. You're police officers. How could you not know that?'

'They didn't record you, Sergeant,' Baxter said calmly. 'I did. I'm not a police officer, and in my line of work we don't worry so much about whether recordings would be admissible in court. We have other uses for them.'

'Such as what?'

'Playing them to whoever may be interested in hearing them – employers, colleagues, family, members of our sister services, perhaps even the press in certain circumstances. And actually, since you've raised the question of admissibility in court, it probably would be admissible in Yugoslavia, if we were to send you over there to stand trial. The rules of evidence aren't quite as strict there as they are here, I'm told.'

Sean pointed a finger. 'You can't do that.'

'I don't see why not. The Yugoslavs would be delighted to get their hands on one of Dragan's crew. They've been turning a blind eye to him for years, but apparently there's about to be a change of plan. They think he's got a bit too big for his boots, you see; he's becoming an embarrassment to them. They'd love to get rid of him, and it would be quite a feather in their cap to announce that they've broken up his British operation. That would put the wind up his people everywhere, wouldn't it? The dominoes might start to tumble very quickly, once word of that hits the streets.'

'What do you want?' Sean had collapsed back into his chair. His defiance had begun to subside.

'Well, first,' Baxter said, 'can you confirm for us that you are "Sean" – and I think you know what I mean by that?'

'Yes. I'm Sean.'

'Thank you. Who are Wally and Franco?'

'I don't know.'

'This is no time to get all coy with us, son,' Webb said. 'You're in enough trouble already.'

'I swear to God: I don't know.'

'I find that hard to believe,' Webb said. 'I know that's what you told Maggie last night. But here you are, in the Drug Squad, getting your instructions – to fit Imogen Lester up, for example – and obviously those instructions are coming from Dragan's other little helpers. They have to be officers in the Drug Squad, don't they? Do you see what I'm saying? How could you not know who they are?'

'I'm telling you, I don't know. My instructions from Dragan come down through one of the DIs or DCIs, like any other instructions. I don't know where the DI or DCI gets his instructions from, and I don't care. It doesn't matter to me.'

'How do you get your drink?' Raymond asked. 'I assume that matters to you.'

'In cash. Brown envelope in my desk. I don't see who puts it there.'

'But there must have been a first time,' Raymond pointed out. 'When an officer's taking a drink, there has to be a first time, doesn't there? Someone has to make the first offer to him. Who would that have been in your case?'

'Mellor,' Sean replied after some time.

'Doesn't that suggest that Mellor is either Wally or Franco?' Baxter asked.

'It might.'

'And by the way, which of the two is in command, Wally or Franco? Do you know?'

'My impression is, Franco is in charge. But nobody has ever told me who Franco is, or who Wally is. I always assumed it was on a need-to-know basis: and for obvious reasons, I've never asked.'

Baxter allowed some time to elapse.

'Assuming that we were to make it worth your while,' he said, 'would you be prepared to work with us to see if you can find out?'

# 55

'Cross-examination, Mr Norris?' Andrew Pilkington asked.

'Much obliged, my Lord.'

Ben glanced behind him. 'This could be a long afternoon,' Clive Overton whispered with a thin smile.

Ben nodded. After the excitement of being nominated to become head of the set of chambers that had almost rejected him when he was starting out, and pleasant memories of an impromptu celebratory dinner with Jess and Joshua the previous evening, Monday morning had seen him fall back down to earth with a bump. The early morning chambers meeting had been fraught. The decision that Ben should take over with immediate effect had gone down well enough with the younger members. Apart from shadowy but persistent rumours, they had known nothing about the peril in which Aubrey Smith-Gurney found himself until Harriet summarised it for them and swore them to silence. Knowing the truth had brought them some measure of relief, and Harriet's confident, soothing manner reassured them that the silks had made the right decision. But Anthony Norris was having none of it. He had stormed out without a word, bringing the meeting to an abrupt, jarring end.

'Well, look on the bright side, Ben,' Aubrey had said once the silks were left alone together in his room. 'At least he didn't object because you're Jewish.'

It was meant as a light remark, and Ben had duly laughed, but it did nothing to allay his fears about what he had to look forward to. Norris had failed to get silk and he had used up the three applications barristers were customarily allowed before accepting that they had been rejected; but he was still senior to Ben in chambers, and although there were several good reasons for having a QC as head of chambers, there was no formal rule that it must be the case. Norris was not going to accept the situation gracefully; he was going to be a thorn in Ben's side for the foreseeable future. And as if that wasn't enough, he now had to face Norris in court for the remainder of the trial of Imogen Lester. Norris was about to close his case; and Ben was about to call Imogen to give evidence in her defence. Her evidence had taken all morning. Norris had not spoken a single word to him during that time.

'Miss Lester, let me see if I understand what you told the jury this morning,' Norris began. 'Correct me if I'm not doing justice to what you said. You told the jury that you had no knowledge that your brother was allowing Sean to use your basement to store drugs: is that right?'

'Yes, it is.'

'Damian was able to get away with it because you were in Sarajevo and you had no idea what was going on?'

'That's correct.'

'Even though, according to Damian, it wasn't the first time he'd looked after drugs for Sean?'

'If that's true, I had no knowledge of it.'

'He never told you about it?'

'No. He knew I would never have had anything to do with it.'

'You were never aware of anything untoward going on, no smell of cannabis, for example?'

'No. I wasn't there very much. I was working long hours. All I did at home was eat and sleep, and quite often not even that – I often stayed in town with my employer, Julia Cathermole. It wouldn't have been hard for Damian to do it without my knowledge, if that's what he did.'

'That's what Damian told the police he did, Miss Lester.'

'After he'd been punched in the face, yes.'

'Well, so you say. The officers told the jury he came into contact with a door, quite accidentally, didn't they?'

'That's what they said, yes.'

'You weren't present when he got the cut on his cheek, were you?'

'No. I was not.'

'The second thing you told the jury was that two senior officers, Detective Chief Superintendent Mellor and Detective Inspector Beech, have fabricated evidence against you. They've attributed statements to you that you never made: is that right?'

'That's correct.'

'Not to put too fine a point on it, these two senior and highly experienced officers verballed you, did they? Do you understand that expression, Miss Lester, to "verbal" someone?'

'I understand it very well.'

'And that's what they did, is it?'

'Yes, it is.'

'And you remember, before Superintendent Mellor gave evidence, your learned counsel asked you to read aloud from *A Tale of Two Cities* – "It was the best of times, it was the worst of times," and so on – you remember doing that, don't you?'

'Yes.'

'And the purpose of that wasn't just to provide us with our moment of cultural inspiration for the day, was it? It was designed to suggest to the jury that you're not the kind of young woman who would speak in the way described by the officers?'

'Exactly. That's not the way I speak, and it's not the kind of language I use.'

'You'd never heard vulgarities like the "Old Bill" and a "good drink" before, had you? Not the kind of thing one is exposed to when one is properly brought up in Hampstead and then goes up to Cambridge?'

'I didn't say I'd never heard those expressions. I said that isn't the way I speak.'

'Were you an actress during your time at Cambridge?'

'I did a number of shows with ADC, the university theatre, yes.'

'Does acting involve the ability to modify the voice, to adopt an accent or manner of speaking, to fit the script?'

'Yes, sometimes, of course.'

'Was that what you were doing when you read Dickens for us so demurely? You were trying to pull the wool over the jury's eyes, weren't you – acting the part of the innocent young girl unsullied by the vulgarities of underworld lingo?'

'No. I wanted the jury to hear my voice. I wasn't acting when the police came to the house at four in the morning, believe you me.'

'That's nonsense, Miss Lester, isn't it? You made some remarks which, quite understandably, you later regretted; and to get yourself out of the corner you'd painted yourself into, you chose to smear these two distinguished senior officers by accusing them of serious misconduct?'

'That's not true.'

'Well, let me ask you about something that apparently you don't dispute at all. When the officers interviewed you in your kitchen before you were arrested, you introduced two words into the conversation: "innkeeper" and "*gostioničar*", which as the jury has heard, is the Serbo-Croat word for "innkeeper". You were the first person present in the kitchen to use those two words, weren't you?'

'Yes, that's correct.'

'No one else mentioned them until you brought them up, did they?'

'No.'

'And when the officers asked you how you were familiar with the Serbo-Croat word, you told them that you must have picked it up at the Holiday Inn in Sarajevo while you were staying there: is that right?'

'That is what I said, yes. Please understand, I didn't intend to talk to the police about innkeepers in English, never mind Serbo-Croat. I wasn't thinking clearly. I wasn't feeling well.'

'Oh yes, of course, you were feeling faint and disorientated?'

'Yes, I was – and I told PC Roberts so at the time, as she said when she gave evidence.'

Norris nodded. 'But whatever you intended, or didn't intend to talk about, you did tell the police about innkeepers, didn't you? And when challenged about it, you came up with this story of picking it up at the Holiday Inn. Why? Because it was the first thing that came into your head?'

'I said that because I couldn't tell them the truth about it.'

'So that we're clear: you agreed this morning, in answer to your learned counsel, that the explanation you gave the police was a lie: yes?'

'Yes.'

'Are you feeling faint or disorientated today?'

'No.'

'Well then, now that we're in court, and you're feeling well, and you've taken an oath to tell the truth, why don't you tell his Lordship and the jury how you came to learn the word "*gostioničar*?"'

'I can't,' Imogen replied quietly.

'You can't? Or is it simply that you now realise what a silly story it was?'

'My Lord…' Ben said, rising to his feet.

'And it is silly, isn't it? I've stayed in hotels in several different countries over the years, as I'm sure have some members of the jury, and I don't recall learning the word for "innkeeper" in any of the languages concerned.'

'My Lord,' Ben said, 'perhaps my learned friend would like to ask a question instead of giving evidence…?'

'I don't need my esteemed head of chambers's advice about how to conduct a cross-examination,' Norris almost snarled.

'My Lord…'

'Let's get on with it please, Mr Norris,' the judge said.

'Yes, my Lord. Why did you lie, Miss Lester?'

'I've told you. As I explained this morning, there are certain things I'm not allowed to talk about.'

'Ah, yes, of course. This mysterious man you and Julia Cathermole met in Sarajevo – all very hush, hush?'

'I'm not allowed to talk about it.'

'My Lord,' Ben said, throwing down his notebook in frustration, 'there's a matter of law I need to raise in the absence of the jury.'

# 56

Andrew Pilkington looked briefly at Ben and at Anthony Norris, and then turned to the jury.

'Members of the jury, apparently, there's a matter of law I have to discuss with counsel. As you know, matters of law are for me to deal with, so I'm going to ask you to retire for a short time and we'll bring you back as soon as we can.'

He watched the jury file out of court.

'Miss Lester, please return to the dock for now. Mr Schroeder?'

'My Lord, may we go into chambers? There are some sensitive matters.'

The judge nodded. 'Yes, very well. Clear the court, please, usher.'

Ben waited for Mary to usher the few members of the public, including Julia and the two reporters taking an interest in the proceedings, out of court; and to put the 'Court in Chambers: No Admittance' sign up on the door.

'My Lord, I'm disturbed at the direction my learned friend's cross-examination is taking. I told my learned friend last week what Miss Lester was going to say during her evidence, and I thought we had an agreement: as long as Miss Lester admitted that she lied to the police, and explained that her knowledge of the word 'gostioničar'' came from a man she and Miss Cathermole interviewed in Sarajevo, my learned friend would allow the matter to rest there.'

Norris shrugged. 'I've reconsidered my position since then, and I've concluded that, in order to do justice to the prosecution's case, my professional duty is to pursue the matter further.'

'In that case,' Ben retorted at once, 'my learned friend should have told me that he had changed his mind before I called the defendant to give evidence.'

'Why? What difference could it have made? My learned friend couldn't have changed the evidence his client was going to give.'

'I have to say, Mr Schroeder,' Andrew Pilkington said, 'I'm having some difficulty in following all this.'

'That's because the position is rather more complicated than my learned friend would have your Lordship believe. The interview in Sarajevo involved the British embassy and the security services. Matters were discussed which may affect our national interest, matters the government may wish to protect from disclosure under Crown privilege. In addition, Miss Lester's employer, Julia Cathermole, was present in her professional capacity as a solicitor and was actively advising a client, so whatever passed between them is privileged. Your Lordship may have to hear evidence and legal argument about all this. I had hoped that my learned friend and I could avoid taking up the court's time if we had an understanding about it. Unfortunately, it appears that my hopes were misplaced.'

'Apparently so,' the judge agreed.

'Miss Lester was in Sarajevo with Miss Cathermole to get information about the progress of the investigation into the death of her parents. In the course of their inquiries they spoke with an individual who had knowledge of what had happened to Mr and Mrs Lester, but who also asked Miss Cathermole to represent him in connection with other matters. This man was not involved in any way with the murders, let me make that clear, but there were matters on which he required urgent legal advice. Miss Cathermole agreed to represent him.'

'So you're saying that whatever was said during the interview was a privileged communication between lawyer and client,' the judge asked, 'and that, as Miss Cathermole's employee, Miss Lester would have a duty to claim the privilege on the client's behalf?'

'Yes, my Lord.'

Norris leapt to his feet. 'The problem with that, my Lord, is the presence of this other mysterious man, who everyone's being very coy about but who was presumably a member of the security services. He wasn't employed by Miss Cathermole or by her client. If a third party is present who is not involved in the legal communication, there's no privilege in what was said.'

'Not if his presence was essential to the interview,' Ben countered immediately. 'No one's being coy about anything. The man being interviewed was being run as an agent, and the third party was an officer of the Service. The Service made it quite clear that they would not allow Miss Cathermole access to its agent unless that officer was also present. The officer is in the same position as an interpreter where the client doesn't speak English. He's a third party, but his presence is essential to the interview.'

'And you have evidence to that effect?'

'Yes, my Lord, but it may well be subject to Crown privilege. The government may feel compelled to intervene, to protect the national interest.'

The judge thought for some time.

'I must say, Mr Norris,' he said eventually, with a smile, 'this is a rather odd case, isn't it?'

'I'm not sure I follow, my Lord.'

'Well, you've done cases involving Crown Privilege before, I'm sure – as have I, and as has Mr Schroeder.'

'Yes, my Lord.'

'Looking back on the cases I've been involved with, I can't remember a single one in which Crown Privilege was asserted by the defence. It's always been the prosecution that raises it. That's natural enough, isn't it? After all, the Prosecution represents the Crown. It's the prosecution's duty, isn't it, to uphold Crown Privilege in cases where it applies? It's not something the defence should have to do.'

Norris hesitated. 'If your Lordship is suggesting that the

prosecution is not entitled to question Miss Lester's story simply because there is a suggestion of the Security Services being involved...'

'Not at all, Mr Norris. But I do find it surprising that you are cross-examining Miss Lester about it, and apparently suggesting that she is not telling the truth, without taking steps to ascertain what view the Security Services take of it. What happens if they agree with the version of events Mr Schroeder has suggested? I prosecuted in many cases while I was at the Bar, as you know. I'm not sure I would have wanted to put myself in that position as prosecuting counsel.'

Ben looked down, unable to suppress a smile. He watched the doubts grow in the mind of Anthony Norris, who was silent for some time.

'My Lord, I'm not sure how to respond to that,' he admitted. 'If your Lordship takes that view, I might have to ask your Lordship for some time to consider my position.'

Ben stood. 'My Lord, perhaps I can assist my learned friend,' he said. 'I would be happy to arrange for him to speak to Miss Cathermole – whom I shall be calling as a witness on this point, if necessary – and if that's not enough, I know that Miss Cathermole can put him in touch with the senior officer responsible for the case of the agent in question. If my learned friend will speak to them, I have no doubt that he will be satisfied.'

'Mr Norris?' the judge inquired.

Norris shook his head. 'In the light of what your Lordship has said, it may be that I have no real choice in the matter.'

'It's not a question of what I say, Mr Norris,' Andrew Pilkington replied. 'It's a matter for you how you conduct your case. I'm simply trying to be helpful.'

'I will do as your Lordship suggests,' Norris said, ungraciously.

'Mr Schroeder,' Andrew said, 'I'm thinking about the jury. Obviously this will involve some delay to the trial, and I'm anxious to keep it to a minimum. How long will you need?'.

'My Lord, I see no reason why we would need any longer than

tomorrow,' he replied. 'May I invite your Lordship to release the jury until Wednesday morning? We will do our best to be ready by then, but if we can't – if my learned friend wishes to make further inquiries, for example - we will let the court know.'

'Yes, very well,' Andrew Pilkington replied. 'It's disappointing that we have to keep the jury waiting like this, but if there is no way to avoid it, then that's what we must do. Usher, please tell the jury that they are free to go, and they should be back for ten thirty on Wednesday morning. Miss Lester, don't discuss your evidence with anyone, and don't forget that you may not speak to any of your legal advisers while you are giving evidence. Do you understand?'

'Yes, my Lord.'

'Very well. I will rise for the day.'

When the judge had risen, Clive and Ben gathered up their papers to leave court. Anthony Norris passed in front of them.

'What was all that about, Anthony?' Ben asked.

'What was all what about?'

'Making an agreement with me and then ambushing me in front of the judge and the jury? Is that really your idea of your professional duty?'

Norris smirked. 'All airs and graces, is it now, Ben, now that you're head of chambers?'

Ben stared at him. 'Is that what this is about?'

'It's about making sure the jury understand the prosecution case,' Norris insisted. 'But since you raise the matter, what do you expect me to think about what happened this morning?'

'It wasn't my decision,' Ben pointed out. 'It was a decision taken by all the silks in chambers, based on what we thought was best for chambers.'

'It was a *coup d'état*, plotted behind closed doors, in the absence of the next most senior member of chambers. I may go to the Bar Council about it.'

'Look, Anthony, I understand you may feel you've been overlooked, but everyone wanted a silk as head of chambers, and it was important that Aubrey should step down without delay.'

'Is that supposed to be an excuse for not consulting me? I am the next senior member of chambers after Aubrey, and I'm left in the dark like some bloody pupil, while some self-appointed group decides the future of chambers behind closed doors? It wouldn't have happened in Bernard Wesley's day, I can tell you that.'

'It wasn't anything I expected or wanted,' Ben replied. 'It should have been Kenneth, and would have been, but for his illness.'

'I'm senior to Kenneth,' Anthony insisted. 'Anyway, I'll save any further comments for the Bar Council. Suffice it to say that I'm no longer in the mood to cooperate with you.'

Ben shook his head. 'You'd allow what happened in chambers to interfere with your work on a case? You think that justifies you in wasting the court's time?'

'You shouldn't have gone behind my back,' Anthony said. 'I know all about your secret meetings. That's how you people took over the City. Don't think I don't know that. But I'm not having it in my chambers.'

'Anthony…' Clive said quietly.

'"You people?"' Ben said. 'What do you mean by that?'

'What do you think I mean?'

'If you mean that you object to having a Jewish head of chambers, why don't you just come out and say so?'

Norris smirked again. 'I rather thought I had.'

The two men suddenly lunged at each other. Mercifully, Clive Overton stood between them. A Cambridge rugby blue in his younger days, he was still fast enough and strong enough to hold them apart before any blows could be exchanged. Mary approached quickly from the judge's bench, where she had been arranging his papers.

'Stop it, both of you,' she commanded imperiously. 'Now. What do you think you're doing? I will thank you to remember that you are at the Central Criminal Court, not in some cheap dockland bar. I will ask you kindly to leave court now, or I will have to inform the judge and see what he wants to do about it.'

Clive put an arm around Ben and pulled him away, pushing

Norris in the opposite direction at the same time.

'Time to go, Ben,' he said. 'Come on.'

'You haven't heard the last of this,' Norris snarled on his way out of court.

'If that's how you feel, Anthony,' Ben replied, 'perhaps you might be more comfortable in some other set of chambers.'

Norris stopped briefly as if to turn back, but thought better of it, and walked away.

'Let him go, Ben,' Clive said.

# 57

Tuesday 21 February 1984

'A pint of Special, is it, Dougie?'

'Please, sir.'

'Let's get some crisps in as well, shall we? Salt and vinegar all right?'

'Yes, sir.'

It was against Baxter's instincts to use the same venue twice in such a short space of time. But Sean had suggested it, and he wanted Sean to feel as comfortable as possible. There were a few potential complications Baxter would have preferred to avoid. The Lamb had a sizeable early-evening crowd on weeknights. He'd had to instruct his Special Branch officers to arrive early to make sure of a table – not that they seemed to object to that particular tweak to the schedule – and Baxter had resigned himself to a cold, uncomfortable couple of hours perched on a stool, up against the window ledge at the front of the bar, by the left-hand door. Continual observation was not guaranteed under these conditions, and there was significant background noise that might contaminate the recording if the microphone happened to get covered. But he had less safety concerns for Sean than for Imogen, and he was not planning to detain Mellor this evening, regardless of what was said. A lengthy conference with Webb and Raymond had convinced him that Mellor might be their only link to Franco, and the preferred plan was to keep him under surveillance, in the hope that any anxiety Sean induced in him might lead him to break cover. Raymond had assembled a team of watchers, which was in place and ready to go as soon as Mellor left the Lamb. He had also discreetly arranged for a rotation of armed officers to keep an eye on Julia's house around the clock.

Mellor brought the drinks and crisps over to the table.

'Haven't seen you in a while, Dougie. What have you been up to? Still supporting Chelsea, are you? I still can't tempt you up to White Hart Lane to watch a proper team?'

'Afraid not, sir, no. We're playing well at the moment. I reckon we'll get promoted and we'll be playing your lot next season. No, I haven't been around much lately. I've been assigned to DCI French for the last couple of months. We've been up and down to Oxford, chasing a couple of gangs who've been peddling meth to the students.'

Mellor nodded and tore open a packet of crisps, which he placed between then on the table. 'Yeah, I was reading about that. French is doing all right, is he? You can tell me, Dougie – I know, and I know you know, he's had a few problems of his own.'

'He seems fine now, sir, and he's been on top of the cases. We've nicked four of the ringleaders and six or seven of their little helpers, and the trade's been significantly reduced, so we're well pleased with it. Mind you, you wouldn't believe the problems we've had with one or two of the colleges – not wanting to let us in, in case the parents find out what their kids have been up to, and start panicking. Sometimes you think they don't care if their students get hooked on meth, as long as it doesn't cause bad publicity for the college. It makes you wonder.'

'Yeah, well, it's always like that with our Squad, isn't it? It's all right when Mr Plod the Policeman comes round in his uniform to make sure they're looking both ways when they cross the road, but anything to do with real crime, they don't want to know, do they? Sort it out, but don't tell us all the murky details. Well, anyway...'

They both drank and took a handful of crisps.

'Well, French is lucky to have you, and you did do that one job for me, Dougie, which I appreciate.'

'Oh, you mean the Hampstead job, sir? Lester? That's in trial now, isn't it?'

'Yeah, the girl's giving evidence now. I don't know how it's going to go – you never do with these bloody juries these days, do you? But at least we've got the lad bang to rights. He pleaded, and with any luck he'll go down for a decent stretch.'

Sean took a deep breath. 'Actually sir, that's what I wanted to talk to you about.'

'Oh yeah?'

'Yeah… Let me get another round in for us. Same again?'

'Don't mind if I do, Dougie, and some more of those crisps would go down a treat too.'

'The thing is, sir,' Sean said, depositing the pints on the table and prising the packets of crisps loose from under his arms, 'she came to see me – the girl, Imogen.'

The glass in Mellor's hand froze in the air on its way to his mouth.

'What do you mean, she came to see you? When was this? You mean, since the trial started?'

'A couple of days ago, sir. She left a message for me at the nick saying she wanted to see me urgently.'

'Why didn't you come straight to me?'

'Well, it's your case, sir, and I didn't want to put the trial at risk by getting you involved if she was just going to say something stupid. You know what judges can be like if they think anything's going on behind the scenes. So I thought it was better to see her myself and report to you afterwards.'

'All right. Go on.'

Sean took a long drink.

'I think we may have a problem, sir.'

# 58

'What do you mean, a problem? What kind of problem?'

'Well, you remember she'd been to Yugoslavia for a few days just before you raided the house and nicked them?'

'I couldn't forget it if I wanted to, could I? I'm hearing about it every day in court. Her brief's saying there are questions of the "national interest" involved, and he's trying to stop us asking her about it. God only knows what he's up to. Our brief doesn't seem to know what he's on about anymore than I do. Anyway, what about it?'

'She told me she went over there to ask the local police what they were doing to find out who killed her parents. She was with that solicitor she works for, what's her name, Cathermole.'

Mellor nodded. 'Yeah. She told us that when we nicked her. It would have been nice if our friend had tipped us off about it before we went in, but that's the way it goes. You can't have everything. So what? I'd be surprised if the local coppers gave her much information.'

Sean leaned across the table and lowered his voice.

'She got quite a bit of information from somebody, sir,' he said confidentially. 'She says she knows it was Dragan who ordered the hit on her parents, and she knows that her and her brother getting nicked for the drugs was to show her father that Dragan was serious about it, just in case they didn't manage to take him out. And she knows that I'm Sean.'

Mellor stared at him for a second or two, but then shrugged.

'Whatever she thinks she knows, she can't prove a word of it. Why is that a problem for us?'

'I don't think we should underestimate her, sir. She's pretty determined. I don't know whether she saw Dragan himself or one of his people, but whoever she saw, she confronted them and told them they'd made a big mistake taking her dad out, and now they needed to either do the same to her, or make a deal with her. That takes a bit of nerve.'

Mellor laughed out loud. 'Leave it out, Dougie. How would she ever get that close to Dragan? And even if she did, if she came on to him like that, she'd turn into one of those tourists who disappear without trace every year while on holiday abroad, wouldn't she? Never heard from again until a wolf digs up their remains in the woods years later. He wouldn't think twice about it – you know that. No, she's winding you up, my old son.'

They both took a drink.

'I don't think so in this case, sir. Her dad was a diplomat and apparently the diplomatic service or whoever are very upset about it, and they've been putting Dragan under a lot of pressure. They've got Interpol involved, they're asking a lot of questions, and he's getting worried.'

Mellor shook his head. 'Interpol's a joke. Dragan's not going to lose any sleep over them. What he has to worry about is his own people doing him down, not Interpol. There are a lot of men who would like to have the kind of empire he's built up, and they'll be lining up three deep to take it over if he shows any sign of weakness. That's what keeps Dragan up at night, I guarantee it.'

'That's as may be, sir. But there's something else. She knew that her and her brother getting nicked was only in case they didn't get her dad. When they got him, it was supposed to have been called off. I'd got the brother eating out of my hand by then – he'd already done a couple of innkeeper jobs for me – so it was easy enough to set them both up. But we weren't supposed to go through with it. Dragan had given orders to call it off, but somebody over here wasn't listening. It got screwed up at our end, and now Dragan thinks the authorities are coming after him even harder, and he's blaming us for it.'

Mellor seemed poised to reply, but instead sat back in his chair nursing his pint and chewing on a crisp.

'Imogen says he offered her a deal,' Sean said.

'What kind of deal? She's on trial, for God's sake. If she goes down, the only deal she's going to be interested in is keeping her sentence as short as she can.'

'She says Dragan is seriously pissed off about his orders not being followed, and he thinks he owes her something. He's made her one of his innkeepers, and he's asked her to take a name. So she has: Maggie, after her mother, she says. She wants to cut me in on it, sir, to work with her. She thinks she's going to get off at the Old Bailey, so we can start more or less straight away. I said I'd think about it.'

Mellor laughed incredulously. 'Little Miss Previous Exemplary Character Cambridge Grad, butter won't melt in her mouth, and she wants to be an innkeeper? I must be getting old. Maybe it's time I called it a day. What is the world coming to, Dougie?'

'It's straight up, sir. Think about it for a minute. Why would she take the risk of meeting me while she's on trial for drugs and tell me a story like that if it wasn't true?'

Mellor thought for some time. 'Tommy and I tried it on with her when we interviewed her at Hampstead nick, didn't we? We offered her a walk on the charges, her and her brother both, in return for a good drink – which was a good offer considering we'd got her verballed up enough to convict Mother Teresa. We even offered to make sure the odd bit of merchandise came her way in the future if she needed it. She didn't want to know, did she? Little Miss Prim and Proper. And she wasn't calling herself Maggie then, I assure you.'

Sean leaned forward again.

'She wouldn't, sir, would she? She thinks you're the one who got her nicked after Dragan had told you to pull the plug. She thinks you're in a lot of trouble, sir, that you're history and she's the changing of the guard, as you might say. She also says you're "Wally", by the way. Where would she have got that from if it wasn't someone close to Dragan?'

'She thinks I'm "Wally", or just "a wally?" If she means "a wally" she's probably right.'

They laughed.

'She told you that?' Mellor asked, after a pause.

Sean nodded. 'Are you, sir? I know I'm not supposed to ask, but now...'

'Yes, I am. But I didn't get any message about calling it off, did I? Look, the way it works is that everything from Dragan comes down to us directly from Franco – and don't ask me about him because I'm not going to tell you. And I swear to you, Franco didn't say a bloody word. I'm not going to do something like that if Dragan's called it off, am I? Give me some credit.'

Sean nodded. 'That's what I would have assumed, sir. But that's the impression somebody's given him.' He paused. 'So, what do you want me to do?'

Mellor drained his pint. 'Nothing for now. If she asks to see you again, you let me know, and I'll take care of it. Understood?'

'Yes, sir.'

'Good lad. Right, well thanks for the drink and for letting me know.' He got to his feet. 'I must have a word with DCI French. He can't have you all to himself in Oxford forever. I've got some things for you to do down here.' They shook hands 'Mind how you go, won't you?'

'Nicely done, Sean,' Baxter said as DS Isherwood jostled his way past him through the throng of drinkers on his way out of the Lamb.

Sean held out his hand. 'That will be thirty pieces of silver, your Grace.'

# 59

'My Lord,' Anthony Norris said, 'I'm grateful for the time your Lordship has allowed to us to consider our position.'

'A day longer than anticipated,' Andrew Pilkington observed.

'Yes, my Lord. The officer I needed to speak to was not available until yesterday because of a professional assignment.'

'I am happy to confirm that, my Lord,' Ben added. 'We had to wait for him to return from a trip somewhere in Europe.'

'The time has not been wasted,' Norris continued. 'I was able to consult with the officer concerned. As a result of what I was told, I now accept that the Sarajevo interview is, in fact, covered by Crown privilege. So I find myself in the difficult position of having to defend the Crown's wider interests, in addition to prosecuting this case.'

Andrew Pilkington nodded,

'Which leaves us where, exactly, Mr Norris?'

'It leaves us in this position, my Lord: that I cannot compel Miss Lester to provide any details of the interview between Miss Cathermole and her client in Sarajevo. I think I could have made an argument against legal professional privilege, both because a third party was present and because Miss Cathermole's client has died since the interview. But there is nothing I can do about the Crown Privilege, and in those circumstances I do not propose to pursue my proposed line of inquiry about Sarajevo any further.'

Ben turned behind and shared a surreptitious grin with Clive and Barratt.

'And as I have already put my case to Miss Lester as clearly as I can, I do not propose to continue my cross-examination.'

Andrew Pilkington was shaking his head. 'Perhaps Miss Lester should have read to us from *Alice though the Looking Glass*, Mr Norris,' he suggested, 'rather than *A Tale of Two Cities*. Anyway, there it is. If nobody has any further objections, perhaps we could actually make some progress with the trial. Mr Schroeder, do you want to re-examine Miss Lester?'

'No, my Lord.'

'Have you any witnesses to call?'

'Yes, my Lord,' Ben said. 'I had intended to call Julia Cathermole to deal with the events in Sarajevo, but in view of the prosecution's change of heart on Crown privilege I don't think that will be necessary. I have five character witnesses, who won't take very long.' Ben took a deep breath. 'I then propose, my Lord, to have Detective Chief Superintendent Mellor recalled, so that I can put some further questions to him.'

Norris stood immediately. 'Again, my Lord, my learned friend did not tell me about this before we came into court, and I object to it. My learned friend has already subjected Chief Superintendent Mellor to a long and extremely hostile cross-examination, in the course of which he has accused him of very serious misconduct. He should not be allowed a second bite of the cherry.'

'I'm not asking for a second bite of anything,' Ben replied. 'I have no intention of repeating myself. But further facts have been brought to my attention, facts I was unaware of when I cross-examined. Mr Mellor is intimately involved with these facts, they are important, and I thought it only right to give him the chance to deal with them.'

'When can Superintendent Mellor be here?' the judge asked Norris.

'I'm surprised he isn't here already,' Norris replied. 'He's usually very punctual and he's been in court almost the whole time during the trial. I'm sure he can be brought within a short time.'

'Have him here not later than twelve o'clock, please.'

'Do I take it that your Lordship is against me on my objection?'

'That is correct, Mr Norris. I will rise for a short time to allow the jury to be brought down and for Mr Schroeder to organise his character evidence. Superintendent Mellor will be recalled as soon as we have finished with the character witnesses. Will ten minutes be enough, Mr Schroeder?'

'Would your Lordship say fifteen? I haven't been able to speak with Miss Lester since she began her evidence three days ago, and I would appreciate the chance to have a quick word with her.'

'I will rise for half an hour,' Andrew said. 'We can all have a quick cup of coffee before we start, can't we? But then we need to make some progress.'

'Much obliged, my Lord,' Ben and Norris replied in unison.

# 60

'My Lord,' Ben began, 'I've asked for the jury to retire and for your Lordship to sit in chambers, so that I can mention certain matters before I recall Superintendent Mellor.'

'Yes, Mr Schroeder.'

'I'm going to be quite candid with your Lordship and with my learned friend about what I intend to do. I am in a position to prove that a colleague of Superintendent Mellor in the Drug Squad, whom for the time being I shall call Detective Sergeant X, had a conversation with the Superintendent on Tuesday evening. In the course of that conversation, Superintendent Mellor admitted to Detective Sergeant X: firstly, that the drugs found at Miss Lester's home during the raid on 4 December last year were brought there as part of a deliberate plot to incriminate her; and secondly, that he and DI Beech had "verballed" Imogen Lester.'

Norris stood at once. His irritation was obvious.

'My Lord, I've been given no notice of any of this. I am taken completely by surprise. It's outrageous...'

'That's why I'm addressing your Lordship now,' Ben interrupted smoothly, 'so that both your Lordship and my learned friend are fully aware of the circumstances. I'm sorry there hasn't been time to deal with it before, but this has all happened within the last forty-eight hours, and there really hasn't been any opportunity. I do, however, have copies for your Lordship and my learned friend of a statement made by Detective Sergeant X – if the usher would be so kind...

'In essence, Superintendent Mellor accepts that the drugs found in Miss Lester's house during the raid were placed there deliberately to incriminate her; and that this was a plan devised by the drug dealer Dragan to discourage Miss Lester's father from investigating him, and carried out by Dragan's agents in this country. Dragan's instructions were that the attempt to frame Miss Lester was only to go ahead if he failed in his primary goal of having Mr Lester killed. As we all know, tragically, Dragan succeeded in his primary goal. But the plan to incriminate Miss Lester went ahead anyway, because of an error on the part of someone working for Dragan in this country. You will see from the statement that Superintendent Mellor ascribes that error to a particular person – I will not mention the name because I'm conscious of the prosecution's concerns about Crown privilege, but you will see it in the statement.

'Detective Sergeant X was "Sean", the man who recruited Damian Lester in his local pub and induced him to store drugs at the house in Willow Road just before the raid on 4 December, and so he was an integral part of the plan. Superintendent Mellor accepts that he was known by the name of "Wally" which, like "Sean", was a code name. He was fully aware of the plan, and indeed played a major role in carrying it out.

'Finally, you will see that Superintendent Mellor makes the clearest possible admission of having "verballed" Miss Lester. As he so eloquently puts it, they had, "got her verballed up enough to convict Mother Teresa."'

'My Lord, the first application is that I should be allowed to ask the Superintendent to reveal to the jury the identity of Detective Sergeant X.'

'The identity of police informants is generally protected from disclosure in court, Mr Schroeder,' Andrew Pilkington said. 'With your considerable experience of these cases, I'm sure you're aware of that.'

'My Lord, that rule does not apply if withholding the identity would make it impossible for a defendant to receive a fair trial. In this case, the evidence will be that there was a conspiracy to have Imogen Lester arrested for, and if possible convicted of, serious drugs offences. The evidence will be that this conspiracy was carried out by members of the Drug Squad acting together, and it is crucial that the jury should know who they were and what they did. Detective Sergeant X is a key player.'

Andrew Pilkington nodded. 'Mr Norris?'

'My Lord. I've been looking at the statement my learned friend has given us, and I'm wondering how it happens that this very convenient meeting took place on Tuesday, two days ago, in the middle of this trial, and how it happens that we so conveniently have such a clear record of it?'

'I don't know,' Ben replied, 'but I shall be calling Detective Sergeant X and my learned friend will be free to ask him.'

'In particular, I would want to know if any recording was involved,' Norris continued, 'because if so, and if Mr Mellor did not know about it, it would be illegal and any such tape would be inadmissible.'

'I don't know,' Ben replied. 'The meeting had nothing to do with Miss Lester's defence team. We were advised of it, and provided with this statement, only after the event. I assume that the meeting was arranged either by the police or the security services. In either case, my learned friend is far better placed to get the information he wants than I am.'

'In the circumstances,' Andrew Pilkington said, 'I will allow evidence to be given of Detective Sergeant X's identity. I agree with Mr Schroeder that it may well be impossible for Miss Lester to have a fair trial otherwise. I note that the informant himself seems to have no objection to his name becoming known. He has signed a witness statement, and apparently, he is prepared to give evidence. No harm can come of it as far as I can see, but in deference to the prosecution's concerns about Crown privilege, the evidence of both Superintendent Mellor and Detective Sergeant X will be given in chambers.'

'If I may, my Lord,' Ben said, 'I would also suggest that your

Lordship will have to make clear to both witnesses that they have the right to decline to answer any question they believe may incriminate them; and that your Lordship should allow them the opportunity to seek legal advice before giving evidence.'

# 61

'Mr Schroeder, would you prefer to treat Superintendent Mellor as still being under oath, or would you like him to be sworn again?'

'My Lord, I would ask that he be sworn again.'

Mary approached the witness box with the New Testament, which she handed to the witness. With a dark look in Ben's direction, he took it in his right hand and read from the card Mary held up for him.

'"I swear by Almighty God that the evidence I shall give shall be the truth, the whole truth, and nothing but the truth."'

'Chief Superintendent Mellor,' Andrew Pilkington said, 'will you please confirm for me that earlier today, when the jury were not in court, I advised you of your right to decline to answer any question if you think the answer to that question may incriminate you with respect to a criminal offence?'

'Yes, my Lord.'

'Do you understand that right?'

'Yes, my Lord.'

'Have you had the opportunity to consult a solicitor before being recalled to give further evidence?'

'Yes, my Lord.'

'Very well. Thank you. Mr Schroeder?'

'Chief Superintendent Mellor, you told the jury when you gave evidence previously that the raid on number 102 Willow Road on 4 December last year was based on information received, to the effect that drugs were being stored at the property: is that right?'

'That's correct.'

'Who was the source of that information?'

'Detective Sergeant Doug Isherwood.'

'Is DS Isherwood an officer assigned to the Drug Squad under your command?'

'He sometimes works under my command, and sometimes under the command of other officers.'

'In relation to this case, was he working under your command?'

'Yes, he was. DS Isherwood was assigned to work undercover by visiting a public house in Hampstead, in which we had reason to believe trafficking in illegal drugs was occurring.'

'Assigned by you?'

'Yes.'

'And in due course did DS Isherwood report to you that he had made the acquaintance of Damian Lester, the defendant's brother, and that Damian was prepared to allow drugs to be stored at his family home in return for money?'

'Yes, he did.'

'And were the drugs found at the house at 102 Willow Road during the raid on 4 December taken there by Damian for storage, in return for a payment of £200?'

'Yes.'

'Who handed those drugs over to Damian and paid him his £200?'

'DS Isherwood.'

'Is DS Isherwood also known as "Sean?"'

'That was the name DS Isherwood used when working undercover.'

Ben stole a glance at the jury box, and saw that the jurors were staring at Mellor as if totally absorbed in his evidence, some leaning forward in their chairs.

'Where did the drugs come from – the drugs found during the raid? Who supplied them?'

Mellor focused a hard stare high up on the wall of the courtroom opposite the witness box.

'I decline to answer on the ground that it may incriminate me.'

The jury gave an audible collective gasp.

'Did they come from a drug dealer known as Dragan, or someone acting on his behalf?'

'I decline to answer on the ground that it may incriminate me.'

'Is it within your knowledge that agents working for Dragan do so using code names?'

'I decline to answer on the ground that it may incriminate me.'

'Was "Sean" a code name used by DS Isherwood because he was working for Dragan?'

'You'd have to ask DS Isherwood.'

'Have you ever heard of someone working under the code name "Wally?"'

'I decline to answer on the ground that it may incriminate me.'

'Is "Wally" your code name, Chief Superintendent Mellor?"

'I decline to answer on the ground that it may incriminate me.'

'Are you aware that Imogen's parents, Michael and Margaret Lester, were murdered in Sarajevo in October of last year?'

'I am aware of that. I believe the case remains unsolved.'

'Are you aware that Dragan is believed to have instigated those murders because Michael Lester was investigating his drug activities?'

'I'm aware that has been alleged. I'm not aware of what evidence the Sarajevo police may have to back that theory up, if any.'

'So, it's just a theory, Superintendent, is it?'

'As far as I know, yes.'

'Bur you do know, do you not, that Dragan made an alternative plan to hurt Michael Lester in the event that the attempt on his life failed?'

'What plan would that be?'

'The plan to plant drugs in the Lester family home at 102 Willow Road and attempt to incriminate Imogen Lester on the charge she's now facing?'

'She's saying we fitted her up, sir, is she, as well as verballing her?'

'Are you saying under oath, Superintendent – and I will remind you that you are under oath – that you are not aware that Dragan had made such a plan?'

'I decline to answer on the ground that it may incriminate me.'

'You are aware, though, are you not, that Imogen travelled to Yugoslavia to try to find out what was going on with the investigation into her parents' death, and that she returned to London on the evening of 3 December, the evening before the raid?'

'Yes.'

Ben paused.

'Superintendent Mellor, did you have a meeting with DS Isherwood on Tuesday evening of this week at the Lamb public house in Lamb's Conduit Street, in Bloomsbury?'

# 62

Mellor seemed to stagger for a moment before leaning against the back wall of the witness box to support himself, his hands on the ledge in front of him.

'That was a private meeting,' he protested. 'It wasn't even a meeting. We were just two colleagues getting together for a couple of pints after work.'

'A couple of pints after work, Superintendent?'

'Yes. What's wrong with that?'

'Didn't DS Isherwood tell you that he needed to talk to you urgently?'

'I don't know about urgently. He did say he wanted to see me, yes. But that happens all the time in the Squad. Things come up, and you have a chat over a pint or two to sort them out.'

'When you met for your pint or two after work, did DS Isherwood tell you what it was he wanted to talk about?'

Mellor turned to the bench.

'Is he allowed to ask this, sir? This was a private get-together between two colleagues. Is he saying it was recorded or something?'

'Why would you ask that, Superintendent?' Andrew Pilkington asked.

'Well, if it was recorded, that would be illegal wouldn't it?'

'Are you going to produce a recording, Mr Schroeder?' the judge asked.

'No, my Lord.'

'Well, there we are, then. Answer the questions put to you, please, Superintendent.'

'What was the question?'

'I asked you whether DS Isherwood told you what he wanted to see you about.'

Mellor drew himself up to his full height defiantly.

'Yes, he did. He told me that the defendant, Miss Lester, had made an appointment to see him – while she was on trial in this court – and they had had a discussion between the two of them.'

'Yes,' Ben said calmly, noting a few raised eyebrows in the jury box. 'I'm not going to ask you what was said between Miss Lester and DS Isherwood, because, of course, you weren't present. But over your couple of pints in the Lamb, did you and DS Isherwood talk about a plan made by Dragan to incriminate Miss Lester if he was unable to kill her father?'

'I decline to answer on the ground that it may incriminate me.'

'DS Isherwood asked you whether "Wally" is your code name, didn't he?'

'I decline to answer on the ground that it may incriminate me.'

'And you told him it was, didn't you?'

'I decline to answer on the ground that it may incriminate me.'

'And that's true, isn't it, Superintendent? You are "Wally" aren't you?'

'I decline to answer on the ground that it may incriminate me.'

'And then you said this, didn't you? "But I didn't get any message about calling it off, did I? Look, the way it works is that everything from Dragan comes down to us directly from Franco – and don't ask me about him because I'm not going to tell you. And I swear to you, Franco didn't say a bloody word. I'm not going to do something like that if Dragan's called it off, am I? Give me some credit." Is that what you said, Superintendent?'

'I decline to answer on the ground that it may incriminate me.'

'When you said, "I didn't get any message about calling it off", was that referring to the attempt to incriminate Imogen using the drugs given to her brother by DS Isherwood, working as "Sean?"'

'I decline to answer on the ground that it may incriminate me.'

'Who is "Franco", Chief Superintendent?'

'I decline to answer on the ground that it may incriminate me.'

'Why does everything from Dragan "come down from Franco?" What does that mean?'

'I decline to answer on the ground that it may incriminate me.' He again turned to the bench. 'This is ridiculous. He's verballing me. Where's he got all this from if there's no tape?'

The jury sniggered.

'Verballing the verballer?' Ben said. 'That would be a new twist, wouldn't it?'

He glanced over towards Norris, expecting some kind of riposte, but his opponent showed no interest whatsoever in intervening to protect the witness.

'Let's avoid comments, shall we, Mr Schroeder,' Andrew Pilkington suggested.

'Yes, my Lord. "I swear to you, Franco didn't say a bloody word. I'm not going to do something like that if Dragan's called it off, am I? Give me some credit." Did you say that?'

'I decline to answer on the ground that it may incriminate me.'

'What was that referring to? Was that referring to the plan to incriminate Imogen Lester?'

'I decline to answer on the ground that it may incriminate me.'

'And finally, Superintendent,' Ben asked, 'did you say this to DS Isherwood: "Tommy and I tried it on with her when we interviewed her at Hampstead nick, didn't we? We offered her a walk on the charges, her and her brother both, in return for a good drink – which was a good offer considering we'd got her verballed up enough to convict Mother Teresa. We even offered to make sure the odd bit of merchandise came her way in the future if she needed it. She didn't want to know, did she?"'

There was another gasp from the jury box.

'I decline to answer on the ground that it may incriminate me.'

'Is "Tommy" how you refer to DI Beech?'

'Yes. Tom, Tommy is his name – well, Thomas…'

'What did you mean when you said you "tried it on with Imogen at Hampstead nick?"'

'I decline to answer on the ground that it may incriminate me.'

'You offered her and Damian "a walk" on both charges. Does that mean you were offering to ensure that they were not prosecuted, that the charges were dropped?'

'I decline to answer on the ground that it may incriminate me.'

'You offered them a walk "in return for a good drink." The jury has heard that one before. A good drink means a substantial bribe, doesn't it?'

'That's a phrase used by criminals, yes.'

'Yes. And you thought that was a good offer because you'd got Miss Lester "verballed up enough to convict Mother Teresa." Would you explain that to the jury, please, Superintendent?'

'I decline to answer on the ground that it may incriminate me.'

'Chief Superintendent, when you gave evidence to My Lord and the jury for the first time, why did you tell them that you had no idea who Sean was?'

There was no reply.

'I have nothing further, my Lord,' Ben said, resuming his seat.

'Mr Norris?'

'No, thank you, my Lord.'

'You may step down, Detective Chief Superintendent,' Andrew Pilkington said. 'I think that's enough for today, members of the jury. Ten thirty tomorrow morning, please.' After they had left court, he added. 'I've sent the jury home early because I imagine both sides would like to reflect on where the case stands. It would be helpful to me if we could meet at ten o'clock so that you can indicate to me where we go from here, and when we can expect the jury to retire.'

'Yes, my Lord,' Ben replied.

Andrew made as if to rise, but then resumed his seat.

'Is anyone going to ask me to send a transcript of this afternoon's evidence to the Director of Public Prosecutions?'

Ben and Norris exchanged brief glances.

'My Lord, may we think about that overnight?' Ben asked. 'There may well have been discussions about Mr Mellor's position – and about DS Isherwood's – elsewhere, to which we are not privy. If so, it may be just as well for your Lordship to be aware of them before sending anything to the Director.'

# 63

Webb and Raymond parked outside the building and hurried through the cold driving rain to the entrance, tucked a few feet away behind the miniscule fenced-in grassy border that passed for a front garden. The building was called Kipling Mansions. Situated in Hungerford Road in Camden Town, it was an eminently respectable Victorian edifice containing four floors of spacious flats, recently renovated with all mod cons. Like other similar buildings it was popular with the new class of affluent young City workers with the means and the inclination to prefer the faster-paced lifestyle of inner London to the humdrum of the suburbs. A uniformed constable, who looked as if he was in danger of freezing to death, was standing by the door, the collar of his raincoat pulled up tightly around his neck, his hands encased in thick black gloves. They flashed their warrant cards in his direction.

'Morning, sir,' he said, through chattering teeth. 'Flat sixteen, top floor.'

'There's no reason to stand out here, constable,' Webb said. 'Wait inside in the corridor. Just make sure you leave the door ajar.'

'The DS told me I had to wait here, sir,' the constable replied dutifully.

'And I'm telling you not to be so bloody silly. You're no use to anyone frozen. Get yourself inside in the warm.'

'Right. I will. Thank you, sir.'

They made their way up the flights of broad white stone steps.

'Why these things always have to happen at this time of the morning, I'll never know,' Webb complained as they arrived at the landing for the fourth floor.

'They say it's the most difficult time, don't they, if you're having problems?' Raymond replied.

'That's no reason to deprive the rest of us of our beauty sleep, is it?'

The door to number sixteen was open. They knocked and entered. Two younger plainclothes officers stood together talking, just inside the door. They looked up as the visitors entered.

'DCI Webb?'

'Yes.'

'Good morning, sir. DS Henderson, from Camden nick. This is DC Goodwin.'

'This is DCI Phil Raymond,' Webb said, as they all shook hands briefly. 'So, what have you got?'

'This way, sir.'

Henderson led the way into a bedroom. A man's lifeless body was lying, face up, on the bed, the head turned to the left, the face contorted, evidence of vomit on the lips and cheek and on the sheet on which he was lying. An empty pill bottle and the remains of a quart of whisky stood on the bedside table to the man's left.

'His girlfriend found him, round about three, four o'clock – she thinks; she's very upset, and she's a bit vague on time at the moment,' Henderson said. 'She's in the kitchen, name of Lucy Squires. We'll know more once Harold can give us an estimated time of death.' He pointed to the forensic medical examiner kneeling by the top of the bed, who briefly raised a surgically gloved hand in greeting, without interrupting his examination of the pillow on which the man's head rested. 'We found his warrant card lying by his body, sir. That's how we knew he was one of ours.'

'Where, by his body?' Webb asked.

'On the pillow, to the right of his head, about three inches from the ear,' Harold replied without looking up.

Henderson walked over to a desk against the wall opposite the bed. 'The reason I called you, sir, is that we found a piece of paper with your name on it.' He showed it to them. 'As you can see, there's just the name, no number, but I asked my Chief Super if he could run one down for me – I hope you don't mind.'

'Not at all,' Webb replied.

'There's another name, too – Baxter – again with no number. Does that mean anything to you, sir?'

Webb and Raymond exchanged quick, furtive glances.

'Common enough name,' Webb observed. 'Any suspicious circumstances?'

'Nothing on the body that I can see,' Harold called back to them, 'nothing to indicate a struggle. I can't confirm that until I get him on the table, of course, but nothing obvious.'

'There was no sign of a forced entry or disturbance, sir,' DC Goodwin added.

'Did he leave a note?' Raymond asked.

'No, sir,' Henderson replied. 'But he did leave something else – it's a bit weird.' He picked up an evidence bag from the far end of the desk. 'At least, I've never seen anything like it before.'

'What is it?'

'These were lying on top of his body, sir. We did photograph them before we removed them and bagged them. They're fifty pence coins. Thirty of them, exactly.'

# 64

'Were they just lying there randomly,' Webb asked, 'or were they arranged in a pattern of any kind?'

Henderson looked at Goodwin. 'They were just lying on him,' he replied, 'I think, weren't they, Steve? I didn't spot a pattern, but I suppose I didn't really look for one. We can check once the pictures are developed.'

'Some of them had fallen off the body, sir,' Goodwin said. 'They were just lying by his side. Do you think they're significant?'

'What do you think?' Webb asked.

Goodwin shrugged. 'We thought he might have been playing the slot machines somewhere. You know, you need a lot of coins for that, don't you? Perhaps he had a gambling habit, and he was down to his last fifteen quid. That might explain why he... you know, if he had nowhere to turn to...'

Harold looked up and gave Webb a knowing smile, shaking his head.

'You should have paid more attention in Sunday school, son,' Webb observed, 'shouldn't he, Harold? I take it you'll be printing all the coins – together with the whisky bottle and the pill bottle, this piece of paper with the names on it, his warrant card, and anything else you can find?'

'We will,' Harold said. 'Don't worry about it. I'd recommend printing the bedposts and the bedding too. I'm sure we'll find the girlfriend's prints everywhere, but if any others come up it might be useful.'

'Quite right,' Webb said.

They heard the sound of the front door opening, someone entering the flat. Goodwin walked quickly back into the hallway. There was some conversation, not loud enough to allow those in the bedroom to hear what was being said. Goodwin returned moments later with a well-built man wearing a dark overcoat with a bright green scarf and gloves.

'This is Detective Chief Superintendent Mellor, sir. He's a colleague of DS Isherwood – was a colleague of DS Isherwood – in the Drug Squad. DCIs Webb and Raymond.'

'Yes, I know,' Mellor replied. 'How's it going, Johnny? Phil, isn't it?' Raymond nodded.

'Can't grumble, Alf,' Webb replied. 'You?'

'Fair to middling.'

'Right. Well, let's talk through there, shall we, and let them get on with it in here?'

They walked back into the hall.

'What are you doing here, Alf?' Webb asked.

'We worked together,' Mellor replied. 'We were colleagues, Dougie and me.'

'I know that. What I'm asking is: what are you doing here now?'

'He was supposed to be working a job with Tommy Beech this morning,' Mellor replied, 'but he didn't show and he wasn't answering the phone. Tommy was busy, so he asked me to come round and check on him. I had nothing on except the Old Bailey today, and I've finished with my evidence, so that can wait. I knew Dougie hadn't been feeling too well. I thought he might have had a few pints and had trouble getting up, or something. But this... I suppose I'll have to notify his next of kin.'

'His girlfriend's here,' Raymond said. 'I daresay these officers will take care of it.'

'What do they think?' Mellor asked. 'Has he topped himself, or is there more to it?'

'Why would there be more to it?' Webb asked.

Mellor shrugged. 'I don't know. But he had things going on,

didn't he? I had to tell the Old Bailey a few things about him yesterday, getting himself involved with the wrong people, you know...'

'So we've been hearing,' Raymond said.

'There's always a lot of money changing hands in drugs cases, especially with people like the lads Dougie was involved with, and you can't afford to cross them. I worried about him, but I never thought...'

'There's no indication that it was anything other than suicide,' Webb said, 'but it's early days yet, isn't it? So we'll have to see. What concerns me at the moment is why you would turn up here, unannounced, within a couple of hours of Doug Isherwood dying.'

'I told you. Tommy Beech asked me to check up on him.'

'Was it Tommy Beech who asked you,' Webb asked, 'or Franco?'

'Who? Oh, for God's sake, Johnny, don't you start. I had enough of that yesterday at the Bailey, with that bloody defence brief, Schroeder, trying to accuse me of playing away from home. He was trying to bloody verbal me, saying I'd told Dougie I was working with some foreign dealer – Dragan or somebody.'

'Yes,' Webb replied, 'we were hearing all about that last night.'

'What we heard,' Raymond said, 'is that you and DS Isherwood were both working for Dragan, and you were refusing to answer questions in court because you thought it might incriminate you.'

'The court was sitting in bloody chambers,' Mellor protested. 'How the hell do you know what I said?'

'We've been asked to consult on the Crown privilege thing, Alf,' Webb replied, 'so we get to hear everything, including the fact that you're refusing to answer questions whenever anyone even mentions the name Dragan.'

'I had to, Johnny. My brief told me. He said I had to protect myself.'

'And now, of course,' Webb added, 'no one's ever going to know what you said to DS Isherwood, are they? Not from him, anyway. You can't get any better protection than that, can you?'

'What are you suggesting?' Mellor asked angrily.

'What made you come here at this exact time, Alf? Just a couple of hours after DS Isherwood died? It's quite a coincidence, isn't it?'

'I've already told you: Tommy asked me to check on Dougie. We were worried about him.'

'Or perhaps you knew he was supposed to be dead by now, and you wanted to check?' Raymond said. 'Or perhaps you did for him? You had every reason, didn't you?'

Mellor turned red and clenched his fists. 'What are you saying? You are well out of order, mate.'

'Is he?' Webb asked. 'You'd better hope the medical examiner doesn't come up with any reason to suspect foul play, Alf, because if he does I would have to agree with Phil – I would really have to fancy you for it.'

'Are you supposed to report back to anyone?' Raymond asked. 'Is somebody waiting to hear from you? And don't tell me Tommy Beech.'

'I'm not saying any more,' Mellor replied. 'You're as bad as that lot at the Bailey, Schroeder and the rest of them. I expect it from him – he's the Lester girl's brief, isn't he – but I don't appreciate it from my colleagues on the job. You are bang out of order, the two of you. I'm on my bike, I'm gone.'

'I don't think so, Alf,' Webb said quietly as Raymond placed himself between Mellor and the front door of the flat. 'I think we should have a chat, just the three of us. A colleague of ours on the Crown privilege side of things has a nice, quiet place available where we won't be disturbed.'

Mellor stared at him.

'Am I being nicked, Johnny? Is that what you're telling me?'

'No. I'm not nicking you – well, not unless I have to. You're not going to give us any trouble, are you, Alf? We don't have to put the cuffs on, do we?'

Mellor shook his head.

'All right, then. We have a car outside. Shall we go?'

Webb poked his head through into the bedroom.

'We're off, and we're taking Superintendent Mellor with us.

Let me know if you find anything interesting, won't you? By "interesting" I mean anything suspicious, anything, however small.'

'Of course, sir,' Henderson said.

'Leave it to me,' Harold added.

'Oh, and by the way, I'm going to borrow the constable you've got stationed on the door outside – assuming he can still move his arms and legs. I just need a bit of company until we get to where we're going. We'll keep him warm and look after him, and we'll make sure he gets home safe and well.'

'Right you are, sir,' Henderson said.

# 65

Imogen covered her face with her hands and sank into a chair.

'Oh, my God,' she said, 'was this because of me?' She made narrow gaps between her fingers to peer up towards Julia. 'It was, wasn't it? I lured him into a trap, and now he's killed himself. It's my fault.' She allowed her head to sink down on to the table.

They were in a conference room at the Old Bailey. It was nine thirty, half an hour before their day in court was due to begin. Julia walked around the table to stand behind Imogen and rested her hands gently on her shoulders.

'It's not your fault, Imogen. Nobody could possibly blame you for this.' She gave the shoulders a squeeze. 'Whatever trouble Isherwood was in, he got into all on his own. It was his choice to break the law and it was his choice to confront Mellor. He knew exactly what he was doing. It was his own betrayal that brought him to this – nothing to do with you.'

'Are the police satisfied that it was suicide?' Ben asked.

'Not a hundred per cent. They haven't found any evidence of foul play, but Webb and Raymond were pretty shocked when Mellor turned up right on cue – that was quite a coincidence, any way you look at it – so they haven't ruled it out. All the signs suggest suicide, but they're keeping an open mind for now.'

'Either way,' Clive said, 'it's a blow. We can't call him as a witness. We no longer have evidence of what Isherwood and Mellor discussed, what they were getting up to.'

'We have Isherwood's written statement,' Barratt pointed out.

'Hearsay,' Clive replied.

'Yes, but, hang on...' Ben said after a silence. 'Wait a minute. Isn't there an exception if the maker of the statement dies, and the statement would have been against his own personal interests? Where's *Archbold*?'

'I have it,' Barratt said. 'Give me a moment.'

'The exception doesn't apply to statements that expose him to criminal liability,' Clive replied.

'What about a statement against his financial interests?' Julia asked.

'That would do,' Ben said. 'Actually, I think that's what the rule was originally designed for.'

'Here it is in *Archbold*,' Barratt said. Ben and Clive stood behind him to look over his shoulder.

'Yes,' Ben said, 'against his financial interests works.'

'What about the financial loss of losing his job?' Julia asked. 'There's no way he could have continued as a police officer after this, is there? They were bound to sack him.'

Ben smiled. 'Good. I think we have a shot at it. I'll ask Andrew to admit the statement in evidence, and we'll see what he says.'

'Norris will complain that he can't cross-examine Isherwood,' Clive pointed out. 'It puts him at a huge disadvantage.'

'Which Andrew will explain to the jury and tell them to make allowances,' Ben replied, 'but if it's an exception to the hearsay rule, we're entitled to admit the statement and Norris just has to live with it. But let's not get too carried away – Andrew also has to direct the jury not to draw any conclusions from Mellor's exercise of his right not to incriminate himself, and he hasn't made any admissions of misconduct in court.'

Ben looked at his watch and picked up *Archbold*.

'Clive, if you will come with me, I want to talk to Norris before we start. I don't want him to whine about being taken by surprise again, so we'll tell him about the statement against interest exception and give him a few minutes to think about it before we go into court.' He turned to the others. 'We'll see you in court in a few minutes.'

'There's something else I want to ask Norris as well,' Ben said to Clive as they walked towards the entrance to the courtroom. 'But it's a long shot, and I didn't want to raise any false hopes in the conference room.'

'What's that?'

'Well, if Andrew Pilkington was still prosecuting and we had him on the other side in this case, I would expect him to be thinking about throwing his hand in. Even taking into account that he can't cross-examine Isherwood, we've done so much damage to his case, I can't see how it can recover. Can you? How can you ask a jury to convict based on Mellor and Beech? And that's what the case comes down to, isn't it? It's the kind of case where any fair-minded prosecutor must be thinking, perhaps it's time to call it a day.'

'If we had a fair-minded prosecutor, perhaps,' Clive agreed, 'but I'm afraid Anthony Norris is no Andrew Pilkington.'

'Very true,' Ben said.

'What about asking Andrew to stop it?'

Ben shook his head. 'There's a case to answer,' he replied. 'A judge can't stop a case just because he thinks it may be a weak one. No, it's the kind of case where you have to rely on your prosecutor to use some discretion, and in Norris's case, I'm afraid you're probably right.'

'Perhaps you could use your influence as his head of chambers,' Clive suggested with a grin.

# 66

Norris was leaning against a pillar just outside court, finishing a cigarette before making his entry.

'Morning, Anthony,' Ben said, approaching briskly. 'Can we have a quick word before we start?'

'Of course,' Norris replied, 'but if it's about Isherwood's statement, you needn't bother. I can save you the trouble. It's obviously a statement against interest, and I'm sure Andrew will let it in. Morning, Clive.'

Ben's eyes opened wide in surprise. 'So you won't oppose my application to admit it?'

'I have no legal basis for opposing it. Do you have any other evidence to call?'

'No.'

'So I suppose we will be moving straight on to closing speeches.'

'Yes,' Ben said, 'I suppose so. Do you want to go straight on? I wouldn't be against putting it off until Monday, when we're all fresher and we've had a chance to think about where we are with the evidence.'

'No, I'm ready to go. My case hasn't really changed. I have a few minor irritations to deal with, such as Isherwood's statement and Mellor taking the Fifth, but I have all the same evidence I started with, and the jury just have to decide who they're going to believe – nothing terribly complicated about it. Besides, Andrew isn't going to want to keep the jury waiting any longer. They've been sitting around doing nothing, and getting sent home early, often enough as it is. He'll want us to get on with it.'

Ben shifted uncomfortably. 'I would have thought that Isherwood and Mellor were more than minor irritations. To be frank, Anthony, I would have expected most prosecutors in your position to be considering whether, in all good conscience, they should even leave this case to the jury or whether the right thing is to stop it now.'

Norris smiled. 'Why on earth would I want to stop it now? Your girl might get off on a sympathy vote, I can see that, but I think I'm still in with a fighting chance.'

'Anthony, the officer in charge of your case has admitted to being in league with Dragan, fitting the defendant up on Dragan's behalf, and verballing her up enough to convict Mother Teresa. If that's not reason enough to stop a case, I don't know what is.'

'That's only if you believe Isherwood; and Isherwood isn't exactly a stellar source, is he? He was desperate – as he's now proved to us by taking his own life. He would probably have said anything to save his own skin if he could – and now I can't even cross-examine him about it.'

'That's an incredible story to make up if you're just a DS,' Clive suggested.

'It's a pretty good verbal,' Norris replied, 'I'll give him that. But according to you and Ben, that's just par for the course in the Drug Squad. That's what they do, isn't it? Perhaps, with his skills in that department, he should have been promoted to DI.'

'You still don't have a case anymore, Anthony,' Clive said.

'Really? Look, Clive, at the end of the day, your girl was in the house when the police found a commercial quantity of class A drugs with a high street value. She'd been smoking cannabis with her brother – which the jury aren't going to like, whatever she says about it now. She'd just got home from Dragan's HQ, Sarajevo; and she knew how to say "innkeeper" in Serbo-Croat. The jury may think she's not quite the innocent young thing she pretends to be. No, this case was properly brought, and the prosecution is still in with a chance.'

He smiled. 'Tell you what, Ben, it's not too late. If she pleads now, Andrew wouldn't be too hard on her for one count of permitting, would he? She'd be out after a couple of months, with time off for good behaviour. She could teach the other inmates to read Dickens while she's inside, couldn't she? They'd have to give her some credit for that. She should think about it.'

He turned towards the door of the courtroom. 'No? Oh, well, thought it was worth a try. Actually, I was hoping you'd say no. It will give me a chance to win a big case against my head of chambers. That would be quite a feather in my cap, wouldn't it?'

Ben exploded. 'For God's sake, Anthony, don't make this into a personal issue between you and me. You must have some sense of professional pride left. Letting our personal feelings run our cases is not the way we do it at the Bar.'

'My dear chap,' Norris replied, still smiling, 'it's nothing personal, I assure you. It just occurred to me that if I were to win a good high-profile case against my head of chambers, a silk, perhaps I might just have one last chance of getting silk myself. You can't blame me for trying, surely?'

# 67

'Members of the jury,' Andrew Pilkington began, 'you've now heard all the evidence you're going to hear in this case, and on Friday you heard Mr Norris and Mr Schroeder make their closing speeches. So all that remains now is for me to sum the case up to you. I hope not to be too long about it, and then you will be able to start your deliberations.

'Let me begin with two basic matters. The first is, what your job is in this case, and what my job is. My job is to deal with the law. When he opened this case to you, Mr Norris described it as "straightforward". But it's turned out to be anything but straightforward when it comes to the law, and I'm afraid you've had to spend quite a bit of time waiting around while I dealt with the legal questions with counsel. It's nobody's fault, members of the jury. Some cases are like that. But the good news for you is that you don't have to worry about the law. That's my job. You have to accept the law from me, as I say it is, because that's my responsibility.

'On the other hand, when it comes to the facts of the case, when it comes to deciding where the truth lies, what evidence you accept – and what evidence you don't accept – it's quite different. You, and you alone, are the judges of the facts. It's your job to decide where the evidence leads, to draw whatever conclusions you think proper from the evidence, and then to reach your verdict. That's your job, and nobody else's opinion about the facts of the case – including mine – matters at all.

'The second basic matter is what we call the burden and standard of proof. As in all criminal cases, it is for the prosecution to prove its case against Miss Lester if you are to convict. The defendant does not have to prove her innocence; in fact, she doesn't have to prove anything to you at all. Miss Lester chose to give evidence. She wasn't obliged to give evidence, but she chose to do so, and because she did, you will consider her evidence as part of the case, and evaluate it as you would the evidence of any witness. That doesn't affect the burden of proof at all: it remains on the prosecution from first to last.

'The standard to which the case must be proved, if you are to convict, is a high one. You may not convict unless the prosecution has proved the case against Miss Lester beyond reasonable doubt. If, on the evidence as a whole – the evidence for the prosecution and the evidence for the defence – you have any reasonable doubt, any reasonable doubt at all, of her guilt, you must find Miss Lester not guilty. Only if the evidence drives you to conclude that the case has been proved beyond reasonable doubt does it become your duty to convict.

'Now, members of the jury, if you will turn to the indictment with me… you will recall that Miss Lester faces a single count of knowingly permitting the house at 102 Willow Road to be used for the supply of illegal drugs. What does the prosecution have to prove before you can convict on this count?

'Members of the jury, there were only two people who were occupiers of 102 Willow Road, and so were in a position knowingly to permit those premises to be used for the supply of drugs. Those two people were this defendant, Imogen Lester, and her brother Damian. You know that Damian Lester agreed to do so in return for money – nobody disputes that – and you know that he has pleaded guilty to the count his sister faces. But the question you have to decide is: has the prosecution proved beyond reasonable doubt that this defendant, Imogen Lester, permitted the premises to be used for that purpose, and that she did so knowingly. Damian's plea of guilty is not evidence against his sister. The prosecution must prove the case against her by adducing evidence against her, and that evidence must persuade you of her guilt beyond reasonable doubt. Damian's plea of guilty can play no part in that at all, and you must disregard it in considering the case against Imogen.'

'So, what happened in this case?'

# 68

'As you know, police officers from the Drug Squad, backed up by uniformed officers from Hampstead Police Station, raided the Lester home at about four o'clock on the morning of 4 December 1983, a Sunday. It is not in dispute that they found a large commercial quantity of illegal drugs in the basement, and it is not disputed that Damian Lester had agreed with Sean to store those drugs in the basement in return for a payment of £200. It's what has become known in this trial as acting as an innkeeper. It is also not disputed that Miss Lester had been away in Sarajevo for several days, returning to London on the previous evening, Saturday 3 December. There is no direct evidence that Miss Lester played any part in dealing with Sean, or in the arrival of the drugs in the basement.

'You may think that the case against Miss Lester depends mainly on the statements she is alleged to have made to Detective Chief Superintendent Mellor and Detective Inspector Beech. That evidence, as you know, has been vigorously disputed. As Mr Schroeder made abundantly clear, the defence say the officers falsely attributed a number of statements to Miss Lester. In the language you've now become familiar with, the defence say that she was "verballed". Members of the jury, I want to say a few words about that. The word "verballed" is a colloquial expression used by lawyers and by some police officers, which almost suggests that making up evidence in this way is in a sense standard practice, or even that there is something of a game about it. But as I'm sure you will agree, members of the jury, it's not a game at all. It is a serious criminal offence to pervert the course of justice by fabricating evidence, and another serious offence to commit perjury by lying about it under oath in court.

'It would also be a very serious matter for anyone to accuse a police officer of behaving in that way if the allegation were false. Both Detective Chief Inspector Mellor and Detective Inspector Beech are senior police officers with many years of experience and unblemished records. Mr Norris asks whether you really believe that these officers would put their reputations and careers at risk, take the risk of being dismissed with loss of pension, and very likely face criminal charges themselves, for the sake of verballing Imogen Lester. The officers themselves were asked about that, you remember, and both said that they would not.

'On the other hand, Mr Schroeder, while emphasising as he did throughout his speech – very fairly, you may think – that the vast majority of police officers are honest and professional and do not verbal defendants, contends that there is evidence in this case that you simply can't ignore. First of all, he says that much of the language attributed to Miss Lester is completely different from her vocabulary and from the way in which she speaks. She is a young woman of previous exemplary character – I will return to that later – a Cambridge classics graduate, who now works for a leading London solicitor. As you no doubt recall, she read out a passage from *A Tale of Two Cities* in what she said was her normal speaking voice. Of course, Mr Norris made the point about her acting career while she was at Cambridge, so you may wonder how far her reading of Dickens really helps you. But perhaps more importantly, you heard her speak at length while she was giving evidence, and I suggest that you may find that a more reliable indicator. What did you make of that?

'All in all, Mr Schroeder says, she is not the kind of young woman to use the kind of language attributed to her, which is more akin to Superintendent Mellor's east London police officer's accent and vocabulary. You will recall that, when the officers first saw Miss

Lester coming downstairs, it was alleged that she was angry and aggressive, and that she said this: "Who the fuck are you? What are you, the Old Bill? Where's your warrant? You'd better bloody have one, mate, or I'll have your badge. What have you done to my fucking door? I'll have you for that!" Mr Schroeder suggests that it is simply ridiculous to believe that this refined, well-brought-up young woman spoke in that way.

'Mr Schroeder also asks you to bear in mind the evidence of PC Roberts, to the effect that, far from being angry and aggressive, Miss Lester appeared to be, as she told you herself, tired and disorientated. Miss Lester told you that after her experiences in Sarajevo, seeing her parents' effects, being taken to the scene of the crime and so on, she was tired and despondent when she arrived home. She admitted to having drunk some whisky and smoked some cannabis with her brother – herbal cannabis, you remember, members of the jury, not part of the drugs in the basement, but apparently part of Damian's private supply. As a result of all that, and then being woken up so violently at four in the morning – as you recall, members of the jury, the Drug Squad doesn't hang about once they've knocked on the door – she felt tired, faint and disorientated. PC Roberts, a female officer who was there for the express purpose of dealing with any female suspects on the premises, said that she had that very impression of Miss Lester, and you remember, she said that she did not regard Miss Lester as fit to be interviewed at that time. PC Roberts said that she herself would have taken Miss Lester to the police station and had her medically examined before interviewing her. She said she tried to make Superintendent Mellor aware of her concerns, but he seemed uninterested.

'This was just before the interview in the kitchen. During the interview in the kitchen, Miss Lester said something that, in a sense, has become the main pillar of the prosecution's case. She introduced the word "innkeeper" and its Serbo-Croat equivalent, "gostioničar". Mr Norris places great emphasis on that fact, and asks you to consider how this apparently innocent young woman came up with that term, the same term Sean had used to Damian when they spoke in the pub, and the same term used by the Sarajevo-based drug dealer known as Dragan. When challenged about it by the officers, Miss Lester told them a lie – she doesn't dispute that – saying that she must have picked it up while she was a guest at the Holiday Inn. She told you in evidence that it was to do with a meeting she and Miss Cathermole had in Sarajevo, but that she was not at liberty to disclose the whole history. And indeed, I think the prosecution now accepts that Crown privilege does attach to that meeting, because it was attended, not only by a man who had information about Miss Lester's parents, but also by a member of the security services. So you may think, members of the jury – it's a matter for you what you make of it – but you may think that Miss Lester could not tell the officers the real story at that stage, and so had to come up with a story of some kind. But Mr Norris says that doesn't answer the question of why she mentioned the word "innkeeper" in the first place, and that her mention of it remains an important pillar of the prosecution's case.

'When Miss Lester was interviewed at Hampstead Police Station later that same day, she was asked to read the written statement her brother had made. You've seen that statement, members of the jury, and you know that in it he admits his own guilt, but steadfastly maintains his sister's innocence. Nonetheless, the officers tell you that, having read that statement, Miss Lester said, "Look, all right, you've got me bang to rights. It's obvious what's been going on. Will you take a good drink to make this to go away?" Again, the defence say that this is a case of pure verbal. Miss Lester told you that it was the other way around: the officers offered to make the case go away if she gave them a bribe, a good drink. Again, you're going to have to decide where the truth lies.

'What other evidence do you have to help you decide where the truth lies in relation to these claims and counter-claims over alleged verballing?'

# 69

'Well, members of the jury, you have been provided with a written statement made by DS Isherwood, and before you were given that statement, you heard Detective Superintendent Mellor recalled to deal with what DS Isherwood had said. There are one or two important points I need to make about that.

'Firstly, as Mr Norris points out, the unfortunate death of DS Isherwood during this trial and shortly after making the statement means that Mr Norris was unable to cross-examine him and seek to protect Superintendent Mellor's reputation against what is alleged in the statement. Mr Norris also asks you to keep in mind what the statement says about DS Isherwood himself, namely: that he was himself working for Dragan using the name Sean; and that he was party to setting up Damian Lester, and perhaps setting up Damian's sister, the defendant. This, the statement claims, was at the behest of Dragan or his associates, because Dragan was concerned about the investigation being carried out by Miss Lester's father. Mr Norris also points out that, because of all this, Isherwood himself was facing likely dismissal from the police force and criminal prosecution. Who knows, Mr Norris asks, what he might say in those circumstances? And you may think, members of the jury, that this is something you must consider carefully.

'Secondly, I direct you that you may not draw any conclusions against Superintendent Mellor because he declined to answer questions put to him by Mr Schroeder on the ground that his answers might incriminate him in the commission of a criminal offence. Members of the jury, it's important that you understand this. When a witness avails himself of the legal right not to incriminate himself, he is not making an admission of criminal conduct. He is merely saying, as the law allows him to say, "I will not answer because I do not yet know what charges, if any, I will face, and so I have no way of knowing how my answer may be interpreted and possibly used against me unfairly." So bear that in mind, members of the jury. Superintendent Mellor has made no admission of wrongdoing.

'All that being said, Mr Schroeder submits that DS Isherwood's statement, taken with the other evidence in the case, should at a minimum persuade you that you cannot be satisfied of Miss Lester's guilt beyond reasonable doubt. If so, of course, as I said earlier, you would be bound to return a verdict of not guilty. What does DS Isherwood's statement suggest? It suggests, does it not: that Superintendent Mellor knew that Dragan wanted to set Imogen Lester up if he failed to have her father assassinated, which was his main goal; that Mellor himself was complicit in the plan to set Miss Lester up; that an error on somebody's part led to the plan going ahead, instead of being cancelled after Mr Lester's murder; that Mellor worked for Dragan using the name "Wally"; and that Mellor believed that they had Miss Lester "verballed up enough to convict Mother Teresa?"

'Mr Schroeder says that you don't need to believe every word of that to have reasonable doubt about the charges levelled against Miss Lester, which depended ultimately, as everyone agrees, on the work done by DS Isherwood under the name Sean, in recruiting Damian to accept drugs for storage at 102 Willow Road in return for a payment, termed "rent".

'So, there it is. Members of the jury, Imogen Lester is a young woman of previous exemplary character, as you have heard. She is a woman of good character not only in the narrow, technical sense of having no previous convictions, but also in the wider sense that she was able to produce several witnesses to give evidence to you about her general good character, including her reputation for honesty and for having an extremely law-abiding disposition. I would add, members of the jury – it's entirely a matter for you – but I would add that you would certainly be entitled, if you saw fit, not to hold it against her that she smoked some cannabis after the harrowing trip to Sarajevo she described to you.

'In law, you must take her good character into account, together with all the evidence, in considering whether these charges have been proved against her beyond reasonable doubt. In addition, when you consider her evidence, her good character supports her truthfulness, and you must take it fully into account in her favour when considering whether to accept her evidence.'

'Members of the jury, you may know that, in certain circumstances, the court may accept a majority verdict from a jury. If those circumstances should arise, I will bring you back into court to give you a further direction about the law. My direction at this time is that you must return a unanimous verdict, which means, of course, a verdict on which all twelve of you are agreed.

'Now, members of the jury, it's almost twelve thirty. You may retire to begin deliberating on your verdict. I suggest that the first thing you do when you retire should be to elect a foreman – a man or a woman, obviously, despite the term "foreman" – who will return the verdict in due course, and who should send me a note of any questions or concerns you may have while you are deliberating. Bear in mind that, like any criminal case, this is a serious case. There are no deadlines for returning verdicts. Take your time; and when, and only when, you are sure you have the right result, come back to court and do what you have sworn to do – to return a true verdict in accordance with the evidence.'

The judge waited for Mary to take her oath as jury bailiff, and for the jury to follow her to their room.

'Mr Schroeder, I will extend Miss Lester's bail while the jury are out.'

'I'm much obliged, my Lord.'

Andrew looked down at his clerk, seated at his desk below the elevated bench. 'Is the next matter ready?'

'Yes, my Lord,' the clerk replied. He turned back towards the courtroom. 'Call the case of Damian Lester for application to vacate plea of guilty and further directions.'

# 70

Ben had been expecting the next case in the list. He, Imogen, and her whole team would remain in court to observe the proceedings. As Damian was brought up from the cells into the dock, he smiled and gave Imogen a slight, surreptitious wave of one hand. Virginia 'Ginny' Castle, an old friend of Ben's with long experience at the Bar, had been asked to represent Damian and she quietly took her place in court while the jury were leaving. Behind her sat Damian's solicitor, Fahmida Patel.

'May it please your Lordship,' Ginny began, once the case had been formally called on and Damian had identified himself, 'I appear for the defendant, Damian Lester, in this matter. My learned friend Mr Norris represents the Crown.'

'Yes, Miss Castle.'

'My Lord, I know that your Lordship is trying the case of Imogen Lester and is well aware of the facts, so I will keep this application short. Damian Lester has pleaded guilty to the sole count of this indictment, having made a written statement under caution containing a full admission of what he had done. We do not seek to resile from that at all.

'But since then, it has become clear that when Mr Lester was approached by the man calling himself "Sean" to allow drugs to be stored in his house, he did not know, and had no way of knowing, that "Sean" was, in fact, DS Isherwood, a police officer attached to the Drug Squad. As your Lordship knows, an undercover police officer is allowed to join in an offence that is already underway in order to investigate and frustrate the commission of the offence. But he is not allowed to instigate an offence that would otherwise not be committed. The evidence now is that DS Isherwood may well have crossed that line in soliciting Damian to act as an innkeeper – as I believe the terminology has been in the case now before your Lordship. In law, crossing that line would amount to entrapment, and would afford Mr Lester a defence.

'My Lord, I cannot, and do not ask for the charges to be dismissed. I concede that there will have to be a trial to allow a jury to determine whether that defence may be available to Mr Lester. But it cannot be right that he should be denied his day in court. My application is that his plea of guilty should be vacated and that he should now be allowed to enter a plea of not guilty. I would also ask your Lordship to release Mr Lester on bail pending trial.'

Anthony Norris stood immediately.

'My Lord, I can't oppose that application.'

Andrew Pilkington nodded. 'Yes, very well. Stand up, please, Mr Lester. I will vacate your previous plea of guilty. Please listen carefully to the charge as the clerk reads it to you, and enter a plea accordingly.'

The court clerk, a semi-retired barrister, sporting his wig and gown, stood. 'Mr Lester, you are charged in this indictment that between about the first and the fourth days of December 1983, being the occupier of premises at 102 Willow Road, London NW3, you knowingly permitted the said premises to be used for the supply of controlled drugs, contrary to section 8 of the Misuse of Drugs Act 1971. How do you plead? Are you guilty or not guilty?'

'Not guilty,' Damian replied quietly.

'In the circumstances, Mr Lester,' Andrew said, 'I will grant you bail pending trial, on condition that your passport remains in the custody of the police, and that you report to Hampstead Police Station every Monday, Thursday and Saturday between two and five o'clock in the afternoon. Do you understand?'

'Yes, sir. Thank you.'

'Very well. I will rise pending the next matter.'

Ginny walked over to Ben. They exchanged quick kisses on the cheek.

'Thanks for making all that material available to us.'

'It was the least we could do. What's your instinct?'

'I think we have a good shot at it. The weakness in our case, obviously, is that the idiot did it more than once, and that he needed Sean's money to feed his habit – which is not ideal as these things go. But once the jury hear about Dragan having police officers working for him, at his beck and call for capers like this, I think Damian will attract a certain amount of sympathy from any jury.'

'I agree,' Ben replied, 'and I have a feeling that the story of Dragan having his claws deep into the Met is only just getting started. By the time you get to trial it will be much more interesting. I think he has every chance.'

'What about your girl?' Ginny asked. 'It would be ironic if she goes down and her brother gets off, wouldn't it?'

'Ironic wouldn't begin to describe that result,' Ben replied.

# 71

Tuesday 28 February 1984

'Come in, gentlemen. There's coffee and water on the table there. Help yourselves.'

Webb and Raymond gratefully poured themselves large cups of strong coffee. It wasn't yet ten o'clock, but it had already started to feel like a long day even before they arrived at the Director's office. Baxter contented himself with a glass of water.

'All right,' John Caswell said, 'take a seat. What can I do for you?'

'Two things, sir,' Webb replied. 'DCI Raymond and I have our recommendation for you in the case of Aubrey Smith-Gurney; and then there's a matter Mr Baxter would like to mention, which may also involve DCI Raymond and myself.'

Caswell extended his arms. 'Fire away.'

Webb coughed. 'Well, as to Smith-Gurney, sir, we feel that with both Conrad Rainer and Gerry Pole being dead, there's no realistic prospect of a conviction, and consequently we would recommend taking no further action.'

Caswell sat up sharply at his desk, failing entirely in any effort to conceal his surprise.

'But I thought you were keen to go after him? Wasn't Smith-Gurney the one who tipped Pole off that Rainer was in trouble and might need shifting out of the country sharpish?'

'What he told us, sir, was that he only intended Pole to hide Rainer away for a few days on the Isle of Wight because it was too dangerous for him in London. He says he had no idea that Pole was going to whisk him away across the channel.'

'That was a bit naïve, wasn't it? Smith-Gurney knew all about the ocean-going yacht, didn't he? What did he think was going to happen?'

'That would be the crux of the case against him, sir – but it's also as good as the case gets. We can prove that Smith-Gurney knew Pole had the yacht. But we have no evidence that he knew Pole was capable of relocating somebody to Sarajevo, or providing them with forged identity documents. We've checked him out thoroughly, and there's no indication of involvement with anything like that at all. There's certainly no evidence of any connection to Dragan.'

'So what it comes to, sir,' Raymond said, 'is that the case depends on the jury drawing a lot of inferences from Gerry Pole having a boat. Smith-Gurney has an excellent reputation: he's a QC, very civic-minded, highly thought of by all, just an all-round good guy. If we had Pole and Rainer we would certainly convict the two of them, and we might just get Smith-Gurney as tail end Charlie. But Smith-Gurney's the weakest link in the chain, and we don't think the chances of success justify putting him on trial on his own.'

'And the other thing, sir,' Webb added, 'is that Smith-Gurney wasn't wrong in thinking that Rainer was in danger in London. Daniel Cleary, the loan shark he'd borrowed £20,000 from, was after him – and Cleary has a history of serious violence. He got sent down for seven years not long after Rainer disappeared, for something else entirely. It made sense for Smith-Gurney to get Rainer out of town for a few days while he tried to bale him out.'

'Bale him out?' Caswell asked.

'He was trying to talk the three barristers Rainer stole from into not going to the police, to let Rainer pay off Cleary before he tried to reimburse them. We did at one time think that might be acting as an accessory after the fact, as we used to say, but treasury counsel disabused us of that. So it seems that Smith-Gurney may just have been doing his best to help, probably not in the most sensible of ways, but nothing that justifies a charge.'

Caswell sat back in his chair, shaking his head.

'So, what you're telling me,' he said incredulously, 'is that Conrad Rainer murders his mistress, decamps to Yugoslavia under an assumed identity, comes back here when it suits him, and neither Rainer nor either of his two close friends is going to be convicted of anything? Is that right?'

'Yes, sir,' Webb confirmed. 'If it's any consolation, Phil and I are going to look stupid all over again for not going in to get him when we had the chance. It's our fault he escaped – well, mine actually, I was in charge, not Phil.'

'I'm not sure how much of a consolation that is,' Caswell said. He turned to Baxter. 'Do you have bad news for me too?'

'No, quite the reverse, actually, John,' Baxter replied, smiling. 'I had a call from our embassy in Belgrade yesterday afternoon. I don't know whether you know this, but the police in Sarajevo arrested a man in connection with the murder of Michael and Margaret Lester, a character by the name of Miloje.'

Caswell nodded. 'I believe I did hear that somewhere.'

'Well, apparently, Miloje has started singing for his supper, and our man who's in touch with the local *gendarmes* tells me that he's prepared to blow Dragan's entire operation wide open in return for suitable consideration – and this is a senior player on Dragan's team, so they're taking him seriously.'

Caswell raised his eyebrows. 'Are we finally going to find out who Franco is?'

Baxter nodded. 'We're going to find out a lot more than that. It seems that Franco, Wally and Sean are just the London end of the British connection, and probably not even the whole of the London end. Franco was in overall charge, but it also seems Dragan has people in place in several police forces. Sean and Wally are not the only ones.'

'So we have another police scandal on our hands, is that what you're telling me – officers assisting in the movement of drugs and hindering investigations?'

'Plus other malfeasance, such as doing physical harm to Dragan's enemies and rivals, and fitting and verballing people up as required.'

'God almighty,' Caswell muttered. 'We were only just getting over the Flying Squad.'

'Miloje isn't much use to us directly,' Webb said, 'as a witness, I mean. He's going to be a guest of the Yugoslavian government for the foreseeable future. But I've been talking to Alf Mellor for several days now, and I think he's about to give it up. If Miloje gives us enough to convince him we know all about it, my gut says he'll crack and ask for a deal – in which case I'll be back here tomorrow or the day after asking for your approval.'

'What about Isherwood?' Caswell asked suddenly. 'Do you think...?'

'I don't know, sir,' Webb replied. 'But I'm going to ask him.'

'I'll be flying out to Sarajevo myself, probably next week,' Baxter said. 'Even if he's no use to the courts as a witness, Miloje may have a lot of other intelligence to offer, and I'm hoping the Militsija will let me sit down with him and an interpreter for a few hours. It might just make up for losing Conrad Rainer.'

'Everybody will be happy then, won't they?' Caswell said gloomily.

'What about Smith-Gurney, sir?' Webb asked.

'Tell him he's off the hook,' Caswell replied. 'Who knows? Perhaps they'll make him a judge, and he can take over from Conrad Rainer. But make sure you put the fear of God into him about his future conduct.'

'That will be our pleasure, sir.'

# 72

The call to return to court came at eleven forty-five. The jury had been out for the best part of two days, and the team's nerves were in shreds.

'Why aren't they back by now? How in God's name can they even be thinking about this, with what we gave them about Isherwood and Mellor?' Clive had asked Ben just over half an hour earlier, on one of the rare occasions when they found themselves alone together for a few minutes.

Ben shrugged. 'You just never know with juries, Clive. Norris wasn't entirely wrong, was he? There was some evidence that's difficult to explain away.'

'Not after Mellor, surely?'

'If we had actual evidence about Mellor it might be different. Look on the bright side. We may have some by the time we get to the Court of Appeal. And if we go down, at least it will make Norris happy, won't it? He will have won a case against his head of chambers.'

'Oh, God, don't say that,' Clive replied. 'Aren't you surprised that Andrew hasn't given the jury the majority verdict direction?'

'Not really,' Ben replied. 'He will want a unanimous verdict in this case if there's any way to get one. If the jury hasn't sent up any distress flares, he'll give them as long as he can. In his shoes, I'd let it go until tomorrow morning, I think, but I'd probably have to give them the option of a majority verdict then.'

Imogen had been sitting outside court with Julia's arm around her shoulder, mostly silent. Damian, also silent, was sitting close by. As they walked back into court she was shaking visibly. She returned to the dock while Mary efficiently assembled court and went to fetch the jury. Her timing was, as always, perfect. The jury filed into court just after the judge had taken his seat on the bench. The jurors looked exhausted. The clerk stood to take the indictment from Andrew Pilkington.

'My Lord,' he announced, 'just under ten hours have elapsed since the jury first retired to consider their verdict.'

He turned to face the jury box, but glanced over to the dock.

'Would the defendant please stand? Would the foreman please stand?'

The foreman was a woman who appeared to be in her fifties, wearing a formal grey suit and moderate heels. The first time she occupied the foreman's seat, Ben had mixed feelings about her election to represent the twelve. She looked too conservative to approve of drugs in any circumstances. But on the other hand, surely she should have some sympathy for Imogen, if only because of her background. This sequence of thoughts had gone round and round in his head, over and over again, during the jury's retirement. But there was no point in worrying about it now. They would know within moments, and as he had reminded Clive: you never knew with juries. Still, he had never watched and listened when a verdict was returned without having a knot in his stomach and a lump in his throat, and he had long ago realised that he probably never would.

'Madam foreman,' the clerk was saying, 'Please answer my first question just yes or no. Has the jury reached a verdict on which they are all agreed?'

'Yes, we have,' the foreman replied. She sounded tired, but confident.

'Madam foreman, on the sole count of this indictment, charging Imogen Lester with knowingly permitting premises to be used for the purpose of supplying controlled drugs, do you find the defendant guilty or not guilty?'

'We find the defendant not guilty, my Lord.'

'You find the defendant not guilty, and is that the verdict of you all?'

'Yes, it is.'

'Miss Lester may be discharged,' Andrew Pilkington said.

As the judge thanked the jury for their service and asked Mary to escort them from court, Ben heard sobbing from the dock and, turning round to share a congratulatory smile with Clive and Barratt, he saw that Damian had collapsed against Julia, who was holding him while trying unsuccessfully to hold back her own tears.

Andrew Pilkington was leaving the bench. The clerk approached with a note: 'Well done, Ben. Right result. It feels strange being up here on the bench instead of down there prosecuting you. Let's have a glass or two before too long. Andrew.'

Anthony Norris had left court without a word.

'Well, I was going to suggest lunch,' Ben said, as Imogen was released from the dock into Julia's arms. 'But you look as though you've had enough for today. Do you just want to go home?'

She stepped forward and embraced Ben, Clive and Barratt in turn.

'I would like to go home. But it's thanks to you that I can go home. I don't know what to say. I can never thank you enough.'

'That goes for me, too,' Julia said, kissing Ben on the cheek. 'I'll take her home. I'll be in touch in a day or two.'

'Well,' Clive said when they were alone, 'I don't know about anyone else, but I'm definitely up for lunch.'

'As am I,' Barratt agreed.

'Right,' Ben said. 'Let's go and get out of these robes. I'm already tasting my first glass of wine.'

# 73

*Friday 2 March 1984*

Webb put the two cups of coffee he had brought from the canteen down on the table, and went through the daily ritual of shaking hands with the man he had been questioning.

'Cheers, Johnny,' Mellor said. 'No Phil this morning?'

'No. His Chief Super wanted him for another job, something to do with firearms – he didn't have time to tell me the whole story; and in any case, I was planning to see you on my own today anyway.'

'Oh, yes?'

'Well, we go back quite a way, Alf, don't we? I have more of a history with you than Phil does. I thought it might be good if it was just the two of us.'

Mellor tasted the coffee. 'That's very nice. I was ready for that. So, what did you want to say, now it's just the two of us?'

Webb extracted and unfolded the several sheets of paper he had secreted in the inside pocket of his jacket.

'Do you remember that the police in Sarajevo had nicked this bloke called Miloje in connection with the murder of Michael Lester and his wife?'

'I remember hearing about it. I don't know any of the details.'

'Well, this is a report of what Miloje has been telling the police over the last few days, probably in the hope of getting some kind of deal for himself. Our embassy has been keeping tabs on it – well they would, wouldn't they, what with Michael Lester being one of their own? Why don't you run your eye over it for me, tell me what you think?'

Mellor seemed to be reading very slowly, line by line, almost as if he was having some difficulty in understanding the document – or, as Webb finally concluded, was having some difficulty in believing that anyone would have committed what he was reading to paper. Webb sipped his coffee and allowed him as much time as he wanted. When he reached the end of the last page, Mellor put the sheets down on the table, and for a moment seemed to have a faraway look in his eyes.

'How long have we known each other, Johnny?' he asked. 'At least twenty years, must be, probably more like twenty-five.'

'Must be,' Webb agreed.

'I remember we worked a few cases together – not many, because you were always based at Holborn, weren't you, and I was always in the East End before I joined the Squad? But we ran into each other quite a bit, one way or another.'

'We did.'

He laughed. 'It was a different world then, Johnny, wasn't it? They're going to bring in all these new rules now, aren't they – you have to interview all suspects at the nick and record everything that's said; and they're going to have, what do you call them…?'

'Codes of practice.'

'Codes of practice, that's it, for when you do interviews. They reckon it will mean there won't be as many arguments about verballing.' He laughed again. 'We both knew the rules, Johnny, didn't we? The old-time inspectors and supers told you the rules when you started in the job, didn't they? Coppers who verballed villains when they didn't have to were just being lazy. The right way to do it was to go out and get the evidence.'

Webb smiled. 'I remember.'

'The only time you verballed a villain was when you knew he was good for it, but you just couldn't get the proof for love nor money. If the super knew you weren't just cutting corners, you were genuinely trying put some villain away for something you knew was down to him, well, he'd back you, wouldn't he? But, my God, if you tried it on and you were doing it just to save a bit of time, he'd bring down the wrath of God on you. You only tried it on once at my first nick, believe you me.'

'I was always amazed at how many people verballed themselves,' Webb said. 'You know, you'd nick him and caution him, and he'd say, "All right, guv, it's a fair cop, I'll come quietly."'

'Right,' Mellor said, 'and nobody would believe you.'

They laughed together. 'You'd go to court,' Webb said, 'and his brief would say, "Come off it, officer, you're making him look like some pantomime villain, aren't you? Nobody says, 'it's a fair cop,' do they? You verballed him, didn't you?"'

'That's right. They wouldn't bloody believe you, and you were telling them God's truth.'

'What was the best one you ever had,' Webb asked, 'something they actually said?'

'We caught this gang burgling an office, mob-handed. This was when I was still a DC, working out of Whitechapel. We'd had a tip off. Turns out, these geezers didn't know each other that well – they'd just teamed up for this particular job and they weren't very careful about it, and we got them bang to rights. So I nick the ringleader and caution him, and he says, "That's the last time I work with fucking amateurs." Those were the days, weren't they, Johnny?'

'They were.'

They laughed again. Then, Mellor suddenly became more serious.

'So, what happened with little Miss Cambridge? Got off, I assume?'

Webb nodded. 'She got a not guilty, and they're going to let the brother change his plea.'

'Typical,' Mellor said. 'So, what do you want to talk about in this report?'

# 74

'Can I take it,' Webb asked, 'that we don't have to go back to square one? Can I take it that you now admit you are "Wally", and that you've been taking a drink from Dragan's people to do him a few favours over the years?'

Mellor nodded.

'How did it get started?'

'How does it ever get started?' Mellor asked. 'The temptation is always there, isn't it? I mean, when I started out in the East End, the rules were clear. You didn't take drinks, and if you got caught taking a drink it was over for you. But it was like verbals – there was an understanding, you might say.'

'What kind of understanding?'

'All right: say you nicked someone for handling stolen goods – which, in the East End, was an everyday occurrence: I mean all you had to do to make a collar was keep your eyes open when you left the nick – and let's say the bloke had a record and he had a family to support, so he didn't want to go back inside. So he'd offer you a drink to make it go away, and as long as it wasn't too much, it was an accepted thing. You didn't talk about it, certainly not when there was a senior officer around, but everybody knew it went on. And let's be honest, fencing stolen goods was part of the local economy, wasn't it? It was a way of life, and even if you nicked him, he'd probably get a not guilty if he could go for trial by jury – East End juries just wouldn't convict for receiving. They'd convict for violence or sexual stuff, but not for just receiving. So giving you a drink was just a bit of extra insurance, and getting out of having to go to court; it was an expense of doing business.'

'Did this "accepted thing" have limits?'

'Of course, it did; that's what I'm saying. It didn't apply to serious offences, and especially not to violence or sexual offences – not if it was serious: I'm not talking about a punch-up outside the pub on Saturday night, but if it was serious you couldn't do it.'

'So how does the idea of a "good drink" fit into this picture?'

'If there was a lot of money involved, say he was handling a lot of electronic gear or fashion accessories, and he was pulling down a few grand, he'd expect to give you a good drink.'

'Meaning several hundred pounds?'

'Could be. But if there was more than one of you in on the collar, you'd agree to split a good drink. You didn't want to be greedy about it.'

'What were the rules about drugs?'

Mellor nodded. 'Again, if it was just a kid who had a joint on him when he was nicked, that was all right; or even if he had enough for a few of his mates as well as himself. For a more serious dealer who was raking in proper money, you might take a good drink once, but with the understanding that he took himself off your patch and you would never see him again. If you ever caught him on your patch again he'd be nicked, no ifs or buts.'

'What rules applied when you joined the Drug Squad?'

'The first thing they told you was, if you were ever found using drugs or taking a drink, good or otherwise, you were gone. They really put the fear of God into you, and I was a DS by then, so I wasn't easily intimidated, shall we say. But trust me, these guys would scare the life out of you.'

He paused to drain his coffee, making a face as he did so, as if to suggest that it had long since turned cold.

'But after a while on the job, you began to suspect that there were some officers who were taking drinks. It wasn't anything anyone talked about, nothing obvious. But it was just that there were certain cases you couldn't work, and there were certain informants you couldn't use, even when it might have made a big difference to a case you were working. If you ask me how widespread it was, the answer is, I don't know. I don't know how widespread it is now, Johnny – that's the truth. But if you start opening closets, you're going to find a few skeletons, I guarantee you that.'

'What about you?'

He shook his head. 'Until Dragan, never. I was too scared, to tell you the truth. But then Dragan came along, and everything changed.'

'Changed, how?'

'Well, for one thing, look who recruited me.'

'Franco?'

'Yes.'

'Now a Deputy Chief Constable.'

'Yeah. I mean, he was a legend in the Squad, wasn't he? He was my rank at the time, a detective chief super. It started off with him saying that Dragan was useful to us, because he was grassing up some big dealers in this country, so we had to look after him, look the other way now and then when he wanted to move some merchandise. Franco made it sound like it wasn't a big deal – Dragan was good for the Squad because he wasn't doing all that much business in this country, and thanks to him we were taking down some of our major dealers. And Dragan was never going to get nicked here anyway, was he? He was a foreigner.'

'And in return you would get a drink?'

'Yeah. But it wasn't the drink in itself; it was how much of a drink. I couldn't believe it, Johnny. I was a DS, but I was already getting money I would never have had the balls to ask for in Whitechapel, even as a good drink. God only knows what he was giving Franco. And as I got promoted, the drink kept going up – I never had to ask, it just happened.'

'So Dragan had his hooks into you?'

'Exactly. There was no way back, was there? In the end it was greed: that's what it came down to. The wife's got used to an enhanced lifestyle, as you might call it. She's never asked me any questions, poor love, but I'm sure she's had her suspicions. And in addition to that, there were some rumours making the rounds about what Dragan did to people who offended him. But it was basically greed – you got used to the good drink way of life. That's what brought the Sweeney down, wasn't it? It wasn't that you had widespread corruption in the Flying Squad. There were just a few really, but what they got into was spectacular; it was the sheer scale of it that did everyone in. It's going to be the same with us.'

'What kind of drink did you get for the Lester job?'

'Twenty grand in total. But I had to see Sean right out of that.'

He held his head in his hands for some time. Webb sat back and watched.

'Is there any kind of deal I could get, Johnny?'

'I don't know,' Webb replied. 'If you're talking about retirement and a pension, and so on...'

'The main thing is, I don't want to go inside. It's the wife more than me, Johnny. She's got angina and God knows what else. I don't know what she would do if I went in for a long stretch.'

'I will go to the Deputy Director and ask,' Webb said. 'I can't promise you anything. But if I go to John Caswell, it will have to be on the basis that you grass up everyone you know who's ever taken a drink, from Dragan or anyone else, and whether they're in your squad or any other squad, or any other police force. You see what Miloje's saying, Alf. He's saying that Dragan has people everywhere, isn't he, not just in the Met? Sean, Wally and Franco are just the tip of the iceberg, aren't they?'

'It's going to be very ugly when it all comes out,' Mellor agreed.

'In addition, Caswell will expect you to give evidence against any of them who end up being prosecuted, to the extent you can.'

'You'd have to take me into protection – the wife, too. Could you do that?'

'I assume so, if you're cooperating fully. Is that what you're doing, Alf?'

Mellor nodded. 'That's what I'm doing.'

'I'll need that in writing.' He paused. 'And there's one more thing: DS Isherwood...'

'Topped himself,' Mellor replied at once. 'No one took him out, Johnny. If they were going to try that, I would have known about it – and I would have stopped it. Dougie lost his way, poor lad, that's all that happened. He couldn't find a way out.'

'You knew he was dead, though, didn't you?' Webb asked. 'That's why you came to his flat.'

'I was worried about him,' Mellor replied. 'That's the trouble with working for people like Dragan: you stay worried the whole time.'

'You can't rule out that somebody got to him, can you?'

'You can never rule anything out with those people. But I swear to you, Johnny, by all I hold sacred: if he was done in, it was nothing to do with me.'

Webb stood. 'I'll do what I can,' he said. 'I see you have some notepaper, and I assume you have a pen. Start writing.'

# 75

Ben took his seat at the head of the table in the biggest room in chambers. The room used for chambers meetings was officially the pupils' room, but it was the only room large enough to accommodate all members of chambers at the same time – albeit in far from comfortable circumstances. The clerks had to bring in chairs from all over chambers, and they were jammed together around the table, and against the walls. It had been that way for many years, and members of chambers had always agreed that it guaranteed their meetings would not drag on unnecessarily. The pupils, with little regard for their convenience, were told to leave until Alan advised them that they were free to return. Ben had witnessed this ritual many times after nearly twenty years in chambers, but this was the first time he had ever had to preside over the proceedings.

'Welcome, everyone,' he began. 'I see everyone is here, except for Anthony Norris.' There were a number of sniggers around the room. 'No, he sends his apologies; he has a very important cocktail party to attend this evening, he tells me.' This time there was open laughter. 'But in addition to his apologies he has also sent me some news. He's been appointed a metropolitan stipendiary magistrate with effect from 1 June. So he will be leaving chambers, but those of you still plying your trade in the London magistrates' courts will continue to see quite a bit of him, I imagine.'

There were groans from the more junior members of chambers,

whose burgeoning practices still made them *habitués* of the lower courts.

Ben smiled. 'Now, now. Let's not be ungracious. I'm sure Anthony will be a very agreeable tribunal.'

Laughter again.

'To those with masochistic inclinations,' Ann Kemp, one of the younger tenants, muttered to renewed chuckles.

'What this does mean,' Ben continued, 'is that we are getting rather thin on top, in terms of seniority. Kenneth is still recovering his full strength, and it's not very long since we lost Donald Weston, also to the bench. We must keep a steady flow of work at the senior level coming into chambers, so that you all have your chance to move up and eventually take silk. I've spoken to Alan, and he agrees that we need to take on at least two or three senior people with established practices, as soon as we can.'

'How do we do that?' Ann asked.

'I have to ask you to treat this as strictly confidential,' Ben replied, 'but I do have a promising development to report. Harriet and I have recently been talking to Ginny Castle. Many of you know Ginny, and I'm sure everybody knows of her. She has an excellent practice, mostly heavyweight crime these days, but also some civil. She's in your father's old chambers, Clive, but she's always been a good friend of these chambers, and she's sounded me out once or twice over the years. I don't think there are any overt problems in her chambers...'

'Not that I've heard,' Clive confirmed.

'But I've had the feeling for some time that she would like a move. She says she would bring three or four others with her, with between seven and fifteen years experience. She's given me the names. Forgive me if I don't broadcast them now, but Harriet and I know them all, and they have a good range of work, crime, civil and family. We will have to speak to them all individually, and introduce them to all of you in due course. But Harriet and I feel this is worth pursuing. Anything to add, Harriet?'

'No. I agree with Ben. This is definitely something we need to look at.'

Ben paused. 'Before we go any further, I want to thank Aubrey for his service as head of chambers. It's all been a bit hectic since he stood down. This is my first chambers meeting in charge, as you all know. But I am delighted to tell everyone that Aubrey is now officially in the clear. The police have decided not to take any action against him – quite rightly, and not before time, I may say.'

There was a round of applause, accompanied by numerous shouts of 'hear, hear.'

'Aubrey and I spoke earlier today,' Ben continued, 'and I offered him the chance to think again. I do so again now. Aubrey, if you would like to take back the reins, nobody, least of all me, would want to stand in your way for a moment. You've had an unfortunate time of it, but it's behind you now, and...'

Aubrey held up a hand. 'That's very kind, Ben, and everyone,' he replied. 'But we all know how these things work. Yes, the police say they're not going to take any further action. But who's to say that some bright spark trying to make a name for himself may not claim to have uncovered new evidence somewhere down the road? And even if that doesn't happen, the suspicions will remain. Every time someone mentions the name of Conrad Rainer – which they will, because it's a story that will run and run – the name of Aubrey Smith-Gurney will always be mentioned in the same breath. Solicitors are volatile creatures. It doesn't take much to make them change their allegiances. Any whiff of scandal seems to be enough. I've been fortunate to some extent: those solicitors who've been instructing me for many years are my friends by now, and they're not going away. But if I remained as head of chambers, it might attract adverse publicity and discourage other solicitors from sending work to chambers, and we can't take that risk.'

He waited for the reluctant murmurs of assent to die down.

'In addition, from a personal and family point of view, I would much prefer to keep a low profile for the time being. But finally, and most importantly, let's focus on the positive side of this, shall we? Ben will be a magnificent head of chambers. I have every confidence in him, and I intend to give him my full support – as, I hope and expect, will all of you.'

Aubrey stood and led a prolonged standing ovation.

# 76

*Saturday 7 April 1984*

'I've got a job,' Imogen said eventually. 'A real one, I mean.'

They were sitting across from each other at the dinner table, finishing up the Chardonnay Julia had selected to accompany an impromptu dinner of home-made pasta with crab and clams, a dinner during which both their lives were in the process of changing direction. As the change began to make itself clear to them, their conversation slowed.

Julia smiled. 'Have you finally decided what you want to do, or is it change for the sake of change? I wouldn't blame you at all if it's just a change.'

'I hope I've finally decided. I won't know until I've done it for a while, obviously.'

'Tell me.'

'It's a job in journalism,' she replied tentatively.

Julia nodded. 'I'm not surprised. You've told me a few times that you liked the idea of working for a newspaper.'

'Yes. I've always thought I would like to write. But with everything that's happened since my parents died, you know – our trip to Sarajevo, my being arrested and put on trial, seeing what power the police and the courts have, seeing what can go on in countries where they don't have the same laws – well, it's brought it all into focus for me. I've realised that we can't take anything for granted; it's given me more of a sense of urgency. I've realised that I need to kick-start my life, get on with whatever it is

I'm going to do. There's so much going on out there in the world that nobody knows about, Julia – just think about what happened to my parents – and without someone reporting it…'

'You're right,' Julia said. 'The world needs good journalists.' She smiled wanly. 'I had hoped I might make a lawyer out of you, but if I'm honest, I always knew your heart was elsewhere. So, tell me about your new job.'

She poured them the remains of the wine.

'It all started during the trial. I spoke to one of the reporters covering the case one morning before court started – we were running a few minutes late for some reason, and I think you'd already gone into court to talk to Ben. So we got chatting, and I happened to mention that I'd thought about becoming a journalist myself, and he gave me his card. He's with *The Times*. He told me to write to the editor – if I got a not guilty, obviously.'

Julia laughed. 'Obviously.'

'So after it was all over, I wrote to the editor. I didn't hear anything for some time, and I'd begun to think it wasn't going anywhere. But then he wrote to me, inviting me to come and see him – this was out of the blue, a couple of weeks ago. He's a really nice man. We talked for a long time, and just like that, he offered me a job. It was so sudden, I was a bit taken aback, actually, and I asked for a few days to think about it. But I called him the following day and accepted.'

Julia looked up sharply.

'The following day? But you didn't … Why didn't you say something to me?'

'I've been trying to think of the best way to tell you ever since, Julia, and I couldn't think of anything; but I finally decided to talk to you this evening.'

'I don't understand,' Julia said. 'Why was it so hard for you to tell me?'

'*The Times* wants me as a foreign correspondent,' Imogen replied, after a silence.

'Ah,' Julia said. 'I see.'

'I'll be based in Paris. I'll have to do quite a bit of travelling, obviously, but Paris will be my base, and I'll be moving there.'

Again they were silent for some time.

'Well,' Julia said, 'I have to hand it to you: there's nothing like starting at the top, is there? No apprenticeship covering the local council for the *Rochdale Tribune* – not for you. Foreign correspondent for *The Times*, no less. I'm impressed.'

'It's not as grand as you make it sound. I'm going to be *a* foreign correspondent, not *the* foreign correspondent.'

'Even so…' Julia said. 'I'm proud of you. I really am.'

There was another silence.

'What will you do with the house?'

'We're putting it on the market. I sat down with Damian and had a long talk, just after they decided to drop the charges against him. We both thought it was the best thing to do. With the sale price and the money and investments we inherited from our parents, there should be enough for both of us to live independently.'

'Do you think he's ready?'

'I do, actually. The experience of being arrested and spending time in prison has been a wake-up call for him. I think he's realised at last that he can't just sit around drinking and taking drugs, not working and expecting others to take care of him, for the rest of his life. I made it clear that I wasn't going to do that anymore, and I think he's got the message. We shall see. I hope so.'

She stretched out an arm across the table and took Julia's hand.

'Julia, Paris isn't that far away. Perhaps I could…'

'No. We both know that's not going to work.'

'I don't mind trying…'

'No,' Julia replied at once. 'It's all right. Really. We both knew this day would come. You'll find someone for the long term… For God's sake, Imogen, I'm old enough to be your mother. We both knew it couldn't go on forever. It's been lovely, but it was always going to end.'

The silence this time seemed to last forever.

'Shall I stay and help you…?' Imogen asked, at length.

'No,' Julia insisted. 'I can clear up. Take yourself off home.'

'I'll keep in touch, of course,' Imogen promised.

'Of course, you will.' Julia replied. 'And I will make sure I read *The Times* every day. I'm already looking forward to your first dispatch – that's what you foreign correspondents call them, isn't it?'

# 77

By the time she had cleared away and changed for bed, it was almost one o'clock. She poured herself a large glass of single malt, switched off the lights, and made her way upstairs. She lay in bed for more than an hour, listening to the silence and feeling the cold space in the bed next to her. Eventually, she put on her dressing gown, took the remains of the whisky, and made her way to the study. By the light of her desk lamp she picked up the receiver and dialled a number.

'Hello,' she said tentatively. 'It's me. I know it's rather late…'

'Not really, Julia,' Baxter said, 'not by the standards of us poor insomniacs. What can I do for you?'

'Well, I just thought you ought to know that Ronald Reagan is about to bomb Russia and start World War Three.'

'Really? Well, thank you, Julia. That's the kind of thing we spooks like to keep abreast of. We'll need to look into it immediately. Before I wake C up to tell him: how do you know this? Is it rumour, or is this coming from a reliable source?'

'It's coming from an impeccable source,' Julia replied. 'It's the highest grade intelligence, I assure you.'

'Well, that's very concerning.'

'That's why I'm calling at such an antisocial hour. Would you like to hear more?'

'Of course,' Baxter replied. 'Take your time, and tell me all about it.'

# Author's Note

This is a novel. The events and the persons depicted in it are fictitious, and any resemblance to any person, living or dead, is entirely coincidental. I have always believed, and believe now, that the overwhelming majority of police officers are, and have historically been, competent, honest, courageous men and women of the highest integrity. But my story is set towards the end of a turbulent time in policing, in London particularly, but to a lesser extent in the country more broadly. It was a time when the work of the vast majority of police officers was often overshadowed in the public mind by the abuses of the few. This was partly a question of culture, and partly, certainly with reference to the practice of 'verballing', a problem of inadequate legal safeguards, a problem eventually solved decisively by the Police and Criminal Evidence Act 1984 (PACE). The Drug Squad, in which I have set my story, was no different to any other branch of the Met's CID. My characters are archetypal, and certainly do not refer to any officer who served in that Squad – whose main notoriety may have been the astonishingly short space of time they needed to gain access even to the most heavily fortified premises, when necessary to secure suspects and evidence.

There had been a period in post-war policing, which peaked in the late 1960s and 1970s, in which a certain level of corruption and malpractice seemed to be not only tolerated, but expected and even, in certain quarters, furtively admired as an acceptable perk for CID officers, who on the whole functioned well in fighting the alarming epidemic of serious and organised crime then going on in London's streets. The history of the Flying Squad, the notorious 'Heavy Mob' or 'Sweeney' (from the rhyming slang 'Sweeney Todd') is the main case in point, even if it was not the only one. During the 1970s, thirteen officers of that Squad were convicted of various offences involving corruption, notably the head of the Squad, Detective Chief Superintendent Kenneth Drury. Yet between 1978 and 1982 in the subsequent broader investigation, Operation Countryman, led externally by the Hampshire and Dorset Constabularies, which investigated allegations of corruption against 84 officers of the Metropolitan Police and 29 officers of the City of London Police, only two officers were brought to trial and none were convicted; although during this overall period a large number of officers resigned, ostensibly on grounds related to health or personal circumstances. The allegations included the taking of bribes, verballing, the planting of evidence, and conspiring with serious criminals such as armed bank robbers to facilitate their bail or keep them out of trouble altogether. There is appalling evidence of systematic resistance to, and obstruction of, the Countryman investigation within the Met, across all levels of the force.

The full scale of the corruption within the Met's CID, which in 1972 led the incoming Commissioner Sir Robert Mark to describe it as 'the most routinely corrupt organisation in London', will not be known for many years. Many investigative records from this period, including many from Operation Countryman, have been sealed until the year 2067 – for which, in my view, there can at this remove of time be no conceivable justification. Equally unsettling is the tone of much of what has since been written about the Flying Squad, notably by one of its former officers, Dick Kirby, in *Rough Justice: Memoirs of a Flying Squad Detective* (Merlin Unwin Books, 2001). Kirby offers a revisionist, tabloid narrative of life in the Flying Squad which, while justifiably laudatory of the Squad's undoubted achievements in fighting serious crime, seems almost dismissive of any criticism of the corruption, and is at times almost nostalgic about the good old days before people started interfering. Kirby also indulges in one or two baseless attacks on those judges and defence lawyers he perceived to be standing in the Squad's way (by raising tiresome legal questions) and in one or two seriously inaccurate statements about the law itself.

The practice of 'verballing' suspects was simply a form of fabrication of evidence and, therefore, an attempt to pervert the course of justice. It was so ingrained in the minds of the relatively few officers who indulged in it, that it had its own internal code of conduct. It was not to be overdone, and it was not to be done at all if other adequate evidence was available. It was in a sense a weapon of last resort against serious offenders, where the police knew the defendant had committed an offence, but were unable to obtain sufficient evidence to convict; it was not to be used to cut corners, where the officer simply could not be bothered to do it properly. This almost Robin Hood-like code of honour failed to conceal the reality behind verballing, which was that it was a form of corruption. On the other hand, it was not uncommon either for defendants to accuse officers falsely of having verballed them, often as a last-ditch stand against a looming and wholly justified conviction. That, too, was an attempt to pervert the course of justice. And even where there was no dishonest intent, a system in which officers routinely questioned suspects anywhere they happened to find themselves, and then handwrote notes of long conversations from memory hours after the event, after they had returned to the police station, inevitably raised questions of recollection and accuracy.

As a barrister in the 1970s (both prosecuting and defending) I remember hours, and sometimes days, of court time at trial spent poring over officers' notebooks, and then examining or cross-examining the officers about whether they had verballed the defendant. It was a horribly inefficient way to run a trial. Unless the officer gave himself away – for example, by putting an elaborate explanation into the mouth of a defendant who manifestly lacked the vocabulary or command of grammar to have made such a statement – the jury were understandably inclined to believe someone the judge usually painted for them as an officer with an unblemished record, who would be risking his career and pension if he were to do something so dishonest as to verbal a suspect. Of course, there were also cases where the defendant gave himself away, while giving evidence to the jury, by using language almost identical to that noted by the officer.

PACE replaced the iconic and venerable Judges' Rules, first promulgated by the judges of the King's Bench Division of the High Court in 1912. The Rules had served their purpose well for a long time. They began with the proposition that no statement made by a defendant was admissible in court unless it had been made 'voluntarily', in the sense that it was not obtained by any threat of prejudice or hope of advantage, or by oppression. This covered, not only verballing, but also the even more serious practice of obtaining confessions by means of violence, intimidation or unfair pressure – assertions of which also occupied large amounts of time in court. They included a requirement to caution a suspect on arrest, and before questioning, as well as when charged with an offence. A judge was entitled (though not bound) to exclude a statement if there had been a breach of the Rules; for example, where the defendant had not been given the proper caution. But the Rules provided no way to avoid contested issues as to how the statement had been made.

PACE did not come into effect until 1 January 1986 and the new régime it created took a good deal of time to put in place. But once the new provisions took effect, they created a sea change in the practice relating to the questioning of suspects. They corrected the problem of verballing almost overnight, and contributed a good deal to reducing the incidence of complaints about other alleged police misconduct.

The Act introduced Codes of Practice for police officers dealing with investigations. Code of Practice C deals with the questioning of suspects. A judge is entitled, but not obliged, to exclude a statement made by a defendant following breaches of the Code, and the Code may be referred to in evidence. To that extent Code of Practice C effectively mirrored the position under the Judges' Rules. But it then introduced truly radical changes. The Code provided that, except in rare cases, an interview must be conducted at a police station, and must be tape-recorded. The defendant is entitled to have his solicitor present to advise him, before and during the interview. (This was arguably the law even before PACE, though little attention was paid to it in practice, probably for reasons of practicality.) The Code defines an 'interview' as, 'the questioning of a person regarding his involvement or suspected involvement in a criminal offence or offences, which… is required to be carried out under caution.' Questioning under caution is required whenever, 'there are grounds to suspect a person of an offence, and his answers or silence in response to the questioning may be given in evidence if he is prosecuted.'

As a judge, post-PACE, I can only remember dealing with one or two issues involving interviews, and these were cases in which the officer claimed that it was necessary to ask questions before taking the defendant to the police station in response to exceptional circumstances. Even in these cases, the issue was simply whether there had been a breach of the Code, and no allegation of verballing was made. In fact, PACE has always benefited the police as well as defendants. Just as it has now become extremely difficult for an officer to verbal a suspect, it has become no less difficult for a defendant to accuse an officer falsely of verballing him. The Codes have been updated and amended since to deal with changing circumstances, but the underlying principles remain. I am glad that the generation of younger advocates who appeared before me when I was a judge, can read about 'verbal' as a piece of history, and do not have to deal with it in their professional lives.

As ever, my thanks to Ion Mills and Claire Watts at No Exit Press, for their continuing faith in my writing; to my agent Guy Rose, and most of all to my wife Chris, who loves and looks after this self-confessed victim of CWD (Compulsive Writing Disorder) without complaint.